THE WORLD WAR GOES ON.
THE PRIVATE WAR BEGINS . . .

"Good morning, Mr. Campbell."

"Whatever this is about it had better be good. Who the hell are *you?*"

"My name is Trentlyon, Mr. Campbell. Nigel Trentlyon. We're going to be seeing quite a lot of each other, we are."

"Oh? And just how do you figure that?"

"We shall be working together rather closely from now on."

"Then maybe you'd better tell me, Trentlyon, what the bloody hell is going on?"

"I thought you knew. We're going to save England."

CODE OF ARMS

LAWRENCE BLOCK
AND HAROLD KING

BERKLEY BOOKS, NEW YORK

This Berkley book contains the complete
text of the original hardcover edition.
It has been completely reset in a type face
designed for easy reading, and was printed
from new film.

CODE OF ARMS

A Berkley Book / published by arrangement with
Richard Marek Publishers

PRINTING HISTORY
Richard Marek edition / April 1981
Berkley edition / September 1982

ISBN: 0-425-05493-4

A BERKLEY BOOK ® TM 757,375
Berkley Books are published by Berkley Publishing Corporation,
200 Madison Avenue, New York, New York 10016.
The name "BERKLEY" and the stylized "B" with design are trademarks
belonging to Berkley Publishing Corporation.

PRINTED IN THE UNITED STATES OF AMERICA

To Brian Garfield

PREFACE _____

In the late spring of 1940, Central Europe belonged to Adolf Hitler and the Third Reich. Only England and the British Isles were left to stand against Germany. It has been said that the secret war waged in the twelve months following the *Blitzkreig* had more to do with the defeat of Germany than any other period of the war.

What happened between May 10, 1940 and May 10, 1941?

Hitler postponed the invasion of England and turned his thoughts to the conquest of Russia when his Luftwaffe failed to crush the RAF in the Battle of Britain.

The world was stunned when the third-ranking Nazi, Deputy Fuehrer Rudolf Hess, flew to Scotland on a one-man mission to negotiate peace, only to spend the rest of the war in the Tower of London.

In clapboard huts at an undistinguished country estate in Buckinghamshire, MI6's Code and Cipher School made a permanent home for Source Ultra intelligence—the greatest secret of our time—and eventually solved the cryptography of the German High Command's "unbreakable" Enigma coding machine.

History testifies in part through captured Wehrmacht documents and Ultra transcripts how, as a consequence of these events, Hitler's promise of a Thousand Year Reich was ultimately destroyed.

Yet, it is true, what Goethe remarked: "The most important things are not always to be found in files."

What we know is history. What follows is fiction. That anything like this might have happened is not recorded. Still . . .

—H.K.
Shreveport, 1980

In the high ranges of Secret Service work the actual facts in many cases were in every respect equal to the most fantastic inventions of romance and melodrama.

—Winston S. Churchill

Ultra was *the* decisive source of intelligence of the Second World War; and in order to protect its security, some very stern measures were employed.

—RAF Marshal Sir Geoffry H. J. Highsmith, Senior Air Staff, British SIS

Of course it was insane to fight a war on two fronts, and that is what defeated us. If we had not attacked Russia, we would have won England. But you could not have told Hitler that. His mind had been made up—and we lost.

—Field Marshal Eric von Planck, General Staff, Wehrmacht High Command

We beat the bloody Germans, di'n't we? But it was Mr. C and that other gent what done it, the rest is, well, pigeon droppings, ain't it?

—Anna Glebe, domestic

Prologue _____

December 1938

THE HUTS—wooden structures with half-round tin roofs—had been erected across the wide lawns of the estate with no particular thought to beauty or order. That they were strictly functional in design and appearance would have been clear to the casual observer had there been one within range to take notice. Indeed, such an observer, stopped on his bicycle outside the sunken boundary fence to warm his fingers before pedaling on to Bletchley, might have found it a strangely odd sight—huts mingled with cedar trees, spoiling the croquet lawn, their unsightly tin chimneys billowing smoke that left a residue like pepper on the previous night's snow. And all within a stone's throw of the timbered gables of a large and pretentious Victorian manor house. Odd, perhaps, but not remarkable, though it might be subject for passing conversation over a brew and darts at the local Rose and Crown.

Of course that was exactly the reason for their placement on the grounds of Bletchley Park and Reggie Hamilton knew it. He knew it because as deputy assistant chief, section A.6, British SIS, it was his charge to know. And thus it was his position rather than his choice that brought him to be here tonight, giving a look-around like a tour guide, instead of home in Nottinghill in front of a fire, whiskey in hand, gleaning *The Times'* financial pages for evidence of rise in his not considerable investments. Still, there was something invigorating about the mysterious project contained behind the clapboards of these colorless shacks that made it seem tolerable. Not that he got much rise out of his guest for all his trouble, either.

He was a queer, brooding sort, Carstairs was, if Hamilton was any judge. Not that that surprised him, of course. He'd heard about James Trevor Carstairs; a Scot, one of the sons of Eton, Household Cavalry back when, DSO, member of the exclusive Agincourt Club in Chelsea, family estate in Gloucestershire, and SIS with Haig in the World War. He didn't seem particularly ruthless, but then, he didn't talk much, did he?

On that thought, Hamilton stepped out of Hut Three and into a bitter gust of snow and was coldly reminded that it was more duty than honor that required his presence here this evening.

"Interesting, eh?" Hamilton said, pulling on a pair of sheepskin gloves and trying not to grimace from the cold.

"Bloody marvel," Carstairs replied in a breath that was visible against the dim light, "if it works."

"Oh, it'll work," Hamilton said with chattering assurance. "Has to, you know."

They trod silently across the powdery lawn toward the manor house, Carstairs leading. The bugger, Hamilton thought. As if this was his show, as if *he* was the deputy assistant and not the guest. Hamilton pulled up the collar of his tweed overcoat against the chill and hunched up his shoulders to savor what warmth there was to be got. He wished he'd brought his hat.

The Chief's silent lion, that's what Archie Priddy called him. Bring in Jamey Carstairs when there's a piece of nasty to be done. He was an old hand, been here as long as the moon, that's what he'd heard. Talk was all it was, Hamilton had thought, until he'd met him tonight. He was tall—a full head taller than Hamilton—with a Roman nose and the look of God Almighty in his eyes, but he had the wit and charm of a Druid's sacrifice. Qualities you'd expect in a man for this job. An odd one he was too; never questioned why the car was sent for him, never asked what was up or why this chat so far away from his cozy little club. That was the Chief's idea, that was. Have him up for a look around, the Chief had said. Tell him it'd be a change of setting.

Hamilton buried himself as deep into his coat as was possible. *He'd* have asked a few questions. There were all the reasons to decline the invitation and not the least was that ghastly fifty-mile drive out of London in the back of a Bentley that guaranteed to be, if not drafty, then chilly to the verge of shuddering frostbite. Hamilton had made it enough times himself these last weeks. But Carstairs never let on that he minded. A bloody stoic is what he was. And Bletchley—now there was a piece of understatement. Change of setting, was it? True to a fault, that. Squatting on the east side of Buckinghamshire, Bletchley was a place no one of Hamilton's acquaintance would ever have the boldness to refer to as pretty.

They reached the porch of the house with Hamilton a half stride behind. Carstairs knocked his pipe against a timber, then slid it into an outer pocket of his gray chesterfield. It had been a dark, moonless night that might have concealed the flutter of snow had not a few flakes been caught in the glow of light from the bay windows of the study. Hamilton drew his head out from his overcoat slowly, like a turtle testing the air.

"Well, James, what do you think?" Hamilton said. It was all right, he thought, to call him James.

Carstairs shrugged as if that should be answer enough. Then he said, "Enigma. That's what the Wehrmacht calls it—Enigma?"

Hamilton nodded inside his coat. "Suitable name for a cipher machine, that, eh?" He glanced through the window into the study. There was a fire roaring in the study. He put it out of his mind, turned toward his subordinate. "We have their machine and soon, with a pinch of luck, we'll break their so-called miracle of cryptographics." He pointed an elbow at the huts. "Freddy Winterbotham's nut, that is. He and his electronic gadget and his crew of mathematicians. Not that I know what they're doing, mind. Never was one for figures. Strategy blocks and deployment—there's my end of it. I leave the codes and the four-space digits to the boys in crypto. Every man to his right department, I say." Hamilton clasped his arms across his chest, tucking his hands under his armpits. Now's the time, he thought. Now, before his bloody ears and feet freeze up. "You understand what's happening in Europe, do you?" he said, a bit more awkwardly than he had a right to.

"Hitler, you mean?" Carstairs nodded. "I *see* what he's doing, if that's what you mean. I don't understand why he's getting away with it. The Sudentenland was only a test, you know. He'll have the Czechs next and the Poles." He thrust his

hands deep into the pockets of his overcoat. His first cogniz-
ance of the weather, Hamilton noted. "Bohemia *will* be next,
too. President Hácha is sitting in Prague tonight, quivering at
the thought of it. But, yes, I understand what's happening."

"It's only a question of time," Hamilton said. "War is
coming, that's plain. Within a year, the Chief says, certainly
within two. We'll be in it—like the last time—pushed in.
There's too little of it, time, I think."

"And this?" Carstairs gestured at the huts.

"Preparation."

"I assume there's to be a part in it for me."

"What we're doing here, James—you see how important it
can be?"

The taller man nodded but said nothing.

"Security's one thing." Hamilton blew into his gloved
hands. "You understand that, of course. We must have an
impenetrable security."

"Yes, of course," Carstairs glanced across the lawns. "So,
it's to be security is it?"

"What we have in mind is, well, something rather special.
Unique, actually. The Chief's idea from the start. There was
only to find the right man to shape it up." Hamilton hesitated,
but Carstairs only waited. "He wanted you to consider it, as a
matter of fact. Get James Carstairs, he said, truth be told.
Show you around then pop it to you."

Carstairs turned. "Yes?"

"We want a run between Berlin and London," Hamilton
said. "It is not to be connected with SIS or MI-6 and therefore it can't be operated through the Admiralty. The Chief
wants an *independent* espionage network. And you to run it."

"Independent?"

"Exactly. If we actually do break the Enigma code, it will be
the biggest secret of the war. That means special security."

Carstairs shrugged. "If there is a war."

"Do you doubt it's coming?" Hamilton asked.

Carstairs glanced at the line of huts across the lawn. "You
really think they can break the code?"

"The Chief thinks so."

"Then—" Carstairs' gray eyes squinted down at Hamilton
"—what's the point of having a *special* pipeline between
Berlin and London? If you're going to be reading their secret
radio traffic, anyway, what's—"

"Eventually, the German High Command may get suspicious," Hamilton said. "They may begin to wonder why we're second-guessing their tactics in the field. If they suspect that we've broken their Enigma machine, they'll change to something else." He gestured toward the huts. "And all this work will have been lost."

"You haven't answered my question."

"Yes, well . . ." Hamilton didn't look at the other man's eyes. "It'd be a fraud; your end of it. A decoy. The whole network. You see, we have to protect *our* secret." He finally looked at Carstairs. "If Germans do get suspicious, we'll put them on to you. Make them *think* we're getting our information from inside—not because we've broken Enigma." He started to smile then thought better of it. "They'd fall for it too. James Trevor Carstairs, former SIS deputy director. Special network. Special operation. They'd think it was all very clear . . . and they'd believe it."

Carstairs stared at him for several moments but said nothing.

Hamilton licked his chapped lips. "Of course, it means framing up one of the Nazis as our leak, but that shouldn't be difficult. Someone rather high up in the NSDAP, I should think. Inner circle, you know; one of the Goebbels-Goering crowd. Someone close to Hitler, but not a professional military man. Of course, that'll be up to you."

"You don't *have* anyone in Berlin," Carstairs said finally.

"Well, now, that's stretching, isn't it? Of course we have people there, but—"

"But no one you can hand over to me?"

Hamilton raised an eyebrow. "You'll take the job, then?"

Carstairs didn't reply.

"It has to be done, you know," Hamilton said. "If not you then someone else, but you're the Chief's choice. I must say—"

"So I set up one of them to be a traitor."

Hamilton shrugged. "Well, yes. One of the Nazis."

"I see," Carstairs said. "I deliberately blow the run, then?"

"If that becomes necessary, yes. As I say, it's all to protect the project here. But we could wreak havoc among Hitler's cronies. They'd never trust one another again."

"Do they now?"

Hamilton shrugged. "Are you interested, then?"

"A phony run," Carstairs said to himself. He looked at Hamilton. "How staffed?"

"Competent operators, of course. It wouldn't work otherwise."

"Bloody clever of us, isn't it?"

"James—"

"Yes, yes," Carstairs said quietly. "I'll take it."

"I say, good show," Hamilton beamed triumphantly. He clasped Carstairs' shoulder like a brother. "Excellent."

"I suppose you realize that these operators—the ones outside Britain—whoever they are, will be necessarily expendable."

"Quite," Hamilton said, with a suggestion of a smile still on his lips.

"And what of their knowledge of all this?"

"Knowledge?" Hamilton's expression was suddenly puzzled. "No knowledge of the plan, certainly not that. We mustn't have everyone in on our little scheme."

"I see. So it won't be just the Nazis we'll be deceiving."

"If war comes," Hamilton said defensively, "we will *all* be doing disagreeable things, I daresay. I for one certainly don't relish the prospect."

"Quite."

"And keep in mind the task at hand. We are protecting a very important secret. Let that be your guidance. Ultra must never be compromised. We're talking about *saving* lives, in the longer view. You should consider that. Saving lives."

"Ultra?"

"Yes, well, it's what we're calling the Enigma information. Special designation to distinguish it from all the rest. Higher that Most Secret. Only a handful to have access, you know." Hamilton tugged at the collar of his overcoat. The wind was coming up again. "No second thoughts, then?" He stamped his feet to shock the circulation back into his numb toes. "You'll take it without reservation?"

Carstairs didn't answer. He only stared into the shadows. From one of the huts came the sound of a door slamming. Finally, he said, "I know what we'll call him." He didn't look at Hamilton.

"Him?"

"Our nonexistent traitor inside the Third Reich. The one who's passing us secrets—*if* this Ultra scheme works and *if* it all comes to more than throwing sticks and stones in the end. It just occurred to me." He glanced back. "If it takes mathematicians to unravel one enigma, it should fall to an algebraist to safeguard another. That's only right, isn't it?" He smiled.

Hamilton shrank behind the protection of his overcoat and shuddered against the draft on his neck. "You're too much the romantic."

"Bloody right." He looked up into the night. "Numbers are the essence of all things."

"What's that?"

"Pythagoras," Carstairs said, "I'll call him Pythagoras."

January 1939

The chief of the *Sicherheitspolizei*—Reich Security Police —stood at the tall corner window of the office, hands clasped behind his back, staring down three floors at the lamp-lighted Prinz Albrecht-Strasse. It was Berlin's most deserted street, he thought. There was only the snow, the halo of light that surrounded the street lamps, and the phonograph recording of Wagner's *Die Meistersinger von Nürnberg* to inundate his awareness. It was as if the mesmeric effect of the glow of lights and the first act prelude combined to transcend time and he was returned to Saxony as a boy, sitting in the prompt box before the orchestra of his father's conservatory in Halle. There was his love; the euphony and purity of rhythm in the classical composition, the organizing of harmonies into a perfect integral whole.

He closed his eyes as the recording breathed out the soft chords by flutes and violins behind the yearning, luxuriant melody. Wagner was not his favorite composer. There was an incessant quest for relaxation of structural tensions about his work that the Reich security chief found at odds with itself; a longing to be passionate, ever more demanding and never satisfied. Personally, he favored the serenity of Mozart and Haydn. But Wagner was the vogue in Berlin just now, inasmuch as the Fuehrer preferred it, which was the standard against which everything was measured these days.

A figure darted across the wide boulevard and passed quickly between two halos of light, then was swallowed up in the shadows toward the side entrance of the gray building. It was the first sign of life from the street in almost an hour. Not that it was surprising. This particular Berlin address was not likely to be mistaken for any other or visited by any cheerful civilian at this late hour. A former art school, 8 Prinz Albrecht-Strasse, was now headquarters for the Reichsfuehrer Himmler's SS-Central Office. It was also the heart of the security chief's own spheres of influence—residence of the SD, the party's sole intelligence organization; center of the Criminal Police and home of the *Geheime Staatspolizei*, the Secret State Police—Gestapo.

But this meeting tonight had nothing to do with political police business. There would be no recording of this conversation as was usual in the office. This was to be a special interview between the security chief and his personal selection from among agents within the SD—the man who walked empty streets—Johann Regenbauer.

He had never met Regenbauer, though it was not necessary for the mission ahead to have known him before. He knew him through the dossier that had been secretly prepared on his life; a dossier so complete that its thickness would stop a nine-millimeter bullet fired at close range. He knew him to be an excellent pilot. Regenbauer had accounted for himself well in Spain under Richthofen's Condor Legion command where he flew *lounwolf*—sorties against the enemy alone, without the usual wingman formations. The dossier reflected that he was not a gregarious man and scant evidence was found that he had any friends at all. It was precisely this loner attitude that first attracted the Reich security chief's notice. Regenbauer was the son of a Wedel shipping merchant who had suffered the loss of his business after the Great War and committed suicide in 1922. A severe case of acne in his youth had scarred his face into rough pitted skin. In his teens he was a tough and more than once had been picked up by the police. He railed against authority. Though it was never proved, he was suspected of causing the fire that gutted a *polizeiwache* on his seventeenth birthday. If his manner was crude, his mind was not. He placed third in his engineering class at Kiel University, where he also was an exceptional student of languages. It was at Kiel that young Regenbauer first made contact with the National Socialist ideology, and he embraced it, leading scores of night encounters against anti-Nazis. He flew with Lufthansa as an assistant pilot aboard transports, joined the party in 1928 and in

1935 was absorbed into the Luftwaffe. He was assigned to the *Forschungsamt* because the air service's intelligence operation was expanding and searching for translators. He ultimately ended up in the code and cipher section of the *Chiffrierwesen* as an analyst, a post he did well in as long as he was left alone to do his work. Too often, however, he was impatient and contemptuous with his coworkers and insolent toward his superiors. Finally, he was returned to the flying service and duty in Spain where he was judged incorrigible and ordered on missions of an independent nature.

It was then that the SS became interested in Regenbauer. Or rather, the chief of Reich security. In Regenbauer he recognized a man dedicated to the party, yet independent, ambitious, and intelligent. He was also crude and seemingly without pity, but that was all right too. Regenbauer was taken secretly into the SD as a special agent. His job: to observe certain ranking members of the Luftwaffe High Command who were suspected to be critical of party policy. Regenbauer reported to no one. His instructions were mailed to him and his reports dropped at a post box in Berlin. All instructions came directly from the security chief. For more than a year, Regenbauer had done his job flawlessly. Now he was ready for the work the security chief had planned; work that could not be trusted to paper. Now was the time for their meeting. SS-Standartenfuehrer Reinhard Heydrich, Chief of the Reich Security Service, strode, to the Victrola and switched off the record machine. Now.

"You know who I am, Hauptsturmfuehrer?"
"Ja, Herr Standartenfuehrer."
"You know you are acting under my orders alone?"
"Ja, Herr Standartenfuehrer."

Heydrich sat back in his chair and rubbed a long, slender finger along his upper lip as he took in the SS captain standing rigidly at attention before his desk. The man's face was broader than the dossier photos indicated, the horrible scars sharply vivid on his cheeks. His dark, emotionless eyes stared above Heydrich in a way that made Heydrich think he was looking through the building rather than at a wall inside it. Somehow—the SS colonel wasn't sure what it was exactly —Regenbauer had a pall about him as if his soul had been burned out of him. He didn't seem nervous and he didn't perspire. Little wonder he had no friends.

"Sit down, Captain." Heydrich pushed himself up in his chair to better see the man before him. "I have been very pleased with your work in the SD to this point."

"Thank you, sir."

"I thought it was time we met. I wanted to see you face to face." Heydrich leaned slightly across the desk. "There's other work."

"Yes, sir."

"I've kept you out of the regular duties normally undertaken by SD agents. What you've been doing has been done for me personally. No one else knows of your work. I suppose you know that?"

Regenbauer said nothing. He nodded.

"I've been studying your history. It appears that this sort of work suits you." Heydrich paused as if to allow a response, but Regenbauer remained silent. "You are independent—some say arrogantly so—and you do not respond well to authority. Not particularly agreeable qualities for a party member of your rank and certainly not for an ordinary SS officer. Can you imagine the chaos if every SS officer took up your attitude? Still, the state has a place for a man of your ability. I need certain men who seem to be cast from a different mold. Intelligent men. Men who display attributes of leadership and inventiveness and more than a little cunning. But above all, I must have a man who is trustworthy." He slapped his hand against the desk for emphasis. "That is the most important thing. I *must* be able to trust you. Is that clear?"

Regenbauer's gaze had not moved from Heydrich. "Yes, Herr Standartenfuehrer."

Heydrich rose from his place behind the desk and moved to the window where he stared down at the street for several moments. "When I say that I must trust you, of course I am speaking for the Reichsfuehrer and for the Fuehrer himself." He spoke it slowly, without looking back at the man seated before the desk. "And I am pleased with your work to this point, as I said. But we must have this understanding. You will be working for me alone. You will report to me only and you will carry out all my instructions as they are issured by me. You will answer to no one else." He turned to Regenbauer. "Is *that* clear?"

The Hauptsturmfuehrer nodded.

"The penalty for disobedience or failure to follow instructions will be your immediate execution. You will attend to my orders without question. That is the essence of your oath to the Fuehrer. Absolute loyalty. As a special agent of the SD your supreme duty is the security of the Reich. Let that be your lodestar as it is mine. There are enemies within the state and they must be rooted out, their traitorous schemes exposed, their opposition crushed. And it is for a few men—men of an independent nature—to track down these Judases." Heydrich was staring out the window and as he spoke rage boiled within him. His fists were clenched rigidly at his sides and the veins at his temples stood out. Suddenly, he whirled to face Regenbauer. "I will cut them down! I will hang them by their traitorous throats! *The Reich does not tolerate treachery!*"

For an instant Heydrich's eyes were fill with madness, then he took a breath and the moment passed. The Reich security chief wiped a hand across his mouth and walked stiffly to the desk. The outburst seemed to have startled Heydrich more than Regenbauer. The captain remained seated. He had not flinched. His eyes continued to track Heydrich without the slightest hint of emotion behind them.

"How can I be of service to you, Standartenfuehrer?" he asked.

"You are eager to the task, then?" Heydrich nodded approvingly. "Good. I thought as much." He took the folder from the desktop. "You are familiar with the functions of the Abwehr?"

"Military intelligence?" Regenbauer nodded. "Yes, sir."

"Under Admiral Canaris' guidance, the Abwehr is the Reich's primary foreign and counterintelligence agency." Heydrich was uncomfortable to admit it. "I have met some difficulty in transferring some of that responsibility to the SD. Little Willie is quite determined to hold on to his little empire of spies. It is a situation to which, for the moment, the Fuehrer agrees—my security forces within the SS have no official jurisdiction on Abwehr territory." Heydrich nodded confidently to himself. "In time, that will change. For the moment the Gestapo, the Kripo and the SD are essentially occupied with police work. That also will change. I do not like depending upon the good admiral's benevolence—he shares information with me arbitrarily, and only that which suits him to share."

Regenbauer nodded. "You do not trust Canaris."

"I do not trust anyone," Heydrich snapped. He glanced sharply at Regenbauer and his frown dissolved. "Except, perhaps, I shall trust you. You are going to be my spy, Captain. My personal spy."

"But, sir, you don't suspect the Abwehr—"

"We shall see, shan't we?" Heydrich allowed a hollow smile. "There are some members of the High Command in the Wehrmacht who have no vision. Some have not accepted that the destiny of Germany is irrevocably in the hands of the Fuehrer. He *is* the Reich! In five years' time, perhaps less, all Europe will march under the German banner. It is for us in the SS, the protective arm of the socialist state, to guard against treacherous schemes of our hidden enemies within the Reich." He paused, his eyes wild again. "I will stamp them out, Captain. You will . . . act as my instrument in certain instances." Heydrich opened the folder he held in his hands and handed a sheet of paper from it to Regenbauer. "Memorize these names. I will give you specific instructions on what is to be done in each case."

Heydrich walked back to his seat behind the desk. "You are about to become a most powerful man, Captain. I will see to it that the considerable resources of the Gestapo be made available to you on request without question. Do not disappoint me."

The SS captain glanced up from the paper. "These names . . ."

"Yes."

"There aren't only Wehrmacht names on this list." He looked at it. "Party members, politicians, officials in the government . . . an American . . ." He looked at Heydrich and frowned.

"Our enemies are everywhere in Germany."

"And these people? What—"

"Kill them," Heydrich said. "Use your imagination. I want their deaths to appear as accidents, not murder. The American can be first."

Regenbauer nodded. He stared at the list again for a few seconds, then raised his gaze to Heydrich. "When?"

The *Chef der Sicherheitspolizei* laughed out loud and there was only Regenbauer to stare at him and wonder why.

Part One

1 _____

May 10, 1940

TED CAMPBELL COAXED the control column back to the right until the Sprint's artificial horizon plane floated level on the bubble indicator before him on the cockpit gauge. Below him some thirty-five hundred feet was Meersburg on Lake Constance, just awakening to the first light of day. He could see the castle keep of Fürstenhäusle reflecting the sun and casting its long shadow across the four steep gables high on the south side. The Steigstrasse, lined with half-timbered houses, seemed to plunge into darkness as it snaked around the ancient castle and emptied into the Marktplatz.

It was an absolutely beautiful dawn with the sun breaking magnificently through the Alps and the lake glistening serenely in the glow of morning from here to Switzerland. It was exactly what he needed—to get away from Friedrichshafen and the stifling sadness there, and greet the dawn in the plane that had more pleasant memories associated with it.

The Sprint was handling just as it always had; it was like steering an eagle. It didn't seem that it was actually two years since he'd won the Renaix Trophy with her in the Leipzig—Essen—Bern cross-country air race. It was one of the last races on the continent before the world started complicating his life. It was before Germany got so terribly hungry for growing space. It was before the Sudetenland and the Austrian union

union and the Czech occupation and Poland. Before the war. It
was also before the crash.

He banked the Sprint in a steep turn to the north and climbed
at a dizzying angle to twelve thousand feet. It angered him to
be reminded of the accident, and he pushed the plane through a
half dozen loops and rolls until the exercise made him
light-headed. The idea of this spur-of-the-moment outing was
to escape the burden of responsibility that plagued him on the
ground. Up here he was free, if only for a short time. These
were his moments to let his mind soar on the clouds—
emptying out the pain—with just the Sprint to fill his thoughts.
The further away he could get from the aerodrome at Friedrichshafen the better he would feel. He watched the Sprint's
tiny shadow cross the Danube just outside what looked to be
Tuttlingen. The sun was full at his back now, he could feel the
warmth on his neck. The sun glinted off the plastic dive
indicator attached to the canopy slide. Ahead he could see the
Neckar River winding north toward Stuttgart on the horizon.
He checked his fuel gauge. The Sprint could go another hour
before he'd need to return. Plenty of fuel and time to burn.
Follow the Neckar to Stuttgart up the valley of the Black Forest
then back over the Hohenzollerns—and home for breakfast.

He was on the west side of the river, approaching Rotten-
burg from the southeast, when he saw the bombers. He
counted five Dorniers and a Junker "Iron Annie." They were
about four thousand feet below him in a tight formation with
the Junker leading. They were headed almost directly west,
lumbering along obviously loaded to the gills. There wasn't
much mistaking where they were going. The Rhine was less
than fifty miles away and beyond that—France.

They were easy to follow. He stayed four or five miles
behind them and maintained altitude. He knew he was safe
enough because he was in their blind spot with the morning sun
still hot behind him. It was an attack force all right. He could
see the puffs of smoke as the upper gunners fired quick bursts
to check their weapons as they passed over the humpbacks
—7.92-millimeter Rheinmetall MG 15 machine guns, if he
remembered correctly. Goering had been very proud. Spain
proved to be an effective proving ground.

Campbell throttled back a bit. He was catching up to them
and he had to cut the Sprint back nearly to a stall to keep from
overtaking the slower, heavily laden aircraft. He could hear

their engines now, straining under the load; probably liquid-cooled Daimler-Benzes in the Dorniers. He hadn't seen a Junker up close, though it likely used the same or perhaps a Bristol Mercury; they'd need that for a heavy payload. Anything that big would rip itself out of a plane the size of the Sprint due to the torque, but then the Sprint was designed for speed, not bombs; she didn't even carry a radio.

The bombers split into two groups as they came into sight of the Rhine, the Junker taking two Dorniers southeast and the others heading a few degrees north of their original heading. It was then that he saw the artillery. The German guns were blasting across the Rhine.

Jesus! Of course—the Maginot fortifications! This was the breakout! He was watching, he suddenly realized, the invasion of France!

He didn't hear the Stuka until it had gone screaming past him—the pilot must have had it in a nearly vertical dive—and then it was already too late. The Sprint shuddered violently under the impact of the Stuka's strafing, the control column jerked from Campbell's grasp, and the plane instantly heeled over on its back and began a twelve-thousand-foot spiraling plunge toward the snow-crested ridges of the Black Forest.

Campbell fought the gravitational force that slung him back in the seat. Instinct told him to roll the plane gradually out of the counterclockwise spin. He didn't know how badly the Sprint had been damaged and now was not the time to jerk her around and lose what little control he had. One thing was clear: her racing days were over. And his, unless he could set her down quickly. Race pilots, he needn't remind himself, could not afford the luxury or weight of a parachute. Until now, he'd never needed one.

There wasn't time to wonder why he'd been attacked. The worry was not to die in burning wreckage, the conclusion of a very long fall. Through his mind flashed the image of a mangled race car crumpled and jammed upside down against a stone abutment, its petrol tank ruptured, black fuel blazing, and above it all the terrifying screams of a trapped driver. *Edward Campbell ist tot.*

The Sprint tried valiantly to level out, but it just wasn't in her. Campbell could feel the limp rudder pedals under his feet. The Stuka's attack had severed the cable to the tail. No rudder.

No directional control. Bloody goddamn Stuka! He pushed the stick forward, steepening the angle of the dive, and throttled forward, keeping his eyes on the airspeed gauge so as not to suffer vertigo due to the spin. The needle seemed stuck at 210 miles an hour. Then it began to move. The stick was as far forward as he could reach, but he couldn't tell if the nose had dropped, because he was concentrating on the gauge in front of him and fighting the gravitational force that was pressing him back into the seat. The needle touched 220. Without rudder to stabilize a spin, which resulted in a low-speed spiral, the only alternative to regain control was to push the nose down and pour the power to her. He needed speed. And quickly.

Two hundred thirty miles an hour.

He could feel his heartthrob pounding at his temples.

Two hundred thirty-five.

"C'mon, get bloody wings!"

Two hundred forty.

The stomach-knotting whirling sensation dissipated. He could see the blue-green trees of the gently sloping range in his peripheral vision. He'd stabilized the spin but he was in a nearly vertical power dive. *Level out or black out.* He pulled the stick back. The Sprint fought him for control, then, gradually, she responded. It took nearly all his strength, but the control column moved toward him. The Sprint lifted her nose.

The altimeter had been turning backwards crazily and now it stopped at twenty-one hundred feet—he'd dropped almost ten thousand feet in a matter of seconds and the plane was still in one piece. Campbell quickly switched hands on the stick and wiped his mouth. In one piece, but for how long? The canopy window was streaked with lines of shiny black rivulets.

Oil.

The oil pressure had dropped to nothing. He glanced at the oil temp—one hundred degrees Centigrade and receding slightly. The engine temperature was cooking the cylinder heads. He throttled back, adjusted the fuel mixture and opened the propeller pitch, and leaned up in his seat to see where he was.

"We gotta get you down, old girl," Campbell said, studying the terrain below. "You and me both." There were several alpine farms. Plowed fields and fences. Not much bloody good. There was the river, but it would be tricky in a nose-heavy bird like this; besides, there was no telling how fast

he could get out before she sank. He remembered the autobahn. There was the Munich-Stuttgart autobahn, a divided
four-lane bloody wonderful highway not a dozen miles from
here!

He checked the instruments. The engine temperature was
coming down, but the lack of oil only gave him a few minutes
before it overheated and melted the cylinder heads. Four,
maybe five minutes—that was as much time as he had left. If
he was easy and didn't push her too hard, he could make it.
Still, it would be a dicey landing without a rudder. But he'd
just have to take his chances, wouldn't he? First he had to get
her there. He banked the Sprint in a slow, sliding turn over the
river and began his descent.

It wouldn't be such a tough landing after all, he thought.
There wouldn't be much if any traffic this early in the day and
he could slow the little racer to forty or forty-five miles per
hour on the pavement before he'd lose directional control. The
worst would be the plane might nose in or skid on a wing. Not
terribly serious, that, he told himself. Then he caught the glint
of light in the rearview mirror. He'd been so preoccupied
trying not to drill himself into the ground, he'd forgotten what
got him into this predicament. Now he remembered. The glint
was aligning behind him.

The Stuka was coming in for the kill.

There wasn't any mistaking his intentions, Campbell was
immediately aware. Not at that angle of pursuit. *The bastard's
followed me down to finish the job!* Campbell's glance shot at
the instrument panel. The engine temperature was still red-
lined. Oil pressure was gone. He didn't have a rudder. And no
parachute if the Sprint caught fire. Not that any of that
mattered. He'd already seen what a Stuka's twenty-millimeter
cannons could do. It wasn't going to happen twice.

Campbell jerked the control column straight back with his
right hand and jammed the throttle forward to the stop with his
left. The Sprint's nose lifted immediately. Campbell felt his
shoulders bite against the seat harness as the racer shot into a
vertical loop. The horizon mark on the canopy window rushed
through the sun. Then the pale blue cloudless sky. Campbell
held the stick back tight against his thighs until he saw the
green patchwork of the earth roll into view then pressed the

stick forward with all his strength. The river Neckar was dead ahead and he made for it.

The maneuver worked. The Stuka pilot hadn't counted on the little plane swooping up in front of him and curling back into an inverted loop. The Sprint, being a much smaller craft and lighter, had a more compact turning radius and Campbell knew the Stuka pilot could make one of two choices if he intended to press the attack: bank off and return on a new pursuit angle or follow him around the loop. Campbell prayed it was the former. It might give him enough time to outrace the German to safety—if the Sprint's engine didn't blow up first.

Campbell searched the sky frantically for his pursuer. His heart sank when he found him, rolling out of a wider loop, bearing down directly behind him, though at a greater distance than before. He'd make that up soon enough. Campbell's mind raced through the alternatives left him. Another loop would be suicide. The German would be ready for that and, besides, the Sprint couldn't handle the strain. Any sudden turns, without a rudder to stabilize, would only drive him into another spin, and at this altitude, he'd never recover from it. A flat-out dive was his only chance. Point the nose straight down and hope the engine didn't explode in his face. Hope the Stuka pilot would see he was following a crazy man and break off. Hope the G-force wouldn't black him out before he could pull her up. Hope he had an engine left to pull up with. Campbell took one last look at the temperature and pressure gauges then forced the control column forward to the fire wall. The nose dropped. He banged his head against the seat rest as the plane seemed to fall from under him. *It's a hell of a way to walk into a war.*

The altimeter began winding down furiously.

He could feel the sun burning through the top of his head, but all he could see was a bend in the river. It was sparkling. Cool. Inviting. And rushing toward him, getting ever wider.

Campbell let his eyes glance at the mirror. Unbelievably, the Stuka was there. He was following him down! He was ten points off the Sprint's tail and lining up for the killing blow; six, seven hundred yards behind.

Christ, he's crazier than I am! What was a Stuka's median range of fire? Five hundred yards? Four hundred?

Campbell suddenly realized that he hadn't fooled anyone. The Stuka pilot knew that he didn't have turning control. He was forcing him to dive, which was exactly what he'd wanted. *You stupid toad, a Ju-87 is a* DIVE *bomber!*

The altimeter needle wound through six hundred feet. He could see individual trees along the banks of the river, but he held the stick forward. In the mirror, the Stuka was closing. Campbell could only make it out as a blur. There were only a few seconds before it would be perfectly aligned in firing position. There was only to wait for the murderous impact of the bullets. He didn't have to worry about the river. Or catching a wing in the trees. He'd be dead before he crashed.

Four hundred fifty feet, according to the altimeter. An instinctive exercise: checking the instruments. Fuel. Oil. Temperature. RPM count. As if it mattered. As if anything . . .

Airspeed! God Almighty! The loop had slowed him to nearly stalling speed. He was doing just over two hundred miles an hour. No wonder the Stuka was overtaking him! *You bloody idiot!*

There wasn't time to consider what he was doing to the plane. Whatever happened now, happened. It was a matter of survival now. He could sense the Stuka's pilot's fingers on the trigger. He must be in his sights by now. It was just too damned bad.

As the altimeter needle swept through three hundred feet, Campbell yanked the throttle back to idle, punched the gear down button, grabbed the flaps lever and pushed it forward. The little Sprint's engine screamed a deafening whine as the controllable prop straightened to flat pitch. Campbell was thrown forward against the harness webbing as if he'd hit an invisible obstacle. Instantly, the control column took on the weight of the plane as the nose wanted to come up. Campbell frantically wheeled the elevator trim with the palm of his hand —three, four, five times, he rotated the wheel. He thought his right arm was going to break against the tremendous pressure behind the control column as the plane fought to correct for the sudden lift and drag Campbell had given her. He blinked at the altimeter.

Two hundred feet.

He glanced out of the cockpit to see the Stuka flash past, then he released the control column and the Sprint shuddered violently as the nose lifted. Rivets were popping on both wings

and the flaps were bent from the unnatural strain on the airfoil
—but the gamble had worked.

When Campbell created the incredible drag by suddenly
lowering the gear and flaps, the relative effect on the Stuka in
pursuit was as if the Sprint had stopped in midair. To keep it in
his sights, the German pilot steepened the angle of his dive. He
would have done it instinctively, as he was trained to do. He
wouldn't have had time to realize, until it was too late, that he
couldn't pull out of it.

Campbell didn't hear the explosion when the Luftwaffe
attack bomber crashed against the east bank of the Neckar. He
didn't need to hear or see anything. He knew exactly what
would happen. He didn't have any particular emotion about the
Stuka pilot or his crewman. They were dead. What mattered
now was that Campbell not join them.

The engine was on fire. Smoke was pouring out of the
vented cowling and obstructing his view. That last little trick
had done the Sprint. Like it or not, she was coming down.
Campbell bobbed his head to see through the smoke. He was
less than fifty feet from the ground, just above the trees, and
traveling much too fast to land. A moot question, that. It
wasn't an issue of landing anymore. He would be encountering
the ground rather quickly and any second. Through the smoke
he glimpsed a farmhouse to his right and somewhere in his
peripheral vision were images of vehicles. Quite a lot of
vehicles, passing in a blur like a picket fence seen from inside
an accelerating car.

He saw the plowed field first—dead ahead—*then* the low
stone fence that enclosed this end. He was skimmering over the
gently rolling ground at an indicated airspeed of 105 miles an
hour. Suicide. But the fence was upon him before he could
form another thought.

It was his very speed that saved him. There was a terrible
explosion of sound as the Sprint's landing gear was ripped
away when they smashed into the stone barrier. The plane
careened up, sliding slightly sideways in the air, and bounced
on its wounded belly. The prop was wrenched back over the
engine like a peeled banana skin. The Sprint struck the ground
again, the right wing was shorn off at the fuselage, and the
plane skidded on its side nearly sixty yards before it stopped.

Campbell's hand was bleeding from a gash across the palm
and his legs were numb, but it was the choking smoke and

stinging smell of petrol that delivered him to action. The cockpit was on its side at an awkward angle and it took him several seconds to pop the shattered canopy and boost himself over the instrument panel. He fell to the ground blindly, staggered to his feet and commanded them to move until he couldn't take another step and collapsed. The Sprint was nearly consumed in flames by then. With her remaining wing canted to the sky like a dorsal fin, she resembled some great serpent from below floundering on a sea of mud.

Campbell heard the voices then. From over his shoulder he could see them coming, following the trail he'd excavated through the field. There seemed to be a lot of them running, men in uniforms, crying out in German, but he couldn't make out the words. He couldn't keep his head up. It was too heavy. His entire body was too heavy. He rolled on his back and felt the sun warm on his face. He tried to keep his eyes open—he was going to have to explain that awful landing—but they were too heavy. It was much easier to simply lie here. Let the darkness take hold of him. Much easier . . .

2

CAMPBELL WOKE FROM the pain. His hand seemed on fire. Someone had bandaged it with gauze but the wrapping was red across the palm and his fingers were streaked with dried, caked blood. He was lying on a bed in the corner of a large room that was teeming with Wehrmacht officers. A knot of them was huddled around a table crowded with radio equipment, apparently jubilant at the news they were getting. Campbell was still light-headed, but he heard enough to know that a huge operation was on in the north. Armored and airborne divisions were crashing along the frontiers of Holland and Belgium. Paratroops attacking Moerdijk, Dordrecht, Rotterdam. He heard that Gennep Bridge over the river Maas had been taken.

Campbell tried to sit up. He scraped one of his legs against the sideboard and a bolt of pain shot up his shins. He cried out in bleary-eyed agony. Suddenly, he was surrounded by guards.

"So, you are conscious again," said a captain in German as he shouldered his way between two rifle-bearing privates. He stood directly in front of Campbell, the creases in his battle uniform still fresh. "Do you understand German?"

Campbell hugged his aching legs. "Yes."

"What are you doing here? Who are you?"

"Ted Campbell," he said. He looked up at the captain. "I didn't have much choice about where I landed."

The captain's eyes widened. "You are English?"

"American, actually." He sat back against the wall so he wouldn't have to look up at such a steep angle. "Do you think I could have a glass of water, Captain. I'm still a bit foggy-headed."

The German snapped an order and one of the guards handed over his canteen. Campbell took several long swallows.

"How did you do that?" The captain motioned toward the ceiling. "We watched you . . . in the sky. How did you make the Luftwaffe pilot crash?"

Campbell shook his head. "Whatever happened to him was his own doing," he said. "I was just trying not to get killed."

The captain nodded as if that was the answer he'd expected. "What were you doing here?" he repeated.

"I was just—"

"Who are you?"

"I told you. Campbell. Theodore Campbell. I—"

"Where are your papers?"

"Papers?"

"Identity papers," the captain urged. "Identity papers. You have nothing on you. Where are your papers?"

"I guess they're in the plane," Campbell said. He knew they weren't in the Sprint, what was left of her. His passport and German identity papers were in the dresser in his room at Friedrichshafen exactly where he'd left them. But let them look in the plane.

"Your plane burned."

"Yes, well, I can't very well help that, can I?"

The captain drew in a breath. "You are English, I think."

"Christ, I'm American! My name is Ted Campbell. I'm staying in Friedrichshafen at a villa my family owns. I'm a pilot and airplane engineer. I took off this morning on a joy ride around Lake Constance. That's all. Check it out. And while you're at it you might send for a doctor. My legs hurt like bloody hell. I think one of them is broken."

The captain rubbed his jaw. He was distracted by a commotion outside. A car skidded to a stop. Some of the guards turned to look and Campbell had a view of a window. There was a cloud of dust and as it passed he could see the Sprint in the distance, across the field. She was a char of burnt metal; a once beautiful machine now a smoldering hulk. It hurt him to see it.

The man from the car stood in the doorway, looking at

Campbell and listening as the captain explained the situation. He was not in the Wehrmacht, at least he didn't wear a uniform. He was dressed in a hat and a leather coat over a plain gray suit. He was one of the Blacks, Campbell realized with mounting distaste. Gestapo.

The Black took up the same position in front of Campbell as the captain had. He was sinister-looking, Campbell thought. At least that seemed to be the impression he wanted to create. The man folded his arms across his chest and stared down at Campbell. He might have taken off his hat, Campbell thought.

"Who are you?" the Black finally demanded.

"Campbell. Theodore Campbell."

"You have no papers."

"I've already been through that. Evidently, they burned in the plane."

"All foreigners must carry their papers at all times," said the Black. "Where are your papers?"

Campbell drew an angry sigh. "Look, I don't have the bloody papers! My name is Theodore Campbell and I—"

"You came from the west and you have no papers." The Black frowned. "Who are you?"

"I told you who I am. I'm sorry I haven't got a passport to show you, but I didn't know your ruddy air force was going to shoot me down now, did I?"

"You came from the west," the Black repeated. "I think you are a spy."

"*Spy!* Christ, I'm hardly French."

"An *English* spy!" said the Black angrily.

"I'm American, for God sakes!" Campbell was suddenly aware of the dangerous situation he was in. They shot spies these days in Germany. "I'm from Friedrichshafen. My family has a villa there. Seventeen Adlerstrasse. You can check it for yourself. Call them if you don't believe me. The housekeeper's name is Glebe. Frau Anna Glebe. I'm an aircraft designer. Willy Messerschmitt knows me. Call *him*. He's at Augsburg. You can—"

The Black struck him in the face with the back of his hand. *"Halt den mund!"*

Campbell touched a finger to the corner of his mouth and saw the blood. "You stupid bastard."

The Gestapo man turned to the captain. "Put him in my car."

"You can't take me anywhere," Campbell yelled. "I'm a fucking American! I need a doctor! I—"

But two guards jerked him up from the bed.

"We shall see who you are," the Black said. With a cruel smile he nodded to the guards.

Campbell screamed when they set him on his feet. The pain in his legs shot through his brain. He floated off into unconsciousness before he reached the car.

He opened his eyes to the curious sound of something being gnawed. He was lying on his face on a steel-framed cot with a threadbare wool blanket for a mattress. The makeshift bed creaked as he turned on his side and the gnawing stopped. It was an incredibly small room—moist stone walls, a single light bulb dangling from a massive rafter above. A cell, Campbell gradually realized. The only opening in the walls was blocked by a large and very heavy-looking timbered door. There was a tiny opening in the door—a peephole—and through it he heard the monotonous echo of water dripping.

Campbell touched the wall for support and eased himself into a sitting position. The exertion made him dizzy and he decided not to get up. His legs were numb. His shoes had been removed. Someone had cleaned his hand—the dried blood was gone and the crevices between his fingers were sticky with an orange antiseptic—and the bandages had been changed. The pain was gone too, at least the aching of it. He noticed his right trouser leg had been ripped along the seam to the knee, and when he pushed open the flap he sucked in his breath at the sight of the ankle. It was hideously swollen and purplish. The numbness frightened him then until he realized he must be drugged. The medication accounted for the grogginess. He hoped that was what it was. There was no telling where he was or how long he'd been here. He remembered the Black.

A rat fled across the floor to a crack between the stones when Campbell called out. He glanced down at a corner of the cell. The rat had been chewing at his shoes.

"Is anybody out there?"

There was no reply except the dripping water.

"For God sakes, I know *somebody's* out there! Get me out of this bloody hole. Hello? C'mon—Christ, I'm not a goddamn spy! Hey? Hey! *Heeeeey!*"

Campbell yelled for nearly an hour. He was hoarse and

exhausted when he laid his head back against the steel bed brace to rest. Somebody's *got* to be out there, he told himself. If they were trying to provoke him they were damned well succeeding.

He draped his bandage hand across his forehead as shade against the light. "All right. All right." He spoke in a conversational tone. "You've proved your point. I'm tired and hungry. So, let's talk. You out there. You hear me?" He paused and listened to his own silence. "Right."

Campbell exhaled through his teeth. "My name's Campbell. No surprise there, eh? Theodore Campbell, Ted to my friends. I was born thirty years ago this June. In Scotland, as a matter of fact, Edinburgh—but I'm still American, see. My parents just happened to be there at the time. You've probably heard of my father . . . Edward Campbell? Eddie Campbell. You know, the race driver. An ace fighter pilot with the French in the Great War. One of Rene Fonck's and Charlie Nungesser's chums. Remember? I can't help it if he was on the other side, can I? Are you getting all this? Let me know if I'm going too fast, won't you? Because I've heard all this before. Look, you know you could save us both time if you'd just put a call through to Friedrichshafen. I lied about the passport. You might as well know. It's on my dresser, at the villa. I forgot it. Hell, I was just going up for a short ride. I didn't know this was going to happen. Really. You're really taking all this too seriously. Do you hear?"

Campbell shook his head. "You haven't got it yet, have you?" He withdrew his hand from his forehead and pushed himself upright. *"I'm Teddy bloody Campbell, for Chrissakes!"* he yelled angrily. "Eddie Campbell's son? 1911? The great kidnapping? Fifty thousand dollars ransom? Don't tell me you don't remember. It was all in the papers. You do *read?* Missing twenty-four days then discovered in a basket under a park bench near the Louvre? The Campbell baby? Little Teddy Campbell?" Campbell opened his hands out to the door. "That's me! In the flesh."

He let his arms sink to his sides resignedly as there was no reply. "This really isn't getting us anywhere. I mean, what the hell do you want me to do? I've told you who I am. What have I done? If it's the Stuka, well, I'm bloody not going to apologize for that. He was trying to kill me, wasn't he? The Sprint was clearly marked. Any fool would have known it wasn't armed. You can believe I'm who I say I am, you know. This detention is illegal. I'm an American citizen. I demand to see someone from the American embassy. Do you hear me? Do you—*will you stop that ruddy faucet from dripping!*"

Campbell drew his knees up against his chest. He was hungry. His anger had cleared his head and alerted his stomach. How long *had* he been here? Certainly not a day. Hours then. Of course, he'd been drugged, but they couldn't have fed him in that state, could they? Maybe it had been a day. Maybe two days. Christ, what did they *want?* He touched his ankle gently. It was beginning to ache again. He couldn't tell if it was broken, but there was no imagining the pain. It was coming back. The medication was wearing off.

Campbell rested his chin on his knee. "I hope you're enjoying this," he said to the door. "I hope you're getting a big chuckle out of this because I'm going to see that you are busted when I get out of here. We'll see how funny it is after I've had a little chat with Goering. I know him, you know. Spent a week with him hunting at Karinhall last November. I know Goebbels too. And von Ribbentrop and Himmler and Rosenberg and Hess. They're all going to be very displeased with this. Especially the Reichsfuehrer. Heinrich is going to be quite embarrassed, having me thrown into this crappy little cell by one of his police forces. You can imagine how he'll feel about you. We could have settled this. You only needed to make a call. But, no. So, we'll do it your way. Do you hear me?"

There was no doubt about the pain now. His ankle was throbbing. He slid his legs slowly off the bed. When his right foot touched the floor, searing pain shot up his leg. He gasped, glanced at the door. "Look, here, I need medical attention. C'mon, for Chrissakes! I need help!"

It took nearly all his will to stand on his left foot. Using the wall for support, Campbell made his way to the door, hopping on one foot. "Open this door, you sonsofbitches! I've had enough—"

He struck the door with his fist, then banged against it with his shoulder. He needn't have bothered. The door wasn't latched. The heavy timbered door's hinges creaked as it swung open and Campbell fell awkwardly through the opening. He tried to break his fall with his hands on the stone floor. He felt the gash under his bandage split and explode with a burning pain. His ankle scraped the floor as he rolled into a fetal position, and he screamed out what breath he'd saved.

Campbell didn't know how long he'd lain there when he looked up to survey the place he'd stumbled into. He'd heard that if you ignore it, you can stand any pain. That was wrong. He couldn't help the agony, he just had to endure it.

The room he was in was larger than the cell. There were no windows and he couldn't see a door anywhere. There were a table and a chair in the center of the room. No, two chairs. He inched his way to the table and with an extraordinary effort of will, pulled himself into a chair. On top of the table was a metal box with a button in the center. Nothing else. He pressed the button. He was too exhausted and too much in pain to appreciate this little Pavlovian experiment, if that's what it was. He needed help. That was all that mattered now. Someone would come. He didn't care who. As long as they could take away the pain. Campbell folded his arms in front of him and lay his head down. It didn't matter that he'd been talking to himself these past hours. Nothing mattered. Just, someone, stop the hurting. Please . . . someone . . .

He smelled the cigarette smoke first. Campbell opened his eyes and was distantly aware that he wasn't alone. If he'd passed out it couldn't have been for very long. He was still in exactly the same place. He seemed to be floating on the edge of consciousness. He lifted his head. It wasn't easy. He felt drunk. It took a few seconds to realize the pain had subsided. He raised his head, blinked. Someone was standing in front of him before the table. He was smoking a cigarette. He tried to focus on the face, but the features were unclear. Campbell watched the figure drop the cigarette and crush it out with his foot.

"You have been given an injection," the man said. "I imagine the pain was intolerable."

Thank God. Campbell could see him a little clearer now. The room seemed to be very bright. It took a while for his eyes to adjust. The man seemed very tall, but it was difficult to judge at this angle. He was smiling.

"You will be asleep soon," the man said. He had blue eyes, Campbell noticed. "But there are questions that must be answered."

Campbell nodded through the dullness that was overtaking

him. Questions. Of course. Clear up this mess. Somebody cared.

"Do you hear me?"

Campbell offered a weak smile. "S-sure."

The man grasped the corners of the table and leaned forward. The smile disappeared. He needn't get so close, Campbell thought. He needn't—

"Who are you?" the man yelled. *"What is your name? Where did you come from?"*

Campbell blinked his astonishment. "Wha—" He was staring stupidly into the man's face. He could see the blue eyes looming huge in front of him. "I'm—" *Christ, you know who I am!* "I'm . . . I'm Campbell . . . I'm . . ."

The man screamed so loud Campbell's ears rang. "Herr Campbell is dead! You will tell me who you are. You will tell me now."

Campbell was too stunned to speak. It wasn't possible. They didn't believe him!

"Your name! *Now!*"

"I'm not *that* Campbell," he said.

"Indeed not. What is your real name?"

Campbell shook his head. "No . . . I'm his son. Believe me, I—"

The man slapped him. He was wearing gloves, Campbell noticed, and he hit him again and again. He felt something behind him, pinning his arms. Then someone—he couldn't see a face—jerked his head back and he was staring into an incredible brightness. He could hear the Black yelling at him and pounding his face, but he was fading. Everything was fading. He knew he was slipping away from them. They'd stop soon. They'd have to. He was fading away and they couldn't do anything about it. The light was dissolving around him. He didn't know if his eyes were open or shut, but it didn't matter. He was escaping and somewhere in his conscious being he inexplicably thought of Holland—windmills and wooden shoes. An image appeared in his mind of soldiers and tanks and trucks and artillery rushing across fields of tulips. He wondered what the Belgians were doing about it. What were the French doing? And the British? They were going to be surprised, weren't they? Then he remembered the sparkling dawn on Lake Constance and the peacefulness of the Alps majestically holding back the sun—how many eons since he'd seen that? But it was an incomplete thought. His mind was on the brink of consciousness and as it slipped over the edge he was distantly aware of a pair of blue eyes and the quite maddening inquiry to which they sought an answer.

Who *was* Theodore Campbell?

3

November 3, 1939

HE LEANED BACK in his chair, sneaking a glance at his watch in
the process. He was anxious to get moving, but Anne's father
didn't seem capable of understanding that Ted didn't want
anything more to eat or drink.

"Anne, you'll get Ted another piece of trifle, won't you. I
think your young man needs another cup of tea."

The trifle was gooey and it had taken effort to get through the
first piece of it. The tea was good and he'd been learning to
like tea, a necessity since no one on the whole island seemed
capable of producing an acceptable cup of coffee. Still, one
cup after a meal was plenty.

Alfred Bullard was a sly and proper old British gentleman,
Ted reminded himself—everything had a right and orderly
time, as if his life was arranged to suit some methodical
timetable. A habit, no doubt, left over from his years of
service in the government. It was never quite clear to Ted if
that service had been in the Admiralty or the War Office,
though it didn't much matter to him one way or the other. Lord
Bullard was most proud of two things he'd achieved in his life.
First, of course, was Anne. She'd been his life since her
mother died, and if ever he'd harbored a secret regret that the
family name ended with her, it was not a lingering disappointment. As a matter of fact, Sir Alfred (he preferred that form of
address) seemed pleased with the prospect of a union between

33

Anne and Ted. There were times when Ted felt he was being
led down the courtship path to Anne's door, rather than finding
his own way.

Sir Alfred's second most noteworthy achievement was his
admission to an order of chivalry—The Most Excellent Order
of the British Empire—and his knighthood at the hand of King
George V at Buckingham Palace in 1917. His class within the
order was Knight Grand Cross, the first of five ranks. Ted had
never been much impressed by titles and grand honors, which
might have seemed odd for the son of Eddie Campbell. It was a
peculiar morality when men conferred awards on one another
for the business of killing, Ted thought. But his father had
been a genuine American war hero and the proof was at the
family compound at Nantucket Sound: a trophy case lined in
black felt that displayed three medals for valor—*Légion d'Hon-
neur, Croix de Guerre* and the Congressional Medal of Honor.

A competitive spirit and a fierce will to win were a family
tradition instilled in Ted, and trophies and awards were the
necessary chaff of that tradition. His father had been a
world-class race driver before he took to racing airplanes, and
it was after the war that he became a premiere pilot on the
racing circuits. It was, naturally, his father who taught Ted to
fly, and over the last dozen years Ted had added air race
trophies of his own to the family collection.

It was in just the last three years that Ted had taken serious
interest in the politics of aviation. Germany had taken a giant
lead in the acquisition and testing of new airplane designs. In
1936 his father had moved his new aircraft company to
Germany from the United States because the climate for
innovation was much more rewarding there. It seemed that
only Germany realized the potential of aviation in a military
sense. The conviction that the United States needed a strong air
force was what led Ted to write *Beware the Hawk* in 1938.
This was a warning that the airplane was too great an
instrument for destruction to be ignored. The book died in the
bookstores.

Less than six months after the book was published, most of
Ted's troubles began. His countrymen attacked him for being
pro-Nazi, which was absurd. He stopped racing in France
because some idiot had published a story that he cheated to win
the Paris-Brest-Bordeaux air race by bribing an official. But
they were trivial miseries compared with the accident—on

March 3,1939, Edward Campbell was killed in a fiery crash as he road-tested an Italian sports car in Munich.

"Ted? Ted, are you there, boy?"

Sir Alfred was staring at him across the table with a slightly ruffled expression. He'd been talking—God, he was always talking—and Ted had let his mind wander. He glanced quickly at the trifle before him. He hadn't touched it. The whipped cream had separated and slid to the side, exposing the soggy cake and its purplish blueberry center.

"Sorry," Ted said. He looked at Anne and she smiled as if to apologize.

"I said you'll want to hear the war news," Sir Alfred mumbled. He rose, walked to the mantel and switched on the radio. "The PM will be coming on after a bit, you know."

Bloody Christ! He didn't want to hear the war news. He was here to see Anne, for Chrissake! He didn't want to think about the war—if that's what is was. Phony War was right. It was already November, eight weeks since Germany crossed the Polish border, and nothing was happening along the western front. British and French troops sat on their asses in northern France. Germans watched silently from their posts behind the Siegfried line and the massive fortifications of the Maginot line were quiet. It was damned maddening, is what is was, Ted thought. There were things he had to do in Germany—war or no war. As a citizen of a neutral country, he was still allowed to travel to Germany. There were still family business needs to be looked after there. And he had to decide whether or not to close and sell the villa in Friedrichshafen. He should have gone weeks ago. He shouldn't have listened to anyone. He should have just gone to Germany and finished it. He was leaving in the morning.

"And now," the BBC announcer said, "rebroadcast from an earlier dispatch to the States, we will hear from Katherine Buchanan in Berlin."

Ted listened then. He had never been able to ignore that commanding voice. "The Secret Police had shot two men for resisting arrest this morning . . . the editor of the *Contra-Komintern,* heretofore fanatically anti-Bolshevik, announced the magazine would be appearing soon with a new name —Germany's real enemies were not communists, but Jews . . . the ministers were furious that the American ship *City of*

Flint had been seized by the Norwegians before it could reach the Baltic port of . . ."

His mind drifted. Not for the first time he thought of the irony of their lives. Kate, the fiery Irisher from Quincy, Massachusetts, sitting before a Nazi microphone. She'd always been far more politically commited than he. Kate, the green-eyed scrapper, now a reporter for a neutral nation; a dispassionate and disembodied voice delivering undoubtedly censored news from the heart of Hitler's Germany. How she must hate it. And here he was in England, uncommitted and yet sympathetic to both sides. It was decidedly odd, this war.

Then the newscast was over and a cultured voice announced a forthcoming program of Welsh and Cornish folk music. It was with a grateful heart that Ted received the news that Chamberlain would not, after all, make an address.

Sir Alfred snapped off the radio, moved his chair closer to the fire. "So," he said, drawing out the word as he seated himself, "you've convinced yourself to leave tomorrow, have you, Ted?"

Ted nodded. He watched Anne make a secret gesture, pointing toward the hall. "Yes, sir, I have."

"Not advisable," Anne's father said, shaking his head sadly as if any fool would know it was a mistake. "Not advisable at all."

"I really have to go, Sir Alfred. There's the plant to see about and the villa."

"Yes-yes," the old gentleman said with a quick nod. "If you must, then." He glanced up unhappily. "Do be careful, won't you, my boy? I mean, you may be American but you do speak English. They're quite suspicious of our kind just now, you know—the Huns are."

"I also speak German."

Sir Alfred shrugged. "I suspect the two buggers the Gestapo shot this morning spoke German as well." He nodded toward the radio. "You heard what that woman said. 'Resisting arrest,' bloody rot, that."

Ted glanced at Anne. *Get me out of here!*

"Lisbon on the morrow, is it?" Anne's father was fiddling with the doily on the arm of his chair.

"Yes, sir. In the morning." *Early* in the morning, he should have said.

"Nezor Gulbenkian's in Lisbon," Sir Alfred said, adjusting

the doily to the exact position he wanted, then patting it as if to tell it to stay put. He looked up at Ted. "Greek commerce department with the Finance Ministry until thirty-four, I think it was. Retired. Pushed off to Portugal for the climate. Runs a little coin shop in the Rossio—forget the name of the place now. How long do you expect to be there?"

"I don't know. A day, maybe two. Depends on—"

"A week, likely. The city'll be a crunch what with people trying to get *out* of Germany. Jews, you know. You can bet you'll pay a pretty penny for accommodations if you find a place at all. Do call Nezor, will you, Ted? He'll love having you. He'll want to know about Anne, of course. You must see him. As a matter of fact I have a book around here somewhere I must return to him. No telling when the post would reach him. You don't mind, do you?"

Ted sighed. "Be happy to."

"That's the boy. You'll like Nezor. Being Greek, naturally, he'll talk your shorts down, but—"

Anne stepped beside her father's chair, her hand on his shoulder. "Dad, Ted came to see me, remember? We'll be taking a walk now."

Sir Alfred raised his eyebrows as if suddenly remembering. "Oh, yes. Right you are, then. Well, off you go, you two. Mind the blackout. Keep one eye to the street. Don't want some bloody fool with his blinders out whacking you on the pathway."

"Goodnight, Dad."

They walked hand in hand in silence toward the Kensington Gardens. The sky was clear, the air crisp and the moon was a sliver of smudged copper over the city. London was an eerie city without lights, her silhouette like a huge fortress under siege against the faded night. What conqueror could possibly think he could break the will of this place? Big Ben sounded in the distance, its strong, reassuring gongs echoing in the chilly stillness. Ted released her hand and slipped his arm around Anne's waist. He could smell her hair, fresh and clean, a country fragrance in an ancient city.

She was a tall girl, full-bodied but not fat, with red-blonde hair and a pale complexion. She was bright and decent and hearty, the sort of woman any man would be lucky to have whether there was a war on or not.

"Do you think about her much, Ted?"

"Who?"

"Oh, please!" There was a hint of jealousy to her smile. "I saw the way you reacted to her name, the way you listened to her voice. That voice is all I know of her. I never saw her picture."

"Kate?"

"Yes."

"I don't carry a picture of my old flames, you know."

"Good for you. Is she pretty?"

"Who?"

"Ted!"

He grinned down at her. "Of course she's pretty."

"Oh."

"She's a ruddy beauty queen."

"Really, I want to know."

"Why?"

"Well . . ." Anne tucked her head under his arm. "You *are* going to Germany. And she's *in* Germany. And . . ."

"It's a big place, Germany," Ted said. "And getting bigger."

"Will you be in Berlin?"

"Probably."

She was quiet for a time then. "I wish I could go," she said. She looked up at him. "Not that I don't trust you, of course."

"Of course." He pulled her closer, kissed her hair. "You're prettier, for the record."

"You had to say that, didn't you?"

"It happens to be true."

"What's she look like, then?"

"Nothing special . . ."

"Right."

"Red hair . . ."

"Partial to redheads, are we?"

"Your is much lighter."

"What else?"

"Let's see. She has green eyes, I think. A bit shorter than you. A damn good tennis player."

"Athletic, too. My, my. I was hoping she was quite fat with a mole on her chin."

They stopped at a curb. "Actually, she does have a mole," Ted said, rubbing his jaw. "But it isn't on her chin."

"Oh, you are a beast, Ted Campbell!"

Ted smiled, took a slight bow. "You asked, didn't you?"

"You're running off to Germany and you'll see your old svelte and sexy American sweetheart in the middle of a war and here I'll be, little Anne—poor little Anne the fat cow —eating my heart out in dreary London and—"

He shushed her, touching a finger to her lips. "Claudette Colbert should be so lucky to look like you, my little cow."

Anne moved her hands over her breasts, over the bulge in her overcoat. "Do you think . . ."

"Yes, I think."

She sighed and closed her eyes as he took her in his arms and kissed her. Ted could feel the warmth of her body through the clothes and they swayed gently together until the headlamps of an approaching car interrupted the embrace.

"I love you," Anne said as they took up their walk. She didn't look at him because she didn't need to. "Terribly much. Do be careful, my darling. I know you're American and all that, but, still, you are going to Germany. And they are Germans there, after all."

"I will be careful," Ted said. "Promise."

The crowd was light at the Crow's Head. Anne had sweet cider while he drank a couple of pints of brown ale.

They left before the half-past-ten closing time and walked back at a slower pace than they had come despite the slight mist and the accompanying fog.

"I wish there was a place where we could be alone," Anne said, breaking the silence between them as they came into view of her father's flat. "I . . . I wish we had a place that was private."

"I know." Ted pulled her nearer, felt her hair against his cheek. "I know."

"We could go to your hotel, Ted."

It surprised him, not the thought of it but that she should suggest it. How many times had *he* made the same proposal and every time been lovingly though firmly turned down.

"That's a rather sudden change of heart, isn't it?"

Even in the semi-darkness he could see her blush. "Not a change of heart, darling. Never that. Daddy would call it a change of priorities."

"And you the proper young lady."

"I don't care about that," she said suddenly. "How proper was your American beauty . . . your . . . your redheaded friend?"

"That was years ago."

"Not that many years!"

"It isn't the same thing. Christ, it isn't the same at all."

"You loved her, didn't you?" She stopped, looked up at him with tears in her eyes. They were within a few feet of her door. "Isn't that so? What's so different? Am I less a woman than she is? Would it be easier if I were an American too? What is so bloody different!"

"Damn it, Anne, I—*Damn it!* What's got into you?"

She threw her arms around him then, her head against his chest, and he stroked her hair gently to soothe her.

"I'm sorry," she cried. "I'm sorry. I want to hold you, to be touched by you, to be loved by you." Anne wiped her eyes. "I'm afraid. Maybe it sounds silly to you. It's certainly selfish of me. I just don't want you to leave without . . ." She glanced up at him. "What if something happened to you? Oh, Ted, I do love you so. I couldn't bear it if anything happened to you." She laid her head back on his chest. "This is our last night together and look how I'm acting such a fool."

"It isn't exactly our last night together," Ted said. "Not the way I have it planned. And if you're a fool"—he raised her chin with his finger to look in her eyes—"then you are the most beautiful fool on this foolish planet."

"Oh, Ted!" She kissed him, her arms around his neck, and he pulled her off the pavement with his embrace. Ted walked her to the door and as they kissed again he heard the turning creak of the large hinges. The hall was dark due to the regulations of the blackout and the figure that was leaving obviously didn't see them as he walked straight into Ted.

"Oh, sorry there, my fault."

Ted caught himself against the rail, holding Anne so that she didn't tumble down the stoop. Then there was a voice from the hall.

"Hello? Anne, that you?"

Ted recognized Sir Alfred's voice.

"Yes, sir," Ted said. "Just seeing Anne safely home."

"Ah, yes. Good, too, I have the book for you. Packaged it myself." Ted could see him now, standing in the doorway. He felt the package thrust under his arm. "There's the good chap. Tell Nezor to drop me a line. I appreciate this, you know. My God, it's cold as Kinnairds Head out here. You mustn't stand about in this weather, you two."

Ted turned to apologize to the man he'd bumped, but there was no one there. Then he saw a figure in a long coat step quickly to the curb across the street. In another moment he was gone, swallowed in the fog.

"I'll be along, Dad," Anne was saying in that privately indignant tone reserved for daughters to their fathers. *"In a few minutes."*

"You might come into the parlor, then."

"Dad!"

Lord Bullard stood there a moment, befuddled. "Yes, well . . . Right." He glanced at Ted. "I guess it's good night to you, then, Ted, and good luck. You will let us know how you're making it?"

Ted nodded. "Yes, sir. Not to worry."

They held each other against the chill when they were alone again, arms around each other's waists, leaning against the bricks.

"Odd time for visitors, isn't it?" Ted said, staring into the fog.

Anne shrugged. "Not really. I think one never really retires from the government. It's been good for him too, you know. Dad is sixty-six. He doesn't get about like he used to. He doesn't like people to know but his legs are varicose. Old friends come round when they can. Helps him feel he's not left out, especially now."

"Not a well-mannered lot, his old friends," Ted said. "You might have been knocked down the stairs." He nodded at the street. "He was gone without so much as looking back."

Anne sighed. "He's one of the quiet ones, that one."

"Who is he?"

"Look here," she said playfully. "Are you interested in me or—"

"You, definitely," Ted said. He slid his hands inside her coat and cupped her breasts. "No question about it."

She pressed her hands over his, closing her eyes, then opened her coat and unbuttoned the halter of her dress and freed the snaps between the cups of the frilly bra. Ted drew her closer, caressing her, kissing her upturned neck. "Oh, Ted!"

Anne found his belt under his coat, loosened it and unbuttoned the pants. She slid her hands inside, her fingers touching him, massaging.

"You have icebergs for hands," Ted breathed.

"They'll warm up." She arched herself to him, moving her hips to the feel of him, raising the hem of her dress and pressing him against her.

"Anne . . ."

"Please, Ted." Anne's voice was husky, urgent. "Please."

"We'll freeze!"

"No place is that cold."

She wasn't wrong. Ted helped her step out of her panties and they huddled together inside their coats, groping awkwardly for each other, oblivious to the cold, maneuvering for position, determined, like a pair of schoolboys desperately fighting to put up a tent from the inside. It didn't work, of course, and after the frustrating realization came to them they broke into a fit of sweaty, exasperated giggles.

"Quite a pair of desperate lovers, aren't we?" Anne wrapped the unbuttoned flaps of her coat around her. She shook her head, smiled. "Better luck next time, eh, Yank?"

"I think you orchestrated this whole thing," Ted said. He grinned. "Just to be sure I'd get back here as soon as possible."

"You won't forget, then?"

Ted snorted a laugh. "Not bloody likely." He kissed her, held her head against his shoulder.

"Good, because I'm freezing," she said. She pushed herself away from him to see his face. "Anyway, if you don't leave now I won't be responsible. I'm randy as hell, Ted Campbell. It's as good a way to see you off as any, aching for more." She stepped back to the door. "I love you, darling."

"And you," Ted said. "Stay out of dark doorways till I get back, won't you, love?"

"I'll try." Her voice was husky with emotion. Ted saw moisture in the corners of her eyes and he knew it was time to go. She wouldn't want him to see her cry. "Give us a kiss and off with you," she said, taking a breath. Then she opened the door quickly and stepped beside it. "No dark doorways till you're back. Promise." She wiped her eyes with the back of her hand. "I won't be bumped off the stoop with anyone but you." She smiled, but Ted knew she was crying now. "No matter how many times Mr. Carstairs might visit. Goodnight, love."

The door closed quietly in the darkness then and Ted was alone in the mounting cold and fog.

It was Europe's coldest winter of the century and it froze the war to a shuddering halt. He spent much of his time in the comfort of the Friedrichshafen villa because the weather was so wretched and the roads so virtually impassable that he couldn't get out even if he'd wanted.

The German bureaucracy of the Commerce Ministry's *abteilung* for domestic and international business was abysmally slow, as if taking its cue from the weather. For some reason Ted's right to assume control of his father's aircraft design and manufacturing company was limited to a wardship capacity. He had administrative authority—he could hire and fire anyone he wanted—but that was the limit of his dominion until certain technicalities had been settled. And there seemed an ever-growing list of them. What it meant was that without German authorization the company could not be relocated within the Reich or, more importantly, it could not be removed from Germany; all of which required an incredibly complex production of paperwork. His protestations had little effect. Always there was the same maddening excuse: "It is the war, Herr Campbell."

It wasn't anything of the kind, of course, and Ted knew it. Campbell Aircraft was one of the foremost designers of superb flying machines and Germany was in desperate need of private industry to manufacture planes for Goering's Luftwaffe. The message was clear enough. If Ted didn't keep the company in Germany, they weren't about to let it out of the country to build for someone else.

So he waited. Eventually, they would *have* to hand him control of the company. They could, however, court him. He was invited everywhere that the Luftwaffe had a plane to display or an assembly plant to inspect. When he wasn't in Friedrichshafen he was at Augsburg with Willy Messerschmitt or with Georg Wulf at Bremen. He toured plants at Aschersleben, Bernburg, Halberstadt and Leopoldshall. He met Ernst Heinkel at Warnemunde and Heinrich Focke in Munich. And he was impressed. These were dedicated and enlightened men and they were making startling advances. Though he had not seen the designs, Willy Messerschmitt told him privately that work on a jet-powered fighter was underway. It was a heady experience and Ted was made to feel a comrade. He itched to get to work with his own company; it was, he realized, exactly the mood his German hosts had wanted to instill in him.

He met Goering several times and even spent a few days at his lavish estate at Karinhall. It wasn't long before he was being invited to Berlin almost every weekend that the weather allowed a plane out of Friedrichshafen. Often he would go if only to escape the solitude of the villa. He met Goebbels and thought the slight and angular little man obsequious. He met Hess and Himmler and Ribbentrop and Rosenberg. It was amusing, almost comical, that the leaders of the Reich, these leaders of the new Germany with its politically inspired claptrap about racial purity and nobility of Teutonic blood, were so decidedly un-Aryan in look and manner. Of all of them, Ted got on best with Hess. They shared a common passion: flying. The deputy fuehrer had won the 1934 air race around the Zugspitze, Germany's highest peak. He spoke admiringly of the Duke of Hamilton, who'd been the first pilot to fly over Mount Everest, and he seemed genuinely concerned that the war should not go on.

"The British and the Americans are our brothers," he had told Ted. "We must not permit this difficulty to continue between us."

Ted reminded him that the United Stares was not at war with anyone. Hess shrugged his large shoulders, remarking that the real enemy was to the east.

"The Bolsheviks," he said.

It was an odd thing to hear the third most powerful Nazi admit, Ted thought. Russia just happened to be Germany's strongest ally. But there were many things about this mysterious man with the dark, hollow eyes that intrigued Ted. Over the long and dreary months before spring, Ted was a frequent visitor of Hess's home in Munich. He learned to know the private Hess; the vegetarian, the geopolitician, the astrologist. The man was tormented over his loss of influence with Hitler. Goering, Himmler, Goebbels—even Bormann—were usurping his power. It was a bitter realization for the man who was at Hitler's side in the early days, at the Beer Hall Putsch, in Landsberg Prison.

If Hess was Hitler's most devoted follower he was not his most intelligent one, Ted came to realize. Based on his own experience as a businessman, he could see that Hess was neither a competent nor an efficient administrator. He was bored by detail, no doubt brought on by the huge bureaucracy of the party he'd had a hand in creating. He was often lazy and procrastinating, letting subordinates handle his affairs as he whiled away his time studying astronomical charts.

It had been an odd winter for Campbell. He became an isolated alien in a country more at war from within then with its enemies. But spring bloomed bright and welcome across the continent and with it the radiant hope of peace. The news of the occupation of Denmark and Norway did not cause great excitement in the south of Germany. The two nations were guaranteed their neutrality. The move protected Germany's flank. It was a good sign, Ted thought. The indications were the fighting wouldn't go on much longer.

The sweet fragrance of holly was in the air as Ted drove the two miles from the villa to the Campbell hangar. He parked the Daimler Double-Six on the grass apron beside the runway and walked briskly through the hangar doors. It was not yet dawn and the hangar lights glowed down from the rafters, casting pools of light on the oil-stained floor. A mechanic was toiling with the engine cowling of a Campbell racer at the far end of the hangar and Ted waved to him as he went into his office.

A pot of coffee simmered on the pot-bellied stove and he poured himself a cup before sitting behind his desk. He propped his feet on the desk, placed the telephone in his lap and dialed.

"Hallo?"

"Karl, you awake?" Ted said in cheerful German.

"Awake . . ." Campbell Aircraft's chief mechanic repeated the word drowsily. "Yes, awake, Herr Campbell. You are in Munich?"

"No, I'm at the hangar. Drove down a couple of hours ago." Ted glanced out the grime-spattered window behind him. "It's going to be a beautiful day, Karl."

"Yes," the voice replied without conviction. "What time is it? Is something the matter?"

"Everything's fine," Ted said. He leaned back in the chair to stretch. "I drove in from Munich this morning, changed clothes and came here. I thought we'd take the Breguet up for a checkout. Run her around the lake, maybe up to Augsburg, get some chow, then home. It's going to be a perfect day, Karl. What do you say?"

Karl sighed. "The Breguet?"

"Sure."

"Herr Campbell, I didn't know, I mean, I thought you would be in Munich until Sunday."

"I got bored in Munich."

"The Breguet is down," the mechanic said apologetically. "Hans and I began the engine overhauls two days ago."

"Damn."

"I'm sorry, Herr Campbell. I didn't know—"

"No-no, it's all right. Never mind." Ted sat up to look out the glass partition that separated the office and the hangar. A twin-engine Campbell light transport was parked inside the hangar. "Are we still waiting for the replacement control linkage on that Flint?"

"Yes, sir, and a cowling exhaust."

Ted shook his head and scratched anxiously at his chin. "Don't we have anything I can take up?"

Karl paused a moment. "There's the little one."

"That's only a single-seater."

"Yes." Karl cleared his throat. "Excuse me, but I didn't know you would return so soon. Freda and I, we were . . . going to Kaufbeuren today. Freda's sister has a birthday and—"

"Of course," Ted said. "I'm sorry, Karl. I didn't intend to interrupt your day."

"I could telephone Sigel, at Zeppelin-Werke, have them prepare a—"

"No, forget it. It was just a sudden itch. I'll get along." Ted could see the lightening sky to the east. "Don't worry about the Breguet. We'll run her out next week."

"Thank you, Herr Campbell."

Ted walked past the duty mechanic, nodded, and strolled out to his car. He climbed behind the wheel and lit a cigarette. He didn't want to go back to the villa. The place would still be closed up. He'd been in and out this morning and careful not to wake Mrs. Glebe, the housekeeper. Besides, he was sick to death of the villa. It was like an extension of the winter; vacant, dreary and cold. The drive from Munich had been invigorating. He'd looked forward to taking the Breguet out.

Ted glanced over his shoulder. The dark horizon was fading to pink over the Austrian Alps. There wasn't a single cloud in the sky. He swung his legs out of the car and pitched the cigarette into the damp grass. What the hell, he thought. He'd greet the sun by himself.

Ted hurried back to the hangar and pushed open the slide doors. The mechanic glanced up as Ted approached.

"Roll out the Sprint and top off her tanks," Ted said. He grabbed his leather jacket from a hook beside the office door. "I'm taking her up for a ride."

4

TED STIRRED. He was conscious of the sound of birds first, then the light. He was on his back and there was a contraption in front of him of wires and pulleys connected to a bulbous white cylinder with toes exposed at its end. It took him a moment to realize that the toes were his and the contraption was a rigging to support his own left leg set in plaster.

He was in a small white room, his bed near a window, and, from the view, apparently on the second or third floor of a hospital. In the distance he recognized the twin cathedral towers of the Frauenkirche. Munich. A hospital in Munich.

"Ah, you are awake."

Ted turned his head to see a tall, heavyset man with thinning hair and a neatly clipped mustache rise from a chair and fold a newspaper under his arm.

"How are you feeling this morning?" He was smiling as he walked to the foot of the bed.

"Who the hell are you?" Ted said. He remembered now. The Sprint, the crash, the cell, the Black. He'd smiled too, before he'd started beating him.

"We met before"—he frowned slightly—"don't you remember? I am Albrecht Haushofer."

The face was vaguely familiar. Then Ted realized suddenly that the man was speaking English.

48

"I don't—I can't—" Ted glanced at his raised leg. "Where am I? How did I get here?"

"The Eichendorff Hospital in Munich," replied the man in the vested suit. "I'm afraid you've had an unfortunate encounter with the secret police. Tomo asked me to come round to see you." He shrugged, and nodded at his newspaper. "I didn't realize you'd be asleep so long. Medication, I suppose. I've been by two days. As a matter of fact, I—"

"What day *is* it?" Ted said quickly.

"Monday."

"Monday!"

Haushofer sighed and gave a sad nod. "You'll want to know what's happened."

"Bloody right!" Ted tried to raise himself on his elbows but was restrained by the rigging that elevated his leg. "I want a lot of things answered! Why was I arrested? How bad am I hurt? Where is the American ambassador?" He paused to catch his breath, eyes fixed on the man before him. "And who the hell is this Tomo that's so concerned about me?"

"Tomo?" Haushofer raised his eyebrows in surprise. "Excuse me," he said sheepishly. "It is a nickname, forgive me. I meant to say, Rudy, that is, the deputy fuehrer." He smiled apologetically. "Herr Hess."

"Hess?"

"Yes, when he heard what had happened—" Haushofer shrugged again and nearly dropped the newspaper from under his arm. "He is deeply sorry, Mr. Campbell. Believe me. To —Herr Hess is sincerely regretting the injuries you have sustained."

Ted laid his head back on the pillow. The anger in him momentarily quieted by the surprise of his deliverer. So, it *was* true: it pays to know important people. He was placing Haushofer's face now. He *had* met him once. He remembered now. It had been at Hess's home. Albrecht Haushofer, son of Karl Haushofer, the famous founder of the Institute of Geopolitics at the Unversity of Munich. Professor Haushofer believed fervently in the conception of German *Lebensraum*—living space, the need for the nation to expand its national boundaries. Albrecht had followed in his father's footsteps. He was, Ted recalled, professor of political geography at the University of Berlin, and his particular interests were in foreign affairs. Like Hess, Albrecht Haushofer was an admirer of things

British. He also shared another attitude with the deputy fuehrer and Ted had just remembered it—he had very little use for the Russians.

"Is there much pain?"

Ted glanced up, momentarily distracted. "What?"

"The ankle," Haushofer said. "Do you have much pain there?"

Ted frowned at his foot. "No. Is it broken?"

"Of course, you wouldn't know," Haushofer said, shaking his head. He looked at Ted, sighed. "Yes, I'm afraid, broken. I'm told that the ligaments and tendons have been severely distended. Also, the right leg—not broken, I mean, but the tibia was cracked. The doctor tells me that such injuries can be quite painful." He pointed to Ted's bandaged hand. "And the left hand, the palm. There was quite a deep gash there. You were very lucky, it was explained to me, that you survived the crash of your aircraft."

"No thanks to the Luftwaffe. I—" Then he remembered the Stuka. And the bombers. "The war," Ted said quickly. "I almost—what's happened? My God, it's been four days! What's—"

"The blitzkrieg continues." Haushofer handed him the newspaper. "Today Holland surrendered. Soon, I think, Belgium. Goebbels tell us Paris will be won in a matter of days, but I think our little Joseph is caught up in the flush of the army's sudden successes. But not far off."

"But the French army," Ted said unbelievingly. "And the British—"

"Fooled," Haushofer replied. He was staring across the room as if in a trance. "They have taken the bait."

"What are you talking about?"

The professor glanced back at him. "The Ardennes," he said, as if the logic of it was perfectly clear. "At this moment, fifty Wehrmacht divisions are pouring through the Achilles' heel of the French strategy. The Ardennes." Then he shook his head. "With the invasion of Poland to the east, Ribbentrop called me to the Foreign Ministry and asked me to resume my work. I accepted. It was, I thought, the beginning of a strategy to secure living space in the Ukraine, but I was wrong. Now, with the Russians guarding our backs, we attack to the west? *The west!*" Haushofer shook his head again, in a mood of utter frustration. When he looked at Ted again his expression was grave. "The problem is, you see, that because of the monumental stupidity of the French—" he stopped, shrugged "—I am afraid we are going to win this war."

"Afraid?"

"An odd sentiment for a member of the Foreign Office, is it not?" Haushofer smiled but in spite of it Ted had the feeling Haushofer was not a man who displayed pleasure often. "You see, it is my belief that Germany is fighting the wrong people."

"You don't say."

"I do say. As a matter of fact, there are others in Germany who believe strongly as I do."

"Evidently, not the ones who count."

Haushofer raised his eyebrows. "Exactly so."

"Look, ah . . ."

"Albrecht."

"Albrecht, I don't give a damn who wins. I'm not a political animal. I'm a businessman. I design and fly airplanes. And I'd like to get back to it."

"You're saying you take a totally objective view of this war?"

"Yeah."

"How convenient for you, Mr. Campbell."

"Not as convenient as you think," Ted said quickly. "I'm so wrapped up in Reich red tape I can't even run my own company. The war, the war they keep telling me. There isn't any damn war, or there wasn't until—"

"It is a real war now," Haushofer cut it.

"Well, *I'm* not in it," Ted said hotly. "I'm an American." He pointed to his plastered foot with his bandaged hand. "Not that it's done me much good telling anybody. What I'd like to do now is get out of this bloody country before I really get hurt!" He crossed his arms across his chest. "I don't suppose you know why the Secret Police saw fit to beat the shit out of me after I told them who I was, do you?"

"I cannot speak for the Gestapo," Haushofer replied. "However, I understand you crashed your plane in a military zone. As a matter of fact, it was quite near the headquarters of a reserve infantry battalion of General von Leeb's Army Group C. And you had no papers."

"I told them who I was, for Chrissake! All they had to do was call Friedrichshafen and—"

"Such a call was made," said the professor simply. "It was

determined that you were in Munich. Only after further investigation did the police learn that you had returned from your holiday without notifying your housekeeper. Still—" he nodded, emphasizing the word "—you *are* alive. That should count for something."

"Count? You sound as if I'm doing you a favor, being alive."

Haushofer shrugged it off. "Perhaps we are each in a position to help each other."

"Oh?" Ted studied him a moment. "How's that?" There was suddenly something very suspicious about the professor of geopolitics.

"The bureaucracy of the Transportation and Commerce ministries," Haushofer said. "You are having a difficult time —what did you say, wrapped up in red tape?"

Ted nodded. "Miles of it. So?"

"Perhaps I could be of service there."

"Oh, you think perhaps you could?" Ted replied sarcastically. "How, exactly?"

"There are ways. I have influential friends." Haushofer was smiling again.

"Ah-huh," Ted said. He sighed. "How much?"

"Bitte?"

"Don't be cute. How much would it take to enlist the help of your . . . friends?"

"You *are* American," Haushofer said, "No, Mr. Campbell, I do not want your money."

"Then, what—"

"You, also, have influential friends. In the United States, in Spain, in Portugal, in France . . . in England."

"I wouldn't say I was terribly popular anywhere," Ted said. "Except maybe here. There are some people at home who don't exactly like some of the things I've said about the quality of the German Luftwaffe. But what I think is my business."

"A prerogative of your freedom of speech?"

"That's a relative privilege, that is. Speaking up for any merits of the Third Reich, real or imagined, is not a popular trend in the United States at the moment."

"So, it is not entirely the home of the free?"

Ted squinted up at his visitor. "Did I say it was perfect? At least the police don't beat up innocent citizens."

Haushofer nodded, accepting the point. "Still, you know important people."

"Look, I don't know what you're driving at, but whoever I know won't help me much in Germany. I mean, my ruddy company is here, not in Spain or Portugal or bloody Iceland!"

"If it meant getting your company restored to you," Haushofer began in a low voice, "would you be willing to go to Madrid? Possibly Lisbon?"

"Go? For what?"

"To deliver a correspondence."

"To who?"

Haushofer shrugged but he did not answer.

"I know you people are keen on intrigue, but anything you can't trust to the mail, I don't want anything to do with." Ted frowned. He glanced out the window. Haushofer said nothing. After several moments Ted looked back at him. "You must think I'm an idiot. Deliver a correspondence? Christ! From a member of the German Foreign Ministry? I'm neutral, remember?"

"I see."

"Yeah, well, you'd better." Ted shook his head in disbelief. "People are arrested as spies for that kind of thing."

"Yes, they are," Haushofer said calmly.

"Besides . . ." Ted pointed at his leg. "I'm not going anywhere for a while."

"It could wait a few weeks."

"Right!" Ted said loudly. "It can wait till bloody hell is stuck in ice!" He shook his head again. "Why ask me, anyway? That's what I'd like to know. Why did you pick me? Of all the people in Germany, why come to me?"

Haushofer pursed his lips. "Because you are Theodore Campbell," he said patiently. "Becuase you *are* an accepted American neutral. Because, whether you realize it or not, you have influential, even powerful friends on both sides of this war." The professor walked to the chair where he picked up his coat and laid it gently over his arm. When he turned back to face Ted from the door, his eyes conveyed tranquil confidence. "But mostly, Mr. Campbell," Haushofer said quietly, "because you've done it before."

5 _____

"CHAMPAGNE," the waiter said with a broad smile, "for the Fräulein Buchanan and her party." He drew the cork, set out the glasses for the four American correspondents. "With the compliments of the gentlemen on the balcony."

Kate turned to look back over her shoulder. Three German SS officers in their black uniforms smiled back at her; one raised his glass as in a toast.

"The gentlemen instructed me to say that Miss Buchanan and her friends are fortunate to be stationed in Berlin. Soon one will be unable to obtain French champagne anywhere else."

Kate smiled back at them, nodding, and under her breath said, "I hope the pigs choke on it." She turned back to Lowell Grayson of the United Press. "You'd think there'd be at least one decent place in this city that'd keep the black-booted bastards out."

Lowell placed a hand on her arm. "Easy." He glanced up at the waiter and said in German, "Tell the gentlemen we are grateful for the champagne."

The waiter smiled cheerfully. As he left Kate said, "Why don't we tell the *gentlemen* to take their champagne and—"

"Because it's free, Missy," said Neil Manning of the *Chicago Tribune*. He clicked glasses with Chuck Walsh next to him, a freelance reporter and photographer, and sipped his champagne. "It's one of the reasons I hang around with you. You attract such interesting admirers."

"Har-har," Walsh said.

"You're all a crowd of drunken bastards," she said, getting control of herself. "Hacks and drunks."

"Right," Grayson agreed. "And thieves." He took a cigarette from Kate's pack of Chesterfields. "Why else would we be in Berlin."

It was a lie, of course, and Kate knew it. Berlin was the choicest assignment going for reporters. And with the war spreading and continental reporters being either expelled or withdrawn, the Americans were left with covering the biggest news event of the century. As a result, with a few exceptions, many of the best newsmen and women in the States were here. And, Kate was well aware, she was not drinking with any of the exceptions tonight. Lowell Grayson, for example, was one of those geniuses in this business who consistently happened to be on the spot when anything important took place. Neil Manning was another. He'd been Berlin bureau chief for Universal Services for eight years before he took over the German capital beat for the *Chicago Trib*. Chuck Walsh, it was silently understood, was the best photographer-correspondent on the continent. He was the youngest of the veteran reporters (except for Kate, a sin she was to forever atone for whenever someone would bring it up—that and the fact that she was a woman, though no one faulted her professionalism, and the proof of it was her acceptance among these professionals), and had begun in journalism in 1934, standing in the Place de la Concorde in Paris, photographing the fascist mob that tried to storm the Chamber of Deputies. She was a member of an extraordinary clique and if not for these nightly sessions to relieve the tensions in a city dizzy with Nazi madness, she knew she would go crazy.

Kate poured herself another glass of champagne. "Will somebody tell me what we're drinking to tonight? As long as we have the stuff—"

"Maybe you should go easy on it," Grayson said quietly.

"Why would I want to do that? You heard the waiter say it's going to be hard to get this stuff outside Berlin." She gripped the stem of her glass. "Sometimes I think outside of Berlin is exactly where I want to be." She turned to Walsh with a smile, her green eyes sparkling. "But only sometimes. So, what are we drinking to?"

"Truth and beauty." Manning raised his half-filled glass. "To Katie Buchanan."

"Stuff that," she snapped. She touched her glass to Manning's. "Heroic little Holland, what say?"

"That's safe."

"And gallant little Belgium," Kate added after a sip.

"Jesus," Grayson said, "they were drinking to the gallant little Belgians twenty-five years ago."

"And Spain," she went on, eyes shining, spilling champagne as she raised her glass again.

"Kate . . ."

"The dress rehearsal for what's on now," she continued, "when Goering's flying gangsters bombed Guernica . . ." She took a long swallow.

Grayson touched her arm as she poured another glassful. "I think you've had enough."

But she ignored him. "Now Rotterdam's destroyed. You've been there, Lowell . . . Neil? A beautiful old city, wasn't it?" There was silence around the table. "Well I'm glad I've seen it because it'll never look the same again."

"It's war, Kate."

She glanced up at Walsh. "Is it? *Is it?* Murder, I think."

Neil Manning made a face. "C'mon."

"Let's call it what it is," she murmured. "Okay? They bombed the hell out of Rotterdam. You know how many people died? Civilians, I'm talking about."

"The Dutch were warned," Walsh said. "Either they surrender the city or it would be bombed. They had a choice."

"Some choice!" Her eyes were fierce. "The surrender negotiations were already underway when the bombers flew in. Don't you read what comes over your own wires? They *were* surrendering when Goering hit them."

"Look, Kate . . ." Grayson said patiently, "no one here is defending Hermann Goering, for pity's sake."

"Pity's sake is right." She looked at the empty bottle. "Are we out of champagne? Somebody attract that moron's attention."

"You don't want more."

"Christ, no," she said. "I want bourbon, but I might as well wish for wings, hadn't I? Maybe we'll be able to get it here after the Wehrmacht rolls into Kentucky."

"They may have Scotch sooner." Grayson stole another cigarette.

"Meaning?"

"Meaning the Channel is not that deep or wide."

"Invade Britain?" Kate's eyes opened wide. "Shit, he hasn't even taken France yet."

"If Hitler's smart, he won't wait. Face it, France is through and England's asleep. I wouldn't be surprised if they surrender the whole British Expeditionary Force before this thing is over."

Kate nodded, pushed a strand of red hair back from her forehead, and smiled wickedly at Neil Manning. "Wouldn't that just suit Churchill? I can see him now, wading into the water off Dover, carrying the Union Jack, leading a huge band and a puny remnant of the BEF, and all the way hollering over his shoulder, 'I told you so!'"

The restaurant had no whiskey, bourbon or Scotch, so the waiter brought a bottle of cognac. They sipped it from pony glasses and smoked cigarettes, breaking open a pack of Gauloise Bleux after Kate's Chesterfields ran out. French wine and brandy and tobacco. Everything French, she thought, as if they were in Paris, but they couldn't have such a good time in Paris because Paris had nothing to celebrate tonight. She remembered when she was in Paris, the last time. Douglas was there then. He was alive then, a hundred years ago. He was her strength. It was there and he'd introduced her to the uncommonly simple philosophy of the party.

The Communist party of France in Paris seemed like a disorganized bunch of fanatics, judging by the company Douglas kept. Still, there was something exciting about the movement. And for all of her journalistic-bred cynicism she could not dissuade him from his commitment to it. The party could save Europe, he'd said more times than she'd cared to hear, and Kate had resisted his patient socialist lessons as just so much propaganda rhetoric. But the war in Spain was a turning point. By the time civil war broke out, they'd been married less than a year, and he left with the International Brigade to fight the fascist Franco on the side of reason and Karl Marx. She tried to get posted there as a correspondent but no one would give her the assignment. She was a woman and women are not exposed to such dangers. So she waited in Paris for her man and did what party work she could to keep her mind occupied.

He died in Spain. Somewhere in Barcelona, they'd told her. His body did not come home and for months she couldn't believe in her heart that he was dead. Then she spoke to someone who had seen him die, a schoolteacher from Chicago. "He died instantly," the man had said, trying to be kind. "A bullet through the head. He didn't know what hit him."

It was then, with the image of his death scorched into her brain, that his cause became hers. She took up the banner that had been his life, not as a soldier for a fallen comrade, but to insure the memory of one man and his cause. And for that, Kate was more dedicated than most. She could be and was an effective tool of the people through her position as a reporter. If she was a small cog in the machinery against the Nazis, then, at least, she was doing *something*. She was a part of a silent army of pro-Soviets in Germany, *Rote Kapelle*—the Red Orchestra—and eager to serve.

She didn't know how great her contribution was in the overall scheme of things, though as a news commentator she did have access to certain people, and any information, her cell leader told her, was good information. She'd never considered what she did as spying because nothing she passed along seemed particularly worthy. It was the bits-and-pieces work, they told her, that made up the backbone of espionage.

The last several weeks had been exhausting. Something was happening, and if she didn't know exactly what then she was also too afraid to guess. The memory of Douglas was again sharply defined and the mourning of his loss flooded her consciousness. It was part of the reason she needed to be with these men—particularly these men—now; to remind her of her duty.

As the level of the cognac bottle dropped, her mood improved. The conversation turned to the question of American involvement in the war. Eventually, a familiar name came up as she knew it would. What was Ted Campbell doing, running around with these Nazis as if they were long-lost cousins? Did he think he was doing Americans a favor by trucking with the likes of Goering?

Ted Campbell was for Ted Campbell, she might have told them, but then she'd have had to explain how she knew him and Kate wasn't up to that. Ted was as much a part of her past as Douglas, just further back.

It was after midnight by the time they broke up. Kate had a 1 A.M. broadcast that would be received at 7 P.M. in New York the day before, due to the time zones. Lowell drove her to the Rundfunk House for the broadcast and waited outside the soundbooth until she was finished.

He offered her a cigarette as they went down the steps to his car.

"You look beat, Kate."

"You're a little baggy-eyed yourself." She stopped to light the cigarette, drawing the smoke deeply into her lungs then waving the match out. "It's sweet of you to bring me all this way, Lowell. I could have taken the subway."

Grayson shrugged. "I'm a chivalrous bastard, I am." He opened the car door for her. "Anyway, you seemed to need—" he shrugged again "—company, I guess. I don't mind."

They drove most of the way in silence. Kate wasn't in the mood for small talk and Lowell sensed it. They'd played this scene before, she thought, and it usually ended up in an intimate liaison in her apartment that had nothing to do with love. She was an indisputably feminine woman, she knew, but since Douglas's death she had acted as if she were utterly unaware of that femininity, as if it were an evolutionary remnant that no longer had a purpose. But that did not mean she abandoned sex altogether, at least not as a verb. She needed a sexual release as much as any man did and a night unencumbered by commitments was practical and it was certainly more enjoyable than masturbation. She didn't know if Lowell took such a clinical view of their occasional lovemaking but it didn't matter. They gratified each other's needs and they were friends, no more. Neither of them gained more or less than the other in this arrangement. For Kate it was an expedient means to an end. For Lowell, were, it was expedient too, undoubtedly cheaper.

Grayson pulled the car beside the curb in front of her building. He looked sideways at her and didn't shut down the engine.

"You really do look beat."

"Are you trying to convince me?"

He shrugged. Lowell was a great shrugger. He was the best damned newsman she knew, but—damn it—when it came to women he didn't have a single aggressive bone in his body. It was a wonder they'd come to this arrangement at all.

"I wasn't trying to be pushy. I mean, if you'd rather not—"

"Oh, Jesus Christ, Lowell!" She reached over and switched off the ignition. "Let's not sit out here like a couple of teenagers. I'm tired, but not that tired. I could use some companionship tonight. A lot of companionship. I want to forget I'm in this city . . . forget I'm a journalist. Just you and me, love. And in the morning I'll fix us some eggs and coffee." She looked at him in the dark. "Well?"

There was a car on the street and Lowell waited for it to pass. He nodded, then shrugged, then smiled. "I'll fix the eggs," he said. "You can't cook worth a shit."

One wall of the office on Great Portland Street in London was entirely covered with a map of Western Europe. The room was a large one with timbered beams, heavy bookcases set into the rich walnut paneling, shuttered windows leading to a balcony and a view of Regent's Park. But the map was the main feature of the room.

Its upper portion contained the southern half of Great Britain and Ireland, the North Sea, a part of Denmark and the Baltic Sea just east of Bornholm Island. The bottom of the map, which came to about a foot from the floor, displayed most of Portugal and Spain, the western Mediterranean to the boot of Italy at Taranto. Its surface was covered by plastic. Arrows had been drawn indicating positions and movements of German and Allied forces in France and the Low Countries and at several cities were hung yellow cardboard disks.

James Carstairs was standing before it with a long wooden pointer. He towered over the man beside him who was studying the map; Nigel Trentlyon, his aide.

"The shape of things to come," Carstairs said, tracing the lines on the map with his pointer. "Holland is through. The left wing of the Anglo-French line taking position on the Dyle River—exactly what the Jerries expected. Then von Rundstedt's Army Group A hit here." The pointer moved and stabbed the map in northern Luxembourg. "The duchy surrenders at once and the panzers slice through Eupen-Malmedy and the Ardeenes Forest. The French, of course, assured us that the Ardennes was impassable. No way through and no way around the Maginot. They set their ten weakest divisions to guard the

Ardennes as a precaution." He exhaled between his teeth. "And what was the estimated strength of Rundstedt's Group A?"

"Forty-five divisions," Trentlyon replied. "Most of the German armor and motorized infantry."

"Exactly," Carstairs said. "The major thrust of the campaign." The pointer moved again. "Panzers across the Meuse and the two columns link up at Sedan. Andre Corap was supposed to fill the gap there but the Wehrmacht's eight divisions have totally stymied his Ninth Army, and von Kleist's tanks are rolling through like grease through a goose. It shouldn't take a week or ten days to reach the coast. And if that happens—"

"Encirclement."

Carstairs nodded. "The entire British Expeditionary Force, the French First and Seventh armies, and of course the Belgians . . . all neatly roped off in Flanders. Trapped like kitties in a sack."

"Our gallant French allies haven't exactly covered themselves with glory on this one, have they?"

Miserable frogs!" Carstairs clamped the pointer under his arm and began pacing. "The French High Command is staffed by imbeciles. France is finished." He jutted his chin out toward the map. "There's the proof, the bloody maniacs! Forty divisions cut off in Belgium and another forty, thumbs up their arses, hiding behind the Maginot. There's the measure of the French military mentality—the billion-dollar fortress, eighty-seven miles of it with its guns fixed in concrete and trained on Germany. The Neanderthal morons! Bloody Germany is better protected by it than France!"

"Yes, sir," Trentlyon said. He clasped his hands behind him and studied the map. He knew Carstairs well enough not to interrupt or contradict him when he was in one of these moods. He'd been summoned here for a reason, but it wasn't to berate the French. So Trentlyon listened and made agreeable sounds when it was appropriate.

Carstairs went on another ten minutes, talking more to himself than to Trentlyon. Finally he stopped, set the pointer on the ledge by the map and ordered tea. "You are a patient man," Carstairs said. He was standing at the large windows, staring past the balcony at the traffic on Marylebone Road where it crossed Park Square near the Regent's Park underground station, and he held a tea saucer under his cup, as if to catch an imaginary dribble of tea sliding down the side of the chinaware. "Do you wonder why I called you here?"

"I never wonder, sir," Trentlyon said. "I expect you'll tell me when you're ready."

Carstairs turned to regard him a moment, then glanced back at the park. "What would you think if Jerry was down there, directing traffic, running the underground, mucking up the parks?" Carstairs didn't wait for a reply. "That's what'll be next, you know. France will fall and Hitler will drive his black touring car to the shores of Calais and stare across the Strait of Dover with a greedy look in his eye. He'll want to add this island to his collection."

"If he had his way," Trentlyon said.

"Quite so." Carstairs turned abruptly. "I want you to listen carefully to what I have to say," he said. "The future of this island may be decided here in the next hour."

"Sir?"

"Hitler must be stopped from invading England," Carstairs said. "And we can do it."

Trentlyon sat perfectly still after Carstairs had finished his briefing. He could hear the measured cadence of his heartbeat, the flutter of pigeons outside the balcony, the street noises three stories below, but at the moment they all seemed distant, unconnected to reality, as if the dream was outside this room.

He'd never heard of Ultra, of course, or Enigma. Bletchley Park was simply the Government Code and Cipher School, and it was rather a dull place at that, all those message clerks with their strange little code books filled with columns of nonsensical letter groups. Not that it made any difference what he'd heard. This Ultra business was real; Carstairs said it was and that made it so. But what was so astonishing—so incredibly surrealistic—was the lengths they were going to to keep it secret.

"You understand, of course, that what I've just told you is Most Secret, absolutely top priority."

"Yes, sir."

"I doubt that I'd be shot," Carstairs said with a grim smile, "but it wouldn't do either of us any good if it ever got out that I briefed you about Ultra. It is on my own authority that I'm bringing you into the picture. It's important that you understand the reasons because I will ask you to do extraordinary things."

"I understand." Trentlyon had worked eleven months with Carstairs on the Pythagoras Operation. He'd helped select agents from all across Europe—Germany, France, Holland, Italy—to serve in the network. He also knew the network was expendable; it was a ruse of some kind, part of some greater scheme to defeat Germany, but he didn't know why. He did now. Ultra was the reason behind it all; the secret they were protecting.

"I've a new plan," Carstairs continued, "and I need a coordinator to see to the details. You've worked for me before, but nothing like this."

Trentlyon immediately thought the worst: the Germans suspected that their Enigma machine had been compromised. That's why Carstairs had called him in. It was time to expose the network, to let the Germans think a British spy operation was getting top-secret information from inside Germany instead of through their coding machine. It was a brilliant ruse, Trentlyon thought. Ultra remained a secret. He pushed himself forward in his chair. "I'll do whatever you say, of course. I'm sorry it's ending this way. I'm sure you'd have wished the fraud had lasted longer."

Carstairs frowned. "What are you talking about?"

"Exposing the Pythagoras run," Trentlyon said. "Isn't that what—"

"I'm doing no such thing!" Carstairs bellowed. "The Pythagoras network must be maintained at all cost. It's the Ultra project I'm abandoning!"

Trentlyon was startled to silence.

"I'm activating the operation as a full-scale network," Carstairs said. "Ultra doesn't work. I suspected it from the beginning, but now I'm certain. Pythagoras *will* work. I know it will. I designed it. The SIS, in its misguided reliance on Ultra, has given me carte blanche to construct a perfect security. Well, it's better than they know. Ultra is an expensive dream; *it's* the fraud. *The Pythagoras Operation will work.*"

Trentlyon sucked in his breath. Carstairs had wanted to have an active part in this war, that was clear from the beginning. But sending phony messages through an operation created solely to stand by as a red herring for the Germans was obviously not his idea of time well spent. He was famous for

wild and grandiose plans—that must have been why they
picked him for this job—but what he was suggesting now was
out-and-out disobedience. He was defying SIS, the Admiralty,
the prime minister himself, and that was treasonous.

"I know exactly what you're thinking," Carstairs said. "I'm
really not crazy. Just hear me out. Take a day or two to sort
through it, then give me your decision. If you agree with me,
we'll begin immediately."

"And if not, sir?" Trentlyon held Carstairs in his gaze. "If I
report this conversation to Colonel Menzies?"

He made a gesture of indifference. "The chief of British
intelligence would have me locked away. If that's your
decision, then my idea wouldn't work in any case." Carstairs
looked hard at Trentlyon. "For if I can't convince you, the
game's lost anyway."

You had to hand it to the old man, Trentlyon mused, he had
grit. He shrugged. "I'm listening."

"Good chap." Carstairs poured himself more tea. "First,
Ultra doesn't work, that's the plain truth of it. If it did the
British Expeditionary Force wouldn't be fighting for its life in
France. The whole Ultra scheme was to reveal the Wehrmacht's most secret radio transmissions; that is, tactics, troop
movements, panzer disbursements . . . but it didn't tell us
anything. The cryptographic marvel up at Bletchley Park was
silent. So much for the reliability of Ultra."

"Surely Colonel Menzies—"

"Colonel Menzies and the prime minister continue to believe
in it. They consider it bad luck that Ultra was not in full
operation. The consensus is that we rely on Ultra."

Trentlyon shrugged. "Of course, the entire British intelligence system does not rest solely on the benefits of Ultra."

"No, but my part in this war does. And it is my part that
concerns me most."

"You want to activate a network to stroke your own vanity?"

"No. By making the Pythagoras network operational we
have a chance to open a direct pipeline to Berlin. We can do
what Ultra can't. And maybe we can keep Germans out of
England. The key is the run, or course. Pythagoras."

"How?" Trentlyon asked. "We don't have anyone in Berlin.
Pythagoras is a code name for a Nazi double agent who doesn't
exist. There is no Pythagoras."

Carstairs waved him off. "But what if there was? Can you

imagine what that would mean to us? What if we did have a man in Berlin? Just think of that!"

"And what if pigs had wings." Trentlyon moved forward in his chair. He'd heard enough. It'd be an embarrassment to both of them if he stayed any longer. He'd make an appointment with Colonel Menzies this afternoon. "I'm sorry, but I don't think just anyone in Berlin would do the trick. I really must go, I—"

"Rudolf Walter Richard Hess isn't just *anyone*, I don't think," Carstairs said evenly. "Not at all."

"Hess?" Trentlyon was halfway out of the chair. He let himself back down carefully. "Rudolf *Hess!*"

"Exactly right," Carstairs said with a slight smile. "Pythagoras."

6 _____

IT WAS A daring, imaginative, fantastic idea. Use Rudolf Hess. Make *him* Pythagoras; the deputy fuehrer of the Third Reich working for the British, in effect, as a spy, though an unwitting one. If it worked—that was the question now—it would be a coup for Carstairs against which Ultra would pale to obscurity.

If it worked.

Trentlyon was astounded at the audacity of Carstairs' plan. But in a queer sort of way, it made sense. Despite his politics, Hess had always been sympathetic to the British people *and* he hadn't wanted this war. Still, he was a Nazi and no one trusted Nazis. Carstairs had thought of that too.

I don't mean to trust him. He isn't to know that he is being used, of course. The important thing is that Hess is absolutely against an invasion of England. He wants Germany and England united to fight the real enemy—the Bolsheviks.

Hess was losing influence with Hitler—Goering was the favorite now—but Hess's counsel wasn't ignored either, and that made him important to Carstairs.

Hess hasn't many friends these days; the powerful Nazis put up with him because Hitler has affection for him. So he has turned to other friends who will listen to him. People who are not only friends of his, but friends of ours.

They were friends, Trentlyon thought, in only the most liberated sense of that word: a professor of geopolitics who

66

worked for Ribbentrop's Foreign Ministry and an American flier who dined with Goering and called him by his first name. Both had circuitous ties to England; one motivated intellectually and politically, the other through love. Neither of them were now directly involved in the project, but that would change, Carstairs promised.

Circumstances will bring them to help us. Haushofer has already made the first move. We still have to convince Campbell, which means we must get him back to London. And that is a circumstance over which I have some control. But the important thing for you to realize is that this plan can work. It's for you to decide if we try it.

Trentlyon walked the streets of St. James' Park for days, wrestling with the problems and the consequences of his decision whichever way he decided. It was a choice between equally undesirable possibilities. To reject Carstairs' proposal meant reporting a man he had known and worked for for almost ten years, a man he knew to be a dedicated patriot. Then there was the maddening chance that his incredible scheme might just work and to reject it out of hand could conceivably seal the fate of the British people. Yet agreeing to Carstairs' intrigue was tantamount to entering into a conspiracy against the Commonwealth, and whatever disgrace or penalty that entailed for Carstairs would be shared by him. England was at war, which necessarily meant the disgrace would be the charge of treason. Still, if they could pull it off . . . . Carstairs was dead right about Hitler. If Germany couldn't work a peace with England after France's surrender—and that was absolutely out of the question with Churchill as PM—then there would be an invasion. That was perfectly clear, if only for its military logic; one way or another Hitler would have to neutralize England.

Trentlyon had never categorized himself as a particularly patriotic soul; he did his work because he was suited to it. But now for the first time in his life he was faced with the question of loyalty; not to Carstairs or Colonel Menzies or even British intelligence—but to Great Britain herself.

So it was oddly ironic when he made up his mind, because it wasn't a consideration of himself or Carstairs that led to it. The decision was forced on him as surely as if someone had held a gun to his head, and he hurried to the meeting with Carstairs to give him his answer. His decision was clear to him the instant

he read a copy of a dispatch shown him by one of his
colleagues in the Admiralty. It was from a commander with the
Expeditionary Force and the last lines were forboding:

> IN THE FACE OF A SUPERIOR ENEMY FORCE OUR
> SITUATION IS HOPELESS REGARDING CONTINUED
> DEFENSIVE RESISTANCE. WITHDRAWAL TO THE PORT OF
> DUNKIRK FOR POSSIBLE EVACUATION OR RESIGNING TO
> HOSTILE FORCES ARE ONLY REMAINING ALTERNATIVES.
> RECOMMEND FORMER. REQUEST INSTRUCTIONS MOST
> SOONEST BEFORE WE ARE PUSHED INTO THE SEA.

If there had been any hope that the BEF could secure a
stronghold on the continent, it had vanished. Only a miracle
could save the British nation from invasion now. If ever there
was a sign that something extraordinary must be done,
Trentlyon realized with sudden clarity, this was that sign.
Britain's military strategists had done their best and it wasn't
enough. Carstairs must have his chance.

So he sat across the serving tray from Carstairs just as he had
five days earlier.

"You've made up your mind, then?" Carstairs said.

"I've decided to come along with you on it."

Carstairs' face only hinted at a smile. "You've done the right
thing. I promise you that." He poured them both a brandy. "I
think you should begin immediately to know who Mr. Theodore Campbell is. His role in this is extremely important."

"I'm still not sure how you're going to bring him round to
our side. I understand he's fiercely neutral."

Carstairs handed him his drink. "Heydrich's already seen to
that. Campbell will help us because of what the Secret Police
did to his father."

Trentlyon stared at him.

"They murdered him," Carstairs said to answer the silence.
"They assassinated Edward Campbell to get hold of his
airplane plants." He raised the small brandy glass in toast. "To
Pythagoras and all his friends."

Trentlyon downed his drink and set the glass down carefully. "God help us."

Part Two

7 _____

TED ARRIVED HOME at the villa in Friedrichshafen on the day Belgium surrendered. Thousands of British and French troops were slipping in the oily waters at Dunkirk, wading toward the pathetic armada of rescue ships that would take them away from the murderous pounding of German guns. Half a million men, fighting desperately to stay alive, paddling with gun butts and tin helmets and bare hands in frantic little boats and rubber rafts to get away from the carnage—a drama Ted had not even imagined in his safe hospital room. The war was still something distant, a conflict that did not touch him. The villa in southern Germany was as much apart from the war as Nantucket Sound, Ted thought. He was not involved in anyone else's fight.

Ted bumped around the villa in a wheelchair, with his left leg in its plaster cast leading the way like a battering ram. More than once he'd nearly chopped down Mrs. Glebe at the knees, coming round a corner. The first few days home were a welcome change from the hospital; at least he could move around now. But the novelty of the chair soon wore off. His arms ached and he got cramps in his hands from pushing the wheels, a task all the more difficult due to the bandage on his left hand.

He wrote letters to Anne every other day, which were posted through Switzerland. Her letters came by way of Portugal, usually, always a week or ten days after they were written, and, always, of course, censored. What could not be blotted out was that she loved him and missed him and wanted him back. The little war news he had came from the radio and even then it was about somewhere far away.

Visitors were rare at the villa. About his only contacts with anyone outside had been by telephone and correspondence with the unflappable stooges of the ministries of transportation and commerce (he had not progressed an inch on that front still), and evenings with Karl, his chief mechanic, who was trying to teach him chess. So it was a pleasant surprise and something of a social event when the man in the light brown fedora visited him one afternoon when he had just finished a letter to Anne on the patio. Welcome, first, because it had been a boring day and not brightened by Nathaniel Hawthorne's *The Scarlet Letter* and, second, because he was an American and Ted could speak English for a change.

"I'm not sure I understand what you're offering me." Ted had parked the wheelchair beside the garden table and the United Press bureau chief had taken a seat on the wooden bench opposite him. "You want me to be a reporter for your news service, Mr. Grayson?"

"I don't, no. I think we have enough newsmen tripping over each other as it is in Germany. No offense. But evidently the brass in New York think it would be an interesting news angle if Theodore Campbell were to report on the aspects of the air war as an observer. Those were my instructions from London. To ask you, I mean."

"I'm not a reporter," Ted said.

The bureau chief nodded. "Yes, I know." He said it with a sigh as if he'd used the same argument himself. "But you *did* write this." He held up a copy of *Beware the Hawk*. "They think you're uniquely qualified to give insight on the Luftwaffe's overwhelming success in the war."

It was obvious that this fellow was only making the request because he was told to. His manner was abrasively polite, as if he'd rather be some other place or asking this of someone else. And it made Ted angry. He had looked forward to a pleasant conversation with a fellow American and got this sour "you're-not-a-proper-journalist" confrontation instead.

"What would I have to do?" Ted asked.

"You're not *interested!*" the bureau chief said quickly, frowning more than Ted expected he meant to.

"Maybe." Ted indicated his leg with a wave. "This comes off in two weeks so I couldn't start until then, of course." He was really enjoying this. The fellow seemed to have stopped breathing.

"Do—can you type?"

Ted pointed to the typewriter under the shade canopy at the corner of the portico where he'd written the letter to Anne. "I've been a right-handed typist since the accident, but when this comes off—" he held up his bandaged hand "—I guess I could get up to thirty, thirty-five words a minute." He smiled. "Fast enough?"

The bureau chief nodded; reluctantly, Ted thought.

"If it makes any difference to you, every word in that book is mine. I mean, no one ghosted it. That may not be important for a book that went generally unread in the States, but—"

"I read it." Grayson tipped his hat back slightly on his head.

"Oh?" Now Ted was surprised. "And?"

"Well . . ." He shrugged, glanced down at his hands, "It didn't win the Nobel prize, did it?" When he looked up there was a crooked smile on his face. "But, then, I guess it was Pearl Buck's turn. Look, Campbell, I think I started this off badly. I didn't really think you'd be interested. I was afraid I made this trip down here for nothing." He took a cigarette out of a pack he produced from his jacket pocket. "Smoke?"

Ted declined with a shake of his head.

The bureau chief lit up, pushing the smoke away from his face with a wave. "I *really* didn't think you'd be interested. You surprised me there. I didn't expect you cared what anyone thought back home about your impression of the Luftwaffe after the reception you got on this." He tapped the book with a finger and took a deep drag on the cigarette. "You are interested, aren't you?"

Now Ted felt like a fool. "Well, I . . . I . . ."

"You know, I didn't even ask them about a salary." He shook his head. "That's how sure I was you'd say no."

"It isn't the money."

Grayson glanced around the patio, squinted down at the garden on the lower terrace. "I wouldn't think so. You couldn't keep this place in wild dandelions with what UP pays."

"Maybe you'd better tell me what exactly I'd be expected to

do. I mean, don't you have to be registered or something to be a journalist in Germany?"

"It's one of the last professions you don't need a license for, just a press card."

Ted shrugged, feigning disappointment. "Well, there you are then. I don't have a press card. I imagine it would take some time to get that straightened—"

The bureau chief laughed. "You? Theodore Campbell? Why, Goering would have Goebbels' head for dinner if it took five minutes! Maybe you don't realize it, Campbell, but your byline on a story about the mighty Luftwaffe would be a feather in Hermann's rather large bonnet, not to mention ours. No matter what you say about it. With Mussolini in it now, there's—"

"Mussolini?"

"Italy, they—" He stopped, glanced at Ted with a frown. "You haven't heard?"

"Heard what?"

"Italy declared war on Great Britain and France last night." He looked at Ted with an incredulous expression. "Don't you have a radio, see a newspaper?"

Karl had borrowed the radio after their chess game last night. The newspaper was on the table beside the typewriter. He hadn't looked at it yet.

"I guess I missed it," Ted said. "I haven't really been keeping up."

"Haven't been—" He wiped his hand across his face. "You do know there's a war on? Germany against the Allies? Dunkirk fell last week. Paris probably this week. The surrender of France will come any day now."

Ted nodded silently.

"Doesn't that *mean* anything to you?"

"It doesn't matter what it means to me," Ted said. "Obviously, it means a great deal to the United Press. I take it they expect a large battle for England."

"They do."

"And by the look of things the critical confrontation will be in the air—between the Luftwaffe and the RAF?"

"That's right. Of course, I'm no strategist, but any fool can see Germany must have superiority in the air if there's to be an invasion across the Channel."

"I see." Ted reached down to scratch at the tip of the cast

below his knee. "And they want *this* fool to report on that battle for the folks back home?"

The bureau chief exhaled a jet of smoke in a long sigh. "I was right, after all, wasn't I? You're not interested. You don't even care about what's happening."

"I'm not exactly thrilled at the prospect of getting busted up like this again."

"The idea wasn't that you'd be a participant," he said sarcastically. "Just an observer."

"I'll think about it," Ted said noncommitally. "But my first obligation is to my business interests here. I'm an American national in a foreign country at war. I don't want to do anything that might jeopardize my neutrality status in—"

"We're all neutral Americans," the bureau chief cut in angrily. His eyes made a quick sweep of the estate. "But some of us are more neutral than others. Look, if you're interested, you can reach me in Berlin at the Adlon Hotel."

"I'll do that."

"Fine. I can see myself out. I'm sorry if I've wasted your time."

"Not at all," Ted replied. "It was nice to talk to another American."

"I'm sure it was." The bureau chief turned on his heel and started out. He'd taken two or three steps and stopped, then returned to the garden table, offering the book to Ted.

"I wonder if you'd mind signing this for me," he said, fiercely polite. "Some friends of mine would get a big kick out of it, seeing your autograph. It might be valuable some day."

Ted took a fountain pen from his pocket. "I doubt it." He opened it to the title page, hesitated then glanced up at his visitor.

"Grayson," the bureau chief said. "Just say 'To Lowell Grayson from a neutral American' and sign it, if you don't mind." He refused to say please. "You never know when something like this might turn out to be valuable."

A group of Berlin conservatives representing the city's academic, civic and industrial communities formed a club in the late 1930s and met on Wednesdays. The Wednesday Club, as it was called, discussed history, art, science, and literature, and the negative impact on National Socialism on each of them. The group was also a mild forum for the expression of theoretical resistance to the Nazi regime and Albrecht Haushofer was a member. What was not known by the Wednesday Club group was that Haushofer and two other members —Ulrich von Hassell, former envoy to Rome, and Johannes Popitz, Prussian minister of finance—had taken their resistance theories several steps further. Each of them had traveled his own road in his contempt for Hitler; they had opposed him in the early years and that opposition had solidified into active resistance until now they found themselves at the crossroads of conspiracy.

Following the regular Wednesday meeting, the three men strolled through a nearby park to hold a quiet meeting of their own.

It was not an altogether satisfactory meeting, Haushofer concluded as he rode the subway back to his residence. They had each been tentative in their suggestions, as if they had not thoroughly thought through any decisive action. Haushofer had cut Hassell off before he could articulate the complete thread of his thoughts, which would have been the elimination of Hitler through violent means. It was an unthinkable course of action at this point. There were other avenues to consider. And Popitz, he thought, had little more to offer, except the notion of bringing the Hohenzollern crown prince back as successor to Hitler, without any thought as to what to do about the Fuehrer in the meantime.

There would be other meetings of course. Resistance cells like theirs were sprouting up everywhere, though too many were weak-kneed and would disintegrate with the ever-present threat of the Gestapo. It was a question of pace. If a concerted effort to remove the Nazi stranglehold on Germany did not develop soon, then Hitler would surely be unstoppable—

This war must be stopped!

That was the all-important issue. The British are not our enemies. Perhaps if he could contact the British on behalf of the German resistance to Hitler . . .

But hadn't he already written to his friend the Duke of Hamilton in that regard? Hadn't the duke been sympathetic to his general thesis of a negotiated peace? Even so, Hamilton was not Winston Churchill, nor was he an entity to be reckoned with to any substantial degree in the eyes of the British.

This war must end!

Haushofer set his coat and hat in the chair in the anteroom

and made quickly for his study. He unlocked a drawer of his large desk and opened the false bottom compartment where he kept his most secret correspondence and his diary.

The Marquis of Clydesdale, Mr. Douglas-Hamilton, lately the Duke of Hamilton, was not his only friend in England. He withdrew the postcard from his diary and studied it in the light that spilled across his desk from an old brass lamp. During the Olympics of 1936 in Berlin he had met several British MPs, including Harold Balfour, Kenneth Lindsay and the marquis. But he'd also met a man who'd shown an interest in his geopolitical theories. When Haushofer lectured at the Chatman House in London in 1937, depicting the hatred the German people felt for the Treaty of Versailles, he'd been a guest of Sir Alfred Bullard. He was a shrewd old devil, his English friend was, owing to his connection with the less-publicized machinations of the Admiralty, no doubt. But Haushofer saw their friendship also in a more practical light—it never hurt to have friends in the government—and he'd shared many of his private fears of the coming Nazi juggernaut with him in letters, just as he had with the Duke of Hamilton. But where the duke had been politely noncommittal, Sir Alfred had shown a genuine interest. A confrontation between England and Germany would most likely result in war, they had agreed, and the only benefactor in such a circumstance would be the Soviet Union.

And now England and Germany were at war, Aryans fighting between themselves, while Russia quietly, steadily expanded—hadn't they just occupied Lithuania, Latvia and Estonia?

Germany was fighting the wrong war!

Haushofer turned the postcard over between his fingers. The picture was a pastoral setting; a herdsman with his sheep and a thatch-roofed house in the distance. It might have been in England or Germany. He reversed the card and read the short note again.

> It looks to be a long and heavy winter, but we are well and hope you to be as fit. I am returning your book by separate conveyance. God speed.
>
> Yours ever,
>
> B.

Haushofer retrieved the book from the wallcase. It had been delivered some months before. Words and phrases had been underlined throughout the book that, set down in order, became a message. A message of hope. It detailed a plan to rectify the current troubles in Europe, though the plan entailed great personal risk if Haushofer agreed to the terms of it. The message told of a special pipeline that they could communicate through and the arrangements and codes for that communication. If he was willing, the plan could be implemented immediately. He had only to send a postcard to a coin shop in Lisbon requesting a certain coin and it would be understood that he agreed to do his part.

There was no minimizing the danger he would be in if the Gestapo discovered his scheme, Haushofer knew. But was it worth the risk? Haushofer had struggled with his conscience through the winter until his mind was irrevocably made up. He thumbed through the pages of the book, mindful of his responsibility. Only two men could make this plan work. One of them was his friend, the deputy fuehrer. Hess could be convinced, if he wasn't already, that the British would and should accept a proposal of peace. If Hess was not fully informed of the extent of his role in this conspiracy, then it was for a good reason. The man was, after all, a Nazi and devoted follower of Hitler. But it was the second man who concerned Haushofer most—the American.

He found the underlined passages toward the end of the book that described his challenge ahead.

C . . . is . . . unwitting . . . probably unwilling . . . key . . . Yours . . . is to . . . convince.

Haushofer set the book down on the desk. He had given Herr Theodore Campbell something to think about when he visited him in the hospital. Now was the time to visit him again.

8

"I DON'T THINK I can do that," she said. "I don't think I have the stomach to pretend to believe in their bullshit."

"It is not a question of what you *think* you can do, Comrade Buchanan. It is a question of what must be done."

They were in a basement apartment on Kirschenstrasse; Kate and her cell leader, Ludwig Freimark, a short but formidable-looking man with a thick neck who had been born in Warsaw and was now a civilian driver for the Ministry of Propaganda. Kate knew little more than that about him except that he was a chain smoker, that he apparently suffered from tuberculosis, and that he was dedicated in his service to the party. Where in other men she could sense their physical attraction to her, with Freimark there was none; his single interest in her was as a worker for the party.

"You can best serve us now, Comrade Buchanan, by seeming to be one of them," he said through a curtain of cigarette smoke. "They want a pet American journalist for propaganda purposes. Look at the use they make of the America First idiots. They'll open up to you. They'll let you in on matters of importance. They'll give you freedom of movement."

Like a human calculating machine, she thought, adding up all the advantages in neat columns. She watched him stab the remains of the short cigarette between his bloodless lips then use it to light another. He exhaled across the small table and Kate was momentarily repulsed by his breath. His lungs must be rotten with the disease.

"People know how I feel," Kate protested. "How will they think I've suddenly changed?"

"Let them believe what they want. Some will think you sold out. Others will think you had a true change of heart. It will be easiest to convince the hard-core Nazis because they believe it so fanatically themselves that your conversion will only demonstrate the power of their convictions."

Kate clenched her fist. "I *hate* Nazis," she said. She looked up at Freimark. "And I hate the idea of acting like one."

Freimark was silent a moment. His dull eyes locked on her. "Do you refuse, Comrade?"

Kate looked away. He didn't show anger or displeasure in his face and somehow that made her feelings of guilt more acute. She shook her head.

"I did not hear you," Freimark said.

"No." Kate pushed her hair back from her forehead. "No, I'm not refusing. It's . . . it's just going to be difficult."

"These are difficult times, Comrade. We all make certain sacrifices." Freimark touched her then. He reached across the table and set his palm over her hand. His fingers were cold and clammy and Kate shuddered without meaning to. "You are prepared to make some personal sacrifices, for the party?" He gave her a rare smile.

There wasn't any mistaking what he meant. "You want me to sleep with them too." She surprised herself that she would be so calm.

"Not *all* of them, Comrade," Freimark replied. "There are too many even for you." He withdrew his hand from hers. "Do you know Walter Ernst Klaussen?"

"No."

Freimark took a photograph from his notes and pushed it toward her. "He is a new assistant deputy secretary in the Foreign Ministry. His post is relatively unimportant, but he sits in on meetings concerning the Hitler-Stalin Pact. We would like you to make his acquaintance. We would like to know what goes on in those meetings."

"Why should he tell me?"

"We want you to—" Freimark shrugged "—become his friend."

"Jesus, you're really serious! You want me to seduce him?"

"We want the information," Freimark said. "How you get it is up to you."

Kate pushed herself back in her chair but said nothing.

"Herr Klaussen is fond of parties." Freimark extinguished his cigarette. "I think you should meet him at a party."

Today would be the test, Kate told herself. She'd been roused out of bed the night before and told to go to Templehof, where a special plane was waiting to take her directly to Paris. She was being rushed in as replacement for Bill Travers, who had got a sudden attack of appendicitis. She was halfway to the airport before she realized exactly what Travers' assignment had been. Compiègne. The signing of the armistice.

Paris was not the city she remembered. There was a curfew, the blackout was still enforced, no taxis, streets nearly deserted. What people hadn't left already stood about expressionless, as if they were unable to comprehend the terrible swiftness of their defeat and humiliation. Paris, the city where she learned to love and be loved, had had its heart ripped out.

The previous Monday, Marshal Pétain, the new premier, had asked the Germans for an armistice. Two days later Wehrmacht engineers were at work in the Forest of Compiègne outside Paris, demolishing the wall of the Museum that held Marshal Foch's railroad car, in which the 1918 armistice had been signed. It was to satisfy Hitler's sadistic desire for revenge that the French were to surrender to Germany in exactly the same wagon-lit, in exactly the same spot as the Germans had ended the World War twenty-two years ago.

Today would be her test, Kate thought, if she could stomach it, to play her first performance as a Nazi convert. She had already steeled herself to it, but she hadn't planned on it happening here, not in France, not on a sunny afternoon near her beloved Paris. But perhaps it didn't matter; Paris died when the first panzer tank clanked to a grinding stop beneath the Arc de Triomphe.

"What time is it, somebody?"

Kate snapped out of her daydream and glanced back over her shoulder to seek out the voice. She was on the fringe of a group of American reporters and photographers clustered along the perimeter of the clearing. The railroad car was in the center of the circular park, which was about two hundred yards in diameter and lined with cypress trees.

"I've got three fifteen," Lowell Grayson said. He was standing beside her, gazing at the knot of uniformed Nazis milling around the car. "Hitler's late. You'd think he'd be on time for this."

Kate took a breath. It was now or never. "It's his privilege, isn't it? He won. I think he deserves credit when it's due." There was a bitter taste in her mouth.

Grayson turned, gave her an odd look.

"I think the Germans are giving this little ceremony exactly the right touch," she added, avoiding Grayson's eyes. "The perfect ending to the Versailles Treaty."

"Am I hearing right?"

Why did Lowell have to be first. "You have to admire them."

"The French?"

"The Germans," Kate snapped. "You have to give them credit. They've waited a long time for this day."

"Are you nuts?" Grayson shaded his eyes from the sun to glance at her. "They're gangsters. You said that."

"Maybe I've changed my mind."

"Maybe!—"

"Here they come!"

Kate was saved a facedown when three German staff cars pulled up in front of the Alsace-Lorraine monument. Adolf Hitler emerged from the rear seat of the lead car. He wore a double-breasted gray uniform, his single decoration, the Iron Cross, suspended from the left pocket. He stopped to glance at the monument, covered now with German war flags, then walked to the edge of the clearing.

"Jesus, the whole gang's here," said an AP photographer. "I see the Reichsmarshal's wearing sky blue today."

"Goering's got more uniforms than you got flashbulbs," someone else snickered.

"Isn't that Keitel next to him? And who's that—von Rundstedt?"

"Von Brauchitsch."

Erish Raeder was there, too; tall and austere in the blue uniform of the Grand Admiral of the German Fleet, his upturned collar a naval tradition. And Kate recognized two nonmilitary members of the party, both wearing gray. Joachim von Ribbentrop, Reich Foreign Minister, and at his side in a

simple party uniform, squinting in the sun, Deputy Reichsfuehrer Rudolf Hess.

But Kate's attention was on Hitler. She tried to read his face.
He was a solemn, scornful little man; prancing, reveling in this
revenge, the triumphant conqueror basking in the shame and
humiliation of the defeated. What was he thinking now, she
wondered? He'd been a corporal in the World War, a foot
soldier, a messenger. Well, now he was *der Fuehrer*, the life
and breath of the new Reich. It would have been an easy thing
to kill him, she found herself thinking. A gun or a hand
grenade from this distance. It would have been easy.

"What's he doing now?" someone asked.

"He's reading the marker."

"What marker?"

*"Here on the Eleventh of November 1918 succumbed the
criminal pride of the German Empire . . . vanquished by the
free peoples it tried to enslave."*

"Oh, that should give him a chuckle."

Chuck Walsh brushed past Kate and bent to one knee to snap
a photograph of the scene. "C'mon, let's have a smile," he
whispered cynically. "Adolf, you haff gutt no sense of
humor."

Kate watched as the photographers rushed to take their
pictures. The party of reporters drifted closer to the railroad
car, craning for a better view as the German party entered and
took their places. Hitler's chair was the very one occupied by
Marshal Foch a generation earlier.

"Where are the French? You'd think Hitler would have
made *them* wait."

"Not our boy. The French are coming to *him*. Here they
come! Jesus, they don't look very happy, do they?"

Four of the French stepped into the clearing, moving briskly
past the German honor guard. They marched mechanically to
the railroad car, exchanging stiff salutes with the German
officers.

Twelve minutes later it was over. Hitler was on his feet, his
right arm extended in a rigid salute, then he was gone;
Goering, Brauchitsch, Raeder, Hess, Ribbentrop came after
him like children playing follow the leader. Only Keitel
remained behind to face the French over the green-topped
table.

Kate and the band of reporters watched in silence as the

Nazis moved to their cars. The German band started playing "Deutschland über Alles."

A Reuters man groaned softly at the anthem. "I wish they'd play something we could dance to."

Kate swung on her heels to face him. "What the hell are you so smug about, Fielding? You might show a little respect." She'd timed it perfectly. One of Goebbels' aides was passing within hearing distance. It she was going to be a goddamn Nazi lover, now was the time to make if official. "This is a historic day."

"I'm sure," he replied, slightly taken aback, "for Germany."

"For the world," Kate said.

"You're kidding. These guys make Chicago's South Side look like it's run by Boys' Town."

Kate's eyes narrowed. "You're a cynical bastard, you know that? If you used an ounce of the brains God gave you then you'd see how important National Socialism can be in this screwed-up world."

The man from Reuters drew away from her. Lowell regarded her with an astonished expression. This is not going to be pleasant, she told herself. "Look, I'm an American. And we're not involved in this fight. It's not our war. You don't have any business taking pot shots at Germany, because you don't have the vaguest notion of what they've been struggling for."

Grayson took her arm, started to lead her away. "Kate—"

"Don't try to shut me up, Lowell. I have a right to say what I want."

He took his arm away. "Jesus, you're starting to sound like Lindbergh."

"He was everybody's hero a dozen years ago. When did we stop respecting the guy?"

Grayson frowned. "When he suddenly started to be full of shit."

"I don't think so," she said quickly. "You just don't want Germany to move forward. It's people like you who would stifle the Reich. And you make me sick the way you snicker and make jokes. All of you!" She lowered her eyes, engulfed by the silence that had greeted her outburst. They were moving away from her now, but from the corner of her eye she saw the Reich propaganda man standing at the open door of a touring car, taking notes. There would be a report of this incident in

Berlin by nightfall. An American journalist speaking up *for* the Reich. She wondered what they would do with that bit of news. She suddenly felt nauseous.

When she turned back to find Lowell, he was just climbing into one of the press cars. He stared at her for a long moment then disappeared into the rear seat, and she knew she'd accomplished what she'd set out to do. Lowell hadn't looked angry or disappointed or even sad. It was pity that she saw on his face. She knew if she could fool Lowell, she could convince anyone. In that instant she knew that whatever was ahead of her, she would have to face it without the company she desperately needed, without compassion, without tenderness; alone.

9 _____

THE WEEKS OF spring and summer seemed to blur together in
Ted's mind as his convalescence continued monotonously on.
He'd shed the confinement of the wheelchair toward the end of
June and missed celebrating the Fourth of July without a cast at
all by a week. Still, his left leg was weak and he moved about
with the aid of a cane. He got out of the villa as much as
possible, spending so much time at the shop tinkering with
airplanes (and getting underfoot, he imagined, limping around
like a toad) that Karl finally suggested that he take up boating
on Lake Constance. Sailing was a disaster, but he did a great
deal of swimming and ended up renting a cottage on the beach.
He swam in the mornings, lay in the sun and read or wrote
letters to Anne in the afternoons and swam for at least an hour
just before dusk. But the satisfaction of the cottage was that it
allowed him to escape from the villa and he became more of a
recluse than he'd been all winter.

It was about the time that Ted moved to the cottage that
Anne's letters began to come less often. By the first week of
July they stopped altogether. His first thought was that the
mails had been slowed because of the war, but then he realized
he was receiving correspondence from business associates in
London and there shouldn't be any reason that hers would be
delayed. He sent a telegram and waited four days for a reply
before trying to call, but the connection through Geneva could

not be accommodated and he was left frustrated and worried. Finally, he decided there was nothing else to do but go to London. Campbell Aircraft be hanged! If it could survive with him in only the titular position as check signer then it could bloody well carry on without him for a week or ten days.

Ted made several phone calls to Munich: to the Transportation Ministry, to the Commerce Ministry, to his doctor, to the comptroller's office, to the company's federal registry supervisor, the company's accounting and paymaster office. He needed a travel visa to leave the country and another to re-enter.

By the time he'd finished making arrangements for travel (Lufthansa from Munich to Madrid with stops in Bern and Barcelona, then a Spanish line to Plymouth) he'd put in an exhausting day. It was amazing how fatiguing holding a telephone could be. He took a long swim to work out the muscles in his neck, then closed up the cottage. The drive to the villa was rejuvenating, with the cool early evening air sweet and fresh in the open-topped car. He was going back to London, to Anne!

When he got to the villa, Mrs. Glebe was preparing dinner. There had been several calls, she said. One gentleman had insisted that he return his call as soon as possible. It was a number in Berlin.

"Hello, this is Theodore Campbell," Ted said from a telephone in the study. "I'm returning Herr Wagner's call." He didn't know who Herr Wagner was, but he was in Berlin so he was probably another government minion. Ted prayed there wasn't a problem with the travel visa. God knows he'd promised them enough just for this brief holiday.

"Hallo."

"Herr Wagner."

"Ja. This is Herr Campbell, in Friedrichshafen?"

"Yes," Ted said, "I'm—"

"Ein moment, bitte."

Ein moment, bitte. Christ, how many times had he heard that today! There was the greatest temptation to slam the receiver back in its cradle. He was sick to death of their officious goddamn—

"Theodore."

Ted recognized the voice instantly and his rage suddenly evaporated. "Herr Hess?"

"How are you this evening, Theodore?" asked the deputy fuehrer. "How is your leg, getting better I hope?"

"It's much better, thank you. Healed now. I've been swimming."

"What's that—swimming?"

"Yes, to strengthen the muscles in the leg. It's good therapy, swimming is."

"Ah, yes. Good, then. So you're getting around all right?"

"Fairly well, yes, sir."

"And your hand?" Hess seemed genuinely interested. "It is also healed?"

"The scar is barely noticeable—good as new."

"I'm pleased to hear it," Hess said. Ted could imagine him nodding to himself, his sad, searching eyes fixed on some object across whatever room he was calling from. "I'm sorry not to have visited you at the hospital. It's a poor excuse to a friend to say one is busy. I can only hope you'll forgive me."

Friend? Now there was something. Rudolf Hess's friend. Ted realized suddenly that it was true to a point. You don't think of men like Hess as having friends.

"Of course," Ted said. "Anyway, hospitals are lousy places to receive guests."

There was an amused murmur from the other end of the line.

"Still your sense of humor," the deputy fuehrer said. "Herr Haushofer told me you were in good spirits when he visited you in Munich . . . in spite of the circumstances."

Ted would hardly have described his mood that day as cheerful. Professor Haushofer had said he was there in Hess's stead, as a friend of a friend. Odd people, some of these friends of the deputy fuehrer. For an instant he wondered if Hess had any idea what had been discussed that day Haushofer came to see him.

I am afraid we are going to win this war.

Ted dismissed the thought. Haushofer was just thinking out loud, sharing his private thoughts with someone he imagined he could trust.

Germany is fighting the wrong people . . . there are others in Germany who believe strongly as I do.

Not a chance, Ted thought. Whatever Haushofer had said it was no way a reflection of Hess's position; not the second man in line for Hitler's throne. Still, it was interesting, wasn't it, made you wonder what kind of shenanigans were going on behind the doors. Of course there was another possibility, one that made more sense: Perhaps Haushofer was acting for the Secret Police to test Ted; see what his attitude was after the crash. He could believe the Gestapo might pull a trick like that, something Hess might even agree to, as a security precaution. But, then, why would Hess be calling now? Why should he be—

"Theodore? Are you still there?"

Hess's voice brought him back out of his thoughts. He'd been doing that quite a lot lately; talking to himself in his mind. It was an eccentricity of a recluse.

"Excuse me," Ted said quickly. "I guess I'm preoccupied. I'm leaving in a few days, going to see my girl."

"Yes, I heard you were leaving Germany."

He'd heard? Ted had made a few calls to Munich and Rudolf Hess had heard about them? Good Christ!

"When were you planning to leave?"

Oh, shit! Were. He said *were*. "Saturday."

"Saturday." Hess repeated the day with studied thought as if to remind himself that such a twenty-four-hour period existed. "I see. That would be—" he paused a moment and Ted thought he heard the slight rustling of pages turning "—that would be the twentieth."

"Yes," Ted said, "that would be it."

"You are flying, of course."

Ted frowned at the receiver. "Pardon me?"

"I assume you will be flying yourself. To Switzerland, is it, then on to . . . your destination?"

Ted wasn't sure if Hess was just playing him along or if he truly was so uninformed. "I *can't* fly," he said. "I can't take a Campbell aircraft out of Germany. It's one of the regulations I'm committed to as a foreign national with a business enterprise. At least until I have full control of *my* company."

"That's absurd," said the voice from Berlin. "You're coming back, aren't you?"

"I have to," Ted said, without putting too fine a point on it. "I can't very well run a company in Germany from the States."

"Or from London."

Ted took a long breath. "Right," he said.

"I would like to see you, Theodore," Hess said. "Before you leave. Could you come to Berlin? Friday the Fuehrer makes an important speech in the Kroll Opera House. I'l like you to be here. And afterwards Hermann is having a large party at the Leipzieger Palace. Oh, but that's a secret." His voice dropped conspiratorially. "Our Hermann is to be honored personally by the Fuehrer—a decoration." By his tone, Ted couldn't be sure if Hess was pleased or not. "Will you come, then? Please say you will."

Ted hesitated too long. He started to say something but Hess cut him off.

"You're worried about your leaving Germany, is that it? A late party Friday then leaving Saturday on your holiday. I understand. Let me look into it. If necessary I'll fly you to Switzerland myself. There—can you find a better bargain? I promise that there will be no inconvenience for you on your journey. As a matter of fact—" the deputy fuehrer paused, there was a muffled exchange at the other end of the line and Ted was suddenly aware that someone was with Hess. When he came back on the line, Hess was as excited as a child. "Theodore, I have an excellent idea! Have you ever flown a Messerschmitt? The ME-One-Ten?"

"No," Ted said.

"But you could?"

"It's an airplane, isn't it?"

The receiver laughed in his ear. "Yes, of course. You are Theodore Campbell. But let me tell you, I have such an airplane at Augsburg. I am a pilot too, remember. The plane is fueled and always ready. I would be happy to loan it to you. You could leave it in Switzerland until you returned."

Ted was astonished. *Borrow* the deputy fuehrer's personal aircraft so that he could make connections to London! It was an outrageous idea. How long would his neutrality image last (such as it was) if he began piloting German military planes for his own use? He could just see it, climbing out of the cockpit of a sleek, swastika-insigniaed fighter at the Bern airport. Wouldn't the press have a field day with that! It was a preposterous suggestion, more so even that Haushofer's . . . *Haushofer!* Abruptly Ted felt a tremor of apprehension; his back and arms went gooseflesh. Who *had* the professor represented when he came to see him in the hospital? And *who* was with Hess at this moment?

"I—I wouldn't want to take away your only means of flying," Ted finally said.

"It's not an inconvenience," Hess replied. "There are two

aircraft at my disposal. One is a reserve in the event the first is being maintenanced."

"Look, ah, do you think you could square it with the proper authorities so I could use a plane of my own?" It was an audacious request, Ted realized, perhaps even insulting considering Hess's obviously capricious offer.

"I'll see about it." It was practically a guarantee. "So, you'll be in Berlin in two days," Hess added cheerfully. "Good. I am looking forward to it."

"Me too," Ted replied.

Afterwards, he sat at his desk and started at the phone. Hess wanted him to do something, that was clear enough, but what?

The plump figure of Mrs. Glebe appeared in the door and announced dinner. He switched out the light in the study with the thought of Anne on his mind. In a few days they would be together, that's what mattered, not the war or the Ministry of Transportation or Campbell Aircraft. They would pick up where they left off the last time he'd seen her and the promise of the encounter made everything else less significant.

No dark doorways till you're back.

Bloody right.

Rudolf Hess paced back and forth in front of his large desk, hands shoved into the pockets of his party uniform, his dark eyes but bleak shadows on a solemn face.

When he stopped and rested his hands on the desk, he was trembling.

"I am frightened," he said in a low, nearly inaudible voice. "In three days the Fuehrer will offer peace to the British people, an offer to end this fighting. And I'm afraid—mortally afraid—that Churchill will turn away from it." He lifted his head slowly, his eyes nervous, like a man haunted by terrifying nightmares. "And in anticipation of that contingency, the order to prepare for invasion has already been given. Raeder is calling it Operation Sealion." He touched a hand to his forehead, closed his eyes. "The Fuehrer will be forced into the attack and our English brothers will die in a senseless and vain struggle. It is our duty to bring England to her senses. We must try, mustn't we? If the Fuehrer's offer of peace Friday is rejected, then *we* must try, mustn't we?" The question was more a plea.

Hess looked at his friend and confidant. "Do you think

there's a chance that this will succeed?" His voice was pitifully sincere.

"Yes, I believe it." From his place in a Queen Anne chair, Albrecht Haushofer nodded. "I believe Herr Campbell can help us. He has very important friends."

10

JOHANN REGENBAUER paused on the steps of the private gymnasium to watch a train decelerate as it entered the Potsdammer railway station. It had been months since he'd been in Berlin last and his return three days ago had been made more agreeable with the news of his promotion. He was now Sturmbannfuehrer Regenbauer—SS major—and the flat silver wire stitched into the braid of his new shoulder straps gleamed in the morning sun as if illustrating the perfect contrast with the black background of his tailored SD uniform. He'd found a home in the *Sicherheitstienst,* and his promotion only proved to him his acceptance into the corps that was the elite of the elite within the SS guard.

Regenbauer entered the main corridor of the building. His footsteps echoing against the tile floor in the long hall were a cadence that personified the strength and power of the Reich. He stopped before a set of double doors that led into the gymnasium and checked his watch. He was slightly early. Heydrich would like that. The chief of the Security Police admired promptness. Regenbauer removed his hat, taking care to wipe the moisture from the sweatband, and placed it snugly under his left arm. Before pushing through the doors he inspected himself once more and brushed a fleck of dust from the breast of his tunic. It had been more than a year since he'd reported in person and he wanted to make a good impression.

Heydrich was in the center of the gymnasium floor, his foil at the on-guard position, having just scored a point on the prime quarte of his opponent's jacket. Regenbauer moved to the edge of the empty spectators' gallery as the two fencers resumed their starting positions at the center line of the piste.

Regenbauer had an amateur's knowledge of the sport—it was a required course at the University of Kiel—but he had never been much impressed by the exercise. In his school days, classmates thrust at one another in graceless lunges as if the object of it all had more to do with wrestling than coordination. But Heydrich was no awkward student. He moved ever forward, finessing his opponent in the salle, foiling attacks in lightning parries, then recovering, feinting, engaging, pressing his opponent back to the warning line, forcing him to attack from a position of weakness, then feinting a lunge and extending his foil past a misjudged parry to score. The gymnasium rang with the scrape of sword on sword as the two masked combatants maneuvered for positions, blades flashing in the sun's rays that streamed through the windows high on the auditorium walls. Neither swordsman spoke throughout the grunting duel until after Heydrich's fifth successive score, when he stepped back and said, "enough."

He removed his mask and dismissed the opponent with a wave of his hand and walked across the wide floor to Regenbauer, wiping his face with the sleeve of his fencing jacket. He acknowledged Regenbauer's salute with a nod.

"Good morning, Major," Heydrich said, "and congratulations." He touched the braided shoulder strap with the blunted tip of his foil. "It looks fine on you."

"Thank you, sir."

"It must be good to be back in Berlin again."

"Yes, sir, it is."

Heydrich pulled the strings on either side of the fencing vest, loosening the jacket, and shrugged it off. "You may stand at ease, Major, we are alone here. Sit down. If you would like to, you may smoke."

Regenbauer sat down at the end of the first row of bleacher seats. He set his hat beside him. The bench trembled beneath him and he heard the blare of a whistle as another train braked into the Potsdammer station across the street.

"I am told some of our Olympic athletes trained in this gymnasium for the Berlin games," Heydrich said, pulling off his fencing breeches. He was a very neat man, Regenbauer noticed. His uniform was folded and hung on a chair beside a wooden table where his shoes had been placed, heels to the edge, exactly in the center. And as he took off the fencing equipment, each item was set neatly on the table as if it were being laid out for a meticulous matador.

"It was part of a boys' school," Heydrich was saying, "until the main building burned down. That was in 1938. Too bad, but then I've always wanted a private gymnasium. Now I have one. So, Major, how did you enjoy Holland?"

"There wasn't much time to spend touring, Herr General."

Heydrich nodded. "Yes, I saw from your reports that you were busy. The resistance is very active there too." He glanced at Regenbauer. "But less so today, eh, Major?"

"You are displeased with my work, sir?"

"Displeased!" Heydrich frowned. "Hardly that. You are my very best agent, Johann, and I don't mind admitting it to you. That's why I've called you back to Berlin." He took the sword from the other paraphernalia on the table and ran his fingers down the tapered rectangular blade. "You do not fence, do you, Major?"

"No, sir."

"Fencing is a game of skill, speed, finesse . . . there is little advantage in mere brute strength. Control of movement and quick thinking can overcome the lack of height, reach, or strength that would be a severe handicap in most other sports. It's a complex and difficult art to master." Heydrich whipped the blade with a snap of his wrist, cutting an arc in the air a few inches from Regenbauer's eyes. "The coordination of hand and eye do not come naturally to many people." He raised an eyebrow. "Do you agree, Major?"

"From what little I know about the sport," Regenbauer replied, "that sounds logical, yes, sir." He kept his eyes on Heydrich, ignoring the blade that carved circles in front of his face.

Heydrich smiled. He rested the tip of the foil on Regenbauer's shoulder. "You're a cool one, Major. Do you know that you are called the Iceman by some of your colleagues? They say you're cynical, brutal, that you have no compassion, no sense of pity. Did you really strip naked a woman in Utrecht and hang her by her wrists?"

Regenbauer inclined his head slightly. "Yes. She was a

member of the underground. She had information that I wanted."

"So, what they say is true." Heydrich nodded. "You got the information, I assume?"

"Yes."

"And the woman?"

"Sir?"

"She died?"

"Yes," Regenbauer said, "eventually."

Heydrich set the sword back in its place on the table. "You're exactly the man I want," he said. "You have a sadistic nature and you're clever, skillful and dedicated. Would you argue with that appraisal?"

Regenbauer said nothing, he only returned Heydrich's stare.

"Yes," said the chief of the Security Police with a slight smile, "exactly the man. We are much alike, you and I. If you will forgive the analogy, we are each expert fencers. The work we do comes naturally to us. Certain things—footwork, balance, control, ingenuity—they cannot be taught. And in a game of subtlety, bluff and violent action we are uniquely qualified to play." He folded his hands together in front of him. "Does any of this make sense to you, Major?"

Regenbauer paused a moment. "No."

"And unafraid to speak his mind," Heydrich said, amused, as if he was speaking to someone else. "Good . . . within certain limits." He clasped his hands behind his back. "Do you recall our first meeting, Major?"

"Yes."

"What do you most clearly remember of it?"

"The penalty for disobedience is death," Regenbauer said.

Heydrich frowned. "Yes, yes, but we discussed other things."

"It is what I recall *most* clearly."

"But I also made you a promise, did I not? I told you that one day I could make you a very powerful man if your work continued to please me. Do you remember that?"

"Yes."

"That day is drawing near," Heydrich said. "You will not be surprised to learn that the invasion and conquest of England is not far off—a matter of weeks, possibly. And with Europe under our control, you can understand the need to expand the foreign intelligence department of the *Schutzstaffel*. At the moment, Brigadefuehrer Schellenberg heads that department. He is a bright young man but with aspirations in other directions. I am considering you, Major, to fill the vacancy when the time is right."

Regenbauer did not blink. He changed his position slightly on the bench, nodded, continued to stare at Heydrich as if the idea was perfectly logical.

"Haven't you anything to say, Regenbauer? Do you realize what I've just said?"

For a moment only Regenbauer considered it. "Yes, sir, I understand. I agree."

"You *agree?*" Heydrich shook his head. "Does anything touch you, Major? I propose to offer you one of the most powerful positions within the Reich and you can only say 'I agree'?"

"May I speak frankly, sir?"

"Of course."

Regenbauer stood up. "First, you are *not* offering me the job. I am being considered, which indicates to me that there are other candidates or that you have not yet made up your mind as to my experience. You have already mentioned my unique qualifications for this work and, if I may say, you are correct. I do not fence. I do not have time for sports and games. What I do best has to do with pain and death and accomplishing a specific goal in the shortest time. Therefore, I agree that I am the best qualified to oversee the work. Secondly, this is our third meeting face to face. On both previous occasions we met privately and I was given specific tasks to perform that no one else was privy to. They were your orders alone and I carried them out faithfully and exactly. I did not question the fact that what I did for you would not be justified by higher authorities within the Reich. I saw it as my duty and I did it because it afforded me a measure of power and because I like it. You are one of a handful of men who will one day rule a continent. However I can help you can only be helping myself." Regenbauer paused a moment, thoughtfully rubbing the acne scars above the line of his jaw. "I am your devoted servant, Herr General, but I am not an unambitious one. If we are as nearly alike as you suggest then you will understand my fascination and my appetite for power. But not in a political sense. I am content to remain in the Security Service. I only wish to have a measure of control over my own destiny."

Heydrich had been listening carefully, leaning against the table, his left arm folded across his chest supporting his right elbow, an index finger patiently tapping his lower lip. "I see." He pushed himself away from the table. "This is a threat of some kind, Major?"

"Absolutely not. We are both practical men. I am only expressing my assessment of this relationship in the hope that my candidness will lead to a beneficial arrangement between us in the future. I ask only that I be granted certain privileges, because of my unique services, that I believe are due me."

"You know of course that I could have you shot and no one would question it."

"Yes, sir," Regenbauer answered. "But you would lose a very effective instrument. And an utterly loyal subordinate."

"Effective, yes," Heydrich said, "and perhaps loyal, but also arrogant."

Regenbauer nodded. "It is my nature. I have a large ego that must be satisfied." He took an envelope from the breast pocket of his tunic. "As an illustration of my personal loyalty, I have this."

Heydrich took the envelope. "What is it?"

"Among my duties in your service was to be vigilant in the search for suspicious conduct on the part of high-ranking members of the Wehrmacht." Regenbauer watched Heydrich examine the contents of the envelope. "It occurred to me that if there was the possibility of a conspiracy within the military at so high a level then there would be a problem for them of communications. With elements of the High Command spread all over Europe it would be difficult for them, at least those involved in treachery against the Reich, to stay in touch with one another. Couriers would be exceedingly risky, a telephone impossible. Their primary military duties would prevent personal contact on a continuing basis. So, I thought, how could members of the General Staff communicate their plans without being discovered."

"The names," Heydrich said grimly. "If you have proof of a conspiracy, I want the names of those involved. 'Not—" he waved the pages from the envelope "—drawings with footnotes in some foreign gibberish."

"If you will bear with me, sir. The chronology of my investigation is important so that you may understand the full meaning of my discovery."

"All right. But I'm not impressed by melodramatics. Get to the point. Did you find a conspiracy or not?"

"I found more than that, Herr General," Regenbauer said. "I won't bore you with the details of the investigation except to say that I spent a great deal of time monitoring secret coded Signal Corps traffic between the major commands. It was there, I thought, that lay the perfect means of communications for would-be plotters—cryptic messages. If I had not been in Holland, dividing my time between this work for you and my duties for the SD in infiltrating the resistance, I would never had found it or even know what I had found."

Heydrich sighed impatiently. "And?"

"A Pole," Regenbauer said. "I caught an officer in the Polish Secret Service who was cipher clerk in the cryptography section. He had made contact with the Dutch underground and was to have been smuggled in a fishing vessel to Sweden and from there to England."

"So? What has a Pole to do with traitors in the Wehrmacht—"

"Nothing," Regenbauer said calmly. "As far as I know there is no military conspiracy."

"No?" Heydrich squinted angrily up at Regenbauer. "Damn it, Major, I don't have time to waste listening to your inconsequential exploits."

"He was a very stubborn informant," Regenbauer went on, ignoring Heydrich's outburst. "He died, but not before he was persuaded to share with me the secrets of Operation *Wicher*. You see, if this man's dying confession is to be believed, the Polish Secret Service and now the British Secret Service have the means to decipher the Wehrmacht's coding machine. He swore to me that the Enigma machine has been compromised."

"What?" Heydrich looked sharply at Regenbauer. "The Enigma code broken!"

"There are certain indications—"

"Indications!" Heydrich bellowed. "Do you have proof that our code has been broken? The machine is a mechanical instrument with interchangeable rotors to make outside deciphering impossible. I've seen a demonstration of it myself."

Regenbauer shrugged. "Look at the page you hold in your hand. It's a drawing of the Enigma machine. The Pole drew it himself. I've checked it against the actual machine and the drawing describes exactly the way the machine functions."

"That's the proof?" Heydrich shook his head. "If we gave the British one of our machines they would not know how to use it. The rotor codes are the heart of the machine. As I recall, the number of possible permutations for a three-rotor machine is three quadrillion. And Enigma has *five* interchangeable rotors. Knowing the mechanical functions of the machine will not help anyone decipher the sequence of the rotors. No, Regenbauer, you've only succeeded in torturing a false confession from a desperate Pole."

"I was as skeptical as you, General, but his story was too fantastic to dismiss. If he was right, then monumental consequences follow. So I spent every moment for two days with him until he died and his story did not waver. I am convinced he believed what he was saying. The human mind has a limit to its tolerance of pain; beyond that point men will tell you anything they know. He was not lying—he could not. What he told me was the truth as he knew it."

"Ravings of a delirious man pleading for his life." Heydrich shook his head. "That's not proof."

"Perhaps you'll believe that." Regenbauer nodded at the page. "Three days ago—July fifteenth—while I was in Utrecht, I sent a special dispatch coded through the Security Service's own Enigma machine to Gestapo headquarters here in Berlin. The message identified the Polish officer by name and rank. I said that he had escaped and that we had information that he would be aboard a small Dutch trawler leaving Haarlem at midnight and asked for Navy support in tracking it down."

"A bogus message?" Heydrich glaned at the paper. "This?"

"Yes, sir."

"What happened?"

"Two British destroyers were waiting to intercept it in the North Sea."

Heydrich frowned. "A confirmed sighting?"

"I was on the trawler," Regenbauer said. "I saw them myself." He buttoned the pocket of his tunic. "The British could only have known the Pole was supposed to be on that ship by reading my dispatch and since it was sent only through the—"

"Yes, Major, I understand." Heydrich paced through the shafts of light in the empty gymnasium for several moments, then stopped and regarded Regenbauer with an angry stare. "It may have been coincidence . . . about the destroyers. The British have patrols all over the North Sea."

Regenbauer shrugged, but said nothing.

"I don't believe it," Heydrich said. "The coding machine is incapable of being broken."

"Sir—"

"No!" snapped the Reich security lord. "There's another explanation!" The shrill whistle of another train preceded a rumbling that caused the sword to vibrate on the table. "Look, Major, if the Allies have broken the technology of the coding device then why didn't they anticipate the blitzkrieg?"

"I can't answer that."

"Our exact plans for the invasion of France would have been known; where troops were to be deployed against Denmark, Holland, Belgium; the strategy of the Ardennes; the encirclement of the British and French at the coast—" Heydrich shook his head "—all of it! Are you saying that the British would rather save one Pole than all of France?"

"There . . . there must be some other reason, sir."

"Look somewhere else for it, Regenbauer. Could the Pole have been a plant? A means to throw you off your original investigation?"

"No."

"Are you so sure?"

"He told me everything he knew. He . . ."

"You're not thinking, Regenbauer. What if someone inside the High Command were cooperating with the British? A traitor inside the Wehrmacht? Wouldn't the British take precautions to protect such a vital source? Wouldn't that explain the Pole and this incredible scheme to sabotage our secret coding machine?" Heydrich shook his head. "You are a good intelligence officer, Major, but sometimes you lack imagination and the analytical nature to deduce the obvious. But it's clear to me that you've been taken in by a trick. I've always believed there was a spy in the High Command and this confirms my suspicions."

Regenbauer was too astonished to speak. Heydrich had refused to believe the truth; he'd grasped the fantasy, ignored the facts. Regenbauer stood dumbfounded, his mouth gaping. Heydrich didn't understand. *The Pole was telling the truth!*

"Find him," Heydrich said suddenly, pointing his finger at Regenbauer. "Whoever it is, one man or fifty, but find the traitor. Use whatever means it takes. Dig him out. You wanted a challenge, here it is. Find the traitor and bring him to me and you *will* have the Ausland SD as your reward. I will make you chief of the SS foreign intelligence. I promise it!"

"Herr General—"

"Do your duty!" Heydrich's words echoed insdie the gymnasium. "Do you understand?"

"Yes, my general." Regenbauer exhaled slowly to control himself. "I understand my duty perfectly," he replied, but his voice was lost in the roar of another train.

11 _____

IT WAS A subdued Adolf Hitler that Ted watched from his seat in the lower gallery of the Kroll Opera House. This was only the second time he'd seen the Fuehrer in person; he seemed even shorter this time than last. Even the opera house itself, the official meeting place of the near-powerless German parliament since the burning of the Reichstag in 1933, seemed smaller than the newsreels depicted it. Still, tonight it was packed.

Ted recognized some of the luminaries in the diplomatic section: Count Ciano of Italy, Prime Minister Quisling of Norway, and Alexander Kirk, the American chargé d'affaires. Goering sat behind Hitler at the speaker's chair fiddling with a pencil and Hess was also on the dais, sitting solemnly proper, like a dark-eyed sphinx. The press gallery was crowded with reporters. Whatever Hitler had to say, Ted thought, a lot of people had come to hear it.

And what he did was make an appeal for peace with Great Britain, confidently, humbly, in a low moderate voice, as if he spoke for reason and common sense. It was a brilliant speech, Ted thought. At the midpoint in his talk Hitler stopped to make twelve generals field marshals and award Goering the Grand Cross of the Iron Cross. It was curious that in the middle of a plea for peace there should be a special presentation and recognition of the state's most illustrious warriors. But even that maneuver made sense to Ted by the time the Fuehrer finished. He was making it clear to England that he was offering peace from a level of undeniable strength.

I consider myself in a position to make this appeal since I am not the vanquished begging favors, but the victor speaking in the name of reason. I can see no reason why this war must go on.

At the close of the session a messenger delivered Ted a note that Herr Hess would be detained and that he should proceed to the Liepzieger Palace alone, if he didn't mind. Ted minded. He didn't like showing up at these semisocial functions Johnny-come-lately. He walked outside, waiting for a taxi apart from the rest of the crowd that had gathered on the steps of the opera house.

"Well, Campbell, what did you think of the performance?"

Ted turned to see Grayson, the bureau chief he'd met at the villa, cupping his hands together as he lit a cigarette. He tried, but he couldn't remember his first name.

"Hello, ah, Len . . . Lester, is it?"

"Lowell," the newspaperman said, waving out the match. "How's the leg?"

"Fine."

"You favor it a little," Grayson said. "I was surprised to see you here. In Berlin, I mean. I didn't think you ever left Friedrichshafen."

"I do now and then. Now that I can walk."

Grayson nodded. "Fly up?"

"Yes."

"I doubt if you'll find a cab for a while." Grayson took a long drag on his cigarette, nodded up the street. "There's a little place on Behrenstrasse. I'll buy you a beer."

Ted waved at a taxi as it passed, but it was already occupied. "Thanks, but I'm supposed to meet someone." He glanced at Grayson. "You don't happen to know where Leipzieger Palace is?"

"Leipzieger? Sure. You don't know Berlin, I take it?"

"About as well as I know Tokyo."

"Well, then, you just—" Grayson stopped, studied Ted a moment. "Leipzieger. You're going to Goering's little soiree?"

"If I can find it."

"Ah-ha." Grayson flicked an ash toward the street. "Your leg must be much better."

Ted ignored him. He waved at another passing cab.

"You think about my offer?"

Ted shrugged. "I've thought about it."

"And?"

"I'm still thinking. Anyway, it may not be necessary."

"You mean Herr Hitler's little show in there?" The bureau chief smiled to himself. "What did you think of it?"

"The speech?" Ted shrugged. "I was impressed. The Germans don't want to fight a war with the British."

Grayson smiled. "They didn't want to fight a war with France either. Or Belgium. Or Holland. Or Denmark. Or Poland. But it doesn't much matter what the Germans want, does it? The guy with the little brush under his nose is calling the shots."

Ted turned back to peer into the darkness for a cab.

"Everyone I've talked to seems to think it was a very generous offer Herr Hitler made to the British," Grayson said. "What do you think?"

"Are you asking me for a quote?"

"Why not? People might be interested in what Theodore Campbell thinks about this magnanimous offer to settle the war —let bygones be bygones and all that."

"It would be foolish to let this war continue, that's what I think."

"So, you think the British should give up?"

Ted swung around to face the reporter. "I didn't say that."

"No, but it would just about amount to that, wouldn't it? I mean, the chancellor didn't mention any terms, did he? And he didn't have a lot of flattering things to say about Churchill, either. I just wonder how dedicated he is to ending this war."

"You seem to be the one with all the opinions," Ted said. "What do *you* think?"

"I think your Herr Hitler is a very clever fellow," Grayson replied. "By offering peace and making like some sort of humble chieftain he wins support of Germans who really want an end to war and puts the onus of warmonger on the Allies if they refuse it. And they will, too. Nobody's believed Hitler's word since Czechoslovakia."

"Got it all figured out, haven't you?"

"Not quite all. I don't know why he didn't take a couple of shots at Roosevelt, too."

"Why should he?"

"Why?" Grayson frowned. "I forgot, you don't keep up much. The president was renominated for a third term yesterday at the national convention in Chicago. I guess the people approve of his hard stance against the Nazis."

"You mean the Democrats. He hasn't been reelected yet."

Grayson shrugged. "True. But he will be. Just take a look at his competition. The Republicans don't exactly have a powerhouse in Willkie, do they? Hell, he doesn't even have a dog." He took another drag from the cigarette, then flicked it into the street. "I don't imagine your Third Reich friends look forward to four more years of Roosevelt in the White House. The president and Churchill are very chummy, you know—he's half American, too, the prime minister is. I'm sure that makes a lot of the goosesteppers in this town pretty nervous when they stop to think about it."

"Look, Grayson, I've had about enough. I told you before that I'm neutral."

"Sure you are."

Ted forced himself to suppress the sudden urge to punch him.

"I guess it's just you neutral folks who are going over to celebrate Goering's new title as Reichsmarshal," Grayson said. "All the neutrals are going. Goebbels, Himmler, Hess—"

A cab pulled up to the curb and the door swung open, rescuing Ted from the newspaperman's needling. He climbed in quickly, without looking back.

"Can I quote you, then—what you said about being impressed?" Grayson was leaning down to the window, reaching in his pocket for another cigarette. "You don't mind, do you?"

"I don't give a damn what you print."

"Neutral to the end, eh?"

Ted glanced at the driver's face in the front mirror. "Leipzieger Palace, *bitte.*"

"Give my best to Hermann," Grayson said. "I hope you all have a lovely evening." He held out his palm straight and whispered, "Heil Hitler."

"Schnell, treiber . . . schnell!" Ted roared, and the cab lurched forward, leaving Grayson laughing at the curb.

The hostess who greeted him was a tall, stately young woman in a long dress and white gloves. She wore her blonde hair in curls piled high on her squarish head and the cut of her dress revealed a full cleavage. Ted introduced himself and she addressed him in tentative English, then beamed gratefully when he replied in German.

"The Reichsmarshal is so pleased to have American guests," she said. "Will you want a translator this evening?"

Ted shook his head. "Thank you, no. I speak German fairly well."

"*Very* well, I think," she said. Her name was Else and she brought him a drink and introduced him to a Luftwaffe colonel and his wife before leaving him. Goering had changed since arriving from the Reichstag meeting and was now in a light-blue uniform bedecked with a variety of military decorations. The ponderous Commander in Chief of the Luftwaffe disengaged himself from a small group of officers and extended his huge hand to Ted.

"Herr Campbell," Goering said with a beaming smile, "good to see you again." He shook his hand vigorously then looked him up and down. "You're walking again, I see. Good, good. The leg healed without complications, then?"

"Yes," Ted replied. "Good as new."

"Splendid, my boy." He grasped Ted firmly on the shoulder. "So, what do you think? Old Hermann is moving up in the world, eh? And what do you think of my new medal?" He held it up for Ted to see from the ribbon around his neck as if it were his favorite Christmas toy. "The Grand Cross. My trophy for winning France. It hasn't been awarded since von Hindenburg was given it in 1918."

"Very nice," Ted said. He remembered the trophy case enshrining the three medals of his father's back at the family compound on Nantucket Sound. Ted touched the black cross lined in silver. "Just be careful you don't have to give it back."

Goering laughed. "Yes, yes, I shall be careful of that. Tell me, weren't you impressed by the Fuehrer's speech tonight?"

"Yes, very impressed."

"Do you think it will make an impression with Churchill?"

Ted shrugged. "I couldn't rightly say. He's stopped writing to me, you know."

The Reichsmarshal laughed uproariously and slapped Ted on the shoulder. "*Amerikanisch Humor,*" he said to a startled guest, then proceeded to retell the incident, flitting from one group to another.

Embarrassed, Ted lost himself among the guests. He shook

hands with a French representative of Pierre Laval's government at Vichy, kissed the hand of a German motion picture actress who no doubt made the Frenchman more comfortable in his ignoble role. He was introduced to a handful of others, most of them Germans, and found himself forgetting their names as soon as he turned from them. All around him conversations bubbled in the refined German of his hosts and their Berliner friends and the schoolbook German of the foreign guests. He could understand everything that was being said but because it was not the language of his unconscious, it was easy to tune it out as if it were so much background music. He had only come because Hess had asked him to; so, where was he? He really didn't care to be here, there was too much noise and bumping, too much laughing, too much cigarette smoke. If Hess didn't show himself soon—

And then as he was searching the sea of heads he saw her, across the room, her red hair folded in delicate curls around her shoulders.

Kate Buchanan.

It had been five years since Ted had seen her last and yet time had not touched her. She was wearing a black gown with a red belt that accentuated her narrow waist, adding fascination to interest in the well-defined lines of her sculpturesque symmetry. An old yearning, fueled by the unexpected sight of her, stirred inside him. She had been the most important thing in his life once and the memory of their private times together came back to him in a rush. She was the most beautiful woman in the world, his Irish rose, then he felt immediately ashamed at the recollection. Anne was his love now; any comparison wasn't fair or wise. But the point was lost in the moment Kate saw him; she was coming to him.

"Well, well," she said with the same sauciness he had known years ago, "you never know who you'll run into at these little shindigs."

"Kate, I . . . it's—"

"Close your mouth, Ted, it's not polite to stare."

He tried to shrug off his self-consciousness. "What a surprise, Kate. It's good to see you. I'm flabbergasted. My God, but you look . . . good!"

She canted an eye at him. "You mean because I'm American or because you can speak English?"

"Any language will do. What are you doing here, anyway? I

didn't think journalists were invited to this private celebration."

Kate averted her eyes from him a moment then smiled and looked up at him cheerfully. "I'm not here as a journalist. I'm just here."

"With anyone?"

She shook her head. "I gave up escorts when I couldn't get dates to the proms. I thought you were down south somewhere, building airplanes or something."

"The company's been shut down until I can run it on my own authority. The Germans are a little funny about foreign independents just now. We do some charter work inside the country, to keep busy."

"I heard about your little crack-up." She sipped her drink and glanced at his leg. "Busted it, I heard."

Ted nodded. "Shoulda seen the other guy." He moved inside to let the Frenchman and the actress pass on their way to the bar. "Look, Irish, a place like this has got to have a balcony or something. What say we get some air?"

It was a veranda that led to a small garden and there were already half a dozen couples in the courtyard. Ted walked her to the marble retaining wall and they leaned against it.

"What brings you to Berlin?" she asked. "It can't be the night life."

"I was invited to hear the speech tonight."

"Oh?" She glanced him. "And what did you think?"

Ted sighed. "If I knew how much people wanted to know what I thought about it I'd have paid more attention."

Kate nodded. "I thought it was magnificent." She tipped the glass up again and finished it then set it aside on the wall. "Absolutely magnificent."

"Well, I don't know about magnificent, but he made his point."

"You're damn right he did."

Ted turned to see her more clearly in the shadowy light. He didn't know why she was suddenly hostile.

"You okay?"

"I'm fine, just fine."

"You seem mad."

She looked sharply at him. "You haven't changed much, have you, Ted? You still haven't found anything to commit yourself to. You don't seem to care what's going on around you."

"Such as?"

"How about the war!"

A couple that had been sitting on the steps to the courtyard looked up, suddenly startled, then got up and moved away. Ted brushed a hand over his hair. He hoped they didn't understand English.

"Well, one thing's for certain," he said. "You haven't changed."

"Don't be so sure."

"Look, Kate, just because I don't throw up when someone mentions National Socialism to me doesn't mean I—"

"Why should you?" Kate interrupted. "What's wrong with it? What's wrong with a national movement to reclaim its destiny? Germany was falling apart until the Fuehrer forged it into an entity to be reckoned with. I don't know how you can live in Germany and not believe that." She stopped because she was out of breath, then reached for Ted's glass. "Give me that." She drank the rest of his brandy and missed the ledge of the wall when she tried to set it down. The glass tumbled out of her fingers and shattered against the stone floor. "Oh, Christ!"

Ted held her arm. "Forget it," he said. He held her against him a moment, searching her face for some explanation of the sudden outburst. "Kate . . . I—Jesus, what's come over you?"

She twisted away from him. "I'm a little bit drunk, okay? Nothing I can't handle."

"Okay, okay." Ted held his hands up as if to surrender. "I just never expected to hear you talk like that; I mean, you are the most anti-fascist human being I know."

"Autocratic rule and an aggressive nationalistic policy was the only choice left in Germany."

"All right. Christ, I'm not trying to argue with you. Just settle down."

Kate steadied herself against the wall. "Okay. Sorry." She brushed her hair back from her forehead. "Maybe I've been drinking a little much. What was that, anyway—what you were drinking?"

"Brandy," Ted said.

"Are you a lush when you can't tell the difference anymore?"

"No. When you start sniffing corks, then you worry."

Kate tried to laugh. "I guess that'll be next." Her smile faded and she touched his arm. "I'm sorry. I'm a little on edge. It was a shock to see you here. I mean, you don't expect to run into someone who—" She tossed her head back and her hair flew away from her eyes.

"Who what?"

"A face from the past, I guess. It's funny, seeing you again. I was beginning to forget I had a past." She wrinkled her nose and glanced back at the main building. "What a place to run into an old lover from Massachusetts."

Not so long ago, Ted wanted to say, but he hadn't the nerve. "You look terrific. Something must agree with you."

She looked back at him as if she were unaware that he'd spoken. "It's good to see you, Ted. I could use a friend tonight." She gave a little shrug in the direction of the party. "These things bore me silly."

"Then why come?"

"Why?" She said it as if she'd like to know the answer herself. "Look, I suppose I should warn you. I'm one of their pets these days—the Propaganda Ministry's, I mean. There aren't many American reporters who figure Hitler's okay and that Germany has the edge in winning the war. It does me a lot of good as a journalist. They invite me everywhere, let me in on the inside of things. Like this little bash tonight. But it doesn't sit well with some of my comrades—the other journalists in this town don't like the way I pick my friends."

"You really have changed."

"Grown up, maybe."

"What changed your mind?" Ted asked. "Doug?"

Kate withdrew her hand from his arm and turned to face the garden across the retaining wall. "Losing him was—" She took another breath. "Look, it doesn't really matter, does it? Maybe Spain opened my eyes. What was it anyway—a bunch of kids getting conned and manipulated by a batch of Bolshies. We were—" She glanced up at Ted. "Let's forget it, okay? Talk about something else. You, for instance. I thought this sort of think bored you silly."

"It has its compensations."

"Oh?"

"I found you here, didn't I?" He hadn't meant to say it exactly that way, and when she smiled he felt all the more guilty for it. He hadn't any right to come on to Kate Buchanan; whatever they had been before was too long ago to try and revive now. Besides, he was leaving in the morning. Anne was waiting.

"Why *are* you here, Ted? You and the Reichsmarshal seemed to hit it off like old buddies. Has Hermann talked you into designing him a new spiffy fighter plane?"

She must be drunk, Ted thought. She wasn't making sense. One minute she was for the red and black and the next she was the cynical Irisher he'd once loved.

"Well?"

"I'm just a tourist," Ted said. "I was invited up here to hear the chancellor's address. I'm leaving in the morning for London."

"London!" Kate gasped.

"The Luftwaffe isn't dropping me off, don't worry," Ted said. "I'm taking the long way around: Switzerland, Spain, Portugal, all the neutral stops."

"From Berlin—" her eyes were filled with amazement "—you're going to London? My God, the Germans are bombing England already! Of all places, why are you going there?"

Ted shrugged. "That's where my girl is."

Kate raised an eyebrow. "Oh," she said, drawing it out, "your *girl*. So, ole Teddy's not *all* business. How long's this been going on? When I knew you the only thing that really interested you was a radial engine."

"Her father had known my father—you know."

"I see, one of those arrangements."

"No, not exactly. Let's skip it."

"Let's not," Kate replied dryly. "What's this girl's name?"

"Anne."

"Not Boleyn, I trust."

"Bullard. Anne Bullard."

"This is a rather odd time for a long-distance romance, isn't it? I mean, what does her family think with you over here in the hinterland?"

"I thought you were all for the Nazis?"

"Some of the personalities I could live without. Himmler, for instance. Hymie-No-Chin. He and his SS give me the willies. But back to you. How did you manage to get a flight to Switzerland? There are all sorts of restrictions. I'm a journalist *and* an American and I don't think I could get to England in less than a couple of weeks."

Ted shrugged. "I just asked. I didn't know it was such a big deal. Anyway, if it works out, I'm flying my own plane to Switzerland."

"Your own plane! God, you have more pull than I thought."

"I wish."

"You don't mind if I use you as a reference? You must have some damned powerful friends, old Hermann notwithstanding. I could find a use for the contacts you have." Kate smiled. "There, that's my journalistic side coming up for air."

Ted suddenly remembered the bureau chief. "There was a guy who came to see me a few weeks ago, a newsman. Asked me to work for him."

"You?"

"On the strength or weakness of having written a book, he wanted me to write about the Luftwaffe. Maybe you know him. Name's Grayson."

Kate perked up. "Lowell?"

"You know him, then."

"I used to. Don't see him much anymore." She shrugged. "Pushy bastard, isn't he?"

"He's one of the best correspondents in this town. Look, if Lowell Grayson thinks you can cut it then let me put my bid in. You didn't accept his offer, did you?"

"I don't think he wanted me to. Besides, I have a company to run, I'm not a reporter."

"Well, you know how to put a subject and a verb together," Kate said. "I read your book too, you know. It isn't a bad idea, either, working, I mean."

"I'm really not that interested."

"You might change your mind. If you do, call me, not Lowell Grayson. Deal?"

Ted shook his head. "Look, Kate—"

"Deal?" She held out her hand.

"If I'm not a reporter, I'm certainly not a broadcaster."

"Let me worry about that. If you change your mind, you'll call me first. Okay?"

Ted shook her hand. "This is crazy. I won't do it, you know."

"You might surprise yourself. You—" She glanced at Ted's wristwatch and gasped. "Christ, is that the right time?"

"Eleven forty-five? Should be, why—"

"I have a one A.M. broadcast. Damn! Gotta run. All kinds of things to set up." She reached up and kissed him on the cheek. "Call me when you get back, if you come back. We'll have dinner."

He walked her back inside and she squeezed his hand, smiled and slipped away into the crowd.

Ted watched her leave while the touch and scent of her lingered in his senses. Kate was a magnificently beautiful woman. Whatever was it that split them apart? Selfishness? Probably that or plain stupidity from him. She'd been a headstrong idealist with causes to suffer and he'd been unmoved except to take flying as his mistress. It was funny, Ted thought. He'd been faithful to his nature; it was Kate who had changed. Somehow Doug was responsible for her new direction, but it was beyond logic to explain why. Not that it mattered, anyway. Whatever feelings Kate had stirred in him were only twitched nerves from a passion that was best forgotten. You can't go home, Ted Campbell, he told himself, and there was the truth of it.

Ted made his way to the bar and ordered a Scotch and water. The Frenchman was there, getting drunk, and the actress looked bored. From somewhere nearby he heard a man repeating his crack about Churchill. Ted watched a woman with an ivory cigarette holder remove the cigarette with two fingers, drop it on the floor and extinguish it with the toe of her pointed shoe; a Wehrmacht general at a table beside the bar overturned a brandy glass on the white linen tablecloth and as the blonde hostess next to him reached to dab the stain with a napkin, he slid his hand inside her skirt. Else laughed as the general nuzzled his chin under her neck, aiming his face into the V of her dress. She glanced up to see Ted and gave him a radiant, glassy-eyed smile, then closed her eyes and wet her lips as the general's hand caressed her thigh and moved to the prize between her hips.

Ted turned and gulped the rest of his drink. He'd had enough celebrating for one night. He wanted to be away from here, back in the cottage by the lake where there wasn't any smoke or noise or drunken fools. He didn't know where Hess was and didn't care. He could call him in the morning.

"Excuse me, but have you a light, *bitte?*"

Ted turned to see a man tapping a cigarette against a silver case that was engraved with an elaborate variation of the *Hoheitszichen*—the Reich eagle clutching a wreathed swastika.

"Sorry, I don't smoke."

The man returned the cigarette to the case and snapped it shut. "You're Campbell, the American, aren't you?"

"Yes." Ted glanced over the man's shoulder. He thought he'd spotted Hess, but it was a steward in a service uniform emptying ashtrays.

"How do you like it?"

Ted looked at him. The man was determined to have a conversation. "What?"

"The party."

"Very nice." Ted regarded him with more interest. "You aren't German, are you?"

"Not even slightly. I'm from Belfast."

"Ireland?"

"Northern Ireland, if you don't mind. Recently with the Republican Army."

Ted nodded. There were a lot of angry Irishmen in Germany lately. There were rumors that Germany was courting the Irish Republican Army for support against England; it wasn't that they shared politically similar views, just a common foe. "Your German is very good," Ted said.

"My grandmother is German; lived in Bremen when I was a tot. We visited most summers. My mum taught us German and French." He smiled at Ted. "Schoolteacher, she was."

"And your father?"

The man's smile faded. "The British killed him in twenty-one."

Ted sighed. "Sorry, I—"

"Do you live in Berlin?"

"No, Friedrichshafen. I'm just visiting friends in Berlin."

"Ah." The man nodded. "Your wife is with you?"

Ted scanned the faces of a group who entered from the garden. Where the hell was Hess? "I'm not married."

"Then it wasn't your wife I saw you with earlier?"

Ted looked at him quizically. "No."

"Then . . ."

"Katherine Buchanan."

The man's eyes lit up. "Ah, the American radio correspondent. I've heard her broadcasts."

"I'll tell her she has an admirer," Ted said. He turned to set his glass on the bar and as he did he caught a glimpse of a man waving to him from a door across the room. But it wasn't Hess, it was Haushofer. Ted glanced back at the man with the silver cigarette case. "Would you excuse me?"

"Certainly," the man said. "It was a pleasure to meet you, Mr. Campbell."

Haushofer opened the door as Ted approached him. "This way, please, Herr Campbell. The deputy fuehrer regrets that he was detained. If you will come with me, he would like to speak with you now on a matter of some urgency."

"Where is he?"

"At his residence."

Ted had never been to Hess's place in Berlin; they'd always met before at his home in Munich. He wondered if the Berlin Hess was any different from the Munich Hess. "Where does he live?"

"It isn't far."

Ted followed the professor to the street. A car waited at the curb with its motor running. Haushofer opened the rear door. "Please."

"Why didn't he come?" Ted asked.

"We were waiting for some response," Haushofer said.

"Response?"

"To the Fuehrer's speech." The professor twisted his hands together impatiently. "Less than an hour ago Selton Delmer the British broadcaster made a statement over the BBC. It was not an *official* statement, but I'm afraid it reflects the official mood."

"What did he say?"

"He insulted the Fuehrer," Haushofer replied. He took a piece of paper from his coat pocket and handed it to Ted. "Read it for yourself."

Ted held the typed transcript up to the window to read.

HERR HITLER, YOU HAVE ON OCCASION IN THE PAST
CONSULTED ME AS TO THE MOOD OF THE BRITISH
PUBLIC. SO PERMIT ME TO RENDER YOUR EXCELLENCY
THIS LITTLE SERVICE ONCE AGAIN TONIGHT. LET ME TELL
YOU WHAT WE HERE IN BRITAIN THINK OF THIS APPEAL
OF YOURS TO WHAT YOU ARE PLEASED TO CALL OUR
REASON AND COMMON SENSE. HERR FUEHRER AND

REICHSKANZLER, WE HURL IT RIGHT BACK TO YOU, RIGHT IN YOUR EVIL-SMELLING TEETH.

Ted folded the paper and handed it back to Haushofer. "Not exactly complimentary, is it?"

"They are being very foolish," Haushofer said. "The English do not realize how this will enrage him."

Meaning Hitler, Ted assumed. Well, that wasn't any of his concern. Hess could worry about it if he wanted to, but Ted would not. "That's all very interesting, I'm sure, but it doesn't have anything to do with me."

"I understand your position."

"I told you before that I'm not getting involved in anything political." Ted tried to distinguish Haushofer's mood by his expression, but it was too dark to see him clearly in the back of the Mercedes. "If you or the deputy fuehrer have any ideas about me acting as a middleman or something absurd like that, then you can damn well forget it. I'm going to London for private reasons. Nothing else."

"To see your young lady friend." Haushofer nodded. "Yes, of course. Herr Hess mentioned that."

"Just as long as you understand," Ted said.

"Oh, yes, we understand," Haushofer said. He folded his hands in his lap and glanced sideways at his American passenger. "Perfectly."

The deputy fuehrer was waiting in his parlor, a comfortable room with modest, unspectacular furnishings; light years apart from the lusty, sumptuous decor that had come to be Goering's trademark. Ted hadn't expected Hess to live in a place like Karinhall, but he had thought that the number three man in the party would have a more richly embellished Berlin home than the one he found. There was something to be learned about Reich leaders' psyches in visiting their private environments, Ted thought. Goering was loud, gaudy, ostentatious. He liked to show off beautiful things and beautiful people, and his lavish estate was a reflection of that taste. Hess's house, this room, was dark, austere; there was nothing in it that lent itself to gaiety, it was as if the place had been specifically matched to the man, who was a mystery himself. Funny, the things you think about, Ted thought, as he stood shaking Hess's hand in front of an unlit fireplace, and, for an instant, he had an urge to ask what the retreat at Berchtesgaden was like.

"Thank you for coming," Hess said. "I felt I could not face Hermann's throng tonight." He gestured for Ted to sit down. "The news from England is bad."

Ted sat down in a padded wooden chair across a small table from Hess. He watched Haushofer move away to a place beside the fireplace. *Tell him,* Ted wanted to say to the professor; *tell him I won't be party to any monkey business in London.*

"Tomorrow you leave for Switzerland, yes?" Hess said.

"Yes," Ted said, "if I have permission to fly my own plane to Bern."

"Of course." Hess opened a drawer in the table and took out a folded packet of papers. "I had nearly forgotten." He handed them to Ted. "Complete authorization to leave Germany and return in your own aircraft. You will find that the authorization is without restriction; you may use it at any time provided that you submit a flight plan twenty-four hours in advance and that your immediate destination is in a recognized neutral state. I have also included one of my own charts with a suggested route to the Swiss capital."

Ted opened the packet and glanced through the papers. "Thank you, Herr Hess. This is very generous of you."

"There's one favor I would ask in return."

Ted glanced at Haushofer before looking up at his host. "Sir?"

"These are dark days," Hess began. "The Fuehrer has made a generous offer to the British to end this senseless struggle. But the British, I'm afraid, don't understand us. We, the German people, do not want war; we do not want to fight the English."

Ted nodded sympathetically.

"England has been wrested from her true interests and policy of friendship with Germany," Hess continued, "and especially from an alliance against Bolshevism, by the warmongers in the British cabinet." He looked straight into Ted's eyes. "Mr. Winston Churchill is chief among them."

Ted moved uneasily in his chair. "Herr Hess, I—"

"I know and understand the Fuehrer's inner mind, Theodore. No one knows him better or has seen him more often in his unguarded moments. I know of his great admiration for

Britain and his earnest wish to be friends with the British empire. He did not ask for this war; he has no demands to make of Britain. He felt sure that if the German viewpoint were properly explained to the English, it would be possible to conclude an agreement." Hess shook his head. "Now . . . now I do not know. The Fuehrer's patience is nearly gone. If something is not done immediately then he'll have no choice. He will unleash a fury against the English that they had not dreamed of and they will be crushed as surely as were the French."

The packet was moist where Ted held it tightly between his hands. He could feel himself sweating under his arms.

"What is—" Ted's voice was high and he stopped to clear his throat. "What do I have to do with that?"

"I want you to understand the situation, my friend, so you can explain it to your friends in London." Hess's dark eyes were firmly on Ted and the room was suddenly as still as death.

"*My* friends?" Ted said.

"The invasion of England is already being planned," Hess said. "The directive was issued three days ago. A contingency strategy. An operation to eliminate the English homeland as a base for carrying on the war against Germany and, if necessary, to occupy it completely."

"Wait, now!" Ted pushed himself back from the table. "Wait a minute, Herr Hess!" He glanced helplessly at Haushofer then quickly back at the deputy fuehrer. "You can't be telling me this! Good Christ, *I can't be talking to you about this!*"

"Don't worry," Haushofer said from beside the fireplace. "This conversation is not taking place."

"Not taking—"

"No one knows or will ever know that we are meeting here tonight," the professor said. "If that's what bothers you."

The man was insane. He was standing there puffing on his goddamn pipe in this dungeon of a room with its curtains drawn across the windows and he was saying not to worry that the fucking deputy fuehrer of the fucking Third Reich wanted him—Theodore Asshole Campbell—to do something that was not only un-neutral and definitely treasonous for them, but very likely to get *his* head blown off by the Gestapo if they found out! *Don't worry!* Christ!

"I'll tell you what bothers me," Ted said, raising his voice.

"You're fucking crazy!" He got up from the chair. "Excuse me, Herr Hess," he said, shaking his head at the deputy fuehrer, "but . . . God damn! Who in the bloody hell do you think I know?"

"Please sit down." There was a calmness in Hess's voice that sent a shiver through Ted. "You do not yet understand."

Ted wiped a hand across his face. He could leave. He could just turn around and walk away; Christ, he should run, but then what? What would happen tomorrow? He took a deep breath and sat down, still holding the packet.

"Thank you, Theodore," Hess said.

"Yeah, well, I don't seem to have much choice, do I?" He turned to glare at Haushofer. "I'm not agreeing to anything."

The professor nodded. "We're not asking you to do anything that you haven't already done."

"Now listen, goddammit, you said that before and I don't know anymore what you're talking about now than I did then."

"Never mind that, Albrecht," Hess said with a wave. "I believe Herr Campbell did not know he was being used by British Intelligence."

Ted turned his bewildered stare to Hess. "British *intelligence?*"

"It happens more often than you would think. An innocent party delivers something to a contact employed by an intelligence service without the party knowing what he is doing. You were so used."

"Me?" Ted smiled, shook his head. "Look, I may not sound very bright, but—"

"You delivered a book to a man in Lisbon," Hess interrupted. "For a friend in London. True?"

"Yes, but—"

"He was a British intelligence agent," Haushofer added quickly. "The British have several agents in Portugal and Spain and in other neutral countries, just as we do. We watch each other. It's a matter of record that you visited this man in Lisbon."

"If you think I'm some sort of spy, then you're nuts."

Hess shook his head. "No, no, we don't think that. But you are very convenient. For whatever reason, the British have already taken an interest in you."

"Taken advantage, you mean," Ted said shortly, "if it's true."

"I only wish to have you do something similar for me," Hess said, "but with your full knowledge and, I hope, with your willing cooperation."

"Do what?"

Hess glanced at Haushofer before speaking. "End the war."

Ted rolled his eyes at the ceiling. "Oh, right."

"I'm not joking. You have friends in London who would be instrumental in negotiating a settlement to this war."

"Look, Herr Hess . . ." Ted wiped his hand across his jaw. "I don't know who you've been talking to, but I don't have those kind of friends. Christ, you're talking about cabinet level. Believe it or not, I do *not* know Winston Churchill."

"I would not consider approaching that madman Churchill," Hess said. "But you do know the Duke of Hamilton. He's a friend of yours."

"An acquaintance," Ted corrected. "I've been up to his place in Scotland a few times—"

"Dungavel House?"

"Yes, but we're not exactly drinking buddies. Anyway, what has he got to do with this?"

"The Duke of Hamilton is the lord steward."

"Whatever that means."

"It means," the professor said, explaining the obvious, "that the Duke of Hamilton has direct access to His Majesty George the Sixth, the King of England."

Ted was suddenly speechless. They were planning to circumvent Churchill and the entire British government and make their case directly to the monarch. What an idea! Make a secret proposal of peace directly to the king. If it worked, if real negotiations could be initiated, then Hess would be a hero in his Fuehrer's eyes that Goering with all his medals and ribbons could never outshine. Of course, that was the reason for this, Ted thought. Hess was being eclipsed in the inner circle of Hitler's crowd by Goering and the rest of them; the deputy fuehrer's star was fading, but this, if it worked—a single-handed negotiated peace with England—would bring him back as never before.

If Hess, with Haushofer's guidance, was a fool, then he was a grand fool. And so was Ted, if he went along, because this thing was too incredible for words. It *was* incredible, wasn't it? Ted wasn't even sure of that. Christ, what did he know about international politics? He should never have left Friedrich-

shafen, that was his first mistake. He should never have come
to Berlin. And what was that about the British intelligence?
Anne's father? Someone had some explaining to do, that was
damn sure. But in London. The answers were in London.

"You are contemplating the risks?" Hess asked, leaning
forward slightly in his chair. "I can't say there are none,
though I have done all in my power to minimize them. But you
must realize that what we are setting out to do is to put an end
to this war. If we are successful then your part in it will be no
less significant than mine."

"And if it isn't successful?"

The deputy fuehrer sighed. "Then a noble attempt for peace
will have been lost."

"I mean me. What about me?"

"No one will ever know that this discussion took place. I
promise you that."

Ted tapped the end of the packet on the tabletop and stared
at his knuckles. He would be very sorry if he got involved in
this. Something would go wrong. Something *always* goes
wrong when you start making guarantees. It might be different
if he could stay in London or go back to the States, but he had
to come back to Germany. Everything he had was tied up in the
company. Everything.

"All right," Ted said finally, "let's consider this on a strictly
business basis for a minute. Forget about the noble attempt for
peace. You have a lot at stake, Herr Hess. I mean, if it works
then you will have won a victory that'll give Goering nightmares. You'll be the Fuehrer's favorite again."

"The deputy fuehrer does not act for personal gain,"
Haushofer responded angrily.

Hess held up his hand to the professor. His eyes bored into
Ted. "My motivation is to achieve peace."

Ted had poked a stick into a sore spot and he recognized it
immediately. All right, then, if he didn't want to admit it, then
that was okay too.

"Let's talk about *my* motivation then," Ted said slowly. "So
far you haven't given me any incentive to do you this favor. I
have everything to lose and precious little to gain from it."

Hess's eyes opened wide. "We're speaking of ending a
war!" he said loudly. "Does it mean nothing to you?"

"It isn't *my* war. Everyone keeps forgetting that I'm an
American and that I am neutral and that there are certain

regulations regarding violation of that neutrality. Which is exactly what you are asking me to do. If I agree—and that is still a great big if—then I want something more in return."

Haushofer slammed his pipe down on the mantel. "We're asking you to serve in the interest of humanity, to bring peace—"

"You're asking me to risk my neck," Ted interrupted. "It comes down to that. Let's not make any mistake about it. Whatever the reason, you're still asking me to represent you to an official of the British government. I'm not sure what that makes me legally but it sure puts into serious doubt my status as a neutral. If you'll pardon me, Professor, it's my fucking ass and I want something more than a free ride to Switzerland."

Hess laughed. The suddenness of it startled Ted. "Theodore," Hess said, "you are an interesting man."

"Well, practical, let's say."

"Perhaps too practical."

"It's a Campbell trait," Ted said. "We tend to be bull-headed."

"Your father was so?"

"He was bullheadedest."

Hess nodded. "There's something to what you say. I can't expect you to share my deep sentiments in this mission and I don't wish to antagonize you. So—" he took a deep breath "—what is it you want?"

"Campbell Aircraft," Ted replied quickly. "I want my company back. Full control. No strings."

"I see." Hess considered it a moment. "What else?"

"Else?" Ted gave the deputy fuehrer a quizzical glance. "Nothing else. I just want my company back."

Hess was quiet for some time, studying some spot across the room. When he returned his gaze to Ted, he said, "Done."

"You agree?" Ted said.

"Upon your return to the Reich, the aircraft company will be fully and absolutely in your hands. I give you my word." Hess stared at him with solemn purpose. "Is that satisfactory?"

Ted nodded. He glanced at Haushofer then turned back to Rudolf Hess, folding his arms on the table, giving the deputy fuehrer his undivided attention. "So," he said, in the tone of a man well-pleased with himself, "what is it you want me to tell Hamilton?"

* * *

"Repeat the name, Comrade," Freimark said, exhaling a long stream of cigarette smoke in his basement apartment.

"Ted Campbell."

"Theodore Campbell?" The communist cell leader pinched the cigarette from his lips and glanced up. "The American flier?"

Kate nodded.

"What was he doing at Goering's party?"

"I suppose he was invited like everybody else."

"And he's leaving tomorrow for England." He jotted the information down in his notebook.

"This morning," Kate said with a tired sigh. "It's nearly three A.M. Do you mind? I'm dead on my feet."

"Soon," he said, still writing. "It is important that we debrief you as soon afterwards as possible, while the names and faces are still fresh in your mind."

"Nothing is fresh in my mind right now."

"Why did he come to Berlin?"

"To hear the Reichstag address and meet someone."

"Who?"

"He didn't say."

"Why is he going to England?"

Kate tried to wipe the burning smoke from her eyes. "He has a sweetheart in London." She rubbed her forehead. "Maybe he's getting married, I don't know. Look, I have a wicked headache. Do you think we could wrap this up?"

Freimark set his pen aside. "This is an important function to which you were invited," he said patiently. "Important to us because of the number of high-ranking military and party leaders present. Your duty was to make as many acquaintances as possible." He took a last draw on the cigarette. "In that you failed." When Freimark glanced up at her again there was a wisp of a smile on his sallow face. "Instead, you spent most of your time with this American. Please bear with me if I appear tiresomely curious, but we must try to reap *something* from your evening. You see, Comrade Buchanan, though it was you who disregarded your instructions it will be me who must answer for your failure." He took up his pen again.

"Look, I'm sorry, but he came to me. I couldn't very well tell him to go away so I could pump his Nazi buddies."

Freimark lit another cigarette. "Of course."

Kate wanted to scream. She was suffocating in this wretched little room, repelled by Freimark and his rancid breath. She wanted a drink and a bath and sleep. She had a ten-A.M. broadcast, which meant she had to be up and awake by eight. Five hours' sleep, if she was lucky. Freimark had made a page of notes for his report. When he glanced up at her it was an effort to concentrate on his face.

"Now, Comrade," the thick-necked communist said with a cynic's cheerfulness, "if you will be so kind, tell me once more as much as you recall of your conversation with Theodore Campbell."

12 _____

A LUFTHANSA MECHANIC helped Ted preflight the plane—a Bell single-seater with an Allison liquid-cooled V-12 engine mounted behind the cockpit. He'd forgotten it was Saturday, Templehof's busiest day, and he had to wait nearly two hours for his turn to take off. Once, while he was passing the time watching the crowd at the terminal, he thought he saw a face he recognized—the man at the party last night. But a gasoline truck cut off his view and when it had passed the man was gone.

He was in the air shortly before noon and down at Stuttgart's Echterdingen Airport for refueling by two. Surprisingly, there were only an old Blohm and a Junker ahead of him. Surprising, too, was the VIP treatment he'd received from the administrator who checked his exit visa. The man had come to meet him in a car and the paperwork was over in less than five minutes. Apparently, Ted thought, he'd been expected. Hess was making sure he met with no inconveniences.

After thirty minutes, he was airborne again, headed nearly directly south for the border. Over Schaffhausen he took his bearing on the Rhine, according to Hess's personal chart, climbed another thousand feet and followed the Aare to Bern.

It was a beautiful flight over beautiful country, and he could let his mind rest to the rhythm of the revving Allison as he absorbed the artistry of nature's most elegant scenery. He let the view crowd any thoughts of Hess and his mission out of his mind. There was time enough for that later. For now he was satisfied to soar above the troubled continent and dream of Anne.

He rented space at one of the private hangars after he'd been through customs and found a mechanic who would service the plane and watch over it. He used the hangar manager's office to change and had an early supper.

When he presented himself at the Pam American counter at eight o'clock, he was rested, fed and forty minutes early.

"T. Campbell," the clerk said, thumbing through the file of reservations, "to Barcelona and Madrid." He found the ticket, stamped it and made an entry in the passenger manifest, then pushed the ticket across to Ted. "Paid in advance, Mr. Campbell." When he glanced up, recognition dawned on his face. He frowned. *"Theodore* Campbell?"

Ted nodded.

Whatever perfunctory amiable traits he'd shown before suddenly disappeared. "I didn't make the connection before. Now I get it."

"What's that?"

"A couple of your pals were here this afternoon," the clerk said, as if it had been a distasteful experience. "They wanted to make sure your reservation was in order."

"Oh?"

"Germans," the man said with a sneer. "Nazis, by the look of them."

"I didn't know Nazis had a look."

The young man nodded, glancing aloofly down the counter, then back at Ted. "No, I guess you *wouldn't* . . . *Herr* Campbell."

Ted walked away under the reservation clerk's hateful stare. It wouldn't have done any good to start a scene with the first anti-German he ran into. He'd forgotten about the American sentiment against him and he hadn't realized that it stretched all the way to Switzerland. It was going to take some getting used to now that he was out of Germany. To most of his countrymen he was a Nazi sympathizer, to some even a traitor. He was going to have to deal with that, he thought. It was unfortunate that Hess had seen fit to look after him even here —the "Germans" were obviously local agents sent here to make certain he hadn't any problem getting his plane to Spain.

He found a chair near the window in the passenger waiting lounge and glanced through a section of a newspaper that had been left behind. The front-page headlines bannered the Fuehrer's offer of peace to England with a text of the address on an inside page. There was a sidebar story about the mass of field marshal promotions and Goering's elevation to the new position of Reichmarshal. Ted scanned the pages then stopped when he discovered a story with Lowell Grayson's byline. It was an account of the Reichstag speech, but what caught his eye was near the end of the column under the boldface caption, REACTIONS.

There were six brief comments by five party leaders, only two that Ted recognized. The last interviewee was Theodore Campbell.

> *Theodore Campbell, the American aviator and aircraft designer, son of the late Edward "Eddie" Campbell, when asked his opinion of the German chancellor's address said he was "very impressed.*
>
> *"The German people do not want a war with the English," said Campbell, who now resides in a villa in southern Germany. "It would be foolhardy for the British to allow this war to go on."*
>
> *The world-famous aviator, hurrying from the Kroll Opera House shortly after the speech to attend a reception in honor of Reichsmarshal Hermann Goering, had only just been informed that United States President Franklin Roosevelt was nominated by his party for a third term in the White House. Said Campbell, "He hasn't been reelected yet."*

Ted stared at the newspaper in stunned silence. Grayson had engineered a piece of propaganda that would have made Goebbels a happy man. The effect, of course, and obviously the purpose, was to single Ted out of the hundreds of Americans in Berlin. Here is the real Theodore Campbell, folks, Grayson was saying, the Nazi who calls himself an American.

He folded the newspaper and dropped it in the chair behind him as he got up. The fucking bloody bastard! He *should* have punched Grayson in the face when he had the chance. If Ted was going to have a tough time of it outside Germany, Grayson had just made it a hundred times worse. If—

Ted's anger was distracted when he saw the two men. They were standing at the far end of the waiting room, away from the light. The one with the newspaper was not reading it; he was watching Ted. *Now* he was reading it. The taller one—the man in the hat—turned slightly, letting the hat brim shadow his face.

When the flight was called, Ted hurried to board it. At the entry platform he looked behind him. They were still there, standing at a window, watching him. But they didn't get on the plane.

Barcelona was only a long stop on a warm, still night. There was some problem with one of the engines and all fourteen passengers were herded into a tiny airport office until it was fixed. One woman—a girl, really—with an infant son, would not leave the plane. She was German, obviously did not speak Spanish, and defied even the chief police officer to remove her. Ted intervened, acting as interpreter, but it was no use. She would not budge from her seat and the policeman gave up only after the baby woke up and screamed louder than they could argue.

"It is not an uncommon incident," sighed the policeman as he walked with Ted across the cement parking ramp toward the terminal. "They are afraid they will not be permitted to get back aboard the plane."

"Does it happen very often?"

The policeman shrugged. "Often enough. But only the Germans and usually the women. They think they will be sent back."

Ted shook his head. "She was awfully young, didn't you think? I mean, to have a baby."

"Very young," the policeman agreed with a nod. "But then, it may not have been her child, Señor. I have seen it many times. She may not even know the parents."

"I don't understand," Ted said. "Why would she be traveling with someone else's child? What on earth—"

"The parents, the ones who cannot leave Germany themselves, they send their little ones out."

They'd stopped at the boarding gate. The policeman stood under a light pole to dig in his pocket for a cigarette.

"But why?" Ted stared back at the plane. "Why are they so afraid? This war may be over soon."

The policeman glanced up from the business of lighting his cigarette, his face registering surprise. "Señor Campbell, it is not the war that frightens them."

"No?" Ted turned to him. "What then?"

"I thought you had noticed," the policeman said. He nodded at the dark figure of the plane on the runway. "She is a Jew."

The last time Ted had been in Madrid was on his twenty-ninth birthday. He'd won the Spanish National Air Race the day before and he'd celebrated it with champagne and caviar.

But from the moment the plane touched down, Ted found a different city from the one he'd known before the revolution. The airport was a madhouse with people everywhere—passengers scrambling for luggage, refugees carrying their belongings in carpetbags or blankets, and the police madly herding swarms of people away from the boarding gates like cattle at a roundup. The airport restaurant was closed because it had no food.

He got a firsthand view of what a bombed city looked like. Madrid had been a battlefield in Franco's war and entire districts had been wasted in the destruction. His taxi passed people in wobbly farm wagons pulled by emaciated oxen, evidence of the city's severe gas-rationing restrictions. The only victors of this war were chaos and starvation.

"Where are they going?" Ted asked his driver.

"Who can say, Señor?" He shrugged. "People are being shot for stealing horses."

"To get out of the city?"

"To eat."

The center of the city was as if it were in a different country, somewhere unconnected with the rubble in the suburbs. The streets were clean, the trolleys were running, only a few scarred buildings and the peeling blue paint on the overhead street lights showed the slightest evidence that not long ago it was under siege.

The driver pulled the taxi into the circular Plaza de la Lealtad and reached behind him to open the passenger door for Ted, but he did not get out.

The driver turned about in his seat to see his passenger. "Señor," he said, raising his eyebrows, "the Hotel Ritz."

Ted was silent for several seconds. He stared at the elaborately decorated hotel entrance. He could see the front desk inside. He could see the man leaning against the counter, speaking privately to the concierge. It was one of the men from Bern—the one with the newspaper. There wasn't any question, it was the same man. The other was probably around nearby too. It wasn't any coincidence, either. They were following *him*. They'd arrived at Madrid first because Ted's plane was delayed at Barcelona. That meant they had their own transportation. Who would take such an interest in him, Ted asked himself. There was only one answer to that. They weren't curious policemen or anyone from Hess to watch over him —they were Gestapo.

"Señor?"

Ted slammed the car door shut and pressed himself back in the seat. "Take me back."

The driver wrinkled his forehead. *"Qué?"*

"The airport," Ted said quickly. "Take me back."

"You wish to go to the airport? You do not wish to go to the hotel?"

"That's right. I want to get to Lisbon as soon as possible."

"There is no more planes today, I think. Tomorrow, but not today."

"No more flights?"

The driver shook his head. "Not to Lisbon, Señor." He smiled as if to apologize. "But there is the *tren expreso.*"

"To Lisbon?"

"Sí, but to Badajoz first."

Ted stole a glance at the hotel. The man was still at the desk. "How long does it take?"

The driver's forehead furrowed, he glanced at the ceiling. "Not very long time, Señor. Maybe . . ." he scratched his head. "Maybe, four, five hours to Badajoz. Then, maybe, two, three hours to Lisbon."

"When is the next express?"

The Spaniard tilted his head to see Ted's watch. "In two hours from now, I think."

I could be there tonight, Ted thought. He glanced at the driver. "Tonight? I could be in Lisbon tonight?"

"Oh, *sí,"* nodded the driver. "Tonight."

"Does it have private cars, the train?"

"*Sí*, private cars, very expensive." He rubbed his fingers together. "Much pesetas, Señor."

Ted leaned back in the seat. "Let's go then." He waved his hand. "Let's go!"

The express to Lisbon was a sixteen-car train with five eight-compartment private cars. The fare for one of the forty compartments was nearly as much as an air ticket and they were, of course, all sold. As a matter of fact, every inch of space on the train had been bought up.

"We have one hundred people in passenger cars that were built for sixty," the conductor said when Ted cornered him in the station manager's office.

"I have to get on that train."

The conductor shrugged without much sympathy. "So do all of them." He nodded toward a window in the cramped office that afforded a view of the loud and crowded station lobby. "I'm sorry, Señor. There is another train at seven P.M."

"Couldn't I share a private compartment?"

The conductor glanced lazily at his pocket watch. "That you must take up with an occupant."

Sharing a compartment may have been an enterprising idea to Ted, but he wasn't the first to think of it. There were scores of people banging their hands on train windows, some with money in their fists, all with the same objective as Ted.

He knocked on a few windows, but he wasn't having any more luck than anyone else. Mostly, the people inside ignored him. He moved to the next car but the prospect of finding a buyer dwindled with each drawn shade he found. It was beginning to look like a stupid idea.

"Señor . . . Señor Campbell?"

Ted turned to see a woman waving at him from one of the train compartments as the train whistle blew. He ran to her window. The train would be leaving any second.

"You are Señor Campbell, the American aviator?"

"Yes, I'm looking for someone to share a compartment." The steam engine gave another blast of its whistle and the cars shuddered as the train jerked into motion. "I'll pay you! I'll pay whatever—"

"Quickly . . ." She pointed toward the front of the car. "Quickly!"

Her name was Theresa Dumas. She was a French actress who spoke reasonably good English and she was leaving the continent by boat from Lisbon to make a film in South America.

"You're a lifesaver, Mademoiselle Dumas," Ted said, trying to get comfortable in the hard leather seat opposite her.

She smiled. "One does not often have the opportunity to offer assistance to a world celebrity. It will make me the envy of all my friends. It will be marvelous to talk to someone who is so . . . influential."

"Hardly that, I think," Ted said.

"At least you saved me from a long boring ride."

"I'll try not to be too boring."

She smiled again. "Oh, no-no." Then she licked her pink lips and in a low voice asked, "Is it true, what they say?"

"What's that?"

"Is Hermann Goering a homosexual?"

There were still people in the world, Ted learned between Madrid and Lisbon, who had no real conception of the war in Europe, and Theresa Dumas was one of them. She was an actress, which should have explained a great deal, and she found the war more a personal inconvenience to her career than a desperate struggle between nations. She had not been touched by the war just as Ted had not been. But that was before. It touched him now. He'd agreed to act as Hess's messenger to an official of the British government, which was a dangerous thing to do considering the fact that he was also being tracked by Gestapo agents.

It was ironic, too, that he should be explaining the situation in Europe to a woman who simply didn't care. It did not effect her that Madrid might have been Paris or that the destruction that had obliterated whole sections of the city might just be a foreboding of things to come for London or even Berlin. She was leaving Europe and whatever happened there was no more important to her than seeing that her mail was correctly posted to Rio de Janeiro. Ted saw a lot of himself in the attitude of Theresa Dumas. None of it was much to be proud of.

Ted left her at the Lisbon train station as soon as was politely decent. He caught a trolley and sat near the rear door to figure what his next move should be. He couldn't stay at the hotel where he'd made his reservation. With the Gestapo behind him, sooner or later they'd realize that he'd given them the slip in Madrid and they'd start looking for him here. He hadn't understood *why* they were following him. Knowing the Gestapo, if they had wanted to kill him they wouldn't have waited until he got to Lisbon. There was plenty of opportunity in Switzerland—or even Germany. But there wasn't any percentage in trying to second-guess the Gestapo. They made their own logic. So, what he had to do was not give them another chance to find him before he caught a plane to England, and that meant staying out of Lisbon. Ted finally settled on Estoril—a resort town on the western edge of the bay. It was exactly in the opposite direction of the airport from Lisbon, which should throw them further off the track. He'd find a place in Estoril. And use another name.

It was a squalid little shorefront hotel and the room he took was little more than a cabana with a view of the beach, but he took it because it was one of the few that had a telephone. He tried calling London and, of course, could not get through. When he called the British airline office he discovered that it would probably be a day or two before he could book a plane.

Ted went to bed before nine and was up again in two hours. It was like the night before an important race, he couldn't sleep and he wasn't hungry. He tried calling London, again with no success, so he dressed and walked along the beach, then sat in the sand and watched the moon, his mind full of Anne.

He returned to his room, undressed, switched off the light, and was asleep almost immediately.

What woke him was the light. Suddenly, there was a brilliance in the room and when he opened his eyes he glanced up straight into the lamplight. He turned away, shutting his eyes, still sleepily unaware of where he was. It took a moment for the blindness to wear off and the first thing he saw was a very large man standing at the foot of his bed.

"Wha—"

A hand clamped over his mouth. More hands gripped his arms and shoulders and forced him up in the bed.

"Mr. Campbell?" asked the man at the foot of the bed. "You are Mr. Theodore Campbell?" He nodded slightly and the hand over his mouth loosened.

"What the hell—"

The hand tightened again.

Ted was aware now that the hands belonged to two men behind him. The man in front of him wasn't as large as he first seemed, though the light from the lamp cast a huge shadow behind him that covered the wall. Whoever he was his motive didn't seem to be robbery. He was dressed too well to be a mugger. Besides, they didn't usually wake up their victims and ask them their names, did they?

"A simple yes or no will do," the man said. "You are Theodore Campbell, aren't you?"

The hand loosened once more.

"Yes, I'm bloody Th—"

The hand returned.

"Never mind that now, Stevenson," the man said with a wave. "Let him go, please."

The two men released him and stepped away.

"Who the hell are you!" Ted exploded. "What the hell is this!"

"Name's Chrichton, sir," he said. "Sorry about rousting you, but I had to be sure. You're not an easy man to keep up with, Mr. Campbell."

Ted squinted up at him. "You're English!"

"Welsh, actually, sir. We've come to see you off safely."

"Off? Off where?"

Chrichton pointed to Ted's trousers on the back of a chair and one of his men retrieved them, holding them out to Ted. And Ted recognized him. The man Chrichton called Stevenson was the man with the newspaper from Bern.

"*You're* not Gestapo!"

Chrichton smiled. "Indeed not, sir." He nodded at the trousers.

"I'm not going anywhere with you. What the hell is this! Who do you think you are, busting in here like—"

"Someone else will explain. I really don't know why. The gentleman at the plane understands the details."

"What *gentleman?*"

"Please, Mr. Campbell, there really isn't much time."

Ted shook his head angrily. "Look, Chrichton, whoever you are, I'm not going with you or anybody. I'm an American citizen in Lisbon, for Godsakes! You haven't any authority over me!"

"That's quite true, sir—technically." Chrichton arched an

eyebrow as if to consider the point. "However, you are going."
His glance touched the two other men then returned to Ted.
"Now, sir."

The British Halifax was at the end of the runway and ready
to leave as Chrichton escorted Ted in the glare of the car's
headlights to the step-up at the passenger entrance. The
engines were too loud to hear whatever Chrichton said before a
hand reached down and hoisted Ted into the plane. Chrichton
turned away from the wash of the propellers as the plane
started down the runway, then someone slammed the door shut
and guided Ted to a seat. The airport passed below and the
lights of Lisbon receded in the distance as the plane gained
altitude and made for the sea.

He turned away from the window when someone sat beside
him. Even in the dark he was aware that they were the only
passengers.

"Good morning, Mr. Campbell," said a rather heavy man.

"Whatever this is about it had better be good," Ted said.
"Who the hell are *you?*"

"My name is Trentlyon, Mr. Campbell," he said. "Nigel
Trentlyon. We're going to be seeing quite a lot of each other,
we are."

"Oh? And just how do you figure that?"

"We shall be working together rather closely from now on."

"Then maybe you'd better tell me, Trentlyon, what the
bloody hell is going on?"

Trentlyon offered a grim smile in the darkness. "I thought
you knew. We're going to save England."

Part Three

13 _____

THE CITY OF London had not changed much in the last ten months, Ted thought, but her mood had. There was a tenseness in the city as if the great old girl were holding her breath in anticipation of some catastrophe. German planes had already started bombing targets in England and the thousands of barrage balloons that floated over the city were silent reminders that London was waiting her turn.

The plane arrived at Heathrow at dawn. A waiting car took Ted and his slightly balding escort to an address on Great Portland Street. The office was a large one with heavy paneling, large French doors that led to a balcony, and a huge map of Europe that covered an entire wall.

Trentlyon had explained damned little on the plane. Whenever Ted had asked a probing question he had received the same evasive reply, "I'd rather let Mr. C fill you in there, if you don't mind."

Well, he minded, all right. He damned sure did mind. And who the hell was this mysterious Mr. goddamn C? Well, he was about to find that out soon. Trentlyon had told him to make himself comfortable in one of the tall overstuffed chairs and rang for tea. Mr. C would be along any moment, he promised. So Ted waited.

"Good morning, Mr. Campbell. I hope your flight from Portugal was not too uncomfortable."

The man who entered the room was nearly as tall as Ted. As he offered his hand, Ted thought he detected something familiar about him.

"Name's James Carstairs," the man said. "'I see Trentlyon's brought in some tea. Good. I'm sure you have several questions."

"Bloody right I do." Ted declined an offer to sit. "I want to know what the hell is going on here. You haven't any right to treat me like this. Just who the hell do you think you are?"

Carstairs arched an eyebrow. "I thought you wanted to come to London."

"What I do and do not want is certainly no concern of yours."

"Oh, but it is," Carstairs said. "Your reason for being in London is very much a concern to me." He poured himself a cup of tea. "How is Herr Haushofer these days? Still in the Foreign Office, is he?"

Ted looked up suddenly from the spot on the serving tray he had been studying. There was the slightest hint of amusement to Carstairs' expression.

"Herr who?"

"Come, come now," Carstairs said, "surely you haven't forgotten Albrecht Haushofer so soon. Tall, distinguished gentleman. You were with him less than three days ago." Carstairs stirred his tea, set the spoon back on the tray. When he looked up at Ted he raised his eyebrows questioningly, as if to dare Ted to contradict him. "In Berlin," Carstairs added. "With Herr *Stellvertreter* Rudolf Hess. Surely you remember that."

"What I don't remember," Ted said angrily, "is inviting the British Secret Service to spy on me."

Carstairs shrugged. "The important thing is that now you are here."

"Important to you, maybe. I don't know what your sudden interest is in me but I can tell you it is not a mutual fascination. I'm only in London for one reason and it isn't to powwow with you."

"Of course not. You've come to see Anne Bullard."

Ted frowned. "Wait a minute. I *do* know you! That night at Anne's . . . you bumped into us. Carstairs . . . now I remember. What the hell are you—"

"Alfred Bullard is a close friend," Carstairs said. "We were classmates at Eton." He walked to the desk. "We've worked together on one project or another over the past thirty years. He's helping me with this one." Carstairs held up a packet of letters tied together with a string. "So it wasn't especially difficult for him to intercept these for me."

Ted recognized Anne's stationery immediately. Another bundle of letters on the desk were his to her.

"I'm afraid Anne's quite worried that you haven't written," Carstairs said.

"You son of a bitch!" Ted snatched the letters from Carstairs' hand. "You bloody son of a *bitch!*"

"I needed you here," Carstairs said solemnly. "We weren't at all sure how to get you out of Germany without arousing your suspicion . . . Sir Alfred decided the surest way was to simply interrupt those communications." He nodded at the letters. "I must say I wasn't convinced myself, but, then, here you are."

Ted only stared at him in stunned silence. *Sir Alfred!*

"Surprising, isn't it . . . about Lord Bullard, I mean. We've been planning this little exercise from the beginning. His retirement from the Admiralty didn't mean he also retired his resourcefulness. He's very clever, Alfred is. It was his idea to bring you into this."

"Into this?" Ted glanced around the room. "Into *what?*"

Carstairs pointed toward the large map on the wall. "Britain is a hairsbreadth away from being overrun by a megalomaniac. Sir Alfred is an integral part of a plan to resist that German intention. We needed someone in Germany who was beyond suspicion. Someone we could turn to for help. That's why it was imperative that you come to London now. It's time we explained what we want you to do."

It took Carstairs nearly an hour to explain what he called the Pythagoras Operation and Ted's role in it. They needed a deep plant—someone the Germans would not suspect to be working for the British. They needed a link between the network and Rudolf Hess. The man they needed had to have access to the deputy fuehrer, be trusted by him and to pass certain valuable information gotten as a result of this friendship back through the network to England. Hess was the dupe and Ted, according to Carstairs, was the link. He turned out to be at the right place at the right time; his courtship of Anne worked nicely into their plans. Bullard had known Ted would go to Germany sooner or later. There remained only to get Hess and Ted together and Ted had accomplished that without anyone's help. It was a very cozy arrangement, Carstairs said. He even smiled when he'd finished.

"You're crazy," Ted said. "You want me to *spy* for you!"

"It isn't exactly *spying*, is it? I mean, you're not being asked to photograph documents or derail trains. We simply want to groom a friendship with the deputy fuehrer that may prove beneficial in the future. After all, Hess wants the same thing. He doesn't want this war with England."

"It's spying." Ted shook his head. "If the Gestapo found out I'd be a dead man. I don't know what they'd do to Hess, but they'd *shoot* me."

"We'd look after you. It might also interest you that we know about your mission to visit Douglas-Hamilton." Carstairs raised an eyebrow as Ted straightened in his chair. "Oh, yes, we know about that. Technically, I suppose *we* could shoot you too. It cuts both ways, Mr. Campbell." Carstairs shrugged it off. "Of course, we don't want to shoot you. We need you in Germany, in Berlin . . . to work Hess."

"Well, you're nuts if you think I'm going to do it."

"You have a special relationship with him and he trusts you."

The man wasn't listening, Ted thought. He wasn't listening at all. "If you know about Hamilton then you know that Hess is only trying to help save you. You're right, he doesn't want a war with England. And to pay him back you'd betray his trust?" Ted shook his head. "Not with my help, you won't."

"Hess's way won't work."

"Why don't you let Hamilton and the king decide that?" Ted replied shortly. He got up to leave.

Carstairs rose too. He moved to the map and jabbed angrily at the south of England with a pointer. "People are dying—" the pointer moved quickly across the map "—here and here and here. Luftwaffe bombers. Every day there are more. Can you stand there and tell me that calling on the Duke of Hamilton will stop them? Hess's good intentions haven't stopped one of Goering's bombers. I can't feel much sympathy for Hess's political predicament when men and women and children are being crushed to death under the rubble left by five-hundred-pounders."

Ted tried to control his temper. It wasn't his fault that there was a war on. It wasn't his fault that the Germans were winning it. Why was the man climbing all over him about it. It wasn't his fault! "Look, I let myself be used as a messenger, but this is the end of it. I don't like the idea of people dying any more than you do, but I have nothing to do with it. You and the Germans got into this without my help. It isn't my fault that England's getting bombed. I didn't declare war on Germany, did I?"

"Maybe you should."

Ted threw up his hands. "Oh, Jesus!"

Carstairs moved back to his desk. "I won't take up much more of your time."

"You won't take up any more of it. I'm going to see Anne and I have a few things to say to Lord Bullard—"

"And he wants to speak to you," Carstairs interrupted him, "but before you leave I'd like you to see something." He opened the top drawer of his desk, extracted a folder and pushed it across to Ted. "You know Heydrich, I presume. Reinhardt Heydrich?"

"No, I don't *know* him." Ted glanced at the folder; it was gray with a red diagonal stripe across its cover. He was ready to leave. He should leave, he told himself. Carstairs hadn't any legal hold on him. He hadn't done anything wrong.

"SS-Gruppenfuehrer Reinhardt Heydrich," Carstairs said. "Head of the Reich Security Service. The Gestapo, the SD, the—"

"I know *who* he is," Ted said impatiently. "Look, you're wasting my—"

"He's the official party executioner. He draws up lists of names of undesirables and they disappear or die in mysterious accidents." Carstairs handed Ted a batch of photographs from the folder. "These are some of the results."

Ted glanced through the photographs. They were pictures of mutilated bodies; slack-jawed men and women posed obscenely in death by their executioners. Some hung like terrified marionettes, eyes open, elbows splayed out from their bodies, with large curved hooks protruding through their shoulders. One victim was suspended by a rope around the ankles and so grotesquely battered and bloody it was impossible to tell whether it was man or woman. "Oh . . . my God!"

"Of course, they're only the ones we know about," Carstairs

said grimly. "A great many are Jews, but the butchering isn't limited to race alone."

"What . . ." Ted looked at Carstairs with breathless horror. "What are you showing me these . . ." He blinked several times, cleared his throat. "Why are you doing this? Christ . . . I . . . there's nothing *I* can do about it. You act as though I have some spectacular interest, as if I can do something about it." He pointed angrily at the photographs. "There's nothing I can do about *that!*"

Carstairs sat forward and nodded. "You know one of the victims, at least."

"One or twenty-one, it doesn't make any difference!" Ted could feel his face flush. He was nearly shouting at the man across the desk. "I still can't help them, can I?" He scooped the letters from the desk and jammed them into his jacket. "I've had enough of your horror show. I don't want to listen or see any more. I want to leave. If you're going to shoot me you'd better arrest me now because I'm not going to work for you . . . or anyone!" Ted's chest was heaving. He could feel his pulse pounding.

"Your father was one," Carstairs said, in a voice that Ted had to strain to hear.

"One what?"

"Like those others . . . a victim."

Ted let out a long breath. "Don't be an ass!"

Carstairs didn't blink. He took another group of photographs from the folder. "See for yourself."

Ted snatched them defiantly. He shuffled through the photographs angrily. Then his anger dissolved. He studied the photos slowly and more carefully. They were pictures of an automobile crash. A race car. Ted recognized it immediately. It was his father's car. For a moment he could only stare at the pictures with unblinking dread.

"Heydrich had your father killed, just as he had the others murdered."

"I don't believe it," Ted said finally. He crushed the photographs between his hands and threw them on the desk. "You're sick, Carstairs. If you think you can seduce me with a cheap trick like this . . ."

"It *is* true, Campbell. Heydrich had your father's car booby-trapped by one of his henchmen. We know how it was done and why."

"You're lying!" Ted was shouting now. "It was an accident, you lying bastard!"

Carstairs reached for the photographs, smoothed the crumpled edges, but said nothing.

"Why would they do it, then?" Ted demanded. "Why would they care? He didn't care about their politics any more than I do. Christ, they loved him!"

"But they wanted Campbell Aircraft," Carstairs said.

"Campbell . . ." Ted stared at him as if he were an insane man.

"He was going to move it out of Germany." Carstairs set the photos aside and looked at Ted. "At least that was the rumor."

"You're nuts. That was just talk. We weren't—"

"It wasn't just talk to certain influential people in the Reich. It scared hell out of them. They couldn't take the chance that it was 'just talk,' an unfounded rumor. If Eddie Campbell took his aircraft company out of Germany then others would follow. They didn't want that."

Ted shook his head. "No, it—"

"Your father was very important to them. With Campbell in Germany it was the same as an endorsement. If he left it would start a migration. So it was decided that he be eliminated. They couldn't send him to a camp, they couldn't trump up a charge against an international hero, so they divised an accident. They would much rather deal with the son than the father." Carstairs glanced at Ted without emotion. "They could control the son."

"It's not true!" Ted shouted.

"No? Then, tell me, where is Campbell Aircraft today?"

Ted remembered the regulations, the red tape, the delays. The law of the Reich had limited his control to administrative authority. His domination over his own company had been hamstrung by technicalities. He was the figurehead president of a company that did no business.

"You're still the Campbell baby to them," Carstairs said. "You're the spoiled son of a famous war hero and they know exactly how to handle that situation." He got up slowly from his chair. If there'd been a hint of sympathy in his voice before, it was gone now. "You've been used by both sides in this war and I won't apologize for our part in it. We're struggling for our lives here and if we have to use people to get a leg up then that's their lookout. I won't deny that we haven't counted on your cooperation. But you have something at stake

here too, haven't you? It's time you did something for our side
for a change."

Ted had been staring at the floor. He looked up quickly. "I
haven't done anything *against* your side!"

"That's where you're wrong."

"Wrong!"

Carstairs moved to the map. "How many production plants
does Campbell Aircraft have in Germany?"

Ted turned in his chair. "What do you mean . . ."

"How many plants?"

"None. They've been shut down for more than a year. We
only operate the hangar and flight facility at Friedrichshafen."

"Where are these closed plants?"

"Ravensburg and Freiburg, but what's—"

Carstairs' pointer moved on the map. "Here and here, then,"
he said. "Southwestern Germany?"

"Yes, but—"

"Have you been to either of them lately?"

"No. Why the hell should I? Besides, they're being cared for
by—" Ted only just realized what he was saying. An official of
the Commerce Ministry had been in Ravensburg when he
closed the plant. Until the technicalities had been worked out
over proper ownership of the company, Ted had decided to
shut down both plants. Or had he? Whose decision was it
really? The Reich ministry had been very agreeable to his
decision even though it meant unemployment for two hundred
workers. And they manufactured engine parts at the plants.
Parts that could be used in Luftwaffe planes.

"I think you see what I'm getting at," Carstairs said.

"They wouldn't dare." Ted shook his head. "They
couldn't!"

"I can show you copies of shipping invoices to German
aircraft assembly works in Bavaria where they have received
truckload after truckload of the inverted V-twelve stock
engine, all from southwest Germany." Carstairs laid aside the
pointer. "How much convincing does it take?"

"They couldn't! Not without me knowing."

"The fact is they have. England is being bombed by planes
that very likely are kept in the air by engines built by Campbell
Aircraft." Carstairs went to the French doors of the balcony,
stared down at Regent's Park Square. "So, you see, you *have*
made a great contribution to one side of this war." When he

turned back, he clasped his hands behind him and stood challengingly with his feet spread slightly wider than the span of his shoulders. He canted his head a fraction as if to see Ted better. "It's our turn now, Campbell. You'd better think about that. But whatever you decide, your nonpartisan days are over."

14 _____

TED ROCKED ALONG in the backseat of the taxi in silence. The driver had made a friendly attempt to chitchat—something about a soccer game—but Ted ignored him. The grisly images of the photographs lingered in his mind and he tried to block them by staring at lamp posts.

Carstairs was crazy if he thought Ted was going back to Germany as a spy. It occurred to him that he shouldn't go back at all; just wait the war out. It couldn't last forever; hell, it could be over by the end of the summer. Then, too, it might drag out for months and then where would he be? He had to go back. The company was there. Despite whatever Carstairs said, it was still Ted's company.

The pictures of the fiery wreckage returned to his consciousness, the charred and burnt-out hulk overturned beside the road, the figure frozen in death behind the steering wheel.

It was decided that he be eliminated . . . they devised an accident . . . we know how it was done and why . . . you have something at stake here too, haven't you? . . . It's time you did something for our side for a change . . . they would much rather deal with the son than the father . . .

He lay his head back on the seat. His head pounded unmercifully. Why were they doing this to him? Hess had lost his senses on some idealistic notion of reconciliation. And for what? Politics, that's what it was. Hess was less concerned about saving England than improving his favor with a madman who wouldn't care anyway. Haushofer was as much a war-monger as Goering; he wasn't against the idea of war, just the concept of who the real enemies were. Carstairs was just crazy; he was one of the old war-horses, one of the over-the-trenches-and-damn-the-cost veterans who didn't think in terms of individual lives, just objectives. And if Carstairs was crazy what did that make Sir Alfred? Ted closed his eyes and rubbed at his temples with his fingertips. They were, all of them, nuts. He refused to think about his father. Carstairs would have said anything, Ted thought. Well, the hell with them. He only wanted to see Anne now and he voided his mind of everything but the thought of her and touched her letters under his coat.

"She isn't here, Theodore. Anne's gone to the house in Haslemere."

Sir Alfred was in the study, in his favorite chair and smoking his pipe. Ted gave the maid his coat, but kept the letters. When she was gone he said, "I'm going to see her."

"Yes, of course." Sir Alfred motioned for Ted to take a chair. "We'll take the train down together. How was your trip?"

Ted didn't move. "I just came from Carstairs."

"Did you?" The old man inhaled thoughtfully on his pipe. "Interesting man, Jamey Carstairs. A bit abrupt sometimes, still—"

"He said you were responsible for this," Ted said, producing the bundle of letters, in a tone that was both accusing and fearful. He didn't want it to be true.

Sir Alfred's brow furrowed as his eyes narrowed in the subdued morning light. "What's that, letters, is it?" He nodded, motioned Ted over with his pipe. "Do sit down, will you, my boy. Can't talk to you way over there, can I?" Ted walked to the proffered chair. "So, had a chat with Jamey, did you?" The idea seemed to amuse him. "Laid it all out, did he? And you're indignant and ruffled and feeling betrayed. Is that it?" The old man shook his head. He touched the doily on the arm of his chair, straightening it, then his watery eyes glanced up at Ted. "Anne doesn't know, of course, if that's what worries you."

"You really are part of this?" Ted's voice almost cracked. "You and Carstairs and . . ."

"And you," Bullard said, cutting him short. "Yes I'd have thought you'd jump at the chance . . . considering what the Nazis did to your father."

"Photographs of a car wreck aren't proof of anything but a car wreck."

"You don't believe it, then?"

"No," Ted said quickly. "I don't like being used either. Did you really think I was going to join this conspiracy as if it were a parlor game? Good God, Carstairs wants me to act as his spy! He wants me to use Hess like . . . Christ, why am I telling you! You're in it too."

"A peripheral role, actually." Sir Alfred tapped the cinders from his pipe into a free-standing ashtray beside his chair. "It is true about your father, but I won't press it any further. I can understand your suspicions. Even if it weren't true . . . if I had the opportunity to persuade you that the Nazis did murder your father, I'd do it." He gave Ted a shrug. "Not the usual sort of conduct to expect from a future father-in-law, but, then, these are unusual times. Of course, you already know that."

"Just don't ask me to spy for you," Ted snapped. "I'm not involved in this. Not at all."

Anne's father considered it while he loaded his pipe. "Jamey mentioned your aircraft plants, I trust?"

"Yeah, well, he talks a lot. Proving it's something else."

"Would you like to see proof then?"

"I want to see Anne."

"And you will. But if I could show you positive proof that the Germans are using Campbell engines in their Luftwaffe bombers—" he paused to light the pipe "—what would you do then?"

"First, prove it."

Sir Alfred nodded patiently. He didn't smile exactly but his expression seemed to imply that that was precisely what he intended to do. "It's half a day to Haslemere by train, what with the daylight regulations," he said, adjusting the doily again. "We should leave straightaway. Anne will be so pleased to see you."

Wellhurst House was an estate on the west side of Haslemere that had been a horse breeding farm during the reign of Queen Victoria. The horses were gone now and the stables converted into guest quarters and a large greenhouse that were connected to the main house by a vine-shaded arborway. Anne was on her knees in the greenhouse garden, her apron muddied by the soil, picking fruit from a row of tomato plants.

Ted slipped silently into the greenhouse and sat on a bench behind her. The photograph he carried didn't do her justice, he thought. She was so much more than any camera lens could capture. He could distinguish her fragrance from the sweet smell of plants that permeated the air. The light on her hair gave it a wispy reddish glow that was almost dreamlike. She was as beautiful as he remembered and this rustic setting of sticks and leaves and twisted wire only reaffirmed her loveliness.

"Better find one extra," Ted said softly, "there's another place for dinner."

She whirled around, spraying the moist earth with the tomatoes she'd gathered in her lap, and nearly fell over. "Ted!" For a moment she just stared at him. God, she was beautiful, he thought; her hands were grimy and there was a smudge of dirt on her cheek—all the more. She scrambled to her feet and ran to him, almost bowling him over the rickety wooden bench. "Ted!" He held her and kissed her mouth and she melted into his arms, then they did fall off the bench, backwards in a crash of clay pots and spindly plant sticks.

Anne pulled away to catch her breath. She held his face between her hands. "Ted . . ."

"Is that all you can say," he said with a wide grin.

"It's . . . I'm so surprised! When did you get here? Why didn't you call first?" She touched a hand to her face and glanced fretfully at her dress. "My God, I'm such a mess! I didn't have any idea . . . why didn't someone tell me . . ."

"You look wonderful, really." He touched the smudge on her cheek. "Dirt does you proud."

"Oh, Ted." She rubbed her cheek with the hem of her apron. "Is that it? Oh . . . you should have called. Look at me. I should have been dressed. I should have met you. I'm just a mess!"

He kissed her again, then pulled himself up on the bench, holding Anne around the waist. "If you looked any better I'd never control myself."

"I don't *want* you to control yourself." She took his hand, staring into his eyes, and pressed it against the cotton fabric of her dress over her breast. Then suddenly, her expression went cross as if she'd just remembered some sin he'd committed and she pushed his hand away. "You haven't written in weeks! Do you know that, Theodore Campbell? Weeks! I've been sick with worry. I don't know if you've been hurt or, or . . . anything might have happened to you. And suddenly, here you are . . . popping up like a jack-in-the-box. You might have called. You might have *written!*"

For as long as he lived, Ted thought, he would never understand the swift and unexpected change of moods in women.

"I did write," he said, more defensively than he intended. Ted pulled the bundle of his letters from his coat pocket. He'd thought this out on the train coming down. He'd made up a story about a foul-up with British censors. He couldn't tell her about Carstairs or her father's involvement with this ridiculous scheme. He'd read all her letters on the train, some more than once, then discarded them in a refuse bin at the station. He couldn't let her see those letters because none of them had a postmark stamped on them as proof that they'd been mailed. He'd thought it was the wise thing to do, throwing them away, but he wished he had them now. It meant he was thinking like Carstairs might think—blotting out evidence—and he didn't want to do that. Now or ever.

They sat together in the loose ground beside the bench, Anne leaning against Ted's chest while she read his letters, slowly, chronologically, pausing only occasionally to touch his arms that surrounded her waist in a silent gesture of affection. He hadn't realized his own loneliness and the extent of his deep longing for Anne until he saw the words he'd written weeks before. When she'd finished, Anne folded the pages of the last letter and slipped it gently back into its envelope. She held it a moment, staring at his handwriting, then glanced tenderly at Ted. "They're . . ." She tried to smile, but her chin trembled and gave her away. "They're beautiful, Ted. I love you. God, I do." Then her arms went around his neck and she buried her face in his shoulder and Ted knew she was crying.

"I love you too," he said as if he needed to. He didn't think of Carstairs or Hess or the war or anything else but her. He had Anne and nothing else touched him now. Peace was a few meters of dirt in a tiny garden with the woman who wanted him for himself. It was enough; more, even.

15 _____

THE BALLROOM WAS crowded, the air electric with music and laughter. An orchestra played without interruption, breaking into the dance music from time to time for a chorus of the "Horst Wessel Lied." About half the men in attendance wore formal evening dress, but it was the other half, the ones who wore German uniforms, that most interested Kate. Freimark had made his instructions explicit: make friends.

She was dancing with a Prussian officer, perspiring and panting with the effort of the dance. The man moved stiffly, as if he were bound up in too tight a corset, and Kate pitied him. She did not know who he was or what his chestful of medals was meant to signify. He had told her his name when they began dancing, but it had not registered. If she were a good little spy she'd remember everybody's name. She'd draw them all out in turn about their military careers and their perceptions, calculate their weaknesses and report all to Freimark. But the process of deciding which of the officers to make a play for (the highest-ranking ones being the obvious choices) was a laborious task and her intuition did not always prove correct. This Prussian boob was a case in point. Nothing about him suggested that he would provide the slightest interest to Ludwig, the chain-smoker.

The tune ended. As the orchestra struck up another, a monocled man in evening dress asked her to dance. She begged off, pleading exhaustion, and snatched a glass of champagne from a passing tray. She was the Nazis' pet these days. Goebbels himself had publicly praised her as an exemplar of the "finest sort of impartial open-minded journalist," a phrase that was permanently sullied by having been issued from the lips of that malignant dwarf. But it provided her with an excellent cover and made her infinitely more useful to the party. Every day it seemed another correspondent from America was being officially requested to leave Germany because of inflammatory articles or broadcasts that piqued the *Reichspropagandaleiter.* Just a few days ago, Ralph Barnes of the *Herald Tribune* had wired home a story that relations between Russia and Germany had deteriorated. Overnight, Barnes was asked to leave. Other correspondents had their movements circumscribed and their broadcasts heavily censored. In the meantime, Goebbels' underlings busied themselves rolling out the red carpet for Fräulein Buchanan. She was, for example, the only member of the press invited to this party, a celebration of something she only half remembered. But it wasn't important to know why she was invited, just that she attend—and make friends.

"Fräulein Buchanan? I hope I am pronouncing your name correctly."

She glanced up to see a tall man with penetrating blue eyes in the black dress uniform of the SS. A narrow waist, trim hips, a well-developed chest—he was the sort to lift weights in front of a mirror. His commanding presence was typically SS, with one exception: his face had been severely scarred by acne.

Kate returned his smile. "You pronounce it nicely."

"I enjoy speaking English." He raised his champagne glass. "But there are so few to practice it on."

"Your accent is superb."

"Thank you." He gave a slight bow. "English is many ways similar to the Germanic tongue, for all the words are from different sources. In some respects its vocabulary is richer than German, but it has not the purity or orderly grammatical structure of German. In that sense it is a mongrelized language, but I certainly take pleasure in speaking it."

There wasn't any mistaking whose propaganda he listened to, she thought. But she only nodded. "You certainly speak it well."

"Well enough to be on the radio?" His eyes sparkled. "I enjoy your broadcasts."

"You hear them in Germany?"

He shook his head. "Of course they are not carried here. Why would Germans want to hear an English broadcast? But my work often takes me abroad, you see."

A dance number ended. The orchestra struck up another, and throughout the room people began to sing.

> *Our flag waves as we march along.*
> *It is an emblem of the power of our Reich,*
> *And we can no longer endure*
> *That the Englishman should laugh at it.*
> *So give me your hand, your fair white hand,*
> *Ere we sail off the conquer England!*

As the orchestra moved into something else, the SS man turned to her. "A popular march," he said. "You'll hear more of it in the weeks to come."

"You didn't join in," Kate said.

"When it is an accomplished fact," he replied, "I will sing it louder than the rest in Trafalgar Square."

"You sound a little skeptical."

He shrugged politely and changed the subject. "I fear my English has more to recommend it than my dancing. But perhaps you'd like another glass of champagne? And I'm sure the air will be fresher on the balcony."

She could do with a breath of air. And the man was interesting, if more than faintly sinister. She took his arm and let him lead her through the crowd. She learned he was an SS-Sturmbannfuehrer, a rank equivalent to a major in the American army, and that his duties, of which he was careful not to speak specifically, placed him somewhere in the security service. Possibly Gestapo. The chance that he might be was not exactly comforting. Even staunch Nazis found the presence of Gestapo officers disquieting. And this man had singled her out for both barrels of his Teutonic charm. Why? She was in Goebbels' good graces, so why would the Gestapo take such an interest in her? Of course, he might not be investigating her at all. Even Gestapo officers can be attracted by a well-turned calf and, Kate well knew, she had considerably more than that. Besides, wasn't this what she was here for—to make friends?

Kate tried to ignore her paranoia. She'd be more careful with this one, but she'd play him out as she did the others and see where it led. His name was Regenbauer—Freimark would want to know it precisely—Johann Regenbauer. He was polite, but not suave, and had a killer's smile.

"The Gestapo," she heard herself say. "Isn't that part of the Security Service? I'm sorry to be so ignorant, especially for a journalist, but the SS is so large I'm not sure which departments are aligned together." The direct approach, if she was going to learn anything, Kate figured, was as good as any even if she had to lie a little. It was a tactic women could get away with in Germany. "I'm fascinated by the Secret Police, but I don't know much about it."

"Many of your countrymen share the fascination," Regenbauer said. "I'm afraid that they regard it as a sinister organization."

"Americans are traditionally apprehensive about secret police."

"Of course." He nodded. "Americans lack our particular security problems. How can they be expected to understand our methods when they dismiss them out of hand? But I've not been to the United States, either." He smiled. "It's an oversight I hope to correct."

They way he said it, the way he smiled in the dark, made her feel suddenly cold. She was beginning to notice his eyes.

"You . . . travel a great deal, do you?"

"My work demands it."

She realized that he hadn't answered her original question. Try something else, she told herself. "What sort of work is that?"

"Investigative, mostly."

Kate nodded. "Gestapo?"

It wasn't any trick to make herself blush—not the way he looked at her.

"I'm sorry, Major," Kate said behind a nervous smile. "It's my nosy upbringing as a journalist. I guess I just can't stop the habit of asking questions."

"No need to apologize. I don't mind."

He smiled again. He knew exactly who she was and what she was doing, Kate thought.

"*Are* you in the Gestapo?" She was committed to asking him now.

"Not exactly, though I do concern myself with domestic investigations of the type that the Gestapo usually handles."

"Are you working on an investigation now? I mean, in Berlin?"

"My work takes me throughout Europe," Regenbauer said. He leaned slightly toward her. "Do you mind if I call you Katherine?"

"No, of course not. Please."

"And I am Johann," Regenbauer said with a gracious nod. "It is so much less formal than major, is it not?"

"Much," Kate agreed. "It must be exciting work, Johann, what you do."

"Germany's work is its own reward." His expression was cool. "They say that of virtue. But there are rewards besides the work itself. As your own work must be. Far more interesting than mine, I think . . . being here in Berlin in the center of monumental events." He paused a moment. "Very interesting, is it not?"

Kate nodded. "You meet interesting people."

"I'm sure," Regenbauer said. "A woman in your position must be privy to fascinating bits of gossip and rumor. Doubtless you hear far more than you are ever free to broadcast."

"I'm a news reporter, not a gossip columnist."

Regenbauer touched her arm. "I've offended you—please, forgive me. I meant only that your work must give you much insight into German society."

Kate felt suddenly like an idiot. Regenbauer wasn't investigating her, he was doing the same thing she was—groping for informers. The idea was almost funny. As if she knew anything that would interest the Gestapo about German society!

"I think you overestimate me," Kate said. "I'm just a working girl. My circle of friends doesn't include the fashionable, you know."

"It's their loss, then, I'm sure." Regenbauer frowned. "Though I was under the impression that you were a friend of the American aviator."

She gave him a questioning look. "Who?"

"Herr Campbell."

"Ted Campbell?"

"Ah, you do know him." Regenbauer nodded. "I met him

once, briefly. An interesting young man." He smiled again and Kate felt a chill. Of all people, why would he be inquiring about Ted?

"Ted's an old friend," Kate said. She glanced nervously across the city. Why *was* he asking about Ted? Surely, they weren't investigating *him*.

The SS major nodded as if he understood. The killer smile flashed across his face and then was gone. "Pity about his father, wasn't it?"

16 _____

THE DREAM LASTED a week before the war shattered it forever.
They spent every minute together and Sir Alfred did not
intrude except at dinner, and even then he kept his comments
on the war brief as if in passive acquiescence to unspoken
terms. It was only at night that the reality of war could not be
ignored; there were blackout regulations to be obeyed, even at
Wellhurst House, and the droning roar of aircraft engines,
mostly Spitfires and Hurricanes, Ted reckoned, that stopped all
conversation till they'd passed.

But they ignored the reality as much as was possible to
disregard it; they picnicked in the country, shopped in the
town, and spent the evenings together in front of a cold
fireplace in the main house because it was quiet and private and
because no one told them not to. The surprising thing was that
so little conversation passed between them after such an
extended separation—certainly they talked, she told him of her
volunteer work as a letter carrier for the King's Road post
office before she left London at her father's request. London
was a city tensed and ready for Luftwaffe bombers that would
surely come, she told him. Already children had been evacu-
ated from the city and the coastal towns to Devonshire and the
midland counties. Signposts had been removed in southern and
eastern England to confuse paratroopers if they came that way.
When the Germans came (Anne spoke as if the invasion was a

foregone conclusion) the British people would be expecting them. She wanted to know about his accident, of course, and what it was like in Germany. He told her about meeting Goering and Goebbels, but not Hess or Haushofer, and that a news service had asked him to be a correspondent. He described the destruction he'd seen in Spain and the Jewish girl on the plane in Barcelona. The war had touched everything and it was partly due to that that they spoke so little, as if to deny the war and its development any consequence on their time together. Partly that and partly because there wasn't great need for conversation. They had each other and the fact of it made dialogue not unimportant, just not essential.

It was a Tuesday that marked the end of their first week and to celebrate Ted took Anne to Haslemere's most elegant restaurant, such as it was. They had roast hen and red wine because there wasn't anything else and were served by a waiter who was also the air raid warden, and who wore boots under his apron and kept his steel helmet on a hook beside the kitchen door. They held hands when they weren't eating and Ted left a five-pound tip, as much in gratitude for not being interrupted as for the service. Anne snuggled against him in the front seat of the Bentley and it wasn't just the wine he'd had that distracted his concentration on keeping the blinded headlights on the left side of the road.

Wellhurst House greeted them with silence when they arrived. Tuesday was the housekeeper's night off and Sir Alfred had left a scrawled note that he'd accepted an invitation to bridge.

" 'Late, I'll be,' " Anne said, reading the note. " 'Don't wait up.' " She set the note back on the writing desk and stared at Ted with a glint of devilment behind her eyes. "We're alone . . . finally."

"Until when?" Ted said.

"Late." Anne pressed herself against him without inhibition; she held her arms around him, then glanced up at him with a smile that was more than a smile. "He's an absolute fiend about bridge. Loves it more than brandy, I think. Very, *very* late, if I'm to judge."

"Your place or mine," Ted said after a moment. He let his hands drop around her to the small of her back and pressed her even closer.

"Now," she whispered. "Please . . ."

What was intended to be a tender and sensual encounter turned out to be less than either of them had expected. Ted's fantasy of wanting Anne for so long had proved to be somehow unsatisfying in reality and he sensed she had the same feelings. They had been urgent, hasty lovers and their moment had been spent too quickly in the mechanics of lovemaking. In a rush to make up time they had wasted it and the result was an embarrassed aftertime made even more awkward as they dressed themselves in self-conscious silence like puberty-sensitive adolescents at a bathhouse. Ted tried to be consoling, but he did it badly, and Anne compounded the error by admitting they'd tried too hard, that they'd been too eager. She'd likened their attempt to being thrown from a horse, and said the best way to overcome it was to get back in the saddle; which was not exactly an analogy that wonderfully described the situation, she said on reflection, but it was, somehow, appropriate. They laughed because it was what they needed to release their embarrassed energies and rescue what might have been a dreadful end to an otherwise beautiful day. They lay locked in each other's arms, slowly, gently regaining the momentum they had lost when Ted heard the wounded bomber.

The sound of it came to him as if out of a dream; far away like the rhythm of the surf, then nearer, louder, until he recognized the high-pitched whine of an engine badly maimed and sucking against itself as it strained desperately for fuel.

He pushed himself away from Anne, eyes wide and staring at the darkness of the ceiling, but listening as if his ears could do what his eyes could not.

"Ted . . . what—?"

"Quiet!" He was on his feet then. The sound of it was all around him. Ted rushed to the huge bay window and flung back the curtains.

There nearly wasn't time to call out. Ted didn't recognize the burning silhouette immediately except that it was a twin-engine bomber—Dornier, possibly—and its starboard wing was ablaze, lighting the darkness around it like an enormous speeding torch. It was forty yards away and only barely above the ground and headed directly for Ted. Loose window glass vibrated as if in fearful reply to the deafening roar and Ted was momentarily frozen to the spot before the window. For an instant he wondered unaccountably why the pilot hadn't switched on his landing lights as if to tell him that this was not a place to bring an aircraft. Then he saw the pilot, or thought he saw him; a figure behind the slanted Plexiglas, shadowy and animated in the flickering glow of the fire and Ted stood breathlessly transfixed in rigid terror, eyes and mouth wide, as he saw the screaming, ghastly face of death itself. The plane's nose lifted as the pilot made a useless attempt at avoiding the house. The burning wing dipped, nearly touching the ground, then the whole plane disappeared, passing out of the window frames and at the same time exploding into the hundred-year-old stone and mortar walls of Wellshurst House's second story.

Anne's scream, and Ted's, as he spun around, shrieking a warning, were lost in the shattering blast of rocks and timber. The ceiling collapsed with a rush of wind that knocked Ted backwards into the blackout drapes and blew out the bay window.

The seconds it took Ted to come to his senses were like an eternity. He knew somewhere in the depths of his consciousness exactly what had happened, but the sudden shock of it, the numb grogginess, the absurd paralysis, condemned his movements to an awkward dreamlike state that made seconds into hours and bedlam into silence until he was on his feet and the whole dreadful scene came thundering into focus as his senses gripped reality. Sir Alfred's elegant Victorian study had been transformed into burning wreckage. Dust and smoke hung in the air like fog. Through the gaping hole above him Ted saw the silvered moon held in a jagged frame of fire. Then he heard Anne call him in a frightened half-whispered voice and he stumbled across the demolished room toward it.

"ANNE!"

A massive support beam in the ceiling had fallen across the print sofa where Anne had been, crushing one end as if it were a matchbox. Debris littered the place in splintered heaps of chalky rubbish.

"Anne!"

He pushed aside the broken sideboard of a vanity table that had crashed into the hole when the ceiling gave from the room above and found her on her back, under the beam. "Oh . . . God!" In a frenzy he attacked the foot-thick timber and lifted an end and heaved it away with all his strength. It crashed in a flurry of choking dust and he had to wipe his face to see again. Ted knelt beside Anne and his trembling fingers touched her face. "Anne? . . . Anne! . . ." He was afraid to touch her, to move her. He couldn't see her face well in the darkness lit by scattered fires. She wasn't dead, he told himself. He held her hand, then covered her face as another chunk of ceiling gave way and crashed against the fireplace. "Anne! . . ."

When she opened her eyes, her mouth formed a word but there was no sound.

"I have to move you," Ted said close to her face. "I *have* to. We must get out. Do you hear? Where are you hurt? Anne? Anne!" He wiped a hand across his face, glanced around at the shambles of the room. Fires were beginning to spread. Already the blackout drapes were a sheet of flames. He slid his arms gently under her neck and legs. "Hold me," he told her. She gasped when he raised her. "Hold me, Anne!" But her arms hung limply away from him and her face was ugly with a pain that Ted couldn't help.

He half ran, half stumbled out of the house with her in his arms, fleeing down the curved drive until he couldn't walk another step, then set her softly on the lawn beside a fountain. He ripped at his shirt and soaked a strip of cloth in the water to wipe her face. The house was burning furiously now and by its light Ted tried to find a wound to staunch, but Anne wasn't bleeding. Somewhere, Ted heard the wail of a siren, its doleful cadence rising and falling in the heated breeze.

"They're coming," he told her with desperate assurance. He touched the dripping cloth to her cheek. "They're coming, Anne," he said again with tears in his eyes, not knowing who they were. "God! Anne . . . please . . ." He soaked the rag with more water as if that were what she needed most and held it to the side of her face.

But her eyes didn't open and she didn't speak another word and Ted remained beside her in the shimmering light, soothing her, caressing her with his damp cloth, until they came and took Anne's body away.

17
_____

THE FUNERAL WAS held at Sevenoaks, in Kent, at a small Anglican church that had been built of stones from a Roman fortress in the fifteenth century. Anne had been baptized there, and her mother, who was born in nearby Knole, was also buried in the well-kept churchyard. It was a brief service —which was fortunate, considering the number of people who crowded the tiny sanctuary. Mostly, they were old chums of Sir Alfred's who'd come out of respect for him rather than any memory they'd had of Anne. Ted hardly knew anyone, except a few relatives he'd met with Anne in Greenwich once. Not that it mattered to him who came. They were all gone by late afternoon, even Sir Alfred; he'd had a few words with Ted before he left, but the old man's mumblings were barely articulate and Ted could see, in his bearing more than his face, the unsharable grief of a man who'd lost twice. So Ted waited through the end, until the last shovel of dirt was patted in place. Then he went to London. To see Carstairs.

It was after midnight when he found the address on Leinster Mews. He had spent two days in the city before he was ready to see Carstairs. Ted had needed the time to think it out, to know exactly how he would put it to Carstairs and to make peace with himself for the war he was about to declare. He rang the bell and was surprised to hear someone come so quickly; surprised and disappointed, he'd wanted to get Carstairs out of bed.

Carstairs squinted out from behind the door. "Yes? Who's that?"

"Campbell," Ted said. "I want to talk."

"Tonight?"

"Now."

Carstairs nodded disagreeably but opened the door. He led the way down a corridor and into a brightly lighted parlor. Trentlyon was there, sitting in a large chair with a drink in his hand. He frowned at Carstairs when he saw Ted, but Carstairs only shrugged.

"Let me say," Carstairs began as he turned toward Ted, "how deeply sorry—"

"I'm not here about that," Ted said before Carstairs could finish. "I don't care to hear what makes you sorry or glad. I came here to talk about this Pythagoras scheme of yours."

The announcement didn't startle Carstairs but it got a rise out of Trentlyon; the big man set down his drink as if he might otherwise drop it. Carstairs nodded. "I see." For a moment he said nothing, just stared at Ted with the indifferent intensity of a cow. "I take it then that you've given our proposal some thought." It wasn't so much a question as a statement to be acknowledged.

"Yes, I've thought about it. I've decided to play."

"Play?" Trentlyon's face contorted as if repeating some vile oath. "*Play!* Look here, this isn't a bloody circus ride we're talking about!"

"I know exactly what it is," Ted snapped.

"Perhaps not *exactly*." Carstairs motioned for Ted to have a seat. "Can I get you a drink then. Tea, brandy . . ."

"Bourbon," Ted said, "straight up. I'll work with you but only on two conditions. First, I want to know who the network contact is in Berlin. If I get in trouble I want to know who to call to get me the hell out of Germany fast. I don't have any intention of letting the Gestapo shoot me for spying. Besides, if I have an urgent message I'll need to know who to give it to."

Carstairs stood with his back to Ted at the sideboard, pouring Ted's drink. "And the second condition?"

"Let's just take this one step at a time. Who's the agent in Berlin?"

Carstairs brought Ted his whiskey. "I'm afraid it doesn't work that way." He held up his hand before Ted could object. "Listen, please. Knowing who the agent is will not help you and can only endanger him. It will only be rarely, if ever, that you will have a face-to-face confrontation with anyone *in* the network. It's an obvious security precaution. Any messages you have to pass will be handléd through a drop and that will be explained to you in detail, but later. As for being caught, there is always that risk, but it is kept at a minimum by these very precautions."

"You're not going to tell me who it is, then?"

"No."

"Look, you're ready enough to trust me to confide in Hess. I don't see there's much difference if—"

"No one's said we were confiding in Hess," Trentlyon interrupted. He'd had his glass nearly to his lips to take a drink, now he lowered it to give Ted an unobscured view of his scowl. "Why on earth would we do that?"

"This whole setup is engineered for Hess, isn't it?"

"To use him as a source, yes." Carstairs sat in the chair opposite Ted. "We'll allow the deputy fuehrer to *believe* he's corresponding with the Duke of Hamilton when in actual point of fact he will be corresponding with me."

Ted set his whiskey down. "You're not even going to let him try to negotiate!"

"Rudolf Hess," Carstairs began as if everyone in the world knew but Ted, "however much he wishes it were so, does not speak for the Third Reich. Now, you mentioned a second demand?"

"Condition," Ted said.

"Quite."

Ted took a long swallow of his bourbon and set it down again. "When you dreamed up this little scheme you saw it in two phases. One, maintain air superiority over England; two, divert Hitler's attention away from England. Through Hess, you want to persuade Hitler to look to the east, to forget about England as a threat, to concentrate on Russia. Let the RAF take care of the Luftwaffe and let Pythagoras work on Hitler. If the first phase is successful then the second should be easy. Right?"

"An oversimplification," Carstairs said.

"Simple or complex doesn't matter because it won't work,

not the first part. If you believe that a few hundred Hurricanes and Spitfires have the slightest chance of holding back Goering's armada of fighters and bombers—I've *seen* them, Carstairs—then you're the biggest fool since Chicken Little. It won't work because the Luftwaffe is putting the pressure on; they're bombing airfields and shipping yards. Attrition alone will deplete your air defense but at this rate, with skirmishes every day, by the end of summer there won't be enough planes in the air to protect Dover much less the entire coastline. Hitler won't need a peace then; he'll just float across the Channel and *take* England. And you won't need me or Hess or a network of spies in Berlin because the Germans will be *here*."

Carstairs waited until he was sure Ted had finished. "I'm not sure I understand what you expect of me, Mr. Campbell. I am not in charge of the physical defense of these islands. I do not have squadrons of aircraft under my control. That is another department entirely. What is it that you want?"

Ted finished the bourbon all at once then sat slightly forward in his chair, ignoring Trentlyon, focusing on Carstairs. "I have an idea. It's probably crazy but it's as sane as anything I've heard from you. But I'm the only one who can carry it off. That's what I want . . . a chance to try it. If it works then I'll do whatever you want in Berlin. If it doesn't, well, it won't matter anyway."

Carstairs waited. "Well, what is it?"

"Bomb London," Ted said, settling back into his chair. "I want to bomb the capital."

"Good God!" Trentlyon exploded, "He's a bloody lunatic!"

"I've given it a lot of thought," Ted said, his eyes on Carstairs. "I know what I'm talking about. The only way to give the RAF a rest, and time to rebuild and take the pressure off, is to divert the Luftwaffe to a different target."

"London?" Carstairs mused.

"How do you think the Germans would take it if Berlin were bombed?" Ted waited for an answer.

"No one in *this* government would condone it," Trentlyon said emphatically. "The prime minister will not bomb a civilian population. Not even Berlin."

"Exactly," Ted said. "Unless it was an act of retribution. It's an eye for an eye sense of morals you people have. London isn't bombed for the same reason that Paris wasn't . . . Hitler wants it intact for a special victory parade. But the British don't attack Berlin because it isn't a vital military target. There's some sort of stupid unwritten understanding that neither capital will be attacked. One bomber can change all that . . . even one bomb, in the heart of London, from a Luftwaffe plane. It would give Churchill the perfect motive to strike Berlin—and keep hitting it until Goering's forced to respond."

"Goering would never change his strategy," Carstairs said thoughtfully, "if it were working."

"The hell with Goering! Hitler is the one who counts. Look, the RAF raids on Bremen, Hamburg, Paderborn . . . the Germans expect that. But Berlin . . . don't you see? Hitler *lives* in Berlin. It's the *Fuehrer's* city, his sacred domain. Bomb his paradise and you'll enrage him beyond reason . . . he'll demand that Goering retaliate against London to the exclusion of everything else."

Trentlyon couldn't stand it any longer. *"You are* a lunatic! This isn't some Moorish port in Spain, Campbell, it's the capital of the British empire!"

"It won't be much longer at the rate you're going," Ted said sharply.

Carstairs stared at his empty glass. "What you say—" he glanced at Ted "—may be true, about the odds faced by our RAF, I mean." He kept his eyes on Ted with steady coolness. "About the rest of it . . . It's rather speculative, isn't it? Dangerously speculative, I might add."

"I thought you were in the business of taking risks."

"Sensible risks," Trentlyon put in, "not hallucinations concocted by madmen."

Carstairs calmed him with a wave of his hand. "Tell me, if you've given this so much thought, how you intended to get a German bomber over London if it is a forbidden target?"

"Not with a fake," Ted siad. "It would have to be real from the start—a real Luftwaffe bomber from a real airfield in France on an actual raid. An authentic mission. We have to make the Germans believe it was one of their own planes and bomber crews that did it."

"And also Churchill, I think," Carstairs said. His eyes touched Trentlyon.

"Yeah, well, that's your end of it. I'll fly the plane, you just get me the proper identity papers. You have people who can do that, I assume. It should be a junior grade flying officer assigned to the Luftflotte Two . . . a Heinkel bomber group."

Trentlyon nearly choked with amazement. "You're mad!"

"And a disguise," Ted added. "Nothing flashy, mustache and change of hair color should do."

Carstairs said nothing.

"It's the most absurd, insane thing I've ever heard!" The big man was red-faced. "Your responsibility is Rudolf Hess!"

Ted turned to him. "Unless you do something about the Luftwaffe, Hess's part in this won't mean a damn."

Trentlyon shook his head. He looked pleadingly at Carstairs. "Sir . . . *sir,* the man is a bloody lunatic! Fly a Luftwaffe bomber—my God! Campbell is too valuable to risk in a harebrained scheme like this!"

Carstairs finally glanced at Trentlyon. "You're right there, quite right. It would be risky indeed." He let his gaze fall on Ted. "Quite right."

"Look, it's my goddamn neck. I'm willing to take the chances. Considering what's at stake, I'd think you would be too."

"Not if it jeopardizes other *more* important operations," Trentlyon said.

Ted turned to Trentlyon with an incredulous look. "More important? Good Christ, what the hell is *more important* than preventing an invasion! I'm trying to keep the goddamn Germans off your necks!"

For a moment Trentlyon flustered in the icy stare from Carstairs. Ted assumed he'd broken some sworn secret oath forbidding them from even mentioning other intelligence operations even existed. As if Ted cared what else the British intelligence had on.

"I . . . It . . . it would be nothing that concerns you, you may be sure of that," Trentlyon stammered. He was speaking to Ted but he was looking at Carstairs.

"You could be recognized," Carstairs said to break the spell. "Someone might recognize you and then you'd be finished before you began. In that case we couldn't help you at all."

Ted sensed a glimmer of interest. He pushed himself to the edge of his chair. "I don't have that many friends in Germany. And those who do know me well enough to see past a disguise are very unlikely to be strolling around a Luftwaffe airfield in France."

Trentlyon snorted. "You'd be surprised how curious the Gestapo can be."

"The Gestapo is a police organization," Ted rebutted, "not a military one. They have no authority on a military post."

Carstairs acknowledged the point with a nod. "Even if you were successfully infiltrated—"

"Sir!"

Carstairs silenced his subordinate with a look. "We're considering a hypothetical situation," he said patiently. He glanced at Ted again. *"If* we could infiltrate you—and understand, Campbell, it would be dangerous gamble to many more lives than just yours—if it could be done, there is still the considerable risk of your being shot down by the RAF before reaching your destination."

"At night?" Ted shook his head. "Look, I told you I've thought this out. I don't plan to be shot by either side. But you're right, it's a gamble, but the odds are on my side. Unless there's been some astounding development, night fighting between aircraft still relies on visual contact. Even the best pilot can't shoot at something he can't see."

"London is probably the most heavily fortified city in the world at this moment," Carstairs went on. "Even if there hasn't been an armada of planes to shoot at, the city is ringed by antiaircraft batteries just waiting for the chance."

"I'm only talking about one plane," Ted said, " . . . at low level, in the dark. If we were discussing thirty bombers it would be different, but we're not talking about thirty, not even two. One's all it would take . . . with me flying it."

Carstairs considered it in his silent way, fingers laced together, eyelids drooping as he stared thoughtfully at a place on the hardwood floor midway between himself and Ted, as if absorbed in the artistry of tongue-and-groove construction. He poured himself a cup of tea from the table beside his chair, then, ready finally, looked squarely at Ted. "Why?" he said and Ted was momentarily confused.

"Why what?"

"Why did you come here in the middle of the night with this audacious idea? Why do you care now when ten days ago you wouldn't have anything to do with it? Why does it matter to you enough to risk your life even beyond what we've asked?" Carstairs' gray eyes were unblinkingly steady; like a predatory animal, Ted thought. "Why?"

"Because I . . . I want to do it."

"No one *wants* to risk his life, Campbell." Carstairs didn't blink.

"Look, goddammit! I'm volunteering, all right? What difference does it make?"

"Is it because of the girl? Is it because you feel responsible for Anne's death? Is it grief, then?"

"I'm not suicidal, if that's what you're thinking."

"I want to know what *you're* thinking," Carstairs said. *"Are* you a lunatic?" His gaze caught Trentlyon. "Is this a gesture of conscience? I want to know what motivated you to such a radical change of mind."

Anne's scream coursed through Ted's mind like an electric shock. He remembered the chaos, the plane thundering toward him, the frozen moment of terror on the pilot's face. Anne hadn't said a word; he remembered that too . . . *and* the smoldering wreckage of house and plane at Wellhurst the day after she died. He'd gone back to it to see for himself, to prove to himself that it couldn't have been a possibility. The metal of the plane had still been hot as he twisted it back to get closer to the mounts. Carstairs was crazy but he had to know for sure. He had to know positively, to quell his nagging conscience, before they carted off all the pieces and melted them down. He had to know. And he did.

"I went back to the wreckage," Ted said finally, avoiding Carstairs' searching stare. "The Luftwaffe bomber that crashed into the house. I . . ." He glanced at his glass but it was empty.

"What did you find?" he heard Carstairs' voice ask.

Ted looked up at him slowly. At this moment he hated Carstairs more than he'd hated anyone in his life. "A Campbell inverted-V engine."

Carstairs raised an eyebrow and nodded to himself sadly. "I see." Then he looked at Trentlyon. "Nigel, I'll want you to take some notes, if you please." To Ted he said, "Tell me again about the class of bomber you're considering flying. We'll want to have it right."

18 _____

IF THERE WAS a good side to getting back to Germany it was that Ted didn't have any trouble with transportation; all the full planes were on the way *out* of the Third Reich, not heading toward it. He was in Bern twelve hours before arriving in Lisbon from London. He checked the Allison out of the rented hangar space, serviced it for flight and tipped the mechanic an extra hundred francs before he took off for Friedrichshafen.

He hadn't known—rather hadn't realised—that being a spy was such a complicated business. Trentlyon had been his tutor on that account and the first thing he learned was that nothing is ever written down. *(Remember, Campbell, that even if you are an amateur you are no less a spy in the Gestapo's eyes. They will kill you with the same enthusiasm they'd give to our best. So memorize everything, write nothing and perhaps you'll survive.)*

So Ted memorized everything Trentlyon told him: Code names, recognition signs and a particularly ridiculous verbal code that had to be responded to predisely as worded.

> *Do you have an interest in pianos?*
> *I don't play, myself.*
> *Just black keys and white keys, eh?*
> *Fourscore and eight, I think.*

During the flight, Ted went over everything again in his head, running through the list of Pythagoras code names alphabetically and the post office boxes to contact them. He didn't know *who* they were specifically except that they would respond to the verbal code exactly. They also all carried a coin. Ted took his out of his pocket.

Don't lose this coin whatever you do. It's your physical link to the network and part of the recogniton code.

The coin was a 1780 Austrian silver thaler distinguished by the likeness of Maria Theresa, the eighteenth-century empress. Ted shoved it back into his pocket. It wasn't especially reassuring that his life might depend on owning a quarter-sized piece of change. The best thing was not to think about it. He went over the names again. There was Archimedes in Lisbon, Ptolemy in Cairo, Plato in Paris, Seneca in Brussels, Copernicus in Rome . . .

But Ted would not be known as one of the ancient philosophers. He was not an agent of the network and he would not be referred to as one. Carstairs had been adamant on that point. Ted Campbell would simply be "A" for Alfred and none of the operators on the network would have prior knowledge of his real identity, just as he didn't know them. It made for a secure system, Trentlyon had said. No one knew any more than he needed to know.

Just A for Alfred connected by a coin to Plato in Paris. And Archimedes in Lisbon, Copernicus in Rome, Seneca in Brussels . . .

Rudolf Hess stared solemnly at the floor in the same unremarkable room where Ted had seen him last. He obviously had not expected the bad news Ted was delivering. Haushofer, on the other hand, seemed not surprised at all. He sat in the same chair as before as if that was *his* chair, quietly sucking his pipe.

"The Duke of Hamilton would not see you?" Hess said finally.

"I didn't say that," Ted said. "He wouldn't discuss it with me. I explained your concern, your commitment to peace, but further than that, he would not allow me to continue." He was doing this much better than he thought he would, Ted thought. As many times as he had rehearsed this speech—and Carstairs had gone over it with him several times—he still wasn't sure he could pull it off. Give him the bad news first, Carstairs had said. *The Duke of Hamilton would not discuss details of a negotiated peace. Not with you. Not with Ted Campbell, an American. Not with a neutral. Let him chew on that, then spring our idea on him. The idea is to give him some ray of hope to cling to.*

"Hamilton was polite enough with me," Ted continued, "but he really couldn't speak with me, an intermediary, in detail on a matter of such critical importance. I could certainly understand that. Anyway, he explained he was not an official of the government." Ted shrugged and took a breath. Now was the time. Don't make a big deal of it, he told himself. You're supposed to be unaware of the possibilities. Let Hess figure it out.

"The only encouraging thing he said was that he thought it was good to know that someone in Germany actually wanted peace. He said he very much would like to remain in touch. As a matter of fact, he told me he wished there was a way he might correspond with you—in the event the situation changes."

Well, that was it. The much-practiced monologue was finished. It was Hess's turn to react.

But he didn't do anything. The deputy fuehrer just stood quietly, hands clasped behind his back, staring forlornly at the same spot on the floor that he had stared at when Ted began.

"Correspond, did you say?" he said at last.

Ted let out his breath. "Yes," he said quickly. "In secret, naturally."

"I see," Hess said slowly. "Then I will correspond with him, because the situation will change." He shook his head. "Very soon."

Ted nodded gravely, because the circumstances seemed to require it. He didn't know what Hess meant, and Haushofer's expression was impenetrable. Probably, he didn't know either.

"Today is the first day of August," Hess began, speaking to neither of them in particular. "In a fortnight, or less, Goering begins Operation Eagle . . . a massive air offensive against Britain. He promised the Fuehrer he could destroy the entire British air command in two to four weeks." Hess looked solemnly at Ted. "Do you think, Theodore, that the Reichsmarschall knows what he is talking about?"

Ted shrugged. "Anything's possible. Goering commands the most devastating air force in the world." He tried not to let his anxiety show. A massive air offensive in two weeks! He had to find out where, against which targets, in what strength. He had to get the information to Carstairs.

"The plan is to eliminate an air defense of England," Hess said. "Without its RAF, England is helpless."

And the Reichsmarshal was right, Ted thought. Fighter Command could never beat back a sustained all-out effort. Four weeks was not an unreasonable timetable for the destruction of the RAF if the Luftwaffe concentrated on airfields and aircraft factories. By the middle of September it could all be over. It gave Ted precious little time. Carstairs had said it would take weeks to get him the right papers forged—identity cards, squadron assignment, flying orders . . . Well, goddammit, he didn't have weeks. The German High Command was already counting Britain's stubborn resistance in days now. That placed the burden on him. He had to get in a Luftwaffe raid before Goering crushed the RAF. He had to bomb London soon—and the sooner the better.

"You are as distressed by the prospect of a shattered England as I, by your expression, Theodore," Hess said.

It was one of the few things Ted need not fake. "Yes . . . I have friends in England."

Hess gripped Ted's shoulder like a comrade. "All the more reason—" he glanced back at Haushofer "—to stay in touch with the duke."

Ted nodded, but he wasn't thinking of Douglas-Hamilton. His mind was on Goering and how he was going to get on one of the Reichsmarshal's bombers.

Two hours later, Ted was in the bar of the Adlon Hotel. This was the congregation spot for American correspondents, and he ordered a drink then strolled toward a group at a table. Lowell Grayson was there, nursing what looked like a gin and tonic.

"Afternoon," Ted said. "Someone from your office said I'd probably find you here." He smiled, stretching the limit of his self-control. He was still smarting over the article Grayson had written. It would have been easier, at least more satisfying, to break a chair over the bastard's head.

"Well, well, well," Grayson said, rising a little awkwardly from his chair. "The prodigal son returns."

He wasn't exactly drunk, Ted thought, but he wasn't exactly sober either. "I'd like to talk to you, Grayson . . . if you can spare a couple of minutes."

Grayson took a sip of his drink. "I'll bet you would. You'd probably like to separate me from some of my teeth, eh?" He gestured to Ted for the benefit of the others at the table. "Gentlemen, let me introduce you to Theodore Campbell." He let his arm swing wide to include the men at the table in the introduction. "Mr. Campbell—" he bowed slightly "—the press. Also, witnesses, in case you have something physical in mind."

"Maybe I should see you later. Tomorrow, in your office."

"I'm *in* my office, Campbell." He plopped back into his chair. "More stories get written in this bar than have ever seen the light of day. We're thinking of renaming the place the Precensor Pub."

"You're drunk," Ted said.

"Not yet. Not yet by a long shot. But stick around."

"I want to *talk* to you, Grayson!"

"Well, I don't want to talk to you. We're having a wake. We're saying goodbye to a good man, a goddamn good man —Ben Horner—a news correspondent who died in the trenches, and we don't need you—we don't *want* you— especially you—fucking up our sendoff. So why don't you just, just turn your ass around—"

"I want a job."

"—and get the—what?"

Ted glanced self-consciously at the others.

Grayson shook his head as if it would help his hearing. "You want what? A job, did you say?"

"I want to report on the war," Ted said. "The war in the air."

Grayson, in his stupor, couldn't take his eyes off Ted. "For me?"

"You offered it to me. Are you still interested?"

"*I* wasn't interested when I offered it," Grayson said, "but my employers are." He got to his feet, using the table and someone's shoulder for support. "You *want* to work for me?"

"I want a job reporting."

Grayson glanced at the faces around the table, shrugged. "You got it. Now, why?"

"When do I start?"

"Tomorrow suit you?"

"What time?"

"Anxious sonofabitch, aren't you?"

"What time tomorrow?" Ted said.

"Nine o'clock. My office. My office office. What changed your mind? How come you suddenly—"

"I want to cover the air war in France."

"You might get hurt in France," Grayson said. "Correspondents aren't immune, you know." He glanced soberly at the men at the table. "Especially in France, eh? Horner got it in France. Calais. Three days ago."

"I'm sorry."

"You are that, Campbell. You may be a hotshot pilot, but you ain't a goddamn newsman. You aren't a Bennett Horner and you never will be—I don't care how many fucking Nazis you know!"

Ted nodded but said nothing.

"Go away," Grayson said, waving his hand. "This is a private wake. Just go away and leave us alone."

"There's just one more thing," Ted said.

"Jesus Christ! I don't want—"

Whatever Grayson thought wasn't articulated. Ted's punch connected squarely on his jaw and knocked him tumbling backwards over his chair.

With the broadcast completed she was free to have a drink. And, if she had needed them frequently in the past, she damn well needed a drink now. She couldn't take Johann Regenbauer without alcohol to soften the edges of perception, nor could she take the attitude of former friends and colleagues now that she was openly keeping company with an SD officer.

She'd heard some of the rumors. Rumors that the network brass back home were nervous about the pro-German reputation she was getting, so she took pains to keep her broadcasts as blandly impartial as she possibly could.

Still, there'd been some mention of her personal politics in the stateside press. Winchell had slammed her in his column and a few other commentators were following his lead. But it wasn't likely she'd be fired, really, unless she let her private life interfere with her professional one—and that simply was not going to happen.

Their affair, such as it was, was proceeding nicely. He began by sending flowers, which surprised her, since it was not an art of an SS man. He would escort her to receptions, then off to a back-street restaurant for dinner. Two nights ago they'd been to bed together for the first time and she was still unsure how she felt about the experience. Physically, he was an exceptional lover. He'd moved with precision from one sexual posture to another, performing skillfully and retaining complete self-control. He'd brought her to climax time and again until she was exhausted beyond response, then gently disengaged without having reached fulfillment himself. At first she thought he was showing off, demonstrating his extraordinary self-discipline. But it was more than that. Regenbauer's failure to climax was on a plane with everything that made him enigmatic. There was a coldness, a detachment, in his touch, as if he was more an observer than a participant. And if there was anything that frightened her most about Regenbauer, it was this trait of mechanical aloofness to natural sensibilities. The answer, Kate decided, was that nearly all vestiges of human frailty had been bred out of him, except where it was expedient in his work.

It seemed remarkable that Regenbauer had chosen Kate to be his intimate companion. Perhaps, she thought, it was because she was the new darling of Berlin society. Their relationship had grown to the point that he allowed her a glimpse of his ambition. Occasionally, when they were alone, he would speak of his work, but rarely in much detail. However, she did learn that Regenbauer was on a special assignment to seek out a traitor within the National Socialist hierarchy. Their relationship was also a constant reminder to Kate of his nearly unlimited power and of her own dangerously insecure position: If Regenbauer ever suspected her real motivations in seeing him, there wasn't any question he would kill her without the slightest hesitation, and he'd do the job himself, slowly and with sadistic pleasure, an inch at a time.

Following her broadcast they'd attended a reception for a Japanese attaché, another dull party at which she was the only American. Afterwards, they'd gone to Regenbauer's apartment. The furniture, she noted again, was as severely stark and angular as Regenbauer's character—the color scheme for the most part was limited to black and white.

He was in a talkative mood. He was getting close to his quarry, he said, and it put him in a boastful mood. Kate sat on the white sofa with a drink in her hand and listened attentively as his self-confidence displayed itself. His superior recognized his abilities, he assured her. When he finally ran down the traitor his efforts would certainly be crowned with another promotion. He would then be SS-Obersturmbannfuehrer Regenbauer and would probably be awarded the Knight's Cross with oak leaves.

Kate took care to be suitably impressed. Was he making progress then? Had he come closer to finding this traitor? It was worth something, she thought, to ask. Freimark would make use of it.

"Progress?" Regenbauer said. He strode to the sofa, sat beside Kate. "I think, yes." He reached into the breast pocket of his uniform blouse and produced a large silver coin. He handed it to her.

"What's this?" Kate turned it over between her fingers.

"Perhaps nothing. Perhaps something. We shall see."

"You're being very mysterious." She snuggled closer to him, held the coin up against the light. "Is it valuable?"

"The coin itself?" Regenbauer shook his head. "No."

"I guess you're not going to tell me, then."

"The previous owner of that particular issue is now dead," he said. "We discovered it in his wallet after the interrogation."

Kate dropped the coin as if it were suddenly on fire. "Don't do that!"

Regenbauer only smiled. He slid the coin back into his pocket. "You mustn't be offended by my work. I'm proud of what I do."

"Did he . . . was he killed in the course of the . . . interrogation?" She rubbed the palms of her hands down her dress over her thighs as if to wipe away the stigma.

Regenbauer shrugged. "He died."

"Who was he?"

"A spy, we think."

"You think!"

Regenbauer glanced at her with dead eyes. "Don't question my work," he said in a low voice. For an instant he was what he truly was, Kate realized. If ever a man could kill without remorse, she was looking at him at this moment. Knowing it was more terrifying than she could possibly imagine it. He was *here*, next to her.

"I . . . I didn't mean . . ."

"Of course not." He smiled.

"It's just—" Kate had to swallow to get control of herself. "It's just that I'm not used to . . . to that sort of thing." She looked up at him. It took nearly all the courage she had to look into his eyes. "I've never seen a man die."

"You never will," Regenbauer said.

"If you say he was a spy, then he was. I didn't mean to—"

"You're trembling." Regenbauer took her drink, set it aside. He put his arms around her. "I've frightened you."

"No, no, really—" She tried to sit up, but he held her near him. "It's just the thought of a man dying . . . I mean, that coin. He held it in his hand. It's silly, I know. But things like that make me feel spooky."

"So," Regenbauer nodded, "we won't discuss it again."

Oh, Christ, now what had she done! "No, Johann, really, I'm interested." She touched his face, gently caressing the scar tissue on his cheek. "I don't want you to think I'm a child."

His hand pressed lightly against her neck, then slid down inside her dress to cup her breast. "No one could remind me less of a child than you." He bent down to kiss her breast; Kate closed her eyes at the touch of him.

"Then . . . tell me about the coin. What's so special about it?"

"Nothing." He unbuttoned the dress and unclasped her bra, caressing the tip of her nipples with his tongue.

"Please, I'm interested."

Regenbauer sighed. He massaged her breasts with his hands.

"I really am interested."

Regenbauer nodded. "It's a reproduction of an old Austrian piece," he said. "The Maria Theresa thaler. It may mean nothing at all."

"But, again, it might mean something?"

"Perhaps. It's an old trick, to use an outdated coin as a recognition sign among conspirators who do not otherwise know each other on sight." He leaned forward, pushing her back on the sofa and sliding the dress off over her legs. "Tonight I will bring you to climax a dozen times." Regenbauer stood up then peeled off his uniform blouse.

"That's all there is to the coin story?" Kate said.

"It is all you need to know." He was standing beside the sofa, glancing at himself in the mirror. Then he looked down at Kate. "Take off the undergarments."

There was only one left, but she was damned if she would make love as if it was close order drill. "I've been romanced more subtly before. And in a bed, too."

Regenbauer smiled. He reached for her then, grabbed the hem of her panties and ripped them.

"Johann!"

"Open your legs."

"What's the matter with you? I'm not a fucking spigot you can turn on and off."

"I like you to talk that way," Regenbauer said. "It's exciting."

"No kidding."

"I want to give you pleasure." He put his hands on her thighs and firmly pushed them apart. "Much pleasure."

"What about you?"

"The satisfaction is getting *you* there." He lowered himself toward her. "A dozen times, you will see."

19

SHE SAW FREIMARK the next afternoon. There wasn't much to tell him—there never was where Regenbauer was concerned —but it seemed to pique enough interest in Freimark to make him happy.

"So, you think he's not concerned with the Russian espionage?" Freimark asked, making notes as usual without looking at Kate.

"I didn't say he wasn't interested, I just don't think he's looking for Bolsheviks. He's onto something else."

"Find out what," Freimark said.

"If I can. There's a dinner party tomorrow night and I'll see him there. Some professor from Berlin University. Hofhauser . . ."

"Haushofer?"

"Right."

"Why were you invited?"

"I don't know."

"But you accepted?"

"Of course."

Freimark nodded, went back to his notes. "Regenbauer will escort you?"

"Yes."

"Who else will be there?"

"They didn't give me a seating chart. Anyway, Regenbauer was happy with the invitation."

"I should think so. He's moving in high society, thanks to you. Haushofer's a professor of geopolitics and a favorite with the Fuehrer, I understand. There will be important people there. Try to make some new friends." He pinched his eyes, then closed his book of notes and looked at Kate. "We mustn't have Regenbauer take up all your time."

"You're a real sonofabitch, Campbell, you know that? A real first-rate peckerhead."

Ted was in Grayson's office, a tiny square room at the end of a corridor which led to the newsroom. Grayson was in his shirtsleeves. He was holding a cloth icepack to his jaw, which made it difficult to talk.

"All right, I'm a real bastard," Ted said. "Now what?"

"You didn't *have* to hit me." Grayson wrung out a dribble of water from the icepack into his wastebasket. "Maybe I deserved it, *maybe*, I said. But you didn't have to clobber me. You don't have to punch drunks, you know." He winced as he pressed the icepack against the side of his mouth. "I thought it was busted."

Ted smiled. He rubbed the knuckles of his hand. "It's a very hard jaw."

"It isn't funny." Grayson's scowl dissolved in an expression of pain. "Do you always go around beating up your employers?"

"Not always. You're the first one. Does that mean I'm still hired?"

Grayson sneered. "Peckerhead," he grumbled. "You know the answer to that. I got a reply from the powers that be this morning. They are overjoyed to have Theodore Campbell on our team."

"I want to go to France," Ted said. "I want to cover the Luftwaffe's operations against England."

"You're a special correspondent. My instructions are to let you do whatever you want."

"I'll need papers or something. Don't I have to have some kind of UP identi—"

"Already taken care of." Grayson eased himself forward and pushed an envelope across the desk. "I got this from the Ministry of Propaganda this morning. Your journalism identification papers. You are now *officially* a special correspondent for this august news-gathering service. There are certain rules we have to play by here—I'll explain those to you later—but the important thing to remember is not to piss off Dr. Goebbels and make sure you clear all dispatches outside Germany through the military censor."

"When can I go?"

"Go?"

"To France."

"When Goebbels' people say you can. The press have to have travel permits like everyone else. Anyway, I want to see what you can do. I'll keep you busy in Berlin a few weeks, then—"

"I can't wait weeks!"

Grayson stared at him with a quizzical look.

"I mean . . . I want to go to France. The sooner the better."

"You'll go when I tell you to go," Grayson said.

Ted nodded. Don't get impatient, he told himself. Just take this one step at a time. "Okay," he said.

"Now, about salary . . ."

"Is there some sort of widow's fund or pension for families of correspondents who are killed?" Ted interrupted.

"I wouldn't worry about it if I were you."

"Is there?" Ted insisted. "The man you were remembering yesterday? Who was it?"

"Bennett Horner," Grayson said.

"Does his family have any insurance or pension?"

"Insurance, such as it is. We do what we can."

"Whatever my salary is, put it in the fund. All of it."

Grayson's eyes narrowed. For a moment, he said nothing. "All right. I won't argue with you about it. It's a hundred eighty bucks a week, just so you'll know." He took a deep breath. "You know your way around the Air Ministry, I presume?"

"Fairly well."

"Might as well start there. Do a profile on Kesselring and . . . what's-his-name—Sperrle. They're commanding the Luftwaffe forces in France and Belgium. As long as you're so anxious to get into the war you might as well get familiar with the field marshals who are running it."

"I'll do that," Ted said. It's what he had intended to do

anyway. It was the perfect cover to ask a lot of questions about bomber groups.

A Luftwaffe colonel, with jackboots so highly polished they were like mirrors, escorted Ted around the Air Ministry. His name was Junger, and he was somehow distantly related to Greta Garbo, a subject he was constantly returning to—that, and Ted's skill as a racing pilot.

Ted spent the entire afternoon with Junger. He was introduced to the Air Ministry staff and admitted to offices that outsiders were seldom if ever invited to see. Being Theodore Campbell accounted for some of it, but being an acknowledged personal friend and trusted ally of Reichsmarshal Hermann Goering accounted for more. There wasn't a question Ted asked that wasn't answered in detail, though he took care not to inquire into sensitive areas. For the most part he had no difficulty learning what he'd come to learn.

Kesselring's Luftflotte Two was divided into three bomber commands and one fighter division, with the heaviest concentration of bomber fields situated along the Seine near Paris and just west of Reims. Most of the bombers were Heinkels and Dorniers; he was familiar with the Heinkel, since it had been used as a civil airliner, but the Dornier was primarily a military plane and he'd only been inside it twice. The Dornier was lighter, slightly faster and more maneuverable, but the Heinkel, with its elliptically shaped wings and sturdy tail section, could withstand a terrific mauling without falling apart in the air. So, if he had a choice, it was going to be a Heinkel bomber. But, just to be sure, he asked for permission to ride in a Dornier. The request was approved; it just wasn't Theodore Campbell's day to be denied.

Finding where the airfields were wasn't a problem; getting into one was something else. He was going to need identification tags, Luftwaffe papers for a junior flying officer and assignment orders to a bomber group. He didn't even know what these looked like. And there were other things besides —leave warrant, ration cards, a dozen kind of permits—and all of them had to be forged or, rather, stolen and forged.

That part was going to be a problem.

Despite what Regenbauer had told Kate about him, Orin Kepler was not dead. For the last six days he had been confined in a dark cell on a sub-basement level at Gestapo headquarters in Berlin. For three of those days he had not slept and for none of them had he eaten solid food. He'd endured so much pain that he longed for death. But Regenbauer had been a patient and careful interrogator; he knew when to apply pain and for how long and with which instrument.

But Kepler's endurance was nearly over and he was unsteadily aware of it. What terrified him was that he couldn't connect his thoughts and account for the passage of time. He couldn't distinguish what had happened five minutes ago from what had happened an hour ago. He couldn't remember if he was alone or if the voices he heard were real or in his unconscious. He couldn't remember anymore the sound of his own voice or if he'd said anything at all, though he surely must have said something sometime. He was only vaguely sure of who he was . . .

I am Orin Kepler, administrative assistant to the Swiss cultural affairs consul at the embassy in Rome. I was born in Burgau, Austria, on the Attersee, and became a naturalized Swiss citizen in 1931. I am Orin Kepler. *I am Orin Kepler!*

But he wasn't really.

Orin Kepler *was* born in Burgau, Austria, in 1902, in his grandmother's house on Bruneckerstrasse, but he died in less than a week of diarrhea because the midwife was not properly sterilized. His mother died too, but that wasn't important to the British Secret Service, because they were looking for a birth certificate to duplicate for an agent they were planting in Switzerland.

The current Orin Kepler was really Quinby Franks, who wasn't born anywhere near Bavaria.

But that wasn't really important either.

What was important—and especially important to Quinby Franks—was that Regenbauer not get out of him who he *really* was. That was critically important. He must not tell Regenbauer because Regenbauer was the enemy. But the trouble was, he couldn't remember. He couldn't remember if he'd said *anything*. He could barely remember his name, which wasn't that easy because he had three. It wasn't easy because he was dying and he knew it and because the pain in his body was so terrible because they'd broken all his fingers and toes and most of his ribs and one of his knees because he wouldn't talk to them about what they wanted to hear.

Well, he couldn't tell them that. He didn't *want* to tell them about Quinby Franks, but he *couldn't* tell them who he really was. He hoped to God he hadn't told them that. He wished he could die so he wouldn't have to talk to anybody.

And not because he wasn't Orin Kepler or because he was Quinby Franks. Those things weren't important. He wished he could remember what he'd said.

Because he was really Copernicus.

Part Four

20 _____

"WHAT DO YOU mean 'missing'?" Carstairs said as he poured himself his first cup of morning tea. "Whom are we talking about?"

"Our Rome contact," Trentlyon said. "Franks, with the Swiss embassy. Quinby Franks."

"Copernicus," Carstairs said. "How long?"

"A week," Trentlyon said. "He was due to make a station check three days ago. He didn't. The Swiss embassy hasn't heard from him since he left for Lyon on business for the cultural affairs secretary." He started to pace. "I think he's been picked up."

"In France?"

"It's in the occupied zone. The Ausland SD could have snatched him up and no one would have known."

Carstairs pushed his tea aside. "Possibly. But why?"

Trentlyon sighed. "I don't know. I don't think the Germans could have tripped to him."

"Swiss civil servant since thirty-five," Carstairs read from Franks' file. "Placed by SIS in thirty-three. Orin Kepler." He glanced up from the file. "How many of our people are using bogus identities?"

"In the Pythagoras run?" Trentlyon gave a dismal shrug. "Only Franks."

"Could Jerry have discovered the switch?"

191

"I don't see how. The Kepler baby died in a small town in Austria. We were particular to use a birth cirtificate that would be difficult to connect to a death certificate. The Germans have always been very careful to screen their own embassy staffs for this kind of thing, but they haven't been checking foreign staffs as far as I know. It would be an incredible undertaking."

"They're very meticulous," Carstairs said. "Especially the Gestapo."

"You think it's possible, then?"

"Until we know otherwise, I think we should assume that Franks is being questioned."

Trentlyon nodded. "Should we alert the others?"

"No. Let's not yell fire yet. Besides, Franks—Copernicus —doesn't know who the other operatives are. If he's being held by the Gestapo and if they manage to make him talk —what can they learn?"

"Pythagoras."

"Which will mean nothing to them. A code name. And that's all Franks knows himself."

"And they'll kill him," Trentlyon said.

"Yes, they will." Carstairs closed the file. "I'm sorry about that." He looked at Trentlyon. "Truly, I am. But the Germans can learn nothing from him that might jeopardize the operation overall." He took a coin from his watch pocket and rolled it absently between his fingers. "Pythagoras is still safe," he said.

It was a silver coin, a 1780 Maria Theresa thaler, and he rolled it between his fingers with quiet agitation while his tea turned cold and Trentlyon paced silently before the window.

Ted called for his clothes at the little laundry shop on the Unter den Linden a few blocks from his hotel and tried not to look nervous. He was just picking up some shirts, he told himself, nothing suspicious about that. There were two women in front of him and he smiled as one of them inadvertently glanced his way.

She knows! he convinced himself the instant she returned his smile. She knows I'm not here just to pick up some goddamn shirts!

But no one knew. Just Ted and his laundress. And Trentlyon.

"When you return to Berlin," Carstairs' deputy had said, "there is a small laundry shop on the Unter den Linden. The

Kronberg Waschanstalt. Go there. Establish an account. Whenever you have information that you *must* pass to us, put it in a shirt pocket in your laundry and deliver the bundle to the shop. Likewise, if and when we make contact with you, it will be in the same manner. A shirt pocket."

At the time, it had sounded pretty easy.

At the moment, it was sweaty. But no one even looked twice at him, except the woman at whom he kept staring.

Back in his hotel room he ripped into the brown paper parcel of shirts and searched every pocket. Nothing. He'd only just sent the note the day before and it was unlikely he'd get something back so quickly, but Trentlyon had never said how long it would take for messages to be acknowledged.

He showered, shaved and dressed. This evening was a dinner party at Haushofer's, but Ted wasn't exactly in a dinner party mood. He'd heard from another correspondent this afternoon that the Germans had dynamited the French armistice monuments at Compiègne.

He hadn't expected a full-scale dinner party. He'd interpreted the invitation as Haushofer's way of arranging a discreet meeting, but there must have been thirty guests here tonight. Ted resigned himself to an evening of inane chit-chat. Well, that wasn't fair, exactly, he didn't know what sort of people Haushofer associated with socially. Probably an academic crowd or, more likely, cronies from the Foreign Office, since that was the hat Haushofer was wearing these days.

The professor greeted him at the entrance to the large living room, grasping Ted's hand in both of his. He nodded pleasantly to another couple as they entered then, still smiling and in a low voice, said to Ted, "When you leave, wait until the others are gone then come back." Haushofer released his hand and warmly greeted another guest.

Ted gave a startled nod, but Haushofer was already moving away. Wait? Wait where, for Chrissake?

But he didn't have a chance to dwell on it because he saw Kate coming toward him. And there was an SS officer with her.

"I guess they'll let anybody come to these things," she said, extending her hand. "Or did I say that last time?"

Ted took her hand. "Probably. You never were very original. How are you, Kate?"

"I'm eating better." She turned to her companion. "Ted, this is Major Johann Regenbauer."

"An honor to meet you, Herr Campbell," the SS major said with a slight bow. "Katherine has spoken highly of you."

Ted smiled. "Knowing Kate, that's a compliment indeed." He glanced at Regenbauer's diamond-shaped sleeve patch. "SD, Major?"

"Presently."

"I ought to spit in your eye," Kate told him. "I just found out you hooked up with Lowell Grayson at UP. You promised you'd come talk to me first."

"Microphones scare me to death. Besides, I can't read worth a damn."

"Fink."

"How do you like the journalism profession?" Regenbauer asked. "Is it as exciting as it seems?"

"I'm hardly a veteran," Ted said. "Less exciting without a war to cover, I expect." There was something he didn't like about Major Regenbauer. More than something. He was SS, for one. He was with Kate for another. "I imagine your work is much more exciting."

Regenbauer smiled. "At times."

Now he knew he didn't like him. Where did Kate dig this one up?

"Scuttlebutt is you're headed for France," Kate said. "Covering the air war, naturally."

"Naturally."

"Of course there aren't any armies left on the continent," she reminded him. "The next foxhole you see," she glanced at Regenbauer, "will be somewhere around Canterbury or Wimbledon."

The seating arrangement was premeditated to separate couples who came together. Ted was seated next to a fat Italian woman, on his right, a textile manufacturer's wife who spoke practically no German at all. On his left, surprisingly, was Kate. The major, Ted noted, was seated at the other end of the table.

"Look, Ted, I didn't want to say anything in front of Johann, but—" Kate touched his hand. "I don't do this very well and I won't embarrass you by repeating it . . . I just want to say that I'm sorry about your girl. There was a short notice in one of the UP dispatches. I really am sorry, Ted. I know it doesn't help, but . . ."

"Let's skip it then," Ted said solemnly. He squeezed her hand. "Thanks anyway." He took a sip of wine. He didn't want to have Anne on his mind. He had left that in England. "Let's start this over," he said to Kate. "Why don't you congratulate me on my new job?"

"You didn't have to, you know. You promised me. Why'd you go to Lowell anyway?"

"It just seemed like a better offer."

"Better! Since when do you need money?"

"It isn't that. Within reason, I'm allowed to go where I want, develop my own stories. Besides, you're the one who told me Grayson was the best newsman around."

"When did you start listening to me? Okay, okay, it's done. Let's talk about something else." She shifted to one side to allow the waiter to place the soup bowl. "Where do you know Haushofer from?"

"I've run into him a few times. He's a pal of Hess's. How about you?"

"First time I laid eyes on him was when I showed up here. I'm the American social item in Berlin, remember? Half the places I get invited to I've never met the host." She shrugged. "But it's good for business."

"Tell me about bullet head," he said.

"Who?"

"Your friend, the Aryan archetype."

"His name is Johann," Kate said indignantly. "Don't be insulting."

"Sorry. You see a lot of him, do you?"

"And then some."

Ted felt himself flush. "He doesn't seem like your type. You didn't used to go for the Charles Atlas image."

"I don't much care what you think." Anger blazed in her eyes. "I don't know why you're so fucking interested in my private life but it's none of your business."

Ted gave an embarrassed smile. "I'm sorry, Kate. Forget I said anything."

But she ignored him, centering her silent rage on her soup. She didn't speak to him throughout the rest of the meal and

Ted was left to interpret the broken German of the fat woman from Milan.

Kate was gone without a word the moment dinner was finished. The company withdrew to the living room where drinks were served and conversation was brisk, but he didn't see her again until she was saying good night to Haushofer with Regenbauer at her side. There was something the matter; Kate had never acted like this before, it was too sudden a transformation. She'd never have had anything to do with a man like Regenbauer. Never. People change, but they don't change that much. Ted was determined to understand. But it would have to wait. Right now he had to find out what the mysterious business with Haushofer was all about.

He waited until the party had thinned out then took his leave, walking out with an official of the Propaganda Ministry. He took a taxi to his hotel, had a drink in the bar and slipped out of the service entrance, feeling ridiculous. He knew he wasn't being followed, but he stopped frequently to look back over his shoulder. At the Potsdammer railway station he took a taxi to within a block of Haushofer's home, then walked to the next street where he could come up the alley to the courtyard entrance. Berliners, like Londoners, obeyed blackout regulations, and from the outside Haushofer's house appeared dark and forsaken. He lifted the latch on the gate and stepped inside the small courtyard.

No one had told him about the dog.

Ted had taken two steps when he heard it growl—a terrifying, stomach-wrenching sound from somewhere in the darkness behind him. He froze then in a moment of panic, started to turn. That's when the dog attacked. It hit Ted in the shoulder and knocked him to the ground, and Ted madly covered his face with his arms and rolled on his stomach. Evidently, the dog had not been trained to kill. It stood over him, its teeth bared, snapping the air around Ted's head between fierce snarls of warning. Ted didn't move. He didn't breath. He'd caught a glimpse of the animal as he went down. A German shepherd.

It was an eternity before he heard a door squeak.

"Wolfe! What is it, boy? Wolfe?"

Wolfe, for Chrissakes! He'd been attacked by a German shepherd named Wolfe!

"It's me, Albrecht," Ted whispered into the dirt. "Campbell."

"Herr Campbell?"

"Call off the dog!"

Haushofer snapped a command and the dog stopped growling. "Get up please . . . slowly."

Ted obeyed. Wolfe bared his teeth again when Ted glanced back at him from the door.

"Why did you come this way?" Haushofer asked.

Ted brushed away the dirt on his coat in embarrassed silence. Haushofer led the way into a study lined with bookshelves. It was a small room, lit by a brass lamp on a heavy desk. He pulled out a book, retrieved a bookmark and handed it to Ted. "You are to go to this place. Reichdammer Strasse. Number nine. You will meet a man who can help you."

"Help me what?"

"He's waiting for you now," the professor said. He crossed to the door nervously and turned back to Ted.

"I don't know what the hell you're talking about," Ted said. "What man?"

"Please go now. He'll explain it."

"Explain what?"

"You must go to Reichdammer Strasse now!" Haushofer pleaded.

But Ted wouldn't budge. "Is it Hess?"

"No."

"Then . . ."

Haushofer hurried back to his desk. He fumbled with some keys, unlocked a drawer and found something inside. "This will have to satisfy you." He opened his hand. It was the Maria Theresa silver thaler. "You are Alfred," the professor said. "The keyboard had fourscore and eight black and white keys." He clamped his fist over the coin and thrust it hastily into his pocket. "Now will you go?"

"Jesus Christ," Ted said. "You're part—"

But Haushofer didn't let him finish. "This way."

Ted followed him to the foyer and the door.

"When you find the address, don't knock. The door is not locked. Go in. He will be waiting."

Ted nodded as if it made perfect sense. Something brushed against his leg when Haushofer opened the door.

Wolfe.

Reichdammer Strasse was off Hildebrandstrasse, a narrow residential street near the Tiergarten, and he found it without trouble. The door led into a corridor and Ted followed it, feeling his way along the wall in the dark, until he bumped into a step and found another door. It opened before he had a chance to knock.

The man in the doorway shifted slightly so that the light from the room behind him fell on Ted's face and his own. "I expected you sooner," was all he said.

The man stepped back to admit Ted and the light fell across his face. Ted recognized him and stood gaping at him. It was the man from Goering's party. The IRA man who couldn't find a match.

"You!"

"Small bloody world, isn't it?"

"You're part of *this?*"

The man shut the door. "One part. Sit down, we've work to do."

"But . . ." Ted was still confused. "You're not Irish? You aren't with the IRA?"

"I'm from Belfast, true enough, as was that bit about my father. The rest of it is a mix of fact and fiction." He nodded to himself. "Part of the game, you know."

Ted felt like a fool for asking, but he didn't know what he was supposed to do. "Do you have an interest in pianos?" When the man laughed, Ted *knew* he was a fool for asking.

"I think we've passed the recognition stage."

"Look, dammit, I'm new at this," Ted snapped. He was more comfortable being angry because it helped mask his fear. "Who are you and what's the idea of making me sneak around in the middle of the night."

"You may call me Moser," the man said calmly. "It isn't my name, but you ought to call me something. As for why we're meeting, you said you needed some things."

"What do you know about it?"

"My shirts get dirty too." Moser smiled but there wasn't anything endearing behind it. "Now, what sort of identification papers did you have in mind?"

"First, I want to know why Carstairs didn't tell me that Haushofer was part of this Pythagoras setup."

"The professor isn't directly linked to it; he isn't a line agent. I am. He's more or less part of the command apparatus while I'm one of the blokes in the trenches."

"What does that make me?"

"I really couldn't say. Shall we get to business; the sooner we can finish this up, the sooner you can get out of here."

Ted shook his head. "That still doesn't tell me why Carstairs—"

"I don't know anyone by that name," Moser said.

"You don't?"

"Neither do you."

Ted gave him a suspicious look. "Maybe we'd better go back to the recognition sign again."

"If I were Gestapo, you'd already be dead." Moser sighed. "You've already connected Haushofer with the London control. I'd watch that. Now, about these identification papers . . ."

Ted rubbed his face with his hands. "Luftwaffe ID packet."

"Flying officer?"

"Yes, an Oberleutnant."

"Flying specialty?"

"Luftwaffe bomber pilot."

"Yes, I know that. Which bomber?"

"Does it matter?"

"All German pilots carry their flight-school certificates and a rating of the types of aircraft they are qualified to fly."

"I don't know which yet. It'll be either a Heinkel or a Dornier."

"Do you know which series?"

"They're both twin engine," Ted said. "The Heinkel is a one-eleven H series, the Dornier is the seventeen Z. I'll try for the Heinkel, but I don't know for sure."

"Then you'll need a rating for both. If this is a rush job, we won't have time to go back and change it. Don't worry, most pilots are double and triple rated. What else?"

"I'll need orders . . . signed by the previous unit's group commander."

Moser shook his head. "Too risky. If they checked, you'd be cooked. Better if you report to a new unit—they're forming them all over the place—after coming off leave. That way the orders will be signed by some Oberst in Berlin and it would take them days to run it down. Okay with you?"

Ted shrugged. "You're the expert. How come you're not taking any of this down?"

"Don't worry," he tapped a finger to his forehead—"I've got it. You'll also need an ID chain. What's your blood type?"

"O positive."

"Party member?"

"That's important?"

"Only if you know the drill. Do you?"

"No," Ted said.

"Then you're not a member. What are you, about six foot?"

"And a quarter."

"Blue eyes, blonde hair . . . what do you weigh?"

"One eighty-five."

Moser nodded. "Okay. Anything else?"

"I'm not really sure. What about permits and ration cards. Licenses. Incidental stuff."

"I'll see what I can do, but the ID and orders are the priority items, right?"

"Yes."

"I'll need a photograph. In uniform. Can you do that?"

"If I have to."

"Put it in your laundry." Moser leaned against the wall. "Do you know what name you'll use?"

"I thought you'd tell me."

"No. It has to be something familiar to you, something you won't forget. You're the one who has to use it."

"I don't know. I . . . I haven't—"

"Send it in the laundry with the photograph," Moser said. "That'll give you some time to think about it. But don't wait too long—three days at the most. Practice writing the name several times until you're comfortable with it then write it out on a clean slip of paper and put it with the picture. And the picture should be small. Passport size. You got that?"

"Yeah." Ted tapped his forehead. "I fucking better."

"There's one more thing, Campbell. I don't know if anyone mentioned it before." Moser was standing beside the door, his fingers resting lightly on the handle.

"What?"

"If the Krauts ever find out what you're doing, you won't have your American citizenship to protect you."

"Yes, I *know* that, Moser." Ted was anxious to leave. He

wanted to put this grim little man and 9 Reichdammer Strasse far behind him.

"You're not a journalist or a Yank businessman or a flying buddy of Herman Goering's anymore. You're a British agent in Germany and the only friend you have in this town is me. You'd be wise to remember that."

"I haven't *done* anything yet," Ted said lamely.

"You came here," Moser said, "and met me. That's all the Gestapo need. You became a spy and an enemy of the Reich the moment you stepped into this room." He opened the door and with a hint of a smile on his lips he said, "Welcome to M16."

Outside, Ted turned up the collar of his coat against the glow of a street lamp. He kept to the shadows and listened carefully to the sounds of his footsteps on the pavement as he made the long walk back to the Adlon. For the middle of August, it seemed a very cold night.

21 _____

SOMETIME DURING THE night a fire had started in the western
suburb of Ravensburg. It had a peculiar origin, because it
started in the attic of the local volunteer fire station and
because, by the time the alert had been sounded, the station
house and its equipment were consumed in flames and there
was nothing to prevent the fire from spreading before firefight-
ing equipment from Ravensburg proper arrived.

Karl had called first thing in the morning with the news. The
fire station that burned down was adjacent to the Campbell
Aircraft manufacturing plant and when the fire spread it made
an astonishing leap over a metal fence, a forty-yard strip of
barren land and a cement parking ramp to ignite inside a
corrugated metal fuel storage shed. The explosion that followed rained burning fuel on the main complex, which burned
until dawn. What Ted now owned in the western suburb of
Ravensburg was ten acres of severely charried ground.

No one thought it was particularly remarkable that a fire
could do such a thing. No one except Ted and Karl.

Ted got the message. There wasn't anything he could do
about it that wouldn't result in the destruction of what was left
of Campbell Aircraft in Germany. Carstairs was right: it didn't
belong to Ted anymore. When he finally realized the fact of it,
it wasn't so difficult to let go. Campbell Aircraft didn't exist
anymore.

Ted flew to Friedrichshafen, packed up his housekeeper, Frau Glebe, and sent her to Munich with instructions to make travel arrangements to Switzerland as soon as possible. Karl and his family, German nationals, were not as easy to get out of the country, but he knew some people in the appropriate ministries who owed him favors and now was the time to collect on them.

He spent three days in Friedrichshafen, closing up the villa, shutting down the hangar and small airfield to a maintenance-level operation, and seeing that Karl was taken care of. To anyone that asked he explained that he was moving to Berlin to work for the United Press and that the company was in good hands in the meantime.

He spent an entire afternoon in the darkroom at the villa developing film he'd taken of himself. He tried different shades of washable hair dyes, and discarded the idea of a false mustache. There was less risk, he reasoned, in being recognized without one than in taking a chance that the damned thing might come off. He found that he did not need a uniform for the photograph. The Luftwaffe identification picture was taken without a hat and cropped so that the only uniform visible was between the shoulder patches and above the first tunic button. It was fairly easy to make that much of a uniform. He did not have to steal one.

When Ted finally returned to his Berlin hotel room, he found a dozen messages from Grayson. Demands to come to the office. Threats to get in touch with him at once. Well, Grayson was just going to have to wait. Ted had one more item to wrap up.

He'd tried and discarded hundreds of names because they simply sounded phony or were too hard to remember. Nothing seemed to fit Moser's criteria—*it must be familiar to you, something you won't forget.*

When it came to him he wondered why it took so long. He was Alfred to Carstairs and Trentlyon, so Alfred would be his given name. The surname he decided on was one he wouldn't forget because it had come to be an important name to him. To give it a Germanic ring he dropped two letters, but that did not diminish its importance to him. Grayson was responsible for that. *It means something . . . just keep him in the back of your mind . . . you aren't Bennett Horner and you never will be . . .*

He wrote the name out several times until he was comfortable with it, then he wrote it on a clean slip of paper. A for Alfred was going to do something goddamn important in this war even if Ted was the only one who knew it. Then he placed it in a pocket of one of his shirts, just as Moser had instructed, folded around the photograph of the man who was sometime soon to be Luftwaffe Oberleutnant Alfred Horn.

22 _____

HERMANN GOERING CONTEMPLATED one of the new paintings that had just been delivered to his collection in a large room at Karinhall. It was a Rubens, depicting a plump, rosy-fleshed shepherdess leading her flock to a swift-running stream.

He was in robe and slippers, pacing back and forth before the easel, smoking a cigarette.

"It tells us two things about the artist," he remarked to his wife. "He knew how young women ought to look and he knew very little about sheep." He regarded his wife with a stern look. "They won't drink from a running stream. You know the Twenty-Third Psalm? 'He leadeth me beside the still waters.' You must lead a sheep to still water if you expect it to drink."

"What a treasure trove of information you are," she said.

"It is altogether too lovely a thing to languish in a French museum," he said, ignoring her sarcasm, but even now, as he scrutinized the painting, he was suddenly unmoved by the art of Peter Paul Rubens. There was a restlessness within him that paracodeine did not seem to reach. He wondered briefly it it might be sensible to increase the dosage, but was interrupted by a servant who told him the Fuehrer wished to speak to him on the telephone.

It was Bormann on the line first, of course; the Fuehrer did not dial his own calls. Goering forced himself to be civil to the obsequious little toad, biding his time until the Fuehrer came on the wire.

The conversation was brief, but when he returned to the drawing room his eyes glowed.

"The Fuehrer has congratulated me," he announced to his wife. "The leaflet raid was a success. A report filtered back from our agents in London. The propaganda has a definite demoralizing effect on the Londoners as well as the personnel at the airfields."

"That's wonderful, darling," Emmy Goering replied.

"Yes," he said, "wonderful," and then began pacing in front of the painting again.

"Then why are you troubled?"

Goering stopped. "You see straight through me." He sighed. "He's been listening to Hess again, I think. He still believes the English will capitulate."

"And you think he's wrong?"

A pulse worked in his temple and he pressed his fingertips against the pain. "I never think he's wrong," he said fervently. "He is a great man, a genius."

"But you think the British will fight?"

"I don't know. I'm prepared for it. What I do believe—and here we deal with an area where I know what I am talking about—is that the only way to proceed is through the destruction of the British Air Force."

He was striding about the room, slapping at his hip to emphasize the points he was trying to make. "You wish to force the British to accept our peace tenders?—smash the RAF and they will turn peaceable. You wish to invade their island? —smash their RAF and Raeder's invasion fleet sails across the Channel. You wish to destroy their industrial capacity?— smash their RAF and you can bomb their factories to rubble. Air supremacy is everything, Emmy, and until we have it everything else is unimportant."

"You have explained this to the Fuehrer?"

"He knows it."

"Then—"

"And he calls to congratulate me on peppering the British with leaflets. Leaflets!"

Frau Goering said nothing. The Reichsmarschall's hand went to his breast pocket, withdrew the pillbox. He popped one of the capsules into his mouth and swallowed.

"There is a new writer in one of Goebbels' departments at the Propaganda Ministry," he said. "So for a time we must contend with leaflets. I suppose the Fuehrer must toss that yapping Goebbels a bone now and then. Perhaps he has to play us one against the other. It's part of his genius, after all, as a leader of men." Goering's large head nodded. "Still . . . I blame Hess for this. Hess is in love with the British."

"But Herr Hess is behind you, Hermann, in the party order. Surely the Fuehrer doesn't take his advice over yours."

"Hess is an orator," Goering admitted, "while I'm a man of action. But in several days' time I shall have my chance to show him what my air force can do. Then we shall see." He nodded to himself. "Still, one wishes to have representation on all fronts. I wish there were a way to stop Hess's mouth. Something that would convince the Fuehrer how strong the Luftwaffe is."

"Perhaps an article in *Volkische Beobachter* . . ."

Goering shook his head.

"—or *Der Angriff* . . ."

"I would not go to that deformed little mouse-doctor Goebbels for help!" Goering snickered. "Anyway, it should be spontaneous—or seemingly so—from a source unconnected with the party organ."

"There was a very complimentary article a few days ago," Emmy said. "On field marshals Kesselring and Sperrle."

"Yes!" Goering said loudly. "Of course. My friend, the American. He's writing for the news service these days." He clapped his hands together. "Yes! He's an authority on the subject. He knows my Luftwaffe. I must call him the first thing tomorrow. Oh, Emmy, you are a great, dear woman!"

She glanced up. "You are the great one, Hermann." Frau Goering squinted at the painting then as if acknowledging it for the first time. "But I don't think I like the artist so much. Why does he make the sheep so fat?"

Kate lit two Lucky Strikes from the night table, rolled back against Regenbauer under the sheet, and handed him a cigarette. She was exhausted; Regenbauer had been especially ardent tonight and she was sore from their lovemaking. She was learning how to cope with him, she thought. He opened up more after sex. But it was the preliminary stage that wore Kate out. He enjoyed hearing her cry out; he *wanted* it, as if the pain of her sexual ecstasy was the excitement he responded to, not the pleasure of it. He wanted to hurt her, Kate realized, to thrust into her and cause her pain, because it was the ultimate demonstration of his will over hers.

But now was the payoff, Kate thought. She'd suffered through the torture as if she were being interrogated and now it was the time to get to business.

"I'll miss your Lucky Strikes," Regenbauer said. He was lying on his back, his head on the mattress, staring at the ceiling.

Kate lay beside him on her elbow, drawing circles on his chest with a finger. "Why, you going someplace?"

"Yes," he sighed. "Tomorrow."

Her fingers stopped. "You are? Where?"

"I'll be back in a few days. You mustn't worry."

"But when will you be back? A few days? What does that mean?"

"Not long."

"You don't want to talk about it, right?"

"I don't mind talking about it, but you don't need to know where I'll be." He flicked an ash on the floor. "Do you remember the man I mentioned before—the man with the coin?"

"The one who died?" Kate nodded. "I remember."

"He *was* a spy."

"I thought you already established that."

Regenbauer glanced at her. "It's a conspiracy of spies. He was only one of many."

"And you're going to pick up the rest of them?"

He got up from the bed, walked to the dresser where he stubbed out the cigarette. Kate watched as he turned back to her.

"Will you miss me?" He'd come around to her side of the bed.

"You know I will." Kate exhaled a cloud of smoke, then set the cigarette in the ashtray on the night table.

"You'll miss our times together?"

"I just said so."

"Tell me you will miss our fucking." He smiled.

"Johann . . ."

"Tell me!"

"I'll miss our fucking." He was smiling, Kate grew frightened. You couldn't tell what he was going to do.

"Say it again."

"I'll miss fucking you. You're the world's greatest goddamn
fucker. I love the way you fuck me. I won't be able to stand it
while you're gone." Kate took a breath. "How was that?"

She didn't have to ask. Regenbauer had folded his arms
across his chest, but his penis erected.

"Kiss it and tell it how you will miss him," he said.

Kate shook her head. She started to roll away, but Regenbauer caught her by the hair and jerked her back.

"Show me that you'll miss me," he said. He wasn't smiling.

"Why don't you just lie down—"

He yanked her with both hands in her hair. "Now!"

She kissed him.

"Again."

Kate obeyed. There were tears in her eyes; he was holding
her so tightly she couldn't see.

"Now, with your tongue," he said. "We should remember
this. We should have something to remember until the next
time."

She touched him with her tongue. She closed her eyes and
parted her lips. Then Regenbauer started pumping, slowly at
first, but steadily, building a rhythm, sliding willfully in long
measured strikes. Kate couldn't get her breath. She was
beginning to choke, but trying to disengage herself only made
him more determined. He was moving faster now, pushing and
pulling at her head, faster than he'd ever been before and she
was choking, gasping against him, beating with her arms,
flailing at him, fighting for air. He was in a frenzy now, and
she suddenly realized he wasn't going to stop this time, he
wasn't going to hold back, and she tried to grasp him, to hold
something—

When he came it was in three shuddering throbs, then she
felt herself pushed backwards. When she opened her eyes she
was crying hysterically on the bed, rasping for air.

Regenbauer was sitting on the edge of the bed, finishing her
cigarette.

"Baas . . . stard . . ."

Regenbauer glanced at her as if she were a thing to study. "Yes," he said. "I think it was something we shall both remember." He smiled.

That was when Kate decided she would kill him.

23

EAGLE DAY, the date for Goering's air assault on England, was postponed three times.

Electrical storms were the reason for the delay, according to correspondents with contacts inside the Reich Air Ministry, but Ted knew better. To Goering's annoyance, his two Luftwaffe Air Fleet commanders, Kesselring and Sperrle, were quarreling over operational plans of the assault. Kesselring wanted to attack large population centers in terror raids that would force Churchill to the peace table. Sperrle bitterly opposed the idea. RAF bases and supply factories were the heart of England's strength, he argued, and they must be the principal targets if there were to be an invasion of the island.

All of which took time.

All of which was all right with Ted. Every squabble meant another conference between the principals. And every conference delayed the attack.

Ted needed every minute. New airfields in France were springing up nearly every day while others were being closed or moved. Luftwaffe group commanders were reassigned as fast as he could look them up; it was going to be difficult to forge transfer orders to a particular tactical squadron with the correct unit commander's name. And that wasn't the only problem. Each flight of bombers would be using a radio beam transmission system to guide it to targets at night. Ted did not

211

know how it worked: worse, he did not know yet how he would find London at twenty thousand feet in the dark.

The most critical problem had come disguised as a blessing: Hermann Goering.

The Reichsmarshal had called last week. He'd been in a jubilant, cooperative mood and talked for more than an hour. He congratulated Ted and wished him the very best in his new role of correspondent. Would Ted like to see the Luftwaffe in action? Would he care to tour bases in France? Was there anything the Reichsmarshal could do to cut through the red tape normally encountered by a foreign correspondent in the war zones?

Ted at first couldn't believe his good luck. It was manifestly apparent what Goering wanted—glowing press coverage of his mighty Luftwaffe by a man who knew what he was talking about. Without thinking it through, Ted accepted. But it didn't take long to realize just what he'd done to himself. Goering, in his zest to satisfy Ted's journalistic wants and needs, had arranged for him special, uninhibited access to any airfield or unit command in France or Belgium. That part was good. But it also meant that the individual commanders would be expecting him. That part wasn't so good. Not for a man who was trying to sneak into a bomber squadron with phony papers as a Luftwaffe pilot.

The more he thought about it, the more he realized that that part wasn't too good at all. As a matter of fact, it was going to be goddamn bloody hazardous.

Eagle Day came on a Tuesday.

It started at three forty-five in the afternoon; the first wave of 150 bombers struck at Southampton, Britain's largest port.

In all, there were fifteen hundred German sorties against England that afternoon. From a historical standpoint, considering the tonnage of explosives dropped and the loss of life and property, it was the most devastating afternoon in recorded time.

But the next day was even worse and the day after that more brutal still.

What surprised Ted, and what he realized must have been a shock to Goering, was that RAF Fighter Command—out-manned, out-planed and out-gunned—was putting up a tremendous fight. What the British gave up in numbers, they made up in sheer tenacity. And their tactics weren't bad either. Instead of sending up fighters plane for plane, Fighter Command scattered its Spitfires and Hurricanes to attack bomber formations like bees on a bull. After the first week the RAF's losses were staggering, but so were the Luftwaffe's. Hitler was in a rage. Goering had promised to wipe the RAF from the skies in a matter of days, but they were still there, pecking away at the mighty German air force, jeopardizing the time-table for the invasion.

Still, time was against the British and Ted knew it. England was barely hanging on. The final, massive blow was coming. Goering himself had explained it to him.

"The days of mere dogfighting over the Channel are finished," the Reichsmarshal expounded.

They were drinking wine on a second-story balcony at Karinhall with a veiw of Goering's private hunting preserve. Ted had called the day before when he heard the Luftwaffe chief had returned from his command post at Cap Blanc-Nez on the Channel coast. It was to be a private interview with the Reichsmarshal on the conduct of the war, but Goering had dismissed that and rather welcomed Ted to dine with him, not as a journalist, but as a friend. Apparently, Ted figured, he needed one just now.

"The second phase of the grand plan will begin in just a few days." Goering sipped his wine. It wasn't easy to tell when the Reichsmarshal was drunk, but Ted guessed that he was loose enough to risk a couple of probing questions.

"Sounds very ominous," Ted said. "What I hear around the Air Ministry is there is a big gear-up . . . leaves being canceled, air crew reserves being posted to France." Ted shrugged. "Sounds big." Of course, he hadn't heard any such thing.

"Yes, we're going to give the RAF a big surprise."

"Stepped-up bombing raids?"

The Reichsmarshal lifted a finger to his lips. "Shhh—it's a secret." He sipped some more wine. "But I think you can appreciate the situation. You probably can guess what we are going to do."

Ted tried not to hold his breath. "More raids, then."

Goering nodded. "Ceaseless attacks. Around the clock, day and night bombing. We will force the English to use their fighter squadrons and then we will erase their air power from the face of the earth." The Luftwaffe Commander in Chief burped, then covered his mouth. "Annihilation, is what we will do to them."

"I wonder if I have time to still get to the French coast," Ted said, half to himself. "That's a sight I'd like to see, Reichsmarshal."

"You haven't been yet? You haven't gone to tour the airfields?"

"Some," Ted lied. "Haven't you read my dispatches?"

"Oh, yes, of course." Which was also a lie, Ted knew, unless Goering had recently learned to read English. The wire services had not been used in German newspapers since Eagle Day. Biased reporting, Goebbels had pronounced.

"I'd like to be at the Channel to see the first wave," Ted said. "If I left for France in the next day or two—"

"I would not wait too long," Goering said with a wink. "I would want to be there by the weekend, if I were you."

"Saturday?" Ted said, "the twenty-fourth?"

The Reichsmarshal shrugged. "Perhaps." He poured himself some more wine. "But I wouldn't want you to miss it. It will make the Eagle Day raids look like a kite contest."

Ted smiled and toasted his host with his half-filled glass, but his mind was whirling. Saturday was only four more days. He had to get to an airfield by Friday. He had to get in a bomber *and be on that raid!*

"Skoal!" Hermann Goering said, raising his glass. "To Germany."

"Mud in your eye," Ted replied.

24 _____

THURSDAY WAS TENSE from the moment Ted got out of bed. He hadn't slept well, first off, and he hadn't slept long; there was so much to do, to plan, that he'd spent hours last night, after returning from Karinhall, organizing a priority schedule.

Paramountly, he had to have the identity papers. So his first stop in the morning was at his neighborhood laundry. The message his shirt delivered was urgent:

ABSOLUTELY MUST HAVE PAPERS TONIGHT. WILL MEET
MOSER SAME TIME, PLACE. URGENT.

A.

Someone had better know that that meant urgent with a capital U! But meeting Moser was only one of the items on the agenda today. Grayson was next.

"So, you think the main event is going to start Saturday?" Grayson said. "Very interesting."

Ted had found him at the Adlon restaurant having breakfast and browsing through a six-week-old edition of the *Kansas City Star* that had arrived in the mail.

Grayson folded the paper to the editorial page. "I assume your source is reliable."

"I would say so," Ted said.

215

"Dinner at Karinhall go well last night?" Grayson dabbed a napkin to the corner of his mouth.

"Fairly well, I guess."

Grayson regarded him quietly a moment. "You have the best damn contacts of anyone in this city. That makes me jealous, you know that? Hermann Goering, for Chrissake!"

"Maybe you'd rather I worked for someone else."

"Don't be a peckerhead."

"I'm making arrangements to go to France," Ted said. "Okay?"

"Where?"

"Calais, I think. That's where most of the action will be, above the straits. It'll be a front row seat, I expect." Calais would be a good jumping-off place, Ted thought. It was a Luftwaffe staging point for transferring officers, and he'd have an easy time of melting into the mob of troops reporting to their new assignments.

"That's fortunate for us," Grayson said. "Goebbels has authorized a press plane from Berlin to Brussels and Lille. I imagine that is his way of assuring coverage. We don't usually get a plane out of the propaganda minister so easily."

"When does it leave?"

"Tomorrow noon, but we'll have to be at Templehof long before then. I'm sure there will be transportation between Lille and Calais that we can hop."

Ted glanced up sharply. "We?"

"It's a plural pronoun, Campbell. We as in us. You and me. You may be the airplane expert and Goering's fair-haired boy, but I'm the United Press bureau chief and sure as hell not going to miss what may be the biggest Luftwaffe air strike of the war. Of course I'm going."

Of course. Why should anything be easy?

Colonel Helmut Junger was becoming a first-class chum of Ted's lately. The good colonel was his primary font of knowledge, from the location and movement of heavy bomber squadrons in France to the news that Reichsmarshal Goering had returned from his Channel command post two days earlier. He was a talkative fellow, but he had an obsessive preoccupation on the subject of Greta Garbo that bordered on lunacy. He was a good source, but the trouble was getting him around to or back on the topic. Like now.

"I think *Ninotchka* was the best of all," Junger was saying. They were in his office, a respectably large room for a colonel. "They say *Anna Karenina* or *Camille* were her best films, but I think *Ninotchka* shows a fuller range of her talent. Don't you agree?"

"I liked *Grand Hotel*, myself," Ted said, trying not to seem impatient. He'd only gone to see two Garbo films in his life, so he wasn't exactly an expert on the subject. Still, it was useful to humor the colonel. He was more cooperative when humored.

"Yes, but she wasn't quite right for the part, I thought," Junger continued. "Not that she wasn't superb, but a ballerina?" He shook his head.

"I guess it is a little hard to imagine her getting sweaty."

Junger wagged a finger at him. "They should not have put Joan Crawford in the same film, you see."

Ted nodded. "I ran across something that really has me fascinated, but I don't for the life of me understand how the thing works."

Junger raised an eyebrow. *"Bitte?"*

"It's this radio beam guidance system that the night bombers use to find their targets in England."

"Knickebein?"

"Yeah," Ted said. "Why do they call it that—crooked leg?"

The Luftwaffe colnel shook his head. "You know I cannot—"

"You know me better than than," Ted cut in. "I wasn't asking as a journalist. Hell, I know better. But the navigational problems it must solve! Can you imagine what it means to a pilot to know that there is a system that simplifies night navigation? And I hear it's pinpoint accurate."

"Naturally."

"Well?"

Junger heaved a sigh.

"I'm just curious," Ted said. "Hell, no, I'm crazy to know how it works. Besides, who the hell am I going to tell?"

"I don't suppose you know any spies, eh?" Junger smiled.

"Hundreds," Ted said, "but they're so goddamn dumb they wouldn't know a crooked leg from a bent prick. Anyway, do I look like Mata Hari?"

The colonel's smile grew wider. "No, my friend, I cannot imagine that you even slightly resemble her." He laughed then.

"In 1932—she made that film. *Mata Hari*." He laughed again and pointed at Ted. "Yes, *Mata Hari!* I saw it three times, no . . . no, four times. It was her third talking film."

"Well, isn't that swell." Ted felt the conversation get away from him.

"Such a woman . . . such a beautiful woman. And to think that we are related!"

"But the *Knickebein*," Ted insisted. "What about—"

Junger waved him off. "I'll tell you, I'll tell you. It's nothing. Dots and dashes. I can explain it in two minutes."

But he didn't, at least not right off. First there was the tale of Ernst-Carl Arvid, his uncle, and the drama of Greta Garbo's christening in the minutest detail. Ted waited because there wasn't anything else he could do. Just wait and hope he spent as much effort on describing the radio beam because this was the only chance Ted was going to have to learn about it before he had to fly with it.

Ted checked with his laundress late in the afternoon only to be informed that there wouldn't be anything for him until the next day. He didn't know how he was supposed to interpret that. Did it mean there wasn't any message or his shirts weren't clean yet? If the woman who operated the shop was part of the pipeline setup, she gave no hint of it. So Ted nodded and said he'd be back tomorrow. He could only hope that Moser would show up tonight.

He returned to the UP office and spent an hour writing a story on the professional efficiency of the Air Ministry staff. It was a fluff piece that complimented the German penchant for orderliness and competence in the running of a war. He filed the story, met briefly with Grayson about transportation from Lille to Calais, and spent a boring dinner with an aide to the Chief of Air Staff. Afterwards, he had a round of drinks with a group of UP correspondents at the Adlon bar then went to his room and tried to get an hour's sleep. By the time he had slipped out of his room, taking the stairs and leaving by way of the service entrance, Ted was shaking with tension and fatigue. He was more nervous now than he had been the first time he went to meet Moser. He was sure he wasn't being followed, but, then, what did he know about it? He didn't know how to double-check for tails.

Which was why Ted was so goddamn careful. He walked to

the subway station across the plaza from the Brandenburg Gate and took a train to Leipzieger Plaza, came back toward the Chancellery, then through the linden-lined Tiergarten, past the zoo, to the fountain at Gassestern Allee, across the boulevard and around the square to Reichdammer Strasse. It had taken him forty fearful minutes to get from his hotel to this rendezvous point and if anyone had suddenly stepped out of the dark to ask him what he thought he was doing, he didn't have the faintest idea of a logical or coherent reply. At least he'd arrived without being run over or dragged off to a Gestapo torture cell.

The door at number nine was locked.

When he tried it the first time he thought it was only that his hand was sweaty. The second time he used a firmer grip. It was still locked and no amount of wrenching at the handle was going to alter the fact. Moser wasn't here. Nobody was here. He was standing in front of a locked door on a dark street in the middle of goddamn Berlin, his shirt soaked in perspiration after he'd risked his life to get here, and no one was home. He'd come for nothing.

He heard the sound of a door unlatch. A car door.

Without turning around to see, Ted began walking away. When he thought of running, it was too late, because he heard the car start up, saw the glow of headlights reflected against the pavement, and he knew that if he did run the occupant of the car would shoot him down before he got ten feet.

They must have been waiting the whole time.

Christ, why did he come tonight! Moser must have known something and called it off. That's why his shirts weren't ready. Goddammit, she said there wasn't anything for him until tomorrow! He was a jerk for coming; an *idiot*.

"Get in, Campbell."

The car had pulled up beside him. Ted didn't respond. He was too frightened to turn because he knew he'd be looking into a Lüger and he really didn't want to see the flash of light when the gun exploded a bullet into his brain. Well, he wasn't going to make it easy for them. He wanted to run, but his legs disobeyed.

"Get in, for Chrissakes!"

It was Moser.

• • •

"You didn't have to scare the shit out of me, you know. You didn't have to do that. You could have said 'Hey, Ted, it's Moser,' or 'Hey, Alfred.' But—Christ!—you scared the hell out of me."

Ted was in the front seat beside Moser, wiping his face with a handkerchief. They were on the Kurfurstendamm, headed east, and Moser was smoking a cigarette and steering with one hand.

"I wasn't sure it was you," Moser said. "I figured it was, but I wasn't sure until you tried the door."

"Why didn't we meet—"

"I don't like using the same place twice," Moser cut in. "It's a chancy business, us meeting at all." He cast a quick glance at Ted. "And you're only supposed to use the laundry drop when you absolutely have to."

"I had to," Ted snapped back. "The flight, it's on for Saturday. I had to get the papers tonight. I'm leaving tomorrow. Did you bring them?"

Moser slid a small package out of his coat pocket and handed it to Ted. "ID chain, Luftwaffe identity papers, and your orders."

Ted slipped it into his jacket. "Thank God."

"Don't get on your knees yet, Campbell. That's all there is in there. We didn't have time to get out any incidentals like driver's license or civilian work permits. What you have there is strictly your military identification, but it'll have to do. If anyone asks for more than that you'll have to bluff your way out of it. Another couple of days and we could have made you a dozen permits and licenses or promoted you to governor-general of Poland, but there just wasn't time."

Ted nodded. "I'll just have to work with what I've got. What about the orders? Which airfield am I reporting to and which unit?"

"Fliegerdivision Nine, Second Bomber Group, Squadron Four," Moser said. "Soesterberg."

"Soesterberg! Christ, Soesterberg's not in France, it's in bloody Holland!"

"It's also Fliegerdivision headquarters, Generalmajor Joachim Coeler, but it's the best we could so."

"I'm leaving for Calais tomorrow. *Calais!* How am I supposed to get from Calais to goddamn Soesterberg without alerting the entire Luftwaffe in three countries that I'm not who I claim to be?"

"Don't rip a gasket, old man. How are you getting to Calais?"

"Fly to Lille by way of Brussels. Drive from there to the coast."

"Brussels?"

"It's a press plane. We're picking up some more people while we refuel."

"Then that's where you'll have to get off."

"Get off?" Ted exclaimed. "Just like that! I'm traveling with the bureau chief to cover the biggest operation of the war and I should just get off? You're a big help, Moser. I can't hop off a plan in goddamn Brussels and just disappear."

"How were you going to do it in Calais?"

He could get away on his own once he got to Calais, Ted tried to explain patiently, because other reporters would be slipping away to get a private perspective on the war.

Moser listened thoughtfully. "Then we'll have to disable your plane in Brussels. Can you slip away from the others if everyone is suddenly looking for transportation?"

Ted shrugged. "How are you going to disable the plane, first of all?"

Now Moser shrugged. "Belgium is full of patriots who don't care for Germans."

"So?"

"We could blow it up."

"*We* could?"

"I don't mean you; that's our department. Don't worry, one way or another we'll see that you're separated from the rest of the correspondents."

Ted didn't quite like the way he put that, but he nodded.

"How about your flight gear," Moser said. "You got everything you need?"

"Yes, everything." Ted smiled to himself. Goering had made him a present of a complete Luftwaffe flying suit —jacket, gloves, boots, breeches—when Ted was touring the airfields and manufacturing plants last spring.

"Uniform?"

"No, I'll wear the flight suit. With the flying jacket I can get by and—"

"I told you to get a bloody uniform, for Chrissake!" He

glanced sharply at Ted. "You mean you *don't* have a uniform?"

"I'm a lousy thief. Besides, half the crews probably don't have a full uniform. They've been so busy flying combat missions they wouldn't remember what a full—"

"Active duty crew members!" Moser snapped. "You're talking about pilots on active duty. Christ, are you always this dumb?"

"What—"

"First, you're reporting to a line squadron after supposedly being on three weeks' leave. You would not report to the squadron group leader in a goddamn flight uniform. Second, your orders show that you haven't flown a combat mission since May, remember, we couldn't take a chance that you might run into someone who might have been in the same squadron if we said you'd been flying runs over England. That, by the way, should help you if you run into something unfamiliar in procedure—they'll just think you're new. But the point is, Campbell, a new guy fresh in from the hinterland would be dressed in a spiffy, button-polished, clean and creased full Luftwaffe uniform."

Ted opted to stare out the window. "Oh," he managed to say.

"You're a pip, you know that? How the hell did you have that photograph made without a uniform?"

"I made it, the insignias, I mean. " All of a sudden it didn't seem like such an accomplishment. "Out of a piece of cloth."

"Christ!"

"Look, Moser, I'm sorry, okay?"

"You're going to *have* to have a uniform."

Ted nodded.

"Obviously. *I'm* going to have to find one for you."

Ted sighed.

"You *do* know how to fly a plane—a Heinkel one eleven H — or should I help you with that too?"

"Don't be a pip," Ted said.

They drove in silence for several minutes past the Charlottenburg railway station then south to Grunewald and finally north on Potsdammerstrasse, back toward the center of the city and Ted's hotel.

"Do you know what the *Knickebein* is?" Ted said to break the silence.

"A navigational system to home bombers to targets in England," Moser said. "Yeah, I know a little about it. Why?"

"Do you know where the transmitter stations are? If I knew which station was transmitting the beam, it might help me locate London a bit easier." He glanced at Moser. "I'll find it anyway," he added, "but if I knew—"

"They're all over the place. Mostly along the Channel. But the Germans don't make the transmission assignments until a few hours before missions."

Ted nodded. "It's okay." Then he looked back at Moser and said, "Look, I'm sorry about the uniform. I've had a lot on my mind and, well, I just didn't think . . ." He looked away again. "Shit."

"Forget it."

"I'm not too good at intrigue."

"After Saturday, you won't have to be. Besides, I don't think I'd have the balls to try anything as ambitious as what you're about to do—even if I knew how to fly."

"It isn't done yet," Ted said. "And it only counts if it works." He allowed himself a grim smile. "It looked a lot easier, scratching it out on paper, when I was safe in London with a Scotch whiskey to take the edge off."

"I guess I should tell you to keep your chin up or something inspiring."

"Do you know something inspiring?"

Moser steered with one hand as he lit another cigarette. "Good luck."

Ted snorted. "That's inspiring?"

"If we had more time," Moser said with a wry smile, "we'd have brought Churchill over to give you one of his specialities, but—"

They finished together "—there just wasn't time."

It was the first moment Ted had felt untroubled in days. The tension that had built up inside him suddenly drained away and he laughed.

"I'm going to drop you at the Leipzieger bahnhof," Moser said. "You can catch a train back to your hotel."

"I hate to bring it up again, but what about the uniform?"

Moser frowned. "I might be able to get one before you leave, but it'll be a problem—getting it to you. I'll just have to arrange something for you when you get to Brussels. Someone will contact you there. He'll use the recognition code to contact you. Okay?"

"You're the expert."

Moser pulled the car up beside a darkened lamp post near the entrance to the subway station. "There's one other thing," he said. "We've more or less been watching over you since you showed up in Berlin." He held up his hand when Ted started to reply. "Quietly."

"I see," Ted said. "You want to remind me I'm not going to have this 'watching over' when I leave Berlin."

"You already know that," Moser said. "No, I just want to pass some information you should know . . . especially when you return."

"Yes?"

"There's another Yank in this city maybe you shouldn't be seen with any more. Another correspondent. She could make things embarrassing for you if they ever picked her up."

Ted looked sharply at Moser. "She?"

"Katherine Buchanan."

"Kate! But . . . how?—"

"She's a gopher for the Reds, the communist underground," Moser said. "Little stuff, mostly . . . whatever she can pick up at parties or socializing with the Nazi upper crust. She's a listener. She's really small potatoes, but it might be wise to be leery of her since you travel in that same crowd."

"Kate Buchanan?" Ted said again. "I don't believe it."

"Well, it's true."

"How do you *know* it's true!"

"I don't know why it's so upsetting to you. I'm just passing it along."

"I know Kate Buchanan. She's . . . we were pretty close once."

"Well, I'd keep my distance now. There's no sense in jeopardizing you . . . we don't want you being linked to an ill-fated Bolshevik operation."

"What do you mean ill-fated?"

Moser shook his head. "Forget I brought it up. You'd better shove off."

Ted grabbed Moser's arm. "I want to know what you mean by that! Are they in trouble?"

Moser sighed. "Half of them are amateurs, for one thing . . . like your friend."

"I suppose I'm a professional," Ted snapped. He shook his head. "Go on."

"We've known about them for a long time. We'd know more except our people are so afraid to have anything to do with them—their security is a joke. The Red Orchestra is what they call themselves, we've had it penetrated for some time. And if we can do it, it's only a question of time before the Gestapo sniffs them out."

Ted remembered the SD major with Kate. Regenbauer. "Could the Gestapo already know?"

Moser shrugged. "Could be."

"Find out," Ted said. "I want to know if she's in any danger. Will you do that?"

"If she is, there's nothing we can do to help her. You'd better understand that. *Do* you understand it?"

"Yeah," Ted said. "Sure."

He watched Moser's car disappear into the night, then he walked to the subway entrance. The nervousness was back; the sweaty palms and awful fear that tingles the tiny hairs on the back of your neck.

Half of them are amateurs.

Christ, Kate, what the hell are you into? What the hell are you doing!

He took the train to the bahnhof across from the Adlon Hotel and walked down the Wilhelmstrasse to his hotel. He wasn't thinking about the uniform or the radio beam or Soesterberg or the flight to England. He wasn't even thinking about Kate, not directly.

He was thinking about SS-Major Regenbauer and the way the bastard smiled.

25 _____

TRENTLYON HURRIED PAST the wall map of Europe to Carstairs' desk and slapped down the second-copy page from the communications center two floors below.

"Copernicus is alive!" he bleated. He held a hand to his heaving chest and nodded at the wrinkled paper. "He *was* picked up by the Gestapo but . . . but he escaped . . ." Trentlyon stopped to catch his breath. "He's been on the run for five days, but he's made it to Utrecht. God knows how he got a radio. He says he's hurt and wants help and—but he's alive, sir!"

Carstairs smoothed out the copy and read it for himself. "How was this sent?"

"By key, sir."

"Coded?"

"Not likely he still has his code book."

Carstairs nodded. "Of course. Still, rather risky transmitting in the clear, wouldn't you say?"

"Considering what he's been through, I'd say he deserves some lapse in judgment. He did transmit on his assigned frequency and at the correct time . . . if you're thinking it might be a Gestapo trick."

"That's precisely what I'm thinking."

Trentlyon took a long gasp of air and let it out slowly. "Naturally, you may be right, sir. I've no idea how long a man can stand up to prolonged torture, but—" he let out a sigh—"Franks would kill himself if it meant not compromising the operation."

"You know him?"

"We weren't exactly close, I wouldn't say that, but you develop a sense about some of the people in this line. And Quinby struck me as a man who would do whatever was necessary for the mission."

"I see." Carstairs leaned back in his chair. "Then, you think it *is* Copern—uh, Franks?"

"I'm inclined to, yes."

Carstairs got up from his chair and walked to the map. "Well, I'm not convinced. Not at all. Utrecht, he says. The message doesn't say where he'd escaped from." He studied the map. "Paris? Berlin? Hamburg? If he were picked up in Lyon and escaped from them there, why wouldn't he try and make it to Spain?"

"I'd guess if he were picked up in Lyon, the Germans already knew he was a British plant and they whisked him off to Germany. That's their routine. Obviously, *someone* discovered him." Trentlyon moved to the map and touched the pointer to Berlin. "If he went to Gestapo headquarters here . . . and escaped—" the pointer moved in a circular motion "—he certainly wouldn't go east or south; without some sort of help he couldn't get across the Baltic to Sweden . . . There's only west, into the Netherlands. It would be difficult, I'm not saying it wouldn't, but he does speak the language. And he's a competent agent. With a bit of luck, I think he could do it."

"But how did he find a radio?"

"It isn't difficult to make a key set. He's been trained for that sort of thing."

Carstairs studied the map for several moments. "Perhaps so." He turned and went back to his desk. "Before we set up any kind of attempt to get him out, I want solid verification. When's he due to make another transmission?"

"Not for a week, if he continues to stick by his Rome schedule."

"Then we'll wait a week."

"But, sir—"

"If he's survived this long, he can survive a bit longer. If he's dedicated as you say, he'll understand that. And if it's the Gestapo I expect we'll be getting this message every day. They won't be sure that our Copernicus was telling them the truth about his check date and time. In any case, we must wait for some sort of verification. That's all we can do, you know."

Trentlyon nodded. "Yes, sir, I understand."

Carstairs came around the desk and clapped his deputy on the back. "I wouldn't worry so much about our Mr. Quinby Franks. Your instincts are probably right. And when we're sure, then we'll have him out of there straightaway. We'll have old Franks back and chucking mail pouches for putting us through this, eh?

Trentlyon smiled then. "I'll drink to that."

But old Quinby Franks, the one-time administrative assistant to the Swiss cuptural affairs consul in Rome, hadn't escaped from the Gestapo. His interrogators went a step too far and Quinby swallowed his tongue and choked to death. But, by then, there wasn't much more he could have said to them.

He'd already told them about Orin Kepler and how Quinby Franks came to be an infant who actually died in 1902.

He's already told them that he was Copernicus and that he was a British SIS man and that there was someone important in the Nazi party or in the government who was cooperating with the British and that whoever it was was called Pythagoras. After he told them that, telling them things wasn't so hard to do anymore.

He told them a lot of things. About recognition signs and greeting signals. About radio check-in times and dates of transmissions. He didn't tell them who the other Pythagoras agents were because he didn't know, but his interrogators didn't stop asking because they didn't believe him. That was why he had died.

Quinby Franks was buried in a hole somewhere in Berlin without a secret left in him. He was buried with two other torture victims who had died the same day. That was why, two weeks later, it wasn't possible for him to be in Utrecht.

But Regenbauer was.

Regenbauer knew everything that Quinby Franks had known, but he thought he knew a little more. He thought he knew that somehow the British had discovered a way to decipher the German Enigma code. And he suspected that this Pythagoras coalition of spies and traitors was part of it.

That was what Regenbauer was doing in Utrecht. He was

testing his theory. He knew that the British would not act on a single transmission from an agent who'd been taken into custody by the Gestapo and suddenly escaped. After all, even the British weren't fools. They would suspect such a call for help. They would suspect it until they could prove it was genuine. They would wait for something that would confirm that the agent was real.

Well, Regenbauer had the proof for them. It was such an ingenious trick, and so simple, that he longed to tell someone about it. But he couldn't do that. Not yet. He had to be sure. And he would be soon.

This evening, in just a few hours, Regenbauer had arranged for a message to be sent from Berlin to all Gestapo outposts in the northern sector to redouble their efforts to find a British spy on the run. His name was Quinby Franks, but his name didn't matter because he wouldn't be using his real name. He was wanted, the message would say, because he was suspected to be a ringleader in a conspiracy against the Reich.

The message would be sent by way of the Enigma machine itself.

Regenbauer was pleased with himself. The proof of his plan would be when the British fools sent someone to rescue their precious Copernicus. Weren't they going to be surprised.

Because *he* was Copernicus now.

26 _____

KATE WAS THE last person Ted had expected to see standing in the queue of correspondents waiting to board the Junker press plane. She was the only woman correspondent at Templehof this morning and naturally she was the first in line. Wrapped in a light trench coat, her hair done up in a bun under a faded gray rain hat, Kate Buchanan was still one of the most beautiful women Ted had ever known.

It was the rain that held things up; a summer shower, really, but it caused a delay in getting the plane serviced. The longer the delay the more correspondents showed up to claim a seat, and for a time the crowded shelter on the runway was in a state of turbulent confusion as frustrated newsmen harangued the harried representative of the Propaganda Ministry.

But not Kate. She stood off to herself, smoking a cigarette, distant in interest or feeling to the turmoil behind her. If her black-sheep status affected her, she gave no hint of it. Ted wanted desperately to go to her, to tell her he knew why she was playing this role as Nazi-worshiper. He wanted to, but he didn't. This certainly wasn't the place, even if there had been time. But he would. When he got back. If there was any reason to make this scheme work now, it was to return and take her out of danger. Whether she goddamn liked it or not.

Grayson nudged him as he plopped in the seat beside him, jogging Ted out of his preoccupation.

"Well, I guess that's that," the bureau chief said.

"What's what?"

Grayson nodded at the crowd. "The Propaganda Ministry didn't make up a manifest for the flight so naturally everyone is claiming a seat. There are more than forty correspondents to cram into a plane that carries seventeen passengers. It ain't gonna happen."

Ted frowned. Suddenly, he felt his heart rise to his throat. He had to get on that plane! "Who's getting bumped," Ted said quickly.

"Nobody, unfortunately," Grayson said with a sour look. "All of these jerks are going."

"But—"

"They're bringing another plane."

The realization of what that meant didn't register with Ted until he was on the plane. All the correspondents drew a number from a hat with thirty-four pieces of paper. Then everyone was segregated into two groups, one for each aircraft. Ted drew number nine. He would be on the first plane. Grayson drew number twenty-seven. He would be on the second plane, as would Kate.

That was the problem, and it only dawned on Ted when he realized that his name was on a manifest.

There were *two* planes.

Moser had said the plane would be somehow disabled in Brussels. But it was based on *one* plane load of Berlin correspondents. Two was a different story. What if the wrong plane was disabled? Now that his name was on the first plane's manifest, if it wasn't somehow delayed or incapacitated, he would have no excuse not to fly on to Lille. And what if his plane *was* disabled? Grayson might somehow finagle him a spot on his plane. Ted worried about the possibilities from Berlin to Düsseldorf.

But that worry didn't last.

Ted was staring out a porthole when he caught a glint of a wingtip in the sun. There wasn't any mistaking that cigar profile or the butterfly wings when it turned against the sky and banked into the sun. It was a Spitfire and it had brought along three of its friends.

Ted was half out of his seat, pushing a *Herald Tribune*

photographer roughly aside so he could keep the RAF marauders in sight, when someone else saw them.

"Hey, look out there!"

"Jesus. British planes!"

They were, Ted's mind answered, and they weren't out sightseeing. The old Junker was in the middle of a war zone and any plane bearing German markings was fair game.

"They're coming after us!" somebody screamed.

Ted scrambled to a porthole to see aft of the wing, because he knew that's where they'd be coming from. He was right; the first Spitfire came in high, out of the sun.

His first thought was how odd it was not to hear the machine guns fire when he could see them blaze from their recessed mountings in the wings; holes that weren't there a moment before were now gouged into the Junker's wing and engine cowling.

A second Spitfire made its strafing pass and the inside of the plane was suddenly a death chamber. Plexiglas shards from three shattered portholes exploded inward as the fighter's .303-caliber bullets ripped through the fuselage. The door separating the passenger cabin from the cockpit slammed open and broke away from one of its hinges as the impact of two projectiles left a pair of splintered holes in the wood. A correspondent who'd been sitting toward the front choked out a scream as he was lifted out of his canvas seat by the force of the round that struck him in the back and penetrated the magazine he was holding. The photographer who'd been standing beside Ted dropped to his knees with his hands to his chest, then slumped to the floor.

Then the plane seemed to come apart. The floor tilted at a severe angle; people who weren't holding on to something tumbled toward the nose of the plane; papers and bits of Plexiglas and pieces of luggage and hats were swirled and tossed about in a roar of wind. The plane's two remaining engines shrieked from the straining change of pitch and started into a shuddering, stomach-churning, dive.

Ted could see the pilot, through the broken doorway, trying frantically to correct against a slow spin with rudder control, but he wasn't winning.

"Trim wheel!" Ted yelled. He was holding onto a strap above his head and his feet were slipping slowly with the steep inclination of the floor. He had to force his eyes open against

the wind that was blowing through a shattered panel in the
cockpit windshield, but he kept yelling because he knew it was
the only chance this plane had to avoid sliding over on its back.

"Trim wheel, goddammit! Use the fucking trim wheel!"

He could see the right engine burning because he was on that
side of the plane and because black smoke was streaming past
his porthole. But he could also see the ground now and it
wasn't that far away.

In a sudden quirky instant, Ted realized two things. First,
the best pilot the plane had aboard was not in the cockpit and,
second, there really wasn't any need to worry about manifests
or seating arrangements or meeting Moser's man because the
plane was definitely not going to Brussels.

Ted let go of the strap. He bumped against a man holding on
to the overhead luggage rack and slid on his knees to the
cockpit door.

"Trim wheel, trim wheel!"

He pushed himself through the opening and crawled on his
hands to the jump seat between the two pilots.

"Trim wheel, trim—oh, Christ!—*trimmen steuern, trimmen
. . . trimmen!*"

The pilot got the message. But it was the copilot with the
problem. He was dead or unconscious; blood trickled slowly
down his neck from beneath his flight cap. No wonder the pilot
was having trouble fighting the dive; he was pulling against the
dead weight of his second-in-command.

Ted pulled the copilot out of the seat and climbed in. The
hole in the windshield was nearly directly in front of him and
he couldn't see for the force of the wind in his face. But then,
he didn't have to see. The pilot could do that. All he had to do
was pull. Help the pilot get the nose up and work the rudder
pedals.

The nose came up. Ted could feel it, but he also knew they
were losing airspeed. They were going to have to set this old
bird down, and soon. He tried to open his eyes enough to see
where they were headed, but he was being buffeted and shaken
too violently to make anything out. They had to be pretty damn
close to the ground, he realized. He just hoped the pilot knew
enough about forced landings not to try and put the gear down.
He hoped the pilot knew enough to shut the fuel to that burning
engine. He hoped—

"*Halten Sie!*" the pilot yelled again.

That was when Ted suddenly remembered what plane he was in. This was a Junker Ju-52 transport. And Junker Ju-52 transports were fixed-gear aircraft. That meant that the goddamn landing gear was just hanging down out there, which was fine for runways or leveled fields, but if one collapsed or was clipped off by a fence or a boulder or a fallen tree, then the nose-heavy little beauty could flip ass-over-nose, drill a hole in the ground and crush its seven-hundred-pound, two radial BMW nose-mounted engine right through the cockpit, prop and all. Where he was sitting.

Ted opened his eyes.

It wasn't the flattest field he'd ever seen in his life and it wasn't without its share of rocks and gopher holes that jarred your teeth through your gums when you plowed over them in a fixed-gear aircraft, but they didn't call the Ju-52 transport "Iron Annie" for nothing.

The plane bumped to a stop well short of dense hedgerows and Ted took back what he'd thought about the pilot earlier. The sonofabitch hadn't got them all killed.

The pilot was just realizing it himself. He leaned back in his seat and let his head fall against the rest. He let out a long weary sigh, rubbed his eyes and glanced at Ted. He was about fifty, maybe more, and probably too old for a combat job, but he'd earned his pay today, Ted thought.

Then the pilot held out his hand. "*Danke*," he said.

And Ted wondered, what the hell was the fighting all about.

Altogether, the casualty list was less than it might have been. There were two men dead, a stringer for *The New York Times* who'd been sitting up front and the propaganda minister's representative, whose neck was broken when they landed. A photographer had been struck in the stomach by shrapnel from a fighter's guns, but he was more concerned, after he knew he would live, that his camera had been smashed. The most seriously hurt was the copilot, who had a large gash along one side of his head and was apparently in shock.

When it was clear that the Spitfires were gone, Ted helped the pilot evacuate the plane. The engine had burned itself out, but there wasn't any sense taking chances as long as there was still some fuel aboard.

Someone would come along, the pilot keep reassuring Ted. Someone would come because he'd radioed for help, not that he needed to. The second press plane was sure to have seen what happened and called for Luftwaffe escort. None of it was of any help to Ted. He needed to get out now. Before *he* was a news item.

He'd already heard some of the correspondents talking. The plane was in trouble and Campbell pulled it out and saved twenty lives; it would be that or something similar. Heroes, Ted was sharply aware, begat heroes. Especially in Germany. And he just didn't have time for it all. No, he had to go now. It was just too bad about Moser's man with the uniform. Alfred would have to find his own way. The pilot had said they'd gone down somewhere north of the Belgium-Holland border, near Reusel. Fine. Soesterberg was north and it was a long walk.

"Herr Campbell, Herr—" The pilot had been running and was out of breath. "Herr . . . Campbell, where are you going? You must stay with the others."

Ted was carrying his bag and he turned and set it down. "This is where the war started for me," he said. "Shot down by a British fighter plane. So this is where I shall begin reporting the war." He tried to sound as sincere as possible. "I want to see what the people here feel about these raids."

"But, Herr Campbell," the pilot stammered, "you have not permission. You must have—"

"I have Hermann Goering's permission," Ted said. He took a paper from his pocket and waved it at the pilot. "I may go anywhere I like."

"The Reichsmarschall?" That impressed him.

"Yes, Goering himself."

"But—"

"Don't worry about me." Ted patted him on the shoulder. He pointed back to the Junker, parked in the center of the meadow as if it belonged there. "See about them," he said. "You're a damned good pilot, if I didn't mention it before. Don't let anybody try to change what you did up there." He nodded at the sky. "Anyway, don't worry about me. By the way, what's you name? I'll use it in my story."

"Putzier," the pilot said. "Kurt Putzier."

Ted nodded at the plane again as he picked up his bag. "You'd better see after them. Don't worry, someone will come along."

Ted found a narrow road. He followed it north for a mile or so, hiding in the brush whenever he heard a vehicle cominng.

Three civilian cars passed and a Wehrmacht corporal on a motorcycle leading two trucks loaded with soldiers. The sun was out now and it was getting hot, especially lugging the bag, but he wanted to put as much distance between him and the plane as possible before he switched identities. He walked another mile, rehearsing what he would say when he ran into someone, but he didn't see a soul. Finally, after two hours' walking, he saw a house ahead where the road intersected with another. There was a soldier sitting on a wooden stool, leaning back against the side of the building, whittling a piece of wood. It was as good a place as any, he thought. He turned and walked back about two hundred yards until he found a thick growth of underbrush beside the road.

It was cramped sweaty work, but he got out of his clothes and into the Luftwaffe trousers and shirt and leather jacket. It was too hot, really, for a jacket, especially here in the close quarters he'd hacked out with his penknife, but it protected him from the barbs and branches.

He slipped the identification chain tags over his head and tucked them into his shirt then started to dig a hole with a branch he'd cut with his knife. He thought he'd been clever to think of burying his bag where no one would ever stop to look, but he hadn't counted on the roots.

He'd barely dug below the surface and all he had to show for his effort was a pitifully shallow hole, dirty hands and muddy, wood-rot stains on his trousers. The hell with it. He could be here the rest of the war, wrestling goddamn roots.

He crammed his clothes into the hole as best he could and covered it over, then stamped it as flat as possible with his feet. Another pathetic job, but it was the best he could do. He carried the bag farther into the underbrush and kicked it under a log.

When he was on the road again, he studied the place he'd just left and decided it didn't appear any more disturbed than when he went in. He tied the laces of the flight boots together and slung them over his shoulder, stuffed the rolled flying breeches under one arm, took a long breath, and started up the road toward the house and its whittler. He'd get a ride to Reusel on one of the trucks or cars that passed. He wasn't too worried about that part. He wasn't sure how he would explain what he was doing out here in the middle of nowhere, but he'd think of something because he had to.

Just take one thing at a time. That's all he had to do. Just go to the house and make some excuse to the soldier about being lost, then sit and wait for a ride.

Someone would come along.

Someone did.

A doctor, in a ten-year-old Ballot salon car, returning from a call. He'd just delivered twins, but it had taken most of the night and the greater part of the morning while the mother suffered through labor. He'd been hoping to run across a responsible hitchhiker, the doctor said, because he was truly worn out from the experience. Would Ted mind driving?

It would be a pleasure, Ted said.

It turned out that the soldier was not a sentry at all. The house was an abandoned grain mill and the soldier was a young private who'd made the acquaintance of a Dutch girl and was returning to his unit at Arendonk from a thirty-six-hour leave. He was waiting for a ride too. Fortunately, no one asked a lot of questions. The boy sat in the back and promptly fell asleep. The doctor, who was in his sixties, Ted guessed, fought to stay awake, probably to make sure his car was in reliable hands.

"Eindhoven?"

Ted glanced at the old Dutchman. "Pardon?"

"You are going to Eindhoven?" the doctor asked. "The Luftwaffe base?"

Ted nodded. "*Ja*." Eindhoven, he remembered, was one of the seven bomber group bases in the Fliegerdivision command he was reporting to. If he could get to Eindhoven then he could get to Soesterberg. The question was, where the hell was Eindhoven from Ruesel?

"Do you know Eindhoven?" Ted said.

"Not too fast, please." The doctor pointed at the hood of the car. "Old like me . . . overheats."

The car was barely going thirty as it was, but Ted eased down. "Do you know Eindhoven?" Ted asked again.

"Everyone knows Eindhoven," the doctor said. "The trains come to Eindhoven."

Right. That meant no train station in Reusel. "When we get to Reusel, what is the best way to get to the airfield?"

"No airfield in Reusel," the doctor said with a sigh, trying to get comfortable against the door. "Eindhoven."

"How do I get there?"

"The bus," he said as if there weren't any other way to travel. "Everyone takes the bus to Eindhoven. Where the trains are."

Ted nodded, smiled. Of course, the bus, why not the bus; everyone uses the bus, knucklehead. So, he'd take a bus to Eindhoven, find the airfield and get somehow to Soesterberg. "Thanks," he said. But the doctor had nodded off.

Ted pushed the Ballot to thirty-five while the old man slept, then felt guilty and eased it back to just below thirty. And it turned out that it wasn't that far to Reusel, forty-five minutes at the most. There was a Wehrmacht lieutenant checking traffic into town and Ted had no problem passing his first test. The private in the backseat was reprimanded for tardiness and instructed to report to his platoon leader immediately; his thirty-six-hour pass was now in its thirty-ninth hour.

The doctor directed Ted to the bus station, a lobby of a small hotel, and told him there would be a bus at three o'clock. Ted bought a German-edition paper and a chocolate bar and sat on a bench near the door to wait.

It wasn't much of a bus, when it came. Acutally, it wasn't a bus at all but a canvas-topped truck with a Wehrmacht corporal to drive it. Since Ted was an officer, the corporal offered to let him ride in the cab. It was a two-hour trip to Eindhoven, according to the driver; the Wehrmacht, the corporal explained with some displeasure, had taken over several of these rural bus runs to alleviate the shortage of men. So he was happy to talk to a fellow German when Ted climbed in beside him. And he talked a lot. Not that Ted minded terribly; he learned a great deal about Eindhoven and the airfield and a girl named Greta in Antwerp who helped ease some of the corporal's boredom and homesickness. He heard that Eindhoven was full of Luftwaffe air crews and that there were more coming in all the time and that something was going on because a friend of the corporal's who drove armaments for the Wehrmacht was pulling double duty, delivering bombs to the Luftwaffe base.

The Eindhoven station was crowded. Ted pushed through the crowd to the railway entrance, found a policeman and got directions to a bar where he could find some fellow Luftwaffe officers.

The *Goede Nacht* Bar was more than a pub and a hanging-out place for fliers; it was also a fairly classy whorehouse; at least, upstairs was. It was noisy and crowded, but Ted learned that there were as many satisfied customers leaving the bar to return to the base as there were thirsty and anxious ones coming in. He could leave for the airfield almost anytime. He bought a beer and strolled through the throng to the piano where an especially boisterous group was singing. What he noticed and what gave him some relief was that hardly anyone was wearing a complete uniform. There was an even mix of those wearing most of a Luftwaffe dress uniform and those in flight suits. On a table near the door there must have been sixty or seventy caps, and upstairs—what was upstairs? It gave him an idea. Maybe he could get a uniform after all.

He moved to the stairs and stepped up to the first landing, moving aside for a captain and his girl coming down. The second floor had a balcony overlooking the bar and two hallways leading to the rooms. So far, so good. Inside the hall was a small foyer and on two sides of the room were open clothes racks. There must have been two dozen Luftwaffe blouses hanging there.

Ted started trying them on. He took off his jacket and began searching for a good fit.

"Did you lose something, Lieutenant?"

Ted whirled around to see the captain he'd passed on the stairs, leaning against the door jamb. He was drunk.

"Yes, I . . . I . . . my wallet."

"Do you think you left it in my pocket . . . because that's whose blouse you have on." He took a step forward, but he had to hold himself up against the wall.

Ted glanced quickly at the shoulder patch; he couldn't have made a mistake like that. He hadn't. "Herr Hauptmann . . . I . . . this could not be yours, it is a lieutenant's uniform."

The captain squinted at him. "Ah, so it is."

Ted breathed a sigh that aged him five years. It wasn't quite a perfect fit, but he couldn't take it off now. He began buttoning the tunic.

"You're leaving now, Lieutenant?" The captain was still supporting himself against the wall.

"Yes, Herr Hauptmann," Ted said, with as much indignation as he could muster. "One of these women has taken my wallet."

"Swine!"

Ted looked up at the captain fearfully.

"Swine and thieves, these women." He took another step

and held Ted's shoulder for support. "I am leaving also," he said, with breath that clouded Ted's eyes. "I have a driver. Can I give you a ride, Lieutenant?"

"Thank you, sir."

"One thing . . ." He was hanging on to Ted for support.

"Sir?"

The captain bowed his head and belched. "Help me find my tunic, will you?"

They found it and Ted helped the captain down the stairs and out into the heat of the late afternoon, stopping at the table on the way out and picking up a cap for each of them.

The captain's name was Kugel and the fifteen-minute drive to the airfield was interrupted twice so he could stand outside the car to throw up. He was feeling much better, he said, when they reached his quarters, but Ted had to help him inside anyway. Kugel's room was near the end of the corridor in a clapboard barracks that he shared with another pilot in the squadron. The room was empty when they stumbled into it and Kugel was asleep or unconscious even before Ted let him drop onto the bed.

Ted sagged into a chair beside a writing table to catch his breath. Well, he'd gotten to the airfield. That was something, at least. Now he had to get to Soesterberg.

He glanced through the window above the writing table, then he heard the plane. A Heinkel was coming in to land. It was at least a mile away but not too far off to know it was in trouble; Ted could hear the engines straining. He stood up and wiped away a film of grime from one of the window panes. The twin-engine bomber was about two hundred yards from the end of the runway. He's lost coolant in one of his liquid-cooled engines, Ted deduced, but he needs the engine to maintain airspeed. Risky business, landing with an overheated engine like that. He could hear the engines more clearly now —the high-pitched whine of the good one, straining under full power, and the popping, guttural groan of the damaged engine, its cylinders missing.

The starboard engine exploded barely a second before the gears touched the runway and the wing immediately ablaze. Then the outboard fuel tank exploded and the bomber veered a fraction to its right, still at full landing speed, and went into a lazy sort of pirouette, turning sideways against itself and then falling on its burning wing. Finally it slid off the runway, off the shoulder, into an abutment of excavated dirt. A trail of burning fuel led from the spot where the bomber first touched the runway eighty yards to where it finally stopped. Black smoke engulfed what was left of the plane but Ted saw two figures scramble away from the inferno. Two. Judging from the way the plane had slid into that dirt embankment, neither of them was the pilot.

Ted sucked in a breath, exhaled and glanced at Kugel, passed out on his face. The captain had something to get drunk about. If what he'd just witnessed was typical of the sort of mauling the RAF was inflicting on German bombers over England, then Kugel had a right to put it out of his mind any way he could. It led Ted to realize what he was in for once he climbed into a Heinkel cockpit. Over England, even at night, he would be surrounded by enemies.

He undressed and took a long shower, Kugel wasn't likely to mind. Afterwards, he picked a clean shirt and tie from Kugel's roommate's closet and packed his flight gear and some of Kugel's in a canvas bag he found in the closet. He emptied the pockets of the lieutenant's tunic he'd stolen, stuffed the contents down a heating vent and put his own identity papers and orders in a pocket. He still had his Propaganda Ministry press card and the letter from Goering, which he slipped into one of his flying boots. He had to keep those to get back to Germany.

He straightened his tie in a mirror and pulled on the uniform cap, adjusting it snugly on his head. Then he left, taking his canvas bag and leaving Kugel snoring soundly with his face to the wall. Somewhere around here was the flight operations office. That was his next stop.

"Horn! Lieutenant Alfred Horn!"

The group commander was a gruff runt who chewed a cigar and spat words out the side of his mouth. His office was a windowless room adjacent to the flight operations lobby. He looked especially gruff and frazzled now, as he stomped out of his office, chewing madly on the cigar, yelling for Ted.

"Here, sir."

"Come here."

"Sir?"

The Oberst waved the forged orders in Ted's face. "Do you know what these are?"

"My reassignment orders, Herr Oberst."

The colonel nodded with an impatient frown. "Yes, Lieutenant, your orders—to Second Bomber Group . . . Soesterberg!

This is Third Bomber Group, Eindhoven." He bit hard on his cigar. "Did you forget how to read while you were on leave or do you usually report to the wrong Fliegergruppen?"

"No, sir . . . I . . . I . . ."

"Do you know how many air crew pilots have reported for duty here in the last twenty-four hours, Lieutenant?"

"No, Herr Oberst, I—"

"Neither do I, Lieutenant," the colonel snapped. "That's how many there have been. And most of them have seen fit to read their orders so at least they'll know which airfield to report to." He took the mangled cigar from his mouth and used it to point back toward his office. "Soesterberg, for your information, Lieutenant, is that way."

"Yes, sir. I'm sorry, Herr Oberst. I—"

"They—" the group commander swung his arm to indicate a knot of sheepish-looking junior officers sitting together on a long bench. "They, were also sorry. They . . . also reported to the wrong airfield." He turned his acerbic gaze back on Ted. "What is it, Lieutenant Horn, that so attracts you new pilots to Eindhoven? Don't you like Soesterberg? Is there something wrong with the Second Bomber Group?"

Ted straightened. "No, sir, Herr Oberst!"

"Good, because you are going there whether you prefer it or not." He chomped down on the cigar with his teeth. "I haven't enough trouble processing new air crews every hour—now I have to provide you transportation to your *correct* unit which means sending a transport and crew to Soesterberg."

Ted looked properly grieved to have caused such trouble. "Yes, sir, I mean . . . I'm sorry, Herr Oberst."

The colonel sighed and nodded at the others. "Yes, I know that, Lieutenant." He thrust the orders out for Ted to take. "If you wouldn't mind taking a seat there with your fellow officers, I'll see about a plane. Just sit there quietly and—" he gripped Ted by the shoulder and made what must have been a smile "—and Horn?"

"Sir?"

His smile turned to a vicious scowl. *"Don't move* from that spot until I tell you!"

Ted sat down. He tucked his orders into a pocket of the tunic and stared at the floor for fear that if he glanced at any one of his traveling companions, he might smile.

Ted never saw Soesterberg. By the time the transport left the airfield at Eindhoven with its seven silent passengers, it was dark and they flew over the wooded village without ever seeing it. But the airfield itself was much larger than Ted had anticipated. The operations office was in a two-story building that also housed the air division staff and General Coeler's office and quarters, the last being an entire second-floor wing of one of the building's annexes. The Germans were still building barracks—there were half a dozen unfinished structures around the field and more being constructed on the other side of the base.

Ted reported in but had to wait for the group commander to return from a late dinner before he was assigned to a squadron —now officially abbreviated to II/KG 4 Gr2. He was assigned an aircraft, given the names of his crew, whom he would meet at the morning assembly, assigned a barracks room which he would have to share with three other officers, and told if he were going to eat tonight he must go immediately to the officer's mess.

Ted went, ate, and afterwards found his barracks quarters. Two other officers were already asleep and Ted stowed his bag under an empty bed, draped his uniform over a chair and slid wearily between the sheets. He lay there for half an hour, eyes staring in the darkness, letting his body and senses unbend from the strain of tension he'd been through. The meeting with Moser seemed a million years ago, but it was just last night. He wondered where Grayson was tonight. What was Kate doing? And Regenbauer?

He closed his eyes. Just take one thing at a time. In the morning he'd meet his crew and check out his plane. There would be squadron briefings—weather, radio codes, flight routes, primary targets, secondary targets, bomb load, fighter escort, night navigation, formation dispersement. But none of it mattered. He had one route, one target, one goal.

He rolled back on his stomach, punched up his pillow, turned it over to the dry side.

What he had to do was go to sleep. He closed his eyes again. Sleep, goddammit! Forget about the bloody run! Sleep. *Sleep*!

27

THE HEINKEL 111 H series medium bomber was the backbone of the Luftwaffe bomber command. It carried a crew of four —a pilot and three gunners; a top turret gunner in the middle of the fuselage; a ventral or belly gunner who lay on a pad and operated either a forward- or aft-mounted machine gun; and a nose gunner who lay forward of the pilot, and was also the bomb aimer.

The plane carried a maximum of eight five-hundred-pound bombs that were stowed in vertical cells, nose up, in two bomb compartments—a bay on either side of the central gangway —separating the pilot and nose gunner from the other two crew members. The Heinkel had a seven-hundred-mile range fully loaded and fuel enough for over three hours flight time.

Ted met his crew when he found his plane; they were barely more than teenagers. The two aft gunners had flown together before on combat missions over England and had been rescued from the North Sea by a Luftwaffe seaplane with Red Cross markings when they'd parachuted from a dying bomber.

The gunners were all sergeants—*unteroffiziers*—the two veterans more cocky and sure of themselves than the new NCO, who'd transferred directly from a training command at Werneuchen. They treated Ted respectfully if a bit warily, especially the old-timers (they were both twenty), because, Ted assumed, he was new to them and as yet untested in combat over England. Still, Ted felt an immediate camaraderie for his crew which was at once strange and inexplicable, considering the circumstances. They were men like these who had crashed and died at Wellhurst House . . . and took Anne with them.

Shortly after noon, the first squadrons of the bombers left Soesterberg to join the first wave of aircraft from all over the coast to strike into England. Ted stood with dozens of other crew members who would be leaving later in the day, and they cheered each plane through takeoff. Then he busied himself with incidental chores around his airplane, and even watched the loading of the bombs into the bomb-bay cells. He'd never seen a bomb before. They were warm to the touch, for they'd been stacked in carts parked in the sun. They were bigger than he'd thought they'd be, and fatter—not the streamlined missiles with shiny body and fins he'd imagined. Solid was the best way to describe them, Ted thought; solid and ugly.

He was sitting in the grass just off the runway in the partial shade of a camouflage net when the bombers began returning. The exuberance displayed during takeoff had changed to silent anticipation.

How many?

The count turned out not to be encouraging. Six planes were missing. Two bombers were so shot up it was amazing they had returned at all. There wasn't any way to know what they'd been through in the time he sat on the grass. There hadn't been any sound to gauge what it might have been like—no bombs exploding, no echo of machine guns or ripping metal or screams of men dying. Nothing. Just the empty sky.

"I wouldn't worry too much, sir. It won't be like that tonight."

He turned to see that it was one of his experienced gunners who'd spoken.

"The daylight raids are always the worst," the twenty-year-old continued. "Them Spits, they'll rip you up once the fighter escorts have to go back and it's just us and them."

Ted nodded thoughtfully, but said nothing.

"It won't be like that for us, sir. The Spits can't find us at night."

"Let's hope not," Ted said.

"You'll see, Lieutenant." The sergeant offered a smile of

encouragement. "You'll see. We'll all of us come back just fine."

Ted tried to return the smile. "Of course we will."

You'll see.

Ted was to bomb Thameshaven.

The final briefing was at nine fifteen and specific targets were assigned to each squadron. Ted's squadron drew the Rochester and Kingston sector, specifically the oil-tank storage installation at Thameshaven.

Thameshaven was only fifteen miles downriver from London.

His luck was finally changing, Ted mused. Of all the targets posted for this two-hundred-plane raid on England tonight, Thameshaven was one of only a dozen in the London district zone. He might have gotten something in south Kent or Sussex or, God forbid, Scotland. But he didn't. Thameshaven was fine. Thameshaven was goddamn perfect.

"Thameshaven?" The veteran gunner glanced at his mate. Ted was standing with his crew under the wing of their plane, going over the flight route and target with a flashlight and map.

"Thameshaven, did you say?"

Ted nodded. It was dark so he didn't think the gunners saw his reassuring smile. "Yes, oil storage tanks about . . ."

"Shit!"

Ted shown the flashlight at the top turret gunner. "What's the matter, Sergeant?"

The sergeant stared at his feet and let out a long sigh. "We've been to Thameshaven, sir . . . Hans and me." He glanced quickly at Hans, the belly gunner.

"What about it?" Ted said.

"It's on the river, isn't it, sir? In the London district."

Ted frowned. "So?"

"That's where we ran into them Spits and Hurricanes, Lieutenant," Hans said. "Chased us to Norwich—"

"Killed our pilot at Norwich," the other gunner volunteered.

"—and we had to jump in the sea."

"But that was in daylight." Ted could feel his stomach tightening.

"Day or night, it doesn't matter, sir. It's on the river Thames and it's in the London district zone. There's more gun batteries along the river than anywhere else in England. And the RAF patrols that sector heavier than others because it's the most likely approach to London."

"But we're not going to London," said the nose gunner a bit fearfully. "London is off limits. The Luftwaffe is forbidden to approach London." It was probably the most Ted had heard his nose gunner say in the few hours he'd known him. The boy turned to Ted. "Isn't that right, sir?"

"We know that," Hans said, "but the British don't. They don't want any bombs falling on their precious capital." He glanced at Ted. "Or oil storage tanks inside the zone. It'll be a scary ride, sir . . . Thameshaven. We wouldn't be going back if it'd been hit the first time."

Ted nodded. He switched off the flashlight. Some luck he had.

"Sir, permission to take aboard extra ammunition canisters."

"You really think we'll need them, Sergeant?"

His answer was a silent stare from the three gunners.

"You'd better start loading," Ted said.

If there was a consolation in any of this it was that he didn't have to worry about the radio beam guidance system. Ted's squadron was sending four *schwarms* on this raid and only the lead plane of each cell was equipped with *Knickebein* receiver. Ted's Heinkel was the third bomber in his cell of four planes. Each plane behind the *Knickebein* leader would simply use the tail formation of the aircraft ahead as guide in follow-the-leader fashion. It meant he'd gone to a lot of bother and listened to a lot of horseshit about Colonel Jung's life's love for nothing.

When the flight master signaled, Ted waved the all-clear sign and the ground crew yanked the chocks from in front of the main wheels. The bomber eased forward.

They would be taking off in pairs, then head to a rendezvous point in Belgium where the squadron would join a pack of bomber groups from Eindhoven and Amsterdam. Tonight's raid would be made up of four such groups, each penetrating the English coast at staggered intervals between Ipswich and Portsmouth to keep the RAF guessing. There were sixty-three aircraft in Ted's group, not including the Messerschmitt escort, and they'd be striking across the Channel, entering

England between Brighton and Hastings, before splitting into four-plane cells and heading for their predetermined targets.

Ted adjusted his headset, setting one earphone slightly back from his ear so he could hear the engines and the nose gunner, if he had anything to say. He wasn't accustomed to a headset, it chafed his ears and muffled the sound of the engines. He wouldn't have worn it at all except it was his only intercommunication with his aft gunners.

Ted taxied into position. A crowd of officers and crewmen were standing in the grass off the runway to send each pair of bombers out with a cheer. Most of them were drinking; they had already flown their missions for the day. Ted noticed a group of passengers who had just landed in a transport earlier, strolling across the apron from the operations building to watch the takeoffs. VIPs most likely.

When the two bombers ahead had cleared the runway, it was Ted's turn. He gave a hand signal to the pilot in the plane to his right, cinched his seat belt tight across his lap and reached up to close the sliding roof hatch over his head. He waved at the crowd in the grass.

That was when he saw Regenbauer.

Ted only saw his face in the moment it took the SS major to strike a match and hold it to his cigarette, but Ted was sure. He was standing with a group that had just walked from the operations office, and there was no question. He couldn't mistake *that* face. Regenbauer was here. At Soesterberg.

What the bloody Christ was he doing in Holland!

Ted's first reaction was the fear that Regenbauer saw him, recognized him or even had followed him here. His second was to release the footbrake.

The Heinkel lumbered down the runway. Ted could hear the fading cheers from the crowd as the bomber accelerated. He didn't turn to smile or wave or make any acknowledgment. He just watched the runway flag markers.

The two bombers lifted off together. Alfred was on his way.

28

REGENBAUER, REGENBAUER—God Almighty, what was Regenbauer doing at Soesterberg! It was all Ted could think about.

—Had he seen him?

—Would he recognize him even in a place like that?

—What was he doing there anyway? He couldn't have followed him, could he?

—Where was he coming from? Amsterdam? Rotterdam? Brussels, maybe? Or was it a special trip from Berlin?

—He was *supposed* to be in Berlin, right? So why was he here? *Why was he here, goddammit!* And—oh, Christ!—what if he was still there when they returned?

Well, there was one thing for sure. It was going to be a long fucking wait, because Ted wasn't going back there. Not to Soesterberg. Not anywhere near the place.

Ted formed up with the other aircraft over Ghent. The worry about Regenbauer was gradually replaced by more immediate concerns. He calmed himself with the rationalization that Regenbauer couldn't have followed him. It would have been impossible to have known where he was going when he left the crash-landed Junker. And if the SS major did see him in the cockpit he couldn't have been sure it was Ted. Not in the dark at that distance. No, he couldn't have been sure. Could he?

The gunners tested their weapons over the Channel. Even with the engines rumbling in his ears, Ted could hear and feel the vibrations of the short measured bursts. Too, he could see flashes in the darkness ahead as gunners in other planes squeezed off testing rounds.

It wouldn't be long now. There was only a sliver of a moon tonight but it was enough to illuminate the Channel fourteen thousand feet below.

The moment the reflection of the water disappeared, Ted knew that they'd cleared the south coast of England. He heard other pilots ordering gunners' directions through his radio headset. But he didn't see anything. He kept up snugly behind the Heinkel in front of him, holding the preceding bomber's port navigation light squarely in view. There wasn't much else to see or even look for. Not yet, anyway. The planned route would take them inland straight for Tunbridge Wells, veer northeast for Maidstone then on past Rochester to Thameshaven. That was the planned route, the *Knickebein* route, but it wasn't the way Ted was going. The course heading from the coast to Tunbridge Wells was on a line that extended straight through the heart of London.

He wasn't sure yet how he was going to explain his defection to the gunners, but he wasn't too worried about it. They were watching the bomber in front of them as closely as he was, especially the nose gunner. Still, so what? He got nervous, lost sight of the other plane and now they were off course and lost. If they didn't buy that, *even* if they knew who he was and exactly what he was doing, they couldn't do anything about it.

It was one of the few things about this mission Ted was absolutely sure about. Every Heinkel 111 H series medium bomber in the German Luftwaffe had at least three gunners, some had four. But it didn't matter if there were fifty. It only had *one* pilot.

"Sir, Lieutenant?"

The nose gunner sat up from his pad. In the dim light Ted couldn't see him clearly, but his voice was anxious.

"Sir, I don't see the light from the plane ahead anymore!"

Ted shook his head, pointed back at the gunner's position.

"Sir, I—" He glanced back through the nose of the cockpit

then moved closer to Ted. "I said I don't see the lights anymore."

"I've got them," Ted yelled back.

The gunner made a face, cupped a hand to his ear.

Ted pointed to himself, "I . . ." then pointed to his eyes " . . . see."

The gunner hesitated a moment, squinted at the darkness ahead then shrugged and gave Ted a thumbs-up sign before going back to his position. It was the first lucky break Ted had had in two days; the inexperienced gunner had accepted on blind faith the word of an officer. He was sure neither of the veterans would have been so quick to let it go at that. No one but Ted knew they weren't flying with the formation anymore, that the other bombers had made a course change at Tunbridge Wells and Ted hadn't. From now on they were on their own. They were due south of London and headed north.

The only edge Ted had over every other pilot in the Luftwaffe was that he was over familiar ground. Flying over unfamiliar territory, even in daylight with reference points marked on a map, is often tedious and never easy. But Ted had flown across this area of England perhaps a hundred times in air races from Canterbury and Salisbury to Southampton and Winchester. Every major air race in England flew over this area and Ted had been in all of them. He knew every town and river in this part of England like he knew the lines on his face. If he could see a town or city he could identify it and know where he was. Cities here were as distinctive to him as fingerprints to the FBI. Other people studied coins and butterflies, Ted studied towns and how they lay on the land and in the valleys and beside the rivers. He knew Basingstoke from Newbury and Sissinghurst from Bodiam. Bournemouth was shaped like a hound's tooth. Guildford was a pregnant duck; Salisbury, a bloated kidney bean. He'd made a living winning races because he knew landmarks. Show him a town in southern England from fifteen thousand feet and he could give compass headings to nearly any place within a hundred miles. That was why London was a cinch. He could find London in his sleep from here. Or in the dark.

That was his advantage; day or night, he'd find London now and he wouldn't need any directions. The misconception was that you couldn't find landmarks at night because you couldn't see the ground. That was a crock. Oh, you couldn't see people or farmhouses or unlighted landing fields, but you could see cities. Even small ones. You don't hide cities, Ted knew, by turning off the lights. It made them more difficult to find, naturally, but it didn't make them disappear. And you most especially do not hide London. Not with the House of Parliament and Buckingham Palace smack in the middle or the towering dome of St. Paul's or the Thames glistening in the moonlight with the unmistakable shadows of more than a dozen bridges across it. No way. The only way to miss the city of London even on a night like this was to look for it in Ireland.

They should be near Westerham by now. Ted leaned over to see. It wasn't likely he'd see anything, it was a tiny place, certainly no city, but it was where Winston Churchill lived or near enough, at Chartwell estate. Ted wondered briefly where the prime minister was tonight.

Ted was gazing into the darkness below when the attack began.

"Spitfire! Spitfire!"

The nose gunner was screaming and shooting, up on his knees, swiveling the machine gun as far as it would traverse.

It had come from the darkness almost directly in front of them. If Ted hadn't been giving himself a tour of the sights he might have seen it too.

"I think I got it, sir!" the nose gunner screamed frantically. "I think I got it!"

The Spitfire had peeled off to the starboard side; Ted saw it go by, but he didn't think it had been hit. God knows the nose gunner had fired enough rounds at it, but the chances of hitting anything accurately firing from the nose of a moving plane at the nose of another moving plane that was coming at you out of the dark were not especially good. And while the nose gunner was craning to see where his supposed victim had gone, Ted was searching the night ahead, squinting to find the other fighter. Because Spitfires traveled in pairs.

It came, but not where he was looking for it.

"Spit! Spit—Hans, two o'clock, low!"

The voice on the intercom was loud, anxious, but without the edge of hysteria that had marked the nose gunner's inexperience. The two in back were the veterans.

"Now, Hans! Now!"

Ted felt the vibrations of the machine guns firing; he felt them in his seat and through the rudder pedals. He never saw the Spitfire, but he saw the tracer rounds from his gunner's position in the belly gondola as they arched out into the darkness. In the next few seconds the whole plane seemed to be vibrating. The night was suddenly alive with flashes of tracer bullets burning toward the ground. Ted couldn't believe that three machine guns could cause so much noise and create so much brilliance. How could—oh, shit! Of course! He wasn't alone.

He'd forgotten about the Heinkel behind him. It was still there, following him, guiding on *his* navigational lights, shooting at *their* Spitfires.

Ted had switched off the radio when they passed Tunbridge Wells because he wasn't going to talk to anyone, was he? Well, he was now. He switched on the radio.

"Nachtadler fuehrer . . . nachtadler fuehrer! Wohin est sie?"

Ted didn't know where their flight leader was and he didn't care, but the pilot behind him did.

"This is Night Eagle Three," Ted said into the microphone.

The radio voice came back quickly. It was confused and scared. "Three? Why have you not answered me? Where is the cell leader? Where are the other planes?"

"I don't know."

"What!"

"I think we're lost."

"I will follow you, *Oberleutnant*. We must find our target."

"We're not going to find anything," Ted replied. "I think we'd better go home before we run into Spitfires." Ted knew he had to shake this guy. One plane, he thought, might slip through the London defense. But not two. "We'd better split up."

But the Luftwaffe pilot had other things on his mind. "The Spitfires, they did not continue the attack. Why not? Where are we?"

Ted wasn't interested in why the RAF fighters didn't come back, just thankful. But he should have been. And he learned why about ten seconds later.

Flak.

The darkness outside was interrupted by white and orange explosions. He knew then why the Spitfires weren't coming back. They were flying into the perimeter antiaircraft zone that surrounded London. All that the damned shooting back there

had accomplished was to announce themselves to the ground
batteries.

"Lieutenant! Lieutenant! Flak!"

It was one of the gunners on the intercom, his voice wasn't
as calm as it had been.

"We're in a flak box, sir! We're too close to London!"

They were close, but they weren't close enough. Ted could
just make out the irregular outline of the city ahead through the
bursting flashes of the antiaircraft shells—slanted roofs, stee-
ples, towers, a couple of bridges and the river. What little
moon there was gave the city an eerie, deserted, bleak
appearance, but it was there. Straight ahead. Only a few
precious minutes away. If he could make it.

"Where are the other planes?" the turret gunner asked
excitedly. "The other planes are gone! The one behind us just
turned away!"

"I know where I'm going," Ted yelled into the intercom.
"Just sit tight."

If it wasn't clear to his gunners where he was headed, it was
to whoever was directing the ground batteries. The exploding
shells were all around, the barrage more intense the nearer he
got to the city.

Ted reached to the throttles and pushed them to maximum
power. He watched the airspeed indicator begin to climb then
pulled the black-handle lever on the floor beside his seat. There
was a rush of wind as the bomb doors opened; Ted could hear
the reverberating rumble of the engines. He wanted to get rid
of the damn things! The longer he waited to drop them the
more his chances increased of getting himself blown into tiny
pieces. The bombs, he needn't remind himself, were stowed
behind the bulkhead in back of his seat.

"Sir! Sir!"

The front gunner was back on his haunches, yelling at Ted
and pointing ahead.

Ted waved him off, but the nose gunner crawled back to
scream in Ted's ear.

"Sir! That's . . . that's London!"

"I know what the fuck it is! Get out of my way!"

"But, sir!—"

Then Hans was on the intercom, yelling in both Ted's ears.
"London! That's London ahead!"

The secret was out.

"Hang on, gentlemen. Bomb release in ninety seconds."

He could see the Thames clearly now. He figured he was about four miles from the center of the city. He could distinguish buildings. There were barrage balloons all over the sky, floating two thousand feet above the ground. He could make out Chelsea Bridge and Westminster Bridge and Parliament beside the river. Just a couple minutes more. That was all he needed. He knew where he was going to drop. Where there wouldn't be a lot of people. He'd drive right between Albert Bridge and Chelsea Bridge and walk the bombs right through Hyde Park, right through the Serpentine; he'd kill a lot of fish and ducks and some pelicans, but no people. God, he hoped the air raid sirens were scaring Londoners off the streets and out of the parks and into shelters. Hyde Park was perfect because it was in the middle of the city and it was big. He'd use Buckingham Palace as a reference point. When he was abreast of it, he'd unload. At fourteen thousand feet it would take a five-hundred-pound bomb about fifteen seconds to hit the ground, covering about half a mile from the release point to point of impact. That would put his load of bombs almost in the center of Hyde Park. If he could just survive this goddamn flak he could make this mission work. He just needed another sixty seconds; that wasn't so much to ask, was it? Just sixty seconds without a major catastrophe.

He didn't get it.

And instead of one catastrophe he got three.

"Nein! Nein, Leutnant!"

The nose gunner, frightened half out of his mind, grabbed Ted's arm and the control column.

"You cannot, Lieutenant! It is *forbidden* to bomb London! *Forbidden!*"

The Heinkel went into an immediate no-power bank to starboard, tipping down on its right wing and, since the hysterical gunner had not only jerked the control column but also knocked the throttles back to stop, was headed into a high-speed stalling dive.

"You stupid—" Ted tried to hit him, but the sudden inclinations had thrown the gunner back against the blukhead where he slammed his head and fell to the floor dazed and bleeding.

"—sonofabitch!" Ted pushed the throttles back to full power and leveled out the plane. He'd barely had time to glance at the wheezing gunner sprawled beside him when a second catastrophe struck.

An antiaircraft shell exploded no more than fifteen feet off the port wing. The concussion nearly blew Ted out of his seat. It took him at least two seconds to realize that he wasn't dead and another two to know that the airplane was in serious trouble. The explosion had come slightly below and forward of the wing's leading edge and as a result shrapnel had ripped through the lift surface of the wing, exiting through the top, and the jagged edges of the thin metal exposed to the slipstream were being methodically peeled back like the lid of a sardine tin. The strips of metal were trailing the wing, and forcing Ted to correct for the plane's tendency to pull to the left.

But that was the least of his troubles. The port engine, which had saved his life by shielding him from the fragments of the exploding shell, was on fire. Flames shot back fifteen feet behind the wing. He cut off fuel to the engine and tried to take stock of the situation. He'd lost an engine, he was losing altitude; he was fighting to keep the aircraft from stalling and keep it level; he was losing airspeed and he watched the fuel indicator slowly turning down.

But he *was* alive, which counted for something, and the bomber was still flying. As far as he knew he hadn't lost any bombs. Some of them were bound to have holes in them, dents, anyway, but they hadn't detonated because they weren't armed until they'd fallen a certain distance.

Could he still make it to Hyde Park?

He was just passing over the Thames. Chelsea Bridge was directly below him. He was only slightly off course; there was only a mile and a half to go. But it meant he had to do some quick figuring because the trajectory of the bombs would be changed now. And while he was mentally computing his new airspeed and altitude and bomb flight distance, the third catastrophe happened.

A searchlight caught him in its beam.

Unlike the first and second catastrophes, he was not physically threatened. Nothing exploded. No one manhandled the controls. The plane itself wasn't distracted from its course or altitude by any outside influence. But the searchlight illuminating the cockpit, changing night suddenly to day, was the worst catastrophe of all. It blinded him.

Ted shaded his eyes from the sudden glare with his arm. The cockpit, being mostly a Plexiglas shell of windows, was now bathed in a brilliant, window-glossing shaft of light.

"Almighty God!"

Then an instant later Ted heard the other gunner's petrified voice.

"They have us, pilot! *They have us!"*

The nose gunner was too dazed or too terrified to speak. He just lay on his back, staring wide-eyed and wide-mouth at the blaze of light around him.

"They *haven't* got us," Ted shouted, but he knew better. He'd known that there were searchlights, of course; he'd seen them all around London. He had not realized what one could do to a pilot inside a plane caught in its beam. But he knew now. It destroyed your night vision in an instant, for one thing. There was nothing to see except the harsh, glaring reflection of light against the windows—backlighted opaque glass. Ted could see the instrument panel but he couldn't make out the indicator hands behind the gauges. He couldn't see the altimeter or the airspeed or the compass or the fuel indicators. He couldn't see the horizon indicator or the engine temperature gauge. But, now there was something even more important. He couldn't see outside the cockpit. Not ten feet. Or ten thousand feet. He couldn't see the goddamn city anymore!

They hid it.

"Pilot, we are getting out! Do you hear, pilot! We are jumping!"

Some veterans. "No!" Ted shouted. "No one's leaving this plane until I tell you, goddammit!" If anyone jumped now they'd be ripped to shreds by low-detonating flak. "Nobody's going anywhere! Hold on!"

Ted kicked the rudder over, slammed the control column forward and right and gave the only engine he had left all the juice it would take. The Heinkel gave a shudder, dipped its right wing, nosed over and dropped like a lead sinker. They wouldn't be expecting that, Ted told himself. They wouldn't be expecting a medium-weight Luftwaffe bomber with its bomb doors open and one engine gone and half its wing shot off to suddenly bank away against the drag, drop its nose and head into a steep-angled, full-powered dive. But if Ted was going to get out of here, if he was going to drop any bombs anywhere, if he was going to do anything right, first he had to shake that bloody searchlight.

"Pilot! *Oh, God!*—you're going to kill us!"

Ted ignored the intercom. He held his arms straight out on the wheel grips of the control column and kept the aircraft in as steep a dive as he could hold and he closed his eyes as tight as he could squeeze them. So tight he saw red. He had to get his vision back. He had to see the instruments.

One thousand one. . . .

The nose gunner was screaming. He was somewhere on the flight deck with his stomach in his throat, yelling his guts out.

One thousand two . . .

The veterans were making semi-articulate sounds that were garbled together on the intercom; begging, pleading sounds, praying too, but Ted ignored them. It wasn't time yet.

One thousand three . . .

The engine was racing frantically, straining for more fuel, as it bit into denser and denser air.

One thousand four . . .

Ted opened his eyes. The shaft of light was gone. The cockpit was dark again. He could see the city, buildings, roofs —but he was diving too fast to look for reference points. He was over the city, but he didn't know where. He thought he recognized the majestic silhouette of the British Museum, but —no, he couldn't be that far north. He couldn't have missed the river!

He pulled back the power, eased the control column until the bomber was not diving, but still coming down. The searchlights were all over the skies. They'd find him again, but first he had to get rid of these bombs. The plane was too heavy to go on with just one engine. He had to find something, a park, the river, a pond, something—

He saw the playing field almost dead ahead just as a beam of light passed across the cockpit and disappeared again. They'd find him in the next sweep. There wasn't any time to compute airspeed and trajectory or rate of fall. The bombs had to go now.

Ted grabbed the bomb release handle, guessing at his altitude, willing that the bombs be straight on target, then pulled. The plane lightened immediately, bobbing as if in relief that it had finally shed two thousand pounds. Then Ted poured the power on, lifting the nose, and headed directly east by the compass. He climbed to twelve thousand feet through the searchlights, but none of them caught him again. In eight minutes he was out of the London zone, limping along at just over ten thousand feet, heading north of Southend, toward the Channel. The Heinkel was a tough old bird. There wasn't much left of her, but she'd kept him alive and the starboard engine was running. It was going to be a shame to let her crash.

"Gunners?" Ted hadn't heard a word out of them since he'd turned their stomachs into jelly.

The intercom crackled. "Yes, sir." They answered together; two wilted flowers.

"Jump," Ted said.

There wasn't an immediate reply, then: "Sir?"

"Get out. I can't make it to the Channel. You'll have to jump."

Another pause. "Over England? The plane sounds good enough . . . can't we make it to—"

"If you want to fly it," Ted snapped, "it's all yours. I'm leaving in thirty seconds."

"We're jumping, Lieutenant," came the quick reply.

Ted nudged the nose gunner with his foot, pointed a thumb over his shoulder. "Out."

The sergeant nodded. He buckled his parachute, started toward the gangway to the exit hatch, then stopped and looked at Ted with his sad nineteen-year-old eyes. "You shouldn't have done it, sir. You shouldn't have bombed London. It was forbidden."

Ted nodded. Right. He pointed with his thumb again.

"Out."

When he saw the third parachute open, Ted leveled the plane and held it at three thousand feet. There wasn't much fuel left but enough to fly his wounded bird twenty minutes more, set the controls then jump out himself over some deserted spot in Belgium.

Did it work?

Was all this time and planning and effort going to make the slightest difference? What if no one really cared whether London was bombed? And even if they did, was it in time? Was there even going to be an RAF tomorrow? Had he risked his life—had he killed—for nothing?

He tried not to think about it. He pushed it back as far out of his mind as he could, back in some compartment of his brain where he wouldn't have to deal with it. Just not right now. Later tomorrow. After he'd had some sleep. Sometime, but not now. *Not now!*

But it wouldn't go away. It kept coming back to him again and again, the same question.

Did it work?

Part Five

29

It WORKED.

The very next night, Sunday, Churchill ordered a reprisal strike against Berlin and of the eighty-one RAF aircraft dispatched, half found Berlin in the heavy cloud cover. What bombs were dropped fell in the suburb of Ruhleben. The damage was minimal, compared to the risks the RAF had taken to inflict it: the bombers had to fly five times further to reach Berlin than the Germans did to reach Southampton and, because of fuel requirements, carried smaller bomb loads.

But the damage was done, trifling as it was. Hitler had lost face. Bolstered by Goering's repeated guarantee, the Fuehrer had told his Berliners that the city would never be bombed. But the British bombed it Sunday night. Then again Wednesday. And Saturday. And the next Tuesday. One bomb that failed to explode fell in the Chancellery garden.

After the fourth raid, the Fuehrer addressed a mass audience in Berlin's Sportpalast.

He assured his people he would not allow this effrontery to continue. He would raze English cities, he said. If the British dropped three or four thousand kilograms of bombs on any German city, then the Luftwaffe, in one raid, would drop three or four *hundred* thousand kilograms. And the Fuehrer kept his word. On Saturday, September 7, exactly two weeks after Ted's bomb run over London, the Blitz began.

The Luftwaffe was given new orders. Now the German bombers roared across the Channel in wave after wave toward one target and with one objective. Obliterate London. Pound the heart of England to dust. Teach the British a lesson.

The strategy had worked. Luftwaffe planes were diverted from RAF targets to London. Hitler's wrath had saved Fighter Command. The expense was London. More than nine hundred planes attacked the city in the first wave. Three hundred planes in the second wave. There were five hundred people killed that first day, in nearly seventy enormous fires and a thousand lesser ones which illuminated the city like a beacon for the planes that came at night.

It worked. But Ted wasn't crowing. He had helped think it up.

"What do you mean you're quitting?" Moser whispered across the table. "You can't *quit*, for Chrissakes. This isn't like a subscription to the *Saturday Evening Post!*"

They were sitting at a small table outside a café in the Tiergarten near the Siegessaule memorial column. It was a clear, sunny afternoon; the pigeons in the park were oblivious to a patch of newly-turned ground where an RAF bomb had uprooted half a dozen lindens two weeks before. Ted had called this meeting with Moser.

"That's exactly what I'm doing," Ted said. "You can tell Carstairs that. You can tell him anything you like, but as of this instant I'm finished with it."

"Goddammit, Campbell, you can't—"

"Don't tell me I can't quit. I just did."

Moser took a long breath. "Have you discussed this with Haushofer?"

"It isn't a subject I'm willing to discuss."

"Have you *talked* to Haushofer?"

"I haven't seen him since—" Ted paused as a waiter passed with a tray of empty glasses "—since before I went to Holland. I haven't seen *you* since then."

"Is that it, then? You need someone to hold your hand?"

"No," Ted said shortly, "I don't need anything except to be out of this."

"Why?"

"*Why!*" Ted raised his voice. He hadn't meant to. A woman

reading a book a few tables away glanced up curiously. "C'mon." Ted got up. "Let's walk."

"It's better if we stay here."

"Let's walk!" Ted said urgently, then turned and started toward the park.

Moser caught up with him a few yards away. "Campbell, you're a fucking asshole." Moser gave him a grim look. "I don't like working with assholes."

"Then your troubles are over," Ted said. "I've done all I'm going to do. London is pounded every night. My part in it is over."

"*Your* part hasn't even started yet. Hess is your part."

"Was."

"You're telling me you won't do anything?" Moser stopped on the walking path. "Nothing? Not even work Hess?"

"Especially that. Look, you don't need me. I don't think you people really ever did."

"We *do* need you, goddammit!"

"You have Haushofer."

"Haushofer! Good Christ, Campbell, didn't Carstairs explain anything to you?"

"He never mentioned Haushofer . . . not as part of this."

"That ought to tell you something. He isn't. Haushofer isn't part of anything. Carstairs doesn't trust anyone. Do you think he'd trust a German? Hell, he doesn't even trust his own MI-6."

"But . . . Haushofer knows about Pythagoras . . . he showed me a coin, he knows my code name. He—Christ, he *sent* me to meet you! That must mean something!"

"It means something all right." Moser started walking away. "It means Carstairs is using him. Haushofer *thinks* he's part of a plan to eliminate Hitler from German politics. He thinks by embarrassing the Fuehrer militarily—like this bombing of Berlin—Hitler will lose the people's confidence and the military will find the guts to kick him out."

"Haushofer *believes* that?" Ted shook his head. "Nobody's kicking Hitler anywhere."

"Carstairs knows that."

"Then what the hell can I do. If you've got Haushofer—"

"Haushofer isn't against the war," Moser cut in, "he's against Hitler."

"And Carstairs isn't?"

"Carstairs wants what we all want. He doesn't fancy Germans running Parliament. Haushofer believes in *Lebensraum*; he is for expanding Germany's borders, but to the east. Haushofer wants the Ukraine. At least in that respect, Haushofer and Carstairs agree. They both want Germany to move against Russia."

"That still doesn't explain why I'm so essential—"

"Hess," Moser said. "Rudolf goddamn Hess. He's the reason. He's the only leverage we have because he doesn't want war with England and because he hates communism as much as Haushofer. Hess is the only important member of Hitler's inner circle who will speak up against an invasion of England. And he trusts you and Haushofer. That's why you're important to us . . . to Carstairs. If Hitler is convinced that England isn't a threat, if Hess can persuade him that the real enemy is Russia, then the day German troops cross Russian soil is the day Hitler commits himself to a double-front war." Moser glanced at Ted. "And that's the day it all turns around. Germany can't survive a prolonged war. It can't fight two wars at once and win."

"You're nuts! Just leave me alone!"

"We're talking about saving thousands of lives."

"Saving lives! Carstairs has already used that one, Moser! Christ, I dropped eight bombs on London. Eight bombs! Did that save any lives? There may not *be* a London in another week thanks to me!"

"In the long run, Campbell, it—"

"The long run doesn't mean a damn to me. People are dying right now. Right fucking now . . . in London. And you know why—because I listened. I let Carstairs talk to me. Well, I'm not listening anymore. Do you hear? I don't want to see you again. I don't want to find notes under my door or in my shirts. I've quit my laundry and I've quit you and I'm out. I know enough about this setup to destroy it. So just leave me alone. You understand?"

"I understand," Moser said with a hard look. He clasped Ted on the shoulder and they stopped on the walking path under the shade of a linden. "My kid's in London. He's nine and I haven't seen him since he was seven. I can't even carry a picture of him. I know what it is to have my stomach tie itself in knots whenever I see a goddamn Luftwaffe plane. *I know*. So don't ever threaten me. That would be a mistake—a fatal one." He took his hand away. "Okay, you quit." He didn't look at Ted. "I'll pass it on. As of now you're out."

"Thanks," Ted said, feeling his heart jump. But Moser didn't reply. He turned away to light a cigarette, cupping the match in his hands, then walked away without another word, a faint line of cigarette smoke visible behind him until he reached the sunlight.

Ted watched him go until he couldn't see him anymore. "Shit," he said.

30 _____

Nigel Trentlyon cursed his bad luck. It had all happened so fast he wasn't exactly sure what had gone wrong.

He glanced at the man behind the desk across the room who was sorting through a stack of papers, unaware or, more likely, unconcerned that Trentlyon had been waiting on the same wooden bench nearly all morning. Waiting for what?—that was what Trentlyon wanted to know. Whatever it was, it wasn't going to be pleasant. He was sure of that.

Our Quinby Franks will have to be gotten out.

Trentlyon remembered when Carstairs had said that. When was it?—two weeks ago? Three? An age ago, it seemed now. He remembered they were in the office on Great Portland Street. Carstairs was studying the large map on the wall. He seemed always to be studying it, Trentlyon recalled, as if it held the answer to some great mystery that could be solved with enough concentration.

Quinby Franks was alive and if not exactly well at least not in the hands of the Gestapo. That was the analysis they'd come to after the Ultra source had deciphered an Enigma transmission which described a search for an escaped British spy. The reasoning was clear enough. If Franks had been in the hands of the Gestapo when he sent the call for help in Utrecht then the Germans would not have sent a priority message to their security headquarters to find him. It was the verification that

Carstairs had asked for; it was the proof that Franks was not part of a Gestapo trap.

At least Trentlyon had thought it was proof enough. Carstairs was not totally convinced. "There are some very clever people in the German counterintelligence group," he'd said. "We mustn't dismiss that fact."

Trentlyon hadn't dismissed it. Germans could be a devious lot, he knew, still, *he* was prepared to believe that Franks was alive and hiding from the German dragnet in Utrecht. Perhaps it was because he wanted to believe that Franks was alive that he volunteered to get him himself. After all, Trentlyon knew Holland, he'd been posted there for two years in the early thirties, he spoke the language, he could easily pass for a Dutch businessman if need be, but more important, he knew Franks. If Carstairs was hesitant, if he still suspected it was some sort of trap, then Trentlyon argued, let him go and sniff around. A meeting place could be established where Trentlyon could observe who showed up. He knew Franks well enough that if there was anything funny about him he could call the whole thing off on the spot without ever actually meeting anyone.

Carstairs didn't like the idea of sending his own deputy but Trentlyon pressed home the thought that if the man was alive and hiding in Utrecht he couldn't last indefinitely, that they couldn't just leave him there. Perhaps that was what finally stirred Carstairs to relent, that and Trentlyon's persistence.

But that was days ago. Trentlyon had had time to reflect on the decisions and the circumstances that brought him to be where he was today. There hadn't been much else to do but think, actually. What had gone wrong was due, he was convinced, to his bad luck. He was simply at the wrong place at the wrong time.

He glanced up when the door opened behind the man at the desk. An officer spoke to the paper-sorter, who nodded, then pointed to Trentlyon with his pen. "Take him inside," he said, not paying much attention to which of the SS guards responded.

Two German soldiers lifted Trentlyon to his feet. His wrists were handcuffed, his right foot was asleep, and he stumbled between the guards as they led him into the adjoining room. They sat him roughly into a wooden chair. He squinted to make out the figure in the black uniform who was standing in front of him, but the sunlight that poured into the room hurt his eyes.

"What is your name, please?"

Trentlyon turned his face away from the light. Whoever it was, he spoke Dutch very well. "Polder," he said through parched lips. "Claus Polder."

"Your real name, please."

Trentlyon offered a smile. "Still Claus Polder. Somehow there is a mistake, *mein herr*. I do not understand—"

"You will understand, I think." The man had switched to English. "You will understand how much trouble you are in because you are wearing civilian clothes. I know you are a British agent."

Trentlyon looked blankly at the figure as if he did not follow the language. *"Englisch?"*

"You're all alone," the voice from the sunlight said. "No one knows you're here—no one in England. They think you've had an accident."

"Neen Englisch." Trentlyon shrugged. *"Holländisch."*

"And you speak it very well, but you'll get over that. I want you to understand that you're caught. I set a trap and you walked into it. I want you to know that I can be patient, to a point. We will be spending a great deal of time together because you will be telling me whatever I want to know. I want you to understand that. Herr Franks understood it, eventually. And so will you."

"Begrijp niet Englisch!"

The figure pulled the curtains closed and Trentlyon blinked in relief. He could see the man plainly now. He was an SD major and his face was pockmarked.

"Oh, you understand me perfectly," Regenbauer said. He smiled. "Don't you, Herr Trentlyon?"

Carstairs learned the news about Trentlyon an hour before dinner. It was a special dispatch from MI-6 Netherlands Office. Nigel Trentlyon and Quinby Franks, the dispatch read, had been victims of an autocar accident. Fatally injured.

Carstairs was on line to the office immediately for confirmation.

The duty officer repeated exactly what was in the dispatch.

"You're sure, then?" Carstairs demanded. "Both killed?"

"Yes, sir."

"And the bodies?"

"Bodies, sir?"

"Of course, the bodies, man! Were they recovered?"

"There was a fire, sir," said the DO apologetically. "They were both burned to a cinder, the way I got it."

Carstairs nodded into the phone, "I see." He groaned. "Then there wasn't any positive identification?"

"It was the right car, sir . . . and two men . . ."

"Yes, well, right. Thank you, Major." Carstairs rang off. He didn't believe a word of it. Trentlyon was a dead man, that was true enough; he just wasn't dead yet. Carstairs knew it, he felt it. *Why had he let him go!*

He stood on the balcony of his Great Portland Street office waiting for Luftwaffe's night raid to begin, half wishing a five-hundred-pounder would crash through his building. If he was any judge, the entire structure of the Pythagoras network was doomed. Someone had engineered a very clever trap. Someone had baited the snare with a spy to catch a spy.

Carstairs shook his head solemnly at the darkness that covered the city. Whoever it was—the Gestapo or the Abwehr —they'd soon discover what Pythagoras was. They'd know if they could keep Trentlyon alive—they'd *make* him talk. Carstairs closed his eyes. Trentlyon would know what he had to do. He hadn't any choice.

Carstairs blinked back the burning behind his eyes and gripped the balcony railing. Trentlyon knew too bloody much!

"Do it!" Carstairs cried. "You *have* to do it!"

It wasn't because of his concern for the ultimate protection of the Pythagoras scheme that Euclid willed his deputy to commit suicide. It was deeper than that. Trentlyon had unauthorized knowledge of source Ultra. Information Carstairs had given him. Besides Churchill, only two men on the face of the earth could give away the most closely guarded secret the British possessed. And the Germans had one of them.

31

WHEN KATE EMERGED from the basement apartment, Ted was waiting. He'd made himself as comfortable as possible, leaning against the brick wall of a recessed doorway half a block away, watching the apartment she'd slipped into thirty minutes ago. It had been easier to follow her than he'd expected. She didn't take precautions to conceal her late-night rendezvous and that disturbed him. Either she was being dangerously careless or tonight's meeting with the stocky little man named Freimark was entirely innocent. But there wasn't anything innocent about him. Ted had followed her for the past five nights and this was the third time she'd been to this address. He'd checked the name on the mail slot after the first night and discovered Ludwig Freimark was a driver at the Propaganda Ministry. He wasn't the type Kate would go out of the way to meet like this for any romantic dallying. It was, however, very likely that Herr Freimark was her party contact, all things considered. Moser had said Kate was one of them and Ted hadn't any reason to doubt it now. And if Moser was right, Kate was in danger. The Gestapo would find her out eventually, and he knew exactly what they'd do to her. Well, now was the time for a confrontation with Kate. Better now with him than later with the Secret Police. If Ted could get out of his spying role for the British then she could do the same for the Bolsheviks. If he could convince her.

Ted stepped out of his hiding place as Kate disappeared around a corner. She'd be heading back to her apartment. They're all amateurs, Moser had said about the communist underground. Well, there was one amateur Ted was going to rescue from being a statistic. He started walking.

He arrived at Kate's building ahead of her and waited at the lift. Kate entered the lobby fumbling in her purse for her key. When she looked up she was startled to see him.

"Ted? What on earth—"

"I want to talk to you."

Kate made a production of looking at her watch. "Do you know what time it is?"

"I want to talk to you about your friend."

"My friend!" She glanced at the ceiling wearily. "I told you last time it was none of your business. My God, Ted, who do you think you are? My relationship with Johann—"

"I'm not talking about Regenbauer."

Kate frowned. "He's the only *friend* I have."

"Ludwig Freimark," Ted said quietly. "Your *other* friend."

The color drained out of Kate's face. She seemed to have stopped breathing.

"I thought you'd recognize the name." Ted opened the lift cage for her. "Let's talk . . . now."

"Me, a Bolshevik? You've been sitting on your brain too long." She was more composed, sitting in the security of her own flat, Ted thought, but she wasn't at ease. Kate had poured them each a drink, straight Scotch, and sat on the sofa. It was the seat farthest away from Ted.

"It's just occurred to my why you don't take any precautions about being followed," Ted said. "It's because you're *not* followed. At least not by the Gestapo. It must be one of the fringe benefits of having Regenbauer for a playmate." Ted shook his head. "I wonder if you know how much danger that puts you in—if he ever found out about you and the underground."

"I don't know what you're talking about."

"C'mon, Kate! Christ, I've been following you! Who is Freimark?"

"*You've* been following *me*?"

"For the past five nights."

"You've no right—"

"For Chrissake!" Ted exploded. "I *know* you're involved with the Soviet underground! And if I can find it out, how long before Regenbauer does?"

"*How* do you know?"

"It doesn't make any difference. Don't you see that? The underground is a step away from being exposed. The Gestapo is infiltrating it. In less than a year they'll know every goddamn contact in Berlin. How long before they get to you? How's that going to make SS Major Regenbauer feel about you when he learns he's been sleeping with a Russian spy, eh? I'll tell you how he's going to feel. He's going to kill you, that's how he's going to feel."

Kate took a sip of her Scotch. "You're getting bad information from somebody. I'm not anyone's spy. Certainly not for the Bolshies. I believe in the National Socialist—"

"Oh, shit!" He was up from his chair and glaring at Kate. "It's Doug, isn't it? Goddammit, it *is* him! Of course it is! He went off to fight the people's fight in Spain and when he didn't come back, you picked up the banner. That's it, isn't it? You're working for them *because of him!*"

Kate glared back at Ted. "I think you've had enough to drink," she said in a measured voice. "I think you'd better leave."

"I'm not going anywhere. You're going to tell me everything about your involvement with this Freimark . . . everything about your commitment to the party. We're going to get you out. Completely out. Otherwise, you're dead. Do you understand? Like Doug."

She slapped him as hard as she could. "Get out! *Get out!* It's none of your business! You haven't any right—you haven't . . . any right . . ."

Ted pinned her arms under his. "I'm not going to let you get yourself killed." He held her by the shoulders and shook her. "Listen to me, damn it!"

"No!" Kate twisted to get free of him. "Get away! *You're* the Nazi-lover! *You're* the one who sold out to them!" She was screaming now, trying to loosen his grip on her wrists, shouting through her tears. "You're their fucking lackey! You and Goering and Goebbels and—"

Ted hit her. He'd never hit a woman before, but he hit Kate with his open palm across the face and the blow knocked her backwards, nearly lifting her off her feet. She tumbled awkwardly over a small table and landed spread-eagled and unconscious on the sofa.

Ted's first thought in the suddenly quiet room was that he killed her. But she wasn't dead. She was breathing. Her eyes were rolled back when he raised her eyelids to check the pupils, the corner of her mouth was bleeding, and her cheek was taking on the first discolored hints of a nasty bruise, but she wasn't dead.

He lifted her from the sofa, carried her to the bedroom, and lay her on the bed.

It was the damp cloth on her forehead that finally brought her around. Ted was dabbing a moist ball of cotton to the cut on her mouth when she opened her eyes. Kate groaned, touched a finger to her puffy cheek.

"I'm sorry, Kate. I . . . I . . . didn't mean—"

She tried to clear her head by shaking it, blinking. Her fingers found the cloth on her forehead. She slid it down and pressed it against her cheek. "When you get pissed—" her eyes focused on Ted "—you get *pissed*."

"Kate—"

"You're sorry, right?" She grimaced when she touched the cut at the corner of her mouth. "You really are out for blood, aren't you? What're you gonna do, kill me before someone else has a chance? That's what I call fanatic protection." She pushed a strand of hair back from her temple. "God, my head hurts. How do I look?"

"You've looked better," Ted said. He sat on the edge of the bed beside her. "Are you okay now? Can I get you something?"

"A drink."

Ted shook his head. "Sorry, you've had enough booze."

"Hell, I haven't even started." She tried to get up, grimaced, then dropped back on the pillow. "You hit hard!" She held the damp cloth over her eyes and for several moments was quiet.

"Kate—"

"If you apologize one more time, I'm going to scream." She pressed the cloth into her eyes. "I'm not going to get hysterical or anything and I am reasonably composed; enough to finish our . . . talk. You know about Freimark, okay. So let's talk about Bolsheviks." Her fingers slid down her face to touch her tender cheek. "But you can beat on me till Christmas and I won't say another word unless I have a drink." She pointed to the night stand beside the bed. "There's a half bottle of real Kentucky bourbon in the drawer. I've been saving it for something special. This'll do."

Ted retrieved the bottle and found two glasses in the bathroom. He poured her a half measure of the whiskey and pressed the glass into her hand. "Easy, now."

Kate tossed the cloth off the bed and eased herself up against the headboard. She held the glass out to him, then downed the alcohol in one long gulp.

"Take it easy!"

She handed him the glass. "Let's have another."

"I want you talkative, not pickled."

"Another," Kate said adamantly, holding out the glass.

Ted sighed, splashed bourbon into her glass.

"Thank you." Kate nodded. "This is sort of like the old times, huh, you and me sharing a bed and a bottle of booze."

"Not funny."

She considered it, sipping the whiskey. "How did you find out about Freimark?"

"I've been following you."

"That isn't how."

"You've been acting very odd. This cozy little act of yours with the Nazis"—Ted shrugged—"it isn't consistent."

"Consistent? With what, for Chrissake! I told you I didn't—"

"I know you better than that," Ted said quickly. "Maybe you can fool some of these yahoos around here, but not me."

"I don't believe that for a second!" She snorted. "You never knew me. That was the goddamn problem between us. You didn't know me at all!"

Ted set the bottle on the table. "Well enough," he said. "How deep are you involved with the underground?"

"Why do you want to know? You're the one who's chummy with Reichsmarschall and the rest of them."

"I'm not as chummy as it might appear."

"What is that supposed to mean?"

"Let me ask the questions, okay?"

"You're working for someone," she said suddenly. She stared at him, her mouth half open. "Aren't you?" She shook her head. "I'll be damned! Ted Campbell—committed. I don't believe it! You're working for *them*, aren't you? The British!

Or is it the Americans?" She shook her head again. "Christ, I can't believe it!"

"Good, because it isn't true."

"How did you know the party was infiltrated by Gestapo? How did you know about Freimark? *You* didn't figure it out. Somebody told you. If it was Gestapo then we'd be dead, so it only leaves the other side."

"Do you usually hallucinate when you drink Kentucky bourbon?"

"You're a goddamn British spy!" Kate sighed, spilling her drink.

"You're drunk."

"How else could you know? You are, aren't you?"

Ted shook his head. He got up from the bed and began pacing. The change in his pocket jingled as he found a coin and turned it over between his fingers.

"We're on the same side, you know," Kate said. "Theoretically, anyway. We're against the Nazis."

"Will you shut up!"

"Thinking, are we? Wondering what to do with little Katie?"

"You're in a great deal of danger, goddammit!"

"And you're not, I suppose."

"I'm not sleeping with an SS officer."

"You can't prove the Gestapo's infiltrated the underground, can you?"

"Prove it?" Ted stopped pacing. He withdrew the coin he'd been fingering and held it in his fist. "To who—Freimark? I don't give a damn about Freimark. They're using *you*, Kate. You're—"

"Where did you get that?" Kate grabbed Ted's wrist.

"Get what?"

"This!" She snatched the Maria Theresa silver thaler from his hand. "This!" She held it up to him. "Where did you get it?"

Ted looked at her with a bewildered look. "It's a good luck piece."

"Don't give me that bullshit! This is a recognition coin! It's a goddamn 1870 Austrian silver thaler—the Maria Theresa —and it's part of a recognition code for a group—" She stopped to suck in her breath. Her eyes got very wide. "Oh, God, Ted? Oh, Jesus! You're not part of that!"

"I don't—"

"You're the one in trouble, Ted," Kate said. "Not me." She glanced at the coin. "This is what Johann is investigating! He showed me this coin—told me what it meant. He's already caught someone. Someone now dead. He's been in Holland for the past month running it down."

"Holland?" Ted remembered Regenbauer's face in the crowd at the Luftwaffe field at Soesterberg. "Where?"

"Utrecht, I think. God, Ted, you *are* working for the British!"

"What does he know?" Ted demanded. "What does Regenbauer know!" He couldn't know about the flight. Christ, if he —Ted looked quickly at Kate. *"What does he know!"*

"He doesn't exactly confide in me. I haven't seen him for weeks, but . . . but he's very close to something. That's what he said. Breaking up some huge ring of traitors. I don't know much more than that except it doesn't involve us, I mean . . . he's not looking for Russians. I know that. It's something to do with spies in the government, someone close to Hitler. That's all I know. They call themselves by code names, classic Greek scholars, I think. The main one is . . . is . . ."

"Pythagoras." Ted let out a deep breath.

"It isn't *you*, is it?"

"No, it isn't me," Ted said slowly. He ran his fingers through his hair. "Close, you said."

"He thinks he can break it very soon." She shrugged. "I don't know what that means. He's been working on it for months. Some sort of special project. He's Heydrich's man. He's done several special jobs for Heydrich in the last couple of years. Eliminations, he likes to call them. He likes to boast about them. He makes them look like accidents."

"What?" Ted's voice was a whisper.

"He makes them look like accidents," she said. "He thinks he's very clever. He—"

"When!" Ted grabbed her arms. He pulled her to within a few inches of his face. "When did he do these jobs for Heydrich!" His voice was trembling.

"I . . . I don't know exactly, Ted. In the last few years . . . I don't know for sure. Ted, you're hurting me."

"Since the spring of 1938?"

"Before that. Ted, please . . ."

He released her. Then he closed his eyes, covered his face with his hands. "Jesus," he said in a low, trembling voice.

"Ted? What . . ."

He shook his head.

"Does it mean something?" Kate touched his arm. "Ted?"

"Regenbauer, he—" Ted choked on the words. He tried to clear his throat. "Regenbauer killed my father."

He felt Kate's hand stiffen, heard her sudden intake of breath, then softly, as if she understood, "Oh . . . God . . ."

There wasn't any reason that he should cry. Eddie Campbell had been dead for two years and in all that time Ted hadn't cried over the loss. They hadn't ever been close, not the way other sons had been close to their fathers. But he was crying now.

He told her everything then because she was there and because he trusted her now. It was like a time an eon ago when there were no secrets between them. He told her about Carstairs and Hess and Moser and the bombing of London —everything. And Kate listened, quietly, without a word, staring at her hands.

When Ted had finished Kate looked up at him with tears in her eyes. "I'm sorry," she said. "I'm . . . sorry . . ."

They made love to each other finally, not because it was convenient or expected, but because it was the natural progression of their bond of sharing. It was a gentle and considerate lovemaking; not the clumsy and harried experience Ted had had with Anne and not the mechanical and emotionless coupling Kate had endured with Regenbauer. And when they were physically and emotionally spent they lay quietly in each other's arms in the private darkness of her room.

Kate spoke first. Her head was nestled against his chest but she didn't move except to let out a gentle sigh. "What do we do now?"

He didn't answer.

"Ted?"

"I don't know what we do now. I'm too tired to think. I don't want to think about anything. Except you." He caressed her breast with his hand and blew a gentle breath across the nipple.

"Ted, I . . ." Kate sighed.

"What?"

"It's so damned adolescent."

"I feel adolescent. What?"

"With everything else that's happened it . . . feelings seem so trivial." Kate rubbed her hand down the muscles in his back. "Do you—" she sucked in her breath. "Oh, damn, Ted. This isn't the time."

"You *are* being adolescent. What is it?"

"Do . . . do you think you could . . ." She closed her eyes. "Do you think you could ever love me?" She shook her head against the pillow. "Oh, God, listen to me! I sound like a silly deflowered eighteen-year-old in the backseat of a Studebaker."

"It isn't so silly." Ted raised up on an elbow to see her. "And it wasn't a Studebaker, it was a Ford, and we were in the front seat and you weren't anywhere near deflowered." His smile was gentle. "And, yes, I could. I wonder if I ever stopped."

"Now who's being ridiculous?" Kate looked away from him. "This is a hell of a time to be discussing . . . love or . . . or whatever . . ."

"This is exactly the time." He drew her to him.

"Ted, don't . . ."

He kissed her neck.

"—please . . ."

He kissed the lobe of her ear.

"—Ted . . ."

"Ten years ago you said you loved me." Ted brushed her hair back from her face and kissed her high on the cheek. "You weren't interested in settling down, you said. The next thing I know you're off to France."

"I had a career."

"It didn't stop you from getting married."

"You didn't have any goals. You only had your damn airplanes. You didn't need anything—Ted, stop that! I thought you were so tired."

He'd pressed his thighs between her legs. "I guess I wasn't that tired." He kissed her mouth, then looked into her eyes. "Why *did* you marry Doug?"

"He loved me. *Me*, Ted. I don't expect you to understand."

"And you loved him?"

Kate nodded.

"Who do you love now?" He couldn't see her face clearly and wanted to see it.

"You're not being fair," she said after a moment's hesitation. "This isn't fair to you or me . . ."

He silenced her with a kiss. "Whatever is fair or just doesn't make sense anymore. This war has turned everything backwards. Things that used to be important to me aren't anymore."

"Ted, listen—"

"No, you listen. I love you, goddammit, and I'm running out of second chances. I want you to get out of Germany."

Kate tensed. "What?"

"It's dangerous here for you. I don't want to take a chance—"

"Now wait a minute," Kate said, pushing herself up on her elbows. "*You* want *me* to leave Germany?"

"The sooner the better."

"Fat chance."

"Goddammit, it's too dangerous for you here! Don't you see that?"

"I happen to be a news correspondent covering a war," Kate answered quickly. "What would you have me tell my employers—send me someplace safe like Peoria, Illinois? Thank you very much, but I've done my time in the little armpits of the world so I could come here."

"What you happen to be is a woman walking a tightrope with the Bolsheviks on one end and the Gestapo at the other. This isn't a movie. When people get shot in this war they stay shot. People are dying, for Chrissakes. I know. I killed some of them!"

Kate sighed. "Christ, I . . ."

"I don't want anything to happen to *you*. All right? I have something to do and I want you safely away."

Kate's eyes suddenly got wide. "I go . . . *you* stay? Now there's a clever bit of logic. I'm not going anywhere if you're staying in Germany. What's so important that needs you to look after it? You talk about me being in danger! Christ, you're the one walking around with the silver thaler in his pocket!"

"Important people need my help. I'm not going to involve you in it."

"If you're talking about Hess then forget it, he doesn't need a chaperon. He has the British intelligence service to do that. You don't owe him anything."

"I have another debt to pay." Ted lay back on the pillow. He stared at the ceiling. "I owe someone for my father and a hundred others." He looked at Kate. "And for you."

"What are you talking about?"

"Regenbauer," Ted said. "I'm talking about Johann Regenbauer . . . killing him."

32

KILLING REGENBAUER, with all the hazards that that task implied, was an obligation Ted had prepared himself for—he'd accepted the risk. But determining to kill Regenbauer was one thing; finding him was, Ted discovered, quite something else. After a week it seemed as if Regenbauer had never existed. Ted had exhausted every contact he had in the government trying to locate him without success. There were Luftwaffe records (thanks to the officious Colonel Junger in the Air Ministry) that proved Regenbauer had served with the Condor Legion in Spain, but the trail ended there. Regenbauer had joined the SS but those records were not available to Ted. After seven days all Ted had learned for his trouble was that Regenbauer worked alone and he did not have an office anywhere in Berlin. The one place Ted hadn't visited was the one place he hadn't any bona fide reason to ask a lot of curious questions. Gestapo headquarters was not one of his usual watering holes.

But it was one of Kate's and she'd gone there against Ted's instructions to stay out of it. Besides, she had friends in the Gestapo, people she had met at parties who had helped her with other stories. She was, after all, a news reporter and obvious friend of Regenbauer's and it was logical that she could get away with asking questions about the sudden, mysterious disappearance of the SS major. Logical to everyone except Ted.

"Goddammit, Kate! I told you to stay away from the Gestapo!" Ted paced furiously in front of the window of her flat. "What is it that makes you so stubborn!"

"I found out where he is, didn't I?" she replied calmly. "It wasn't all that powerfully difficult. I was careful, believe it or not. I happen to have a good reason to stop at Gestapo headquarters, since I also happen to be a news correspondent and Seven Prinz Albrecht-Strasse is as good a place for news tips as anywhere. Anyway, I've been there before. On top of *that,* who gave you the sudden goddamn power to tell me where I can go!"

Ted stopped pacing. "You've been there before? I didn't know—"

"The sum total of what you know—"

"All right, all right," Ted said, raising his hands. "All right!"

"So, where do we go from here?"

"To Haushofer." Ted moved around the sofa and sat in the overstuffed chair opposite Kate. "I have an appointment to see him tomorrow."

"What can—"

"Your Gestapo friend confirmed that Regenbauer is working on something very secret . . . Pythagoras, very probably. He's doing this solo because he doesn't know yet—let us hope and pray—he doesn't know yet how big the conspiracy is. I imagine he expects to get a lot of mileage from cracking this thing—promotion, glory, leverage . . ."

"Power," Kate added.

"Right. Anyway, Haushofer's my only contact to Carstairs now. He has to know that the network is in trouble."

Kate frowned. "What about the laundry? Can't you send a message to . . . what's-his-name—Moser?"

"No." Ted sipped his drink. "I went to where the laundry used to be two days ago. It's a flower shop now. Different people. After I quit Moser he probably shut it down just to be safe. So, Haushofer it is."

Kate nodded. "What are you going to tell him?"

"Everything. Regenbauer has to be stopped. He'll do whatever he can to protect Hess."

"Are you going to tell him about me?"

Ted was quiet for a moment. "If I have to convince him it's true . . . yes."

"And Freimark? The underground?"

He looked up at her. "I don't want to, Kate."

"But you will?"

"If I *have* to."

"Christ!"

"Do you have a better suggestion?"

"You know what Haushofer will do, don't you? He hates the Russians as much as he hates Hitler. He'll go straight to Himmler."

"I doubt that."

"You *doubt* it? It's one thing to quit Freimark, but it's something else to turn them in. I won't do that and I won't let you do it."

"Kate—"

"I swear to God, if you tell Haushofer . . . I'll . . ."

"All right, goddammit!"

"Promise me."

"Yes," he said, "I promise." It was a lie. Freimark didn't matter to him. Or the underground. Only Kate mattered. He wasn't going to lose twice.

Regenbauer, of course, wasn't in Holland and hadn't been for days. With a handful of SD men he'd moved his base of operations inside Germany, to Wesel, a small town on the Rhine. Regenbauer had prepared for the move some time in advance so that his departure from Utrecht was both sudden and unnoticed. He'd left specific instructions forbidding anyone to contact him other than by radio and then only in extreme emergency. That he could demand and receive compliance to such an irregular order was challenged only once. Some inexperienced officer at Gestapo headquarters in Berlin had brashly and ill-advisedly demanded to know on whose authority such an obvious abuse of procedure was being ordered. His defiant query was quickly settled. Reinhard Heydrich— Obergruppenfuehrer Reinhard Heydrich, *Chef der Reichssicherheitshauptamt*—was authority enough.

So far as the Gestapo or the Reich was concerned, Regenbauer had ceased to exist, until such time as *he* decided to reappear. It was an arrangement that suited Regenbauer and the Gestapo as well. That his secret work, whatever it was, might

last indefinitely was the private hope of more than a few
Gestapo officers who'd toiled under him in the past. He wasn't
well liked, the Iceman wasn't. Especially when he smiled.

None of this would have been much comfort to the heavy-
bellied man with the pale skin, who was now gasping for
breath against the pain in his ribs as he lay nude and shivering
on his stomach, even if he'd known. What he knew and didn't
know was precisely the reason for his being here. He didn't
know, for instance, that he wasn't in Holland anymore. He'd
been drugged to sleep for the trip from Utrecht. He didn't
know that his new home, this dank and windowless cell, was
once an elegant resting place for Premiers Crûs red wines from
the vineyards of the French village Morey-Saint-Denis. He
didn't know that the large stucco and timber manor house that
squatted on its century-old foundation above him had belonged
to a Jewish textile merchant before he and his family were
"relocated" and their wealth confiscated. Not that he would
have cared even if he did know, because he had other things on
his mind. He was obsessed with how he was going to kill
himself.

Nigel Trentlyon knew he had to die the moment he laid eyes
on his interrogator. Even when he realized the SS man with the
cool blue eyes had only bits and pieces of the jigsaw puzzle
that was Pythagoras, he knew. Because sooner or later this
man was going to break him. And when that happened . . .

Trentlyon squeezed his eyes shut.

Cannot think about *it* . . . *cannot think about IT* . . .

Time was important. Time was the only thing left. He had to
hold on to his sanity. He had to beat them at their own game, at
least for a while. Time, he needed it. However much of it he
could squander was that much longer he could keep the secret
inside of him. Time to figure a way to do himself. If that was
possible. They'd taken his clothes. They'd removed everything
from . . . this place. He'd figure something. He had to. It
wouldn't take much. A nail. Something sharp. Because it had
to be quick. Something. A pencil. But they'd taken everything.
There was nothing here but . . . him. Naked.

There had to be a way, bloody Christ, there had to be!

He raised his cheek off the floor and felt a stabbing pain in
his side. He forced himself to look at the door of his cell. A

solid, timber door. Naturally, the pins that held the hinges were on the other side. Clever bastards, weren't they.

They fed him on a wooden tray, the food just piled up on it. That was after he'd tried to steal the wooden spoon. He might have whittled it down to a point against the walls. But they came and took it away. There wasn't any bloody place to hide it!

He'd even tried not eating, to starve himself. That was his first ploy. Five days he tried it. Five bloody days! And he realized almost too late that one of the stages of fasting was delirium. No telling what he might have said in that state. No, he had to eat.

The sound of advancing footsteps touched his recently acquired sense for dread and he pushed himself up on his flabby buttocks to await the jangle of keys, the turn of the bolt echoing in the narrow passageway, the door creaking open to reveal the silhouette of the smartly dressed interrogator in his immaculate black uniform. Trentlyon had weeks ago given up caring about the indignities of his situation. It was more important to conserve his strength and concentration for the interrogation that was coming. He couldn't get up without help anyway. By his own painful examination, touching and probing the swollen rolls of his flesh, he figured he had at least three broken ribs. The routine was fairly well established now. They beat him in the mornings and questioned him in the afternoons.

The blue-eyed interrogator never came to the beatings. At least, he didn't think he did. Perhaps when he'd passed out from the pain. He recognized the method of their strategy. The beatings were just to soften him up, to wear him out, to prepare him for the afternoon sessions of endless questions.

Clever bastards.

They used heavy wool socks filled with sand and there were two beaters and a guard stationed at the door. That was how it began. After half an hour or so, when one of the beaters tired of the sweaty work, he'd trade off with the guard. The morning sessions lasted usually an hour or two, though he couldn't be sure because sometimes they beat him unconscious, then back to consciousness. More than once he'd come around groggily to the *blat . . . blat . . . blat . . .* of sand and wool against the pale, bruised folds of his skin. They concentrated on his sides and shoulders mostly, the socks getting heavier and harder toward the end of the session as they absorbed the perspiration that covered his body. Mercifully, by that time, the beaters had lost their enthusiasm and much of their strength in the monotonous business of whipping this blubberous seal and Trentlyon was spared really serious damage.

Only three broken ribs. It wasn't so bad. He had a few bleeding scabs that had been opened and reopened when a sock broke, spilling sand all over him to be ground into a bruise, and he had a thousand black-and-blue marks. But he'd live. After all, that was the idea. Theirs, anyway.

The door opened outward, moved by some invisible hand, the dry pins screaming against the ancient hinges, and there was Regenbauer, hands clasped behind his back, the silver-threaded shoulder patches of his SS rank glistening in the light, not a thread out of place on his black tunic. Dressed to kill, Trentlyon thought.

The Englishman stiffened slightly from the chill of trepidation that coursed up his spine as a wispy smile touched Regenbauer's lips. The shadow of his cap hid his blue eyes, but Trentlyon knew they were eager too, smiling in their own way. Anxious.

"Ready?" Regenbauer said.

33 _____

TED ARRIVED AT the professor's house late because a traffic
accident on Hermann Goering Strasse had blocked the street,
and Ted had paid the taxi and walked. A tram had struck an
automobile that was crossing a busy intersection against the
yield, and the chain reaction that followed had the intersection
crowded with angry motorists and their bashed motorcars. The
car had careened off another, jumped the curb and crashed
through a storefront window. As Ted was picking his way
through the broken glass, a hand grasped his coatsleeve.

"Help, *mein herr*. Please . . ."

It was the driver of the car that had crashed into the store.
His forehead and nose were bleeding, and his eyes were wild
with terror.

"Please, please, help me with the boy!"

The store was a dress shop. Once inside, Ted realized what
had happened.

A boy who couldn't have been more than eight or nine had
been standing in front of the window watching the cars pass
outside while his mother was shopping. When the car crashed
the boy was directly in its path.

"Please, help him!" the driver was crying. "Please, please,
help this boy!"

Ted knelt down beside the figure on the floor. A woman
—his mother, Ted assumed—was on her knees amid the

broken glass, wiping blood from his face with the hem of her dress. Her voice was quiet in contrast to the excitement of angry voices and blare of whistles and horns outside.

"Hans . . . Hans . . ." She called his name as if he were asleep, gently, so not to startle him awake. ". . . Hans . . ."

The boy was lying only a dozen feet from the crumpled grill of the automobile, both its headlights fragmented in the crash. Ted knew the boy's chest was crushed. Judging by the way he lay on the floor, both his legs were broken. But there was no blood except from the lacerations to his scalp. His face was untouched by the force that had brutalized his body and his blue lips were the only sign that he was dead.

"Please . . . do something for him!" the man with the bloodied forehead pleaded. He was standing over them, his hat crumpled between his hands, pounding it against his chest. "Please, don't let him . . ." Tears welled in his eyes and ran down over the streaks of dried blood on his cheeks. ". . . *mein herr, mein herr, please* . . ."

Ted found the boy's wrist to feel for a pulse he knew would not be there. He looked at the boy's mother. It was the hardest thing he'd ever done in his life. "I'm sorry. He's . . ." Looking into her eyes, he couldn't say it. "I'm sorry . . ."

She took the small hand from Ted and lay it across the boy's chest. "Yes," she said softly. She pushed a lock of her son's blonde hair back from his forehead. When she looked at Ted again her eyes glistened with tears of apology. "He did not mean it . . ."

Ted glanced at the man crying into his hat. "I know. It was an—"

"—he did not mean to die."

Ted's eyes flicked back to her, his breath caught in his throat. He was terribly afraid he'd heard her right. He stared dumbstruck as she took from her purse a metal-wreathed swastika and placed it under her son's lifeless hand. "He didn't mean to," she said, shaking her head slowly. She stared at her son and when she spoke again, her voice was proud. "My Hans, he is a handsome boy, yes?" Her chin quivered when she smiled. "A good Aryan."

When Ted arrived at Haushofer's house he was still trembling. A hundred times he had heard the radio speeches and learned nothing. Hitler, Goebbels, Goering, even Hess—they were just spouting words; a symphony of words. And they meant nothing because he was not German, because he was not a follower, because he did not need a leader or a cause to live for or a symbol to cherish. He hadn't seen it until now. Absolute faith. *Absolute faith!*

As he rang he could not dislodge the image of the woman holding the swastika in her dead son's hand. She believed. Hitler had done that. Hitler, the Nazi machine, the Utopian promise of a new, grand Reich—they were responsible. *They were responsible!* He would never forgive them for that. He would never forgive them for that woman.

Frau Haushofer answered his ring, then escorted him to the study where the professor was waiting. Wolfe was lying in one of the large chairs. He growled a steely-eyed welcome, remembering, no doubt, their last encounter, then hopped down from his place and retreated from the room as his mistress pulled the door closed.

"How have you been?" Haushofer came around the desk to shake hands. "I read something of yours the other day quoted in *Börsen Zeitung* . . . You adjusted to this journalistic business quite well, yes?"

"No complaints," Ted said.

Haushofer gestured to one of the chairs. "Sit down, sit down. Tell me—What's this?" He held his hand out, palm up, and stared at it. There was dried blood on his fingers. "Have you been hurt?"

"No-no, I . . ." Ted shook his head. "There was an accident a few blocks from here. It's nothing." He did not want to talk about it.

"Pythagoras," Ted said quickly. "I have something that must be forwarded to England."

The professor glanced at him. "I see." He nodded. "I also have something important to tell you."

Ted acknowledged him with a shrug. He'd rehearsed this in his mind, how he would tell Haushofer about Regenbauer without implicating Kate. Whatever the professor had could wait. "I have a reliable source who—"

"Correct me if I'm wrong, but I was led to believe that you were no longer connected with . . . our Anglo-Saxon friends. I was told you disengaged yourself from further commitment."

"Yes, I did, but—"

"Then why are you here? I'm not sure we should be discussing a subject that pertains to matters you are no longer a party to."

"If you'd let me explain!" Ted said in a burst.

Haushofer nodded. "Please do. I'd be interested to know the reasons for your sudden indifference to our plan, inasmuch as you played a pivotal role in its execution. Perhaps you don't realize the great amount of trouble you've caused us. Certain plans had to be altered because of your change of heart."

"I know." Ted nodded impatiently. "I know. I'm sorry about that, I—"

"Sorry?"

"Look, Albrecht, I wouldn't have come here if it weren't important! The whole Pythagoras operation may be compromised by now."

"Really?" Haushofer seemed calm.

"Yes, goddammit! There's an SD officer named Regenbauer who's on to it. I don't know how exactly except that he beat it out of some poor bastard who was a network operative. Regenbauer knows! He knows some sort of operation exists, he knows it's code name Pythagoras, he knows code signs and recognition signals, he knows the Austrian coin is—" He paused. "You'll have to stop him."

"Then you're willing to come back with us?"

"I . . . I guess maybe I am. I hadn't thought that through."

Haushofer snorted. "Haven't you?"

"I don't know what's so goddamn funny. Don't you see what I'm telling you?"

"Yes, I believe I do."

"Then . . ."

"Where is this Regenbauer?"

"Holland somewhere."

"Somewhere?"

"I don't know *exactly* where! He's hiding until he can put the pieces together."

"By pieces you mean the Pythagoras puzzle?"

"Yes."

"And who is he hiding from?"

"I don't mean hiding precisely. If there *is* a conspiracy involving a high Nazi official, then it would make sense for him to lose himself until he can figure out how widespread the conspiracy is. He's not going to trust anyone, including the Gestapo."

"An SS officer hiding from his own Secret Police force." Haushofer smiled. "Perfectly logical, isn't it?"

"Jesus Christ! Don't you understand? I'm telling you the operation is in danger of being discovered. You have to protect Hess!"

"Even if it means shutting down the network?"

"Of course . . . at least until Regenbauer can be . . . neutralized."

"Which means he'd have to be found first?"

"Yes." Ted restrained his temper. "It *would* be necessary to locate him. That's what I'm saying. Unless we do something about Regenbauer the operation is in trouble. If he figures out what's going on here he can stop your plans to thwart the invasion of England."

"The invasion is off," Haushofer said.

Ted stared at his host dumbfounded. "What?"

"The invasion of England has been canceled. That is, the Fuehrer has postponed it indefinitely. The first phase of our plan is a success. We are now embarked on the second phase —the Soviet question. The Fuehrer, with Hess's strong support, is now considering what options we have in dealing with the Russians. Which makes this sudden visit of yours so curious."

"Canceled?" Ted leaned back in his chair as the meaning of it sunk in to him. It worked! That outrageous, crazy scheme worked? "I'll be damned," he said.

"Your effort in the execution of the plan was possibly . . . no, it *was* the most crucial element of the success of phase one." Haushofer stared at Ted with a look that defied understanding. He certainly didn't appear very pleased, Ted thought.

"Why are you angry, then?" Ted asked. "If you're so pleased—"

"In light of your activities *after* August twenty-fifth," the professor said, "perhaps it would have been better all around if you had crashed in England."

"What!"

"I'm referring to your relationship with Fräulein Buchanan," Haushofer said. "We know who she is . . . and what she is—"

"Now, wait—"

"—and that you are alive today is due directly to your selfless contribution to phase one." Haushofer leaned forward. "The problem is, what do we do about *her?*"

They thought he was working with the Soviet underground! The more he thought about it, the more he laughed. Haushofer, probably Moser, probably all of them, had interpreted the evidence to conform with the theory that Ted had changed sides. They'd believed something as foolish as that because the nature of the game was to do everything backwards.

Fact: Campbell quit the operation. Why? Because overpowering guilt had influenced his perspective of morality.

Fact: Campbell has developed an intimate relationship with Fräulein Buchanan. Why? Because he's been duped by an agent of the Red Orchestra who's persuaded him to the communist side.

Fact: Campbell claims operation in danger. Why? Because now that Campbell is working with the Soviets he will do and say anything to thwart the operation.

It all made nightmarish sense. "You know, Albrecht," Ted said, "you're a goddamn idiot."

Haushofer spread his hands on the table. "I'm afraid we're not accomplishing anything here. Perhaps you should leave."

"You don't *really* think I'm working with the Russians?"

The professor shrugged.

"I'm not! Good God, Haushofer, I'm telling you the truth! Regenbauer is real! He can cripple your plan. Are you going to pass that on to England?"

Haushofer only stared at him.

"Are you!"

More silence.

"Jesus Christ, why do you think I came here! Why do you think—oh. Oh, right. I'm working for the goddamn Russians to sabotage phase two. Right? Look, just let me talk to Moser. I can straighten it out with him."

"I don't know anyone named Moser."

You may call me Moser. It isn't my name but you ought to call me something.

"You know who I'm talking about!"

"Yes," Haushofer allowed, "but I doubt he wants to talk to you."

"I *have* to see him!"

"A waste of time. The apparatus is closed to you. You're a security risk."

"If I'm such a goddamn risk, why not kill me? Aren't you afraid I might go to the Gestapo?"

"And implicate yourself?"

"Tricky fellows like me have ways of avoiding that."

"And Fräulein Buchanan. Is she also tricky?"

Suddenly it wasn't funny anymore. "Kate has nothing to do with this!" Ted's voice was hoarse with alarm. "She's not a part of this! *She's not a part of this!*"

"My dear Theodore, you are wrong. She is part of you. That makes her important to us. If your own safety is not a concern to you, then perhaps Fräulein Buchanan . . ." He shook his head again. "The thing is, you see, not so much how to use the leverage but where you find it."

"You sonsofbitches!" Ted jumped to his feet. *"You sons of bitches!"*

"We don't *want* to hurt you, but you know too much. Not enough anymore to cause us irreparable harm—we've made certain adjustments—but enough to cause irritation. We have *not* killed you. So, our dept to you is paid. From this moment I would advise you to be careful. If not for yourself . . . then for others. And as for this, this . . . story. This SD major. Regenbauer?" Haushofer glanced at Ted from the corner of his eye. "Did you really think we would have closed everything down on the strength of that?"

Ted couldn't look at him. "You're going to think back on this moment and you're going to . . ." He shook his head. "What about Kate . . . Katherine Buchanan? You won't . . . ?"

"Of course not. She's hardly a threat to us."

"Like me?"

Haushofer shrugged. "Less."

Ted walked to Kate's place and on the way tried to think out a sensible explanation for Haushofer's idiocy so he could explain it to her. Only there wasn't a sensible explanation. Haushofer had simply ignored him. Ted fought not to think about the threat against Kate, but it kept coming back to him. Carstairs must be desperate or just crazy. He wouldn't really harm her, would he? Still, you couldn't guess what these maniacs might do. Haushofer should have listened to him. *He should have!* One day he'll know. One day soon when the world crashed in on him. Then it won't matter anymore. They're going to take over the world, the Nazis are. They're going to run everything one day and the sonsofbitches will have everyone so heel-clicking scared that it all works as efficently as a goddamn Swiss watch.

Ted arrived at the apartment building on Freisingerstrasse just before six. It had been a long walk from Haushofer's and he was tired and his rage hadn't yet subsided. The rush-hour traffic was in its last stage but the sidewalks were still busy with people hurrying home. At the lobby entrance Ted had stepped back to hold the door for an old woman with a can when he glanced across the street and recognized a man smoking a cigarette. He was standing at the corner, away from the other pedestrians at the crosswalk, near the entrance to an old church.

Ludwig Freimark.

He was studying the third-floor windows of the apartment building. Kate's apartment, Ted suddenly realized. The bastard was spying on Kate! It wasn't enough that the squatty little bastard had told her what parties to attend, which Nazis to favor, which SS majors to sleep with . . . now he was following her, recording her movements, watching her.

Without thinking, Ted was suddenly crossing the street, taking long angry strides, his rage rising to his eyes. It was Freimark's misfortune to be on this particular street corner, at this particular time, on this particular day. He was going to be sorry, the little chain-smoking comrade was. Goddamn sorry!

A car screeched its brakes as Ted made his way across the street. Freimark turned toward the noise and his eyes got round as he saw Ted coming for him. So much happened in the next few seconds, Ted never did sort out the chronology of it. He was raging mad, he knew that. And when Freimark saw him coming, apparently he knew it too, because his mouth opened and his face squeezed into a grimace of absolute terror. His arms went up from the elbows, palms out, as if he were making some gesture of defense, and he backed into the iron railing that surrounded the church. Then, Ted thought, the gaping-mouthed commissar cell leader did the most unnatural thing a man in his situation could do.

He looked at his watch.

Freimark clawed at his wrist, frantically checking the time while Ted closed the distance between them. Ted didn't understand it. Then Freimark aimed his terror-stricken face at Ted, then at Kate's windows, then back at Ted.

In that instant, when Freimark's panicked, glassy-eyed stare touched him, Ted suddenly understood with horrible clarity what he was doing there. Freimark wasn't spying at all. He wasn't watching for her. He was waiting for something. He was checking his goddamn watch because something was about to happen!

"Kha—aaaa—ATE!" Ted spun around, shrieking at the shaded windows on the third floor, "KHA—AAAA—ATE —EEE!" Then he started running, screaming with all the power in his lungs, racing to get to the building.

A tiny part of his mind was aware of what happened behind him, but the sounds all rushed together like a stream of nonsensical tunes—the church bell tower chiming out the hour, a frantic flutter of pigeons taking flight to escape the knell, a strident skirl of wheels braking, a man's shrill scream cut short by a loud, sickening thud . . . But the sounds were all fused together by the force ot the explosion. Ted felt the blast in the street, followed by a rain of shattered and splintered glass and bits of wood. When he glanced back at the street from the lobby entrance, people were scurrying for shelter or fright-frozen where they stood. Ted didn't see Freimark at first. Then he saw an ashen-faced truck driver climbing out of his cab and Freimark, his crumpled body sprawled against the curb.

The lobby was filled in seconds with a mob of occupants, clambering to get out. They spilled out of the stairway entrance to the upper floor like a herd of gun-shocked cattle.

"Bombs! They're bombing us!" someone yelled.

"—Fire! fire . . . !" from another.

"—British bombers! It's the bombers . . ."

Ted was nearly carried along with them out the door, but he forced his way back. He shoved his way to the stairs and up. On the second-floor landing, he passed a door that had no room behind it, just a hole where the floor had been and curtains burning on a broken rod before a shattered window. The third floor was on fire. People were lying in the hallway, some dead, crushed in the collapse of the interior brick walls and timbered ceilings. The others were choking in the smoke, whimpering sobs for help. Abruptly Ted's was one of the voices.

"Kate . . . Kate . . . answer me . . . Kate . . . goddammit . . . KATE!"

He called her name again and again. He was crying, stumbling through the thickening smoke, tears blurring his vision until he had to drop to his knees for breath.

She couldn't be dead! He wouldn't allow her to be killed like this! Then he remembered another fire, another woman, another search through burning wreckage and the futile aftermath of it all. It couldn't happen again! They can't take Kate too! *"Kaaate!"*

He crawled on his hands and knees over a sea of broken plaster until he couldn't see anymore and he had to feel his way through the smoke. The corner apartments of these buildings were set into the most structurally sound part of the building. They had steel girder reinforcements, didn't they? Double-thick brick walls, wasn't that right? The corner apartments were the safest part of the goddamn buildings, right? Ted stopped to wipe his eyes. Right? He ripped off his coat and draped it over his head. Goddamn right they are!

. . . she isn't dead . . . she's hurt, but she isn't *dead* . . . *she isn't dead* . . .

When he bumped into the wall at the end of the corridor he thought it was another beam until he felt the exposed ribs of the wood slats in the plaster wall. He felt around for the door. It was here, somewhere, to the right. Right here some—He nearly fell into the gaping hole where the door used to be. Half of the floor was gone and with it half of the outside wall and he could see into the street. That's where they'd put the bomb, in the corner of the adjacent apartment. The blast had disintegrated the walls on two sides and the floor had given way for lack of support. He could look into the hole and see burning rubble two stories below him.

"Oh, Christ, no . . . NO!"

He got to his feet, smashing his fist against the half-crumbled plaster walls, then he stepped back, reeling with unfocused rage, stumbled and fell over Kate Buchanan.

She was lying on her side against the splintered baseboard on the other side of the corridor, which was why Ted hadn't found her before. She must have been somewhere near the door. The blast had blown her and the door into the corridor.

Ted scrambled to roll her gently on her back.

. . . she isn't dead . . . she isn't dead . . . *she isn't dead* . . .

He tried to take her pulse, but he couldn't feel it for the pounding of his own. Her head was bleeding, there was a terrible gash above her right eye. The back of her dress was shredded and she was bleeding from several small cuts. Her right arm was broken. Ted bent down to her face, holding his breath. The sound of sirens outside drowned out anything he might have heard. But he did hear something. He was sure he did. Shallow breathing? The faintest whisper of breath?

. . . she isn't dead . . . she isn't dead . . .

She *was* breathing! He saw the flutter of an eyelid. She wasn't dead. She wasn't dead!

"You're alive, goddammit!" Ted exhaled, suddenly joyous. "You're alive!"

He picked her up carefully, setting her broken arm across her chest, and started back down the corridor. She was breathing deeper now, ragged, but deeper. By the time he got her to the second-floor landing, her eyes had fluttered open.

"Don't worry," he said. "I'm getting you out."

"Ted . . ." She blinked, tried to hold her eyes open.

"Don't talk. You're going to be okay. You're gonna be fine."

"I . . . can't . . ."

"Don't talk!"

He nearly stumbled down the last few steps into the lobby. Half a dozen people were wandering aound. A fireman was rigging a hose.

"Out of my way!" Ted demanded. "Get out of my way!" He carried her out of the building. Several people offered to help, but Ted ignored them and went straight to a truck with Red Cross markings.

"She was in there," Ted said to one of the attendants as if it weren't obvious. "Help her. Quick. She has a head wound and a broken arm and—"

"Set her down here."

Ted lay her carefully on a stretcher. Kate's eyes were open, staring at the sky. He bent down beside her; his eyes welled with tears. "You're going to be okay, okay . . ." He took her left hand and squeezed.

"Freimark . . . did . . . it . . ."

"Never mind." Ted looked over his shoulder at the attendant. "Hurry up, goddammit!"

"Must have . . . been . . . Freimark . . ."

"Forget it. He won't be bothering anyone anymore."

"Told . . . him . . . yesterday . . ." Kate's voice was barely a whisper.

"What?"

". . . that I quit . . ." She tried to smile. "Guess . . . he . . . didn't . . .like . . . it . . ."

Ted brushed her hair back from her forehead. "Don't try to talk . . . please. Later, when we fix you up."

"Where are we?"

"Don't worry about where we are. You're going to—"

She squeezed his hand. "Are we outside?"

"Yes, of course, we're outside. What does it—" Ted stopped. He stared at her staring at the sky. She blinked, but her gaze didn't change. "Kate . . . !"

"I can't see," she said quietly. "I can't see anything at all."

Part Six

34 _____

OCCLUSION OF THE central retinal artery by frenetic cranial distension is what the doctors called it. What it meant was that Kate was completely, permanently blind.

Ted had taken her to the most prominent opthamologists on the continent but the prognosis was always the same. The damage to the retinas of Kate's eyes was irreparable. There wasn't even a slim chance she would see him.

It was Christmas now. Friemark was dead and Kate was blind and none of it would change. He'd brought her to the villa in Friedrichshafen after her discharge from the Berlin hospital and they had lived there alone together except for trips to visit eye specialists. The villa became their new home —without interruption from the outside. For the first several weeks, Kate had used his wheelchair to get around until she was familiar enough with the house to move about on her own. They began with one room at a time, the bedroom first, then the kitchen and the path between them. Ted had moved to storage everything that might cause her to stumble, then put them back one item at a time until she had the entire house and its contents mapped out in her mind.

Kate wore sunglasses always, except in the bathtub and in bed. Her adjustment was slow and sometimes bruising in the early weeks when she bumped into corners or misjudged a piece of furniture. She refused to use the cane Ted got for her.

She learned to cook, after a fashion. Pancakes were her breakfast specialty. She claimed she knew when they were ready to turn just by the sound they made.

They spent most days with Ted reading to her on the patio until the late October cold forced them inside to the fireplace. She taught herself to iron, to cook, to sew. She made the bed every morning and even stoked the fireplace. She began to learn braille.

Eventually, they grew comfortable together, each anticipating the other's needs. They slept together, of course, and made love regularly—passionately, genuinely. By December, Kate said she was ready for visitors. Ted was against it, he didn't want anyone invading their privacy. He was happy and contented and with the woman he loved. But Kate insisted, and had her way.

Lowell Grayson came down from Berlin. The first hour or so was awkward: he was uneasy and nervous and talked about everything but the obvious until Kate put an end to it by telling him to stop acting like an idiot. She was blind and that was that. The rest of the evening went smoothly and Lowell told them the news that they had missed in the last three months.

Italy had invaded Greece. London was still getting pounded by the Luftwaffe, but Berlin was getting some of the same. Most of the action had moved to sea. Dönitz's U-boats were ravaging the North Atlantic shipping, severely threatening England's line to the United States. Roosevelt had been reelected to a third term and the Germans and Italians had made a military pact with Japan. And, of course, there had been no invasion across the Channel. Maybe in the spring.

They had invited Lowell back for Christmas but he called the day before to beg off. His secretary had come down with a severe case of influenza and chances were excellent that he'd caught it too; no point in spreading it around. So they spent Christmas alone, which suited Ted fine. He'd cut a little tree from a stand of pines on the north edge of the estate and set it in the den opposite the fireplace and Kate helped decorate it. The balls of tinsel and the misshapen gingerbread cookie men from Kate's kitchen hung from the branches in dollops rather than with any preconceived notion of orderliness and the angel at the top had only one wing, but it was the most beautiful tree Ted had ever seen.

Christmas night they lay together in front of the fireplace

and exchanged gifts. A pair of mittens for Ted, without thumbs, that Kate had secretly knitted from scraps left in Mrs. Glebe's sewing box. For Kate there was a scratchy phonograph recording of how to prepare *zakuska* and Siberian *pilmeny* for a party of twelve—in Russian. They laughed like children, arms and legs all a-tangle, rolling on the heavy fur rug in the firelight, then made love.

"It's been a lovely Christmas," she said late that night. "The best I've ever had."

"You're not going to cry or something, are you?"

"No, I mean it. It's been wonderful . . . the tree and the dumb record and this . . . us. It's been the best. I love it all. I love you. I . . . oh, Christ, I *am* going to cry."

"Must be my charm." Ted kissed her. "I reduce all my women to tears after the heat of passion finally subsides. Gratitude, I guess."

"Shit."

"Yes?"

She sighed. "I'm trying to be serious and tender and what do I get . . . W. C. Fields."

"You want serious? I'll give you serious." He rolled on his side, crossed his leg over hers. "Marry me."

"Ted—"

"I mean it."

"No."

"You have to. It's insane to be stubborn about this. I love you, for Chrissakes!"

"I don't want to be proposed to. Please. I won't talk about it."

"You think because you're blind it makes any difference to me? I love you! You think it's because I'm sorry for you? Well, you're wrong. Goddammit! You're wrong!"

"That's why you never asked me before?"

"Shit." Ted raised up and clasped his hands around his knees. "Stubborn, goddamn thick-headed . . ." He pushed over her, got up.

"Where do you think you're going?"

"The fire needs another log." Ted went to the bin. "I'm not giving up," he said. "I'm not giving up! Stupid . . . stubborn . . . thick-skulled . . ."

The telephone rang. Ted ignored it.

"You going to get that?"

"No," Ted said defiantly.

"It might be Lowell."

Ted stood over her. "Right! Just what I need, to listen to one of your old flames chatter on about his fucking cold."

She sighed. "Oh, all right, *I'll* get it."

"No, no." He padded across the cold, dry floor to the desk. "Hello!"

"Herr Campbell?"

"Who'd you expect?" Ted barked.

"Excuse me," the professor said. "Did I get you up?"

"As a matter of fact, you did." Ted covered the mouthpiece and turned to Kate. "Haushofer."

"Tell him Merry Christmas."

Ted uncovered the mouthpiece. "What the fuck do you want?"

"I must see you. Immediately."

"Sorry."

"Please. Tomorrow . . . as soon as possible. It's urgent. I can be in Munich by noon."

"No, Professor."

"*Please*! It's urgent!"

"No!" Ted shouted. "I'm having a buffet for my Soviet spy friends and I just can't fit you in."

"I was wrong about that. I was wrong not to have listened. But this is . . . is . . . *I must see you*!"

"Not interested."

"No, wait . . . *wait*! The invasion is . . . on again!"

Haushofer must have been screaming. Ted put the phone back to his ear. "What do you mean the in—"

"We cannot speak on the phone. Please, will you meet me in Munich?"

Ted considered it. He glanced at Kate. "No."

"But, Theo—"

"You want to see me, you come to Friedrichshafen."

"But . . . all right. I will come to your villa. Tomorrow?"

"Any time you like." Ted hung up. He went to the liquor cabinet and got two glasses and a bottle of Scotch.

"What was that all about?" Kate said when Ted returned.

"Company's coming."

"Haushofer?"

"Yeah." Ted slid under the quilt.

"What's he—Jesus Christ, you're cold!"

Ted set the bottle and the glasses on the floor above her head. "I brought something for that."

"What did Haushofer want?"

Ted poured out two measures of Scotch. "He says the invasion is on again."

"*What!*"

"That's what the man said." He handed her a glass.

"What does he want you for?"

"I don't know. But he's going to make a very long, cold trip for nothing if he thinks I'm going to help."

"Help with what?"

Ted shushed her with a finger to her lips. "I don't want to talk about Haushofer. I don't even want to think about him. I want to think about us. Hold up your drink. I want to make a toast." He clinked his glass against hers. "To you and me and the hell with everybody else."

"You're nuts."

"You're not drinking."

Kate took a long swallow. "You're still nuts."

"And you're a goddamn stubborn, granite-headed broad."

She held out her drink. "I'll drink to that."

He was never sure what the time was when they came. It was before dawn because the sky was still pitch black and they threw him in the back of the truck. All he remembered was that he came awake suddenly from the noise of the door being smashed, and that it was dark.

There must have been a dozen of them, maybe more; Ted heard the echoing slap of leather boots reverberating in the halls and the harsh sounds of German voices snapping commands as the strangers invaded his house room by room.

The den was nearly as dark as the outdoors. A figure swept through the room, banged into something, knocked over a lamp, and continued into the kitchen, cursing the darkness. They might not have found them except that Ted got to his feet. Kate was awake by then and he told her to lie still and he stood up. He wasn't afraid so much as he was surprised and angry. His mind still hadn't sorted out a reason for the sudden confusion; he was groggy from sleep and a third of a bottle of Scotch.

Whoever had stomped past on his way to the kitchen now was hurrying back through the den. He should have seen Ted, but he didn't. Ted grabbed him by the collar and swung him around. It was a uniform collar, Ted realized, and that made him more angry. An SS collar.

"*Hey!*"

It was the last coherent thing Ted remembered saying—or hearing. Something smashed into his stomach. It was probably a rifle butt, but he didn't think of it at the time. He was doubled over with pain. Then the second blow hit him high on the forehead. That *was* a rifle butt because he saw it coming and he tried to dodge it but he wasn't in much of a position to dodge anything—and then he was falling.

Everything after that was blurry and painful and chaotic. He couldn't make sense of the sounds. He thought he heard Kate scream, but there was so much yelling and screaming it was impossible to tell what was happening. He thought he reached for her, but he couldn't remember. He did hurt, there wasn't any fantasy about that; someone had just kicked his guts into his throat and he threw up his Christmas Scotch and his dinner. After that he couldn't hear anything but the buzz in his head. Some enormous black boot came at him out of the swirling darkness and cracked him between the eyes. Between the patches of darkness he saw odd, strange, frightening things. The fireplace was on fire, not the wood *in* the fireplace—the fireplace. Kate had her two hands over her ears and at the same time over her breasts and on her stomach and between her legs and some of them wore gloves and some didn't. He smelled smoke; it might have been just a cigarette, but it smelled like pine. Then he saw snow and trucks and a face beside a tailgate and he felt snow on his back and in his hair and suddenly he was terribly cold. The buzzing was still in his head when he tried to blink the whiteness out of his eyes, but the painless darkness inside his head forced his eyelids closed and he slipped away into it.

Ted woke up once, briefly, and saw the swirl of snow behind the truck as it was caught in the headlights of a vehicle racing to keep up. He was lying on a damp mattress with a wooken blanket thrown over him and he was bitterly cold. He was numbly aware that he was in a truck, that his hands and feet were bound, that he was alone and that he was freezing to death. He also knew that he was going to pass out again. The truck bounced and Ted's chin came down hard on the mattress.

His mind raced to understand what was happening before he

succumbed to the whirling, dizzying abyss. He tried to put some sort of order to the jumble of pictures that floated through his consciousness like debris in a raging river. For an instant he saw clearly two faces. Kate was screaming, her mouth was open and her unseeing eyes were wide, but there was no sound except the tremendous pounding in his head. It frightened him, seeing Kate like that, it terrified him; but not as much as the second image that flashed across his mind. It was the face of a man standing beside the tailgate of the truck. A man in a black uniform. And he was smiling. Smiling that horrible, wicked smile.

Regenbauer.

Ted screamed himself back into the darkness.

35 _____

WHEN THE Count von Wurttemberg had the Grafeneck castle built in the last quarter of the sixteenth century he had a hunting lodge more than a residence in mind, though he didn't make that clear to Georg-Friedrich Klee, who actually built it. Consequently, it tried to be both and failed on each count. The rooms were too small to accommodate large hunting parties and too large to live in. The castle was isolated, just set into the foothills of the pastoral buttresses of the Swabian Jura range.

It was a perfect site for SS doctors to work uninterrupted in their experiments on the mentally unfit; Grafeneck was remote, lonely, a fortified prison that did not look like one. Inmates were committed to cells converted from stalls in the estate's stables, and the main complex, the castle itself, had been renovated to house laboratories and living quarters for the physicians. It was a perfect testing facility; it was also an ideal interrogation center.

They called it *Entsetzenhaus*—terror house.

"What is your name!"
"Ca—Campbell . . . Ted Cam—"
"Who is Nigel Trentlyon!"
"I . . . don't know . . ."
"Where is Arthur Spengler!"
"I don't know . . . any Arth—"

310

"Are you Pythagoras?"

"No . . . *Aaaaahgh!* . . ."

"Where is Spengler!"

". . . don't know any . . ."

"Who is Nigel Trentlyon!"

". . . don't know . . ."

"What is your name!"

". . . don't . . ."

"Who are you?"

". . . baby . . . Campbell ba—"

"You are Pythagoras!"

". . . no . . . Campbell . . . Ted Cam—*Aaaaahgh!* . . ."

"Who is your British contact?"

". . . don't hurt . . . again . . ."

"Who is your British contact?"

". . . haven't got . . . contact . . ."

"Who is Nigel Trentlyon?"

". . . Campbell . . . Ted Campbell . . ."

"Who is Nigel Trentlyon!"

". . . don't have contact . . . don't know—*Aaaaahgh!* . . ."

"Your name is Theodore Campbell, isn't it?"

". . . A-mer . . . ican . . . sit . . . zen . . ."

"I will not hurt you if you answer my questions."

". . . A . . . mer . . . a . . ."

"Tell me, who is Nigel Trentlyon? He is your British contact, isn't that so? You are a British spy, isn't that so? You are Pythagoras, isn't that so? Answer me now. What is your name?"

". . . Ka—Kate . . . where iz . . ."

"What is your name!"

"Sim . . . Simple Simon . . . wh—went to . . . pie . . . man—*Aaaaahgh!* . . ."

"Take him back."

Ted opened his eyes even though his brain told him not to. He was lying on his side against a wall made of planks. There was straw everywhere, and the smell of urine was so strong it stung his eyes. He rolled on his back and the effort nearly killed him. He felt like a man who'd only barely survived a stoning. The throbbing in his head couldn't mask the pain in his sides and legs. Nausea rose from the pit of his stomach and he pitched himself over on his side to vomit but the contraction didn't come and the feeling passed. Ted lay there for several minutes, his forehead pressed against the clay floor, laboring for breath; then he tried to get up.

It was a mistake. He got to his knees and pulled himself up the wall but his legs wouldn't support him, and he slipped back to his knees. The nausea returned and this time he did vomit, retching on his hands and knees until his arms wouldn't hold him up and he braced himself against the wall to keep from falling into the slime.

He woke up again. He was sitting against the wall. This time he decided not to move. He took stock of his prison cell. The stall he was in was about six feet wide and ten feet long and the walls extended to the rafters. Some light filtered through the cracks between the planks, but not much. He was in some sort of barn or stable.

He vaguely remembered two men and someone else watching. They beat him up but they didn't use their fists. Something light but hard. He remembered the sound of it, the sound of them hitting him.

It wasn't so bad, the pain, as long as he just sat there. It was the stench of the place that made him nauseous. If only he could . . .

What was that? He heard something, wood scraping wood. It was a sound, a definite sound. Then he heard them coming and his stomach tightened into a knot. The footsteps. It was like before. *Now* he remembered. The footsteps. The guards in black sweatshirts. The questions. The beatings. Ted pushed himself into the farthest corner of the stall. He pushed himself in spite of the pain because the pain now didn't matter. They could make the pain worse, a hundred times. He pushed himself into the corner and drew his knees up in front of him. The footsteps were louder. They'd be in front of his door any second. He didn't want the pain! Christ, they'd nearly beat him to death already! He didn't know who Arthur Spengler was!

Shadows passed over the cracks in the door and Ted covered his face with his hands. The footsteps continued. They walked past. Keys jingled. A door creaked open. Then Ted heard the scream and closed his eyes as if that would block out the sound. They dragged the person out of his cell screaming and Ted listened to the footsteps as they took the poor bastard away, watched the shadows cross his door, until somewhere, someone slammed a heavy wooden door and the terrible shrieking was gone and Ted was alone again.

No one came for him for a week. For three days the footsteps came, but someone else was dragged away. For three days the shadows passed the cracks in the door of his stall, but did not stop. Then for four days there was nothing.

At first, Ted thought he'd been abandoned, that he'd been left there in that putrid cell to die, but every morning when he woke there was a wooden tray of food left just inside his door. *Somebody* was out there.

It took him two days to stand up and walk around his cell without using the walls for support. He tried to exercise the aches out of the muscles in his thighs by doing stretching calisthenics—situps and pushups and, after the cramps went away, jogging in place. The exercise gave him an activity to focus on and a goal: he had to get out of this place, he had to find Kate. He didn't know why they'd left him there but there wasn't time to try and figure a reason. Just get out if that was possible. The questions he could deal with later. Like, where was Kate? Where was Regenbauer? It wasn't Regenbauer who'd asked him the questions or beat him, so where was he? And how did they know about Trentlyon? How did they connect him with Pythagoras? Why did they think Ted was Pythagoras? And who the hell was this Arthur Spengler?

He started with the plank walls. They were old but solid as stone. Near the floor in one of the walls was an open heating vent no longer than the palm of his hand and he worked his arm into it in the hope he might find something he could use as a tool for getting out or even a weapon. But there wasn't anything but a bend in the pipe and the warm flow of air on hot metal.

The door was the sturdiest thing in the stall. It was new, the wood not yet discolored, and the crossbraces of the rough-hewn timber were bolted in place through the three-inch thickness of the individual planks. The lock's turnbolt was enormous and set into a metal housing that even an earthquake wouldn't dislodge.

There was only up or down. Climbing or digging. Ted glanced up at the rafters. Twenty feet. He started digging.

He began with his fingernails, scratching the clay floor, then he used the wooden tray after he'd tried to break it into pieces but it wouldn't even crack. He worked for hours but the clay was too hard; centuries of compaction under the hooves of countless animals had made the clay impenetrable. It would have taxed the strength of a man with a pick.

Ted sat against the wall and stared at the roof. It was the only way left. But even if he could get up to the rafters, what then? He wiped a grimy hand across his face. He had to try. He got up and inspected the corner of the stall. The planks had, over the years, shrunk slightly, allowing cracks between them. They weren't large cracks, not large enough to slip your fingers through, but wide enough to get hold with fingertips and toes. Maybe, if he had the strength and took his time, he could climb up the walls where they joined in the corner. He'd have to press his weight against the walls using his opposite limbs —left hand, right foot— in a coordination of balance and strength while his other hand and foot searched for purchase in the narrow cracks. Then by alternating the process he could —might—crawl up the wall like a crab. It would take strength he didn't know if he had.

Ted started climbing. He lost his balance at the five-foot mark and fell back twice, the second time scraping his shoulder raw against the rough wood. But he was learning the trick of balancing himself by putting more weight on his toes, rather than trying to hold himself with his fingertips. At eight feet a wood sliver jammed under a fingernail on his left hand and he slipped and dropped, slamming hard against the clay floor.

He rested nearly an hour before trying again. He'd considered giving up for the day; judging from the fading light it was getting dark. He could wait until morning, after he'd had something to eat. But he didn't have that option. They might come for him at any time.

He started up again. He almost lost it at six feet when he turned back the nail on his big toe, but he held on against the pain and went to the next crack. At twelve feet his left hand found a knothole. It was large enough to slip two fingers into for a solid grip. It was the only kindness the wall had granted and he indulged himself with a minute's rest. He'd climbed sixteen or seventeen feet when he realized he'd misjudged the distance. There was at least ten feet more to go to the rafters and the light was nearly gone. His arms ached unmercifully, but he knew he could make it now—if he could see. The darkness became his enemy. He had to see the goddamn cracks to position his fingers! Ten minutes was all he needed. Christ, five minutes! He shouldn't have rested. He should have known he was going to need the light.

Ted pushed himself up to the next crack with his toes. The muscles in his arms and legs were almost numb with pain. These were the critical moments. If he got a cramp now he was finished. He'd lose control and fall and from this height, probably break his back. He focused his entire being on the rafter above him. Six more feet. He could feel the cold chill of night seeping through the cracks on his sweaty skin. Five feet. The darkness was nearly complete. He couldn't see the rafter anymore as much as sense it. It was there, just there, above his head, another foot, two feet, he couldn't see it, but it was there, close, very close, just a little farther . . . God, grant me the strength . . .

When the first stab of cramp knotted the calf of his right leg, Ted knew he was finished. He'd tortured his body to the absolute limit of its endurance and now it was rebelling. It had been battered and bruised, then compelled to do the impossible, insane feats of strength and coordination. Ted cried out against the throbbing spasm, shifted his weight and strength to the other foot, straightened, and in one final, desperate push, his hands and arms extended over his head, lunged toward the darkness above him. For an interminable pulse-beat, suspended in midair, he couldn't tell if he'd propelled himself up or backwards. It was too dark, there was too much pain. But he'd know soon enough. If he slammed into the floor he'd know for sure. When he . . .

His right hand slapped wood, closed and held. The rafter. It *was* there! Ted took an excited, relieved gulp of black air and nearly lost his grip. He was dangling from a rafter twenty-five feet above a granite-hard floor by one sweaty palm. The pain from his shoulders to his knuckles reasserted itself and he nearly passed out; another few seconds of this and he knew he would. But he'd come too far now to let himself lose. Get up, he told himself. Get up, goddammit! Get your fucking ass up . . .

He swung his left arm up and over the rafter then, swinging his body in a short arc, kicked his feet to the wall and quickly walked up it, hooking his legs over the adjacent wood beam. He hung between the two rafters, exhausted. His head was swimming. He'd made it. That was all his mind could comprehend. He wasn't dead. He hadn't fallen.

"I'll be . . . a sonofabitch . . ." he whispered to himself, staring over the beam at the darkness below, his chest heaving. ". . . son . . . ofabitch . . ."

The rest he could have done in his sleep after what he'd been through. It was a thatch roof and all he had to do was snap a couple of slat supports, punch through the binding and, with the broken pieces of slats for prods, work his way through the thatch. It was a bit tricky balancing himself on the rafter while he worked, but nothing was hard now. He widened the hole, wriggled his head out, then his shoulders, then, with his arms outside, pulled himself onto the roof.

It was cold. There was only a sliver of moon, but it afforded enough light to make out major landmarks. Ted lay prone on the roof with his head just over the peak so as to get an idea of what kind of place he was in. He'd been imprisoned in a barn or stables all right, it was part of a reconditioned villa or castle. Mountain range behind him, maybe . . . north, northeast anyway. He glanced in the opposite direction. The Bavarian Alps, no mistaking that. Switzerland. Austria to the southeast. Then he wasn't far from home. This place was somewhere in the Swabian Jura range. The Danube was just ten-fifteen miles away. If he could get to the river . . . *Goddamn it was cold.* He wasn't going anywhere until he found some clothes. Ted scanned the grounds. There was a wire fence around the place. That meant guards—a guardhouse and barracks and beds and blankets and clothes. Ted crawled to the edge of the roof nearest the main complex of buildings. All the windows were shuttered and barred as near as he could tell. Whatever they did here, they weren't taking any chances of people getting away.

Ted made his way along the back side of the roof, searching for a place to get down. He wasn't going to jump, not take·a chance on breaking a leg. But he had to do something soon. He was so cold his teeth were chattering. Then he saw the tree, a pine at the end of the barn. Ted felt his way across the roof, glancing behind him to be sure he couldn't be seen in the courtyard. Two of the tree's limbs hung out like open arms toward the barn. One was about two feet from the edge of the roof and four feet down. The other, the heavier branch, was at an angle from the corner of the roof, about five or six feet away but nearly parallel with the roof line. The question was, how lucky did he feel? Ted could get to the smaller limb without much trouble, but would it support his weight? The heavy limb would hold him easily and it allowed a less troublesome access to the ground, but could he jump six feet? And if he could, would he hold on? He could feel his strength draining from the cold. He'd put himself through enough acrobatics for one night. He moved up the roof, positioning himself for the best angle to jump to the smaller branch, then took a couple of breaths, swung his arms back, then forward, and left the roof.

He should have risked the big branch. He realized it the moment he hit the smaller one. His weight plus the momentum of his jump put a sudden strain on the limb and it sagged and swayed. Then Ted heard the cracking; it began slowly, and he could feel it through the limb. Finally, it snapped. If there hadn't been other branches to impede the fall of the damaged limb, Ted might have been seriously hurt. As it was, he was only slapped and scratched by pine needles and small branches. The section of the limb that he clung to hadn't touched the ground and Ted loosened his grip and slid off. The experience had taken the last ounce of strength out of him. He was too exhausted to be frightened, too tired to be cold. He dragged himself to the wall of the barn and sat down against it. The hard part was over. He'd make his way to a village or farmhouse and call Haushofer. Then he had to find Kate. But right now he had to rest, just take a couple of minutes to let his mind clear. He pulled his knees up and rested his arching arms on them. He'd be all right in a minute. Then he heard a sound, a tiny whispering sound like a sniffling intake of breath.

"Amazing. Absolutely amazing."

Regenbaur was seated on a block of wood in the shadows behind the tree. He was wearing a heavy winter SS overcoat and he put his gloved hands on his knees for support as he stood up. Behind him like mute statues stood a pair of guards.

"You tripped a silent alarm when you broke through the roof thatch," Regenbauer said. "We've been waiting here for some time. I didn't think you'd ever come down from there." He nodded at the roof. "It was an amazing display of determination and courage." When he glanced back at Ted there was the hint of a smile on his lips. "Too bad."

They fed him a meager meal. Ted was alone in a large dining room with the two guards who did not speak. They'd provided him with something to wear; thick cotton hospital whites—a jersey and drawstring pants. Also slippers, not shoes, but no socks. He'd been allowed to shower while a guard stood by.

The place smelled like a hospital, which was not what Ted had expected of an interrogation center. He didn't know what was ahead, but they'd definitely changed their tactics. No one spoke to him at all. It was if the guards were there to protect him. It was odd, Ted thought. *Very* odd.

A nurse was admitted when Ted was finished eating. At least, he thought she was a nurse. She was dressed in white and she had the ugly, indifferent disposition of a practical medical assistant.

"Come with me, please."

"Where?"

"She frowned eloquently. "Come."

Ted followed her, with his two SS watchdogs close behind him. They all marched down a corridor, up stairs, down another corridor, like characters in a comedy; Ted slapping along in his slippers, Nurse Ugly walking stiffly in front of him in her squeaky crepe-soled shoes, the two gun-toting Goliaths behind. They stopped in front of a door; she unlocked it and pushed it open.

"Inside," she said, turning her dispassionate eyes on Ted. "Sleep."

"What about Regenbauer? When do I see—"

One of the guards shoved him into the room. The nurse stood at the door and pointed at a table bolted to the wall. On it was a small cup of water and a pill. "Take the pill, please."

Ted glanced around the room. It was small, but clean. There was a window with bars on the outside, a table and a bed, both bolted to the wall and floor, and that was all.

"What—"

"Take the pill," she said admantly. She nodded over her shoulder at the guards. "Or they will give it to you."

"What is it?"

"For sleep."

"Look, I don't—"

She stood aside to let the guards in.

"Okay, okay," Ted said. He tasted the tablet first, then popped it into his mouth and washed it down with the water. They weren't going to all this trouble to poison him.

The woman nodded her approval. She grasped the door handle. "Sleep now."

"What about Regenbauer? When do I see—"

"Tomorrow," she said. "Rest now." The door closed, locked.

He sat down on the bed. They didn't need to give him a pill. He was so exhausted he wasn't going to need any help getting to sleep. All he had to do was close his eyes. He leaned back against the wall. His arms and legs had stopped aching. They were just numb now. He dragged his feet onto the bed. Suddenly his body felt like it weighed a thousand pounds. He hadn't the strength to pull a blanket over him. Fast pill, he thought. Fast . . .

36

THE NOISE OF a klaxon reverberated in the small room as inside a barrel and Ted bolted from the bed in wild-eyed panic, stumbling into the wall. When the clanging stopped he was backed against the window and gasping.

The ringer was mounted above the door; he found it when he had his wits back. He also found breakfast. They'd left a tray of food on the table. There was also a light blue robe. Ted carried the food to the bed and sat down cross-legged, balancing the tray on his lap. He uncovered the dishes and his breath caught: eggs, potatoes, bread, marmalade, bacon—*bacon!*—and in a two-portion silver pot, coffee. His mouth watered at the dizzying aroma before him. His throat was sore from vomiting and his arms and shoulders and legs ached from the strain he'd put them through, but this made all the soreness and pain at least tolerable.

He started eating, forking eggs and potatoes into his mouth as fast as he could. He didn't care if he got sick again. They'd brought him food and he was going to eat it all just in case they'd made a mistake. He didn't care about anything except filling the void in his stomach. They'd brought him a king's breakfast, as far as he was concerned, and he didn't wonder why.

"You were comfortable, I hope. Not too cold? Too warm? I grant the accommodations are small and Spartanly functional, but you won't be spending too much time there."

They were in a room that smelled faintly of antiseptics; the nurse and two guards had escorted him to it and he'd waited about half an hour with the guards stationed at the door until Regenbauer showed up. He sat on the edge of the table, which was the only piece of furniture in the room besides the chair Ted was seated in. The room was white, even the floor, and three of the walls framed large mirrors. Ted spent the time waiting by looking at himself, certain they were two-way mirrors and that someone, perhaps several people, surely Regenbauer himself, was watching him. Well, let them watch. They'd see a man who needed a shave.

"I'd pay attention if I were you," Regenbauer said.

Ted looked at the SS major. "If it gets interesting, I will."

"How are you feeling this morning?"

"Peachy."

Regenbauer nodded. "The aches and soreness will go away in time. Any other complaints?"

"I don't much care for the company."

The major didn't flinch. "Anything else?"

"What am I doing here?"

"I think you know the answer to that question."

"Where's Kate?" Ted tried to keep the worry out of his voice.

"Safe."

"Here?"

Regenbauer didn't reply.

"Where is she?"

"I wouldn't worry about Fräulein Buchanan."

"I don't care what *you're* not worried about. I want to see her."

Regenbauer slipped off the edge of the desk. "You're not in a position to make demands."

"Then what *am* I in a position to do?"

Regenbauer walked to the door and summoned a guard. "To observe," he said. The guard took a stance a few feet behind Ted. Regenbauer stood at the wall, where he turned down the light in the room from one of several knobs. "If you'll focus your attention there, please," he said, pointing to the mirror on Ted's left.

Ted turned to see. It was a two-way mirror, all right, but Ted was on the observer's side. He heard Regenbauer flip a switch and the room behind the mirror was suddenly brilliant with light. It was quite a small room, probably a quarter the size of this one, and in the center of it, facing the mirror, was a man sitting in a chair. He was staring at the mirror, actually at himself, and he was wearing a white hospital dressing gown. His forehead was wrapped in a bandage and he was bald.

"Step up to the window," Regenbauer said, "so you may see better."

Ted felt a shiver through his spine. Whatever Regenbauer was up to, he didn't like it. Ted walked to the mirror and studied the man in the chair. He looked to be in his mid-fifties, his face drawn and wrinkled. Ted noticed that he wasn't actually bald; he could see the top of his head more clearly, and the area above the bandage was covered with short, stubby hairs, indicating that his head had been recently shaved. The man didn't move, his hands rested on the seat of the chair by his sides. He just stared at the mirror, at himself, but as if he saw nothing.

Then Ted recognized him and he sucked in his breath in a trembling, shuddering gasp.

"Oh, Jesus God!"

"Recognize him?" Regenbauer asked.

It was Trentlyon. He must have lost sixty—eighty pounds. The round, fat face that Ted remembered was gone. Now it was long, angular, with deep creases around his mouth and eyes. His face was pale, his neck thin. The gown hung on his bony shoulders like a sheet over the knobs of a wooden chair. It was Nigel Trentlyon, but he was barely recognizable.

"What have you done to him!" Ted whirled around violently, squinting in the subdued light of the room to find Regenbauer.

"The demonstration is not yet ended," Regenbauer said. His voice had lost some of its civility; it was cooler now, more authoritative. "Watch the subject."

"Subject? You son—"

"Watch!"

The guard forced Ted around toward the mirror. Trentlyon was still staring into it. Ted heard the door open and close. A few moments later, Regenbauer entered Trentlyon's tiny room. He walked behind Trentlyon's chair and glanced at him in the mirror. A speaker somewhere in Ted's room replied with tinny resonance when Regenbauer spoke.

"How are you feeling this morning?"

Ted watched in horror as Trentlyon's mouth gaped and his eyes seemed to focus with unbridled fear on the reflection in the mirror. His mouth tried to work but only guttural animal sounds came out. A dark stain formed suddenly on his gown in the folds of his lap and a trickle of urine ran down his legs.

"Now, now, you must not be frightened," Regenbauer said. "I have brought you something." He held out his hand and offered Trentlyon a cube of sugar. Regenbauer glanced into the mirror as if to acknowledge Ted, then looked at Trentlyon. "You may take it."

Trentlyon accepted the sugar with his right hand and pushed it into his mouth. Then his hand returned to its place at his side.

"Do you like my present?" Regenbauer asked.

Trentlyon nodded, his mouth moving, dissolving the sugar. Regenbauer smiled.

Trentlyon smiled in return, syrupy juice running out the corners of his mouth. He hadn't any teeth.

"Tell me," Regenbauer said pleasantly, "what is your name?"

Trentlyon swallowed. He licked his lips and stared at the mirror.

"You may answer," Regenbauer said.

"I am not a cat," Trentlyon responded. His voice was high and sing-songy.

"Who is Pythagoras?"

Trentlyon shrugged. "He is not me and me is not it. But Euclid knows the secret. The secret is the secret. The secret is the secret. Spengler knows Pythagoras but he won't tell any of us . . . which is good, it is good. Jamey told us not to tell and Campbell said to go to hell . . . but we know who he is. Enigma is the secret, the secret is the secret. And Ultra is the code word, all fall down . . ."

"Enough," Regenbauer snapped.

Trentlyon's mouth stopped.

"Who is Campbell?" Regenbauer said to the figure in the mirror. "You may answer."

Trentlyon rolled his tongue around his lips like a two-year-old. "Campbell, Campbell, lit-tle boy," he began in his sing-song voice, "where are you, naughty boy. Caught in the branches, caught in the trees, please don't come out and bomb-bomb me."

"What is the secret, Nigel? Tell me, what is the secret?"

"The secret is the secret. Jamey knows and Euclid knows, count on your toes, ten-seven-nine . . . out of the bloody water and Ultra is inside . . ."

"What is Ultra, Nigel?"

Trentlyon wrinkled his nose, stretched his eyebrows. "Ultra is the answer. Everyone knows that no one knows, Euclid said so."

"What does it mean, Nigel? Who is Ultra?"

"Ultra is the secret, Engima is the question, Campbell is the answer . . . ask me some more, I cannot tell . . . ask me some more and we'll all go to hell . . ."

Regenbauer left the room. Ted rested his head on the glass and closed his eyes. He couldn't look anymore. He could only listen to the tinny, sing-song voice of the broken mind from the speaker until Regenbauer came in and shut it off.

"What did you do to him?" Ted said with a calmness that even surprised himself. The lights were back up, the silvered window to Trentlyon's nightmare a mirror again. Ted was in his chair, Regenbauer perched on the edge of the table. "What have you done to his mind?"

"I'm afraid we went too far with your friend," Regenbauer said. "He was very tenacious in the early months. His resistance was extremely difficult to overcome. Eventually, he did break but unfortuantely, we weren't able to extract everything we might have wished. Still, there was enough to connect you to him."

"Me? With *that* gibberish?"

"It wasn't always gibberish." Regenbauer crossed his arms. "I know that the British have set up a network of spies in Germany for the purpose of breaking the Enigma coding device. I know that it is run by a man code-named Euclid in London with MI-6. I know that the principal agent in Berlin is known as Pythagoras and that he is a traitor, supplying the British with valuable information. I know that you are part of this ring of spies and that Arthur Spengler is England's man in Berlin who acts as liaison between Pythagoras and yourself. I know that Ultra is someone very important in this chain of command, probably senior to Euclid. 'Ultra is the secret.' That was the most consistent phrase our friend repeated. 'Ultra is the secret.' I suspecet he *has* compromised some of our most secret codes, Herr Ultra, that is. And I intend to find out what he knows and how he's done it. I also intend to find out the identity of Pythagoras." Regenbauer stared at Ted a moment. "And I intend for you to help me."

Ted let out a long breath. Trentlyon must really have spun them a tale before they shocked his brain into jelly. What was Enigma? He'd never heard of that one. And who was Ultra? Regenbauer was closer that Ted had realized to uncovering Hess as Pythagoras. But what was all this other? A smokescreen? Trentlyon's cover story mixed in with the facts of Pythagoras? And what was Trentlyon doing here, anyway? How the hell did Regenbauer get Trentlyon out of London? "I don't suppose you'd believe me if I told you I don't have the faintest idea what you're talking about?"

Regenbauer allowed a slim smile. "No."

"This little demonstration—" Ted nodded at the mirror that contained Trentlyon "—I suppose it was to show me what I can look forward to if I don't cooperate, is that it? That I'll be pissing in my shorts at the mere sound of your voice?"

"No. I want you well and healthy, Herr Campbell. You see, you are going to accompany me to Berlin when the time is right . . . when I have all the details worked out. You are going to expose the entire plan at a meeting I will arrange."

"A confession?"

"In a manner of speaking, yes. You will meet Standartenfuehrer Heydrich, chief of the Reich security department. I don't mind telling you, Campbell, that you are the means of my advancement."

"Think you got it all figured out, huh?"

The SS major gave him a confident grin. "With your help."

"Just like that? Without laying a finger on me?" Now Ted smiled. "You ever heard the expression 'not fucking likely'?"

Regenbauer moved off the table and began pacing before the mirror directly in front of Ted. "Herr Trentlyon endured very great pain in these last several months, more than I had expected he would. Much more. Beatings. Isolation. Sleeplessness. Starvation. Sodium pentathol, though that is not always reliable. He was addicted to morphine, then heroin, and put through the unpleasant pangs of withdrawal. We even attempted to trick him into believing the war was over. None of it was totally successful, but we did learn pieces of the truth, bit by bit, week after week, until we lost him."

"You drove him bloody mad!" Ted snapped.

"Then I learned of the work here," Regenbauer continued. "Our own SS physicians are experimenting in the field of mental illness. There was a chance I could unlock all of Trentlyon's secrets with one simple operation. I decided it was worth a chance. The procedure was pioneered by two Portuguese neurologists just five years ago after scores of tests on monkeys." Regenbauer stopped here to smile at Ted. "But we don't have any monkeys here. Just the mentally unfit."

Ted only stared at him.

"It is called a lobotomy, this procedure. It calls for severing nerves in the front portion of the brain, just here—" Regenbauer touched his temples with his index fingers.

Ted squeezed his eyes shut. "Jesus!"

"The result is a subject who is completely passive. He has no more fears, no anxieties, no more obsessions . . . harmless. He is nonviolent and cooperative. Unfortunately, even this measure, in Herr Trentlyon's case, was . . ." Regenbauer shrugged, ". . . disappointing. You saw him. He speaks in rhymes and talks like a child. Some of what he says might one day be decipherable, but the doctors here don't give him much hope. Still, we give him rewards and ask him questions. But I don't intend to wait. He led me to you and *you* will do the rest."

Ted looked at the floor. He couldn't get the vision of Trentlyon's glassy-eyed stare out of his mind. "So . . . you're gonna cut my brain? Sever my nerve?"

"Oh, no. The procedure is not yet sufficiently refined to subject such a healthy specimen as you to experimentation. As I said, Trentlyon's case was a calculated risk. You are something special. No, no, I would not think of handing you to these doctors. You are too valuable to me just the way you are."

Ted frowned. "Then, what . . ."

Regenbauer stopped pacing beside a switch on the middle wall. He nodded at the guard across the room and the lights went out. Regenbauer snapped another light switch and the room behind the second mirror came into view.

Kate was sitting in a chair just as Trentlyon had been, facing the two-way glass. She was wearing the same sort of hospital gown, her eyes just as unseeing, but she was alert. Her arms were folded in front of her and when the lights came on she sensed the change and turned her head slightly. She said something then, but the soundproof room swallowed the words.

The guard grabbed Ted before he could get out of his chair. He fought, but he hadn't any strength. It had been an effort to push himself up from the arms of the chair. Now his head was swimming, he had to blink rapidly to keep Kate in focus. Why couldn't he stand up? Where was his strength? What happened . . . the food! They put something in the goddamn food!

"It's harmless," Ted heard Regenbauer say. "A drug that neutralizes the flow of adrenaline. You needn't try to fight it."

"Don't you touch her!" Ted shouted. *"Don't you bastards touch her!"*

"You might guess that the staff here is eager to do some tests on the mental functions of a blind but otherwise healthy subject," Regenbauer said from the dark corner of the room. *"No!"*

"Perhaps we can work something out."

Ted heard him, but only just. He could feel himself slipping away, slipping into unconsciousness. The drug was doing that, and the more he fought it the more it disabled him. But he heard Regenbauer's offer before the blackness engulfed him. There wasn't time to make an answer to it, but he heard it and understood.

37

He woke up in his room.

For an hour or more Ted tried to raise someone outside his door. He yelled and pounded on the door, but he was just wasting his energy. Then lunch came. The nurse brought it and set the tray on the table.

He didn't eat; he wouldn't let them drug him again. Instead, Ted sat on his bed and concentrated on the line he'd use on Regenbauer. He blanked his mind of Kate, or tried to. He tried not to think of Trentlyon's vacant stare or the look of eager anticipation on that creased, pathetic face when it was offered a lump of sugar. Regenbauer was the thing he had to deal with, he told himself. Only Regenbauer. He was going to have to convince him that he was a little fish he'd caught in the dragnet, a messenger. Sure Trentlyon was a British agent, but Ted didn't know how he got into Germany. Hell, the last time he saw Trentlyon was in London with Carstairs. Might as well tell him that too. Carstairs was Euclid, he was the man from the Secret Service who was running this show. As for Pythagoras . . . what about Pythagoras? Who *was* Pythagoras? If he had to give him a name, who would it be? Not Hess, never Hess. Ted had to try to bluff his way through that. He owed that to Hess. Didn't he? Then if not Hess . . . But there was only one other candidate. There was only one other man who might fit the requirements. Someone in the government.

Someone who would even take the rap for Hess if it meant keeping his secret.

Haushofer.

Ted hated to do it, but who else was there? Then, what about this other stuff? Who the hell was Arthur Spengler? Who was Ultra and what was Enigma? How was he going to deal with that? He'd just have to tell Regenbauer everything he knew, everything except Hess, and hope the bastard believed he didn't know about the other things.

The light came on at dusk and a short time later, dinner. The nurse set the new tray on the table and took the untouched lunch.

"I want to see Regenbauer," Ted told her. "I'm ready to talk."

She didn't reply.

"Did you hear what I said? I want to see Regenbauer. Tell him I'm ready."

At the door she glanced at him without a word, then disappeared behind the guard. Ted leaned back against the wall. "Bitch." She'll tell him, he thought. What the hell else does she have to do?

But no one came that night. No one came the next day except the silent nurse with the food. Despite himself, every now and then, every hour or so, he thought of Kate. After a while he thought of her more often. That's when he sweated.

That night he pissed on the door. He'd been awakened by the urge to relieve himself but had no place to go. So, he pissed on the door and delighted in the thought that his nurse might slip in the puddle when she brought him breakfast. The idea made him sleep better. They *hadn't* thought of everything.

But she didn't slip because she didn't come. No one came all day until dusk and by that time most of the puddle had evaporated and the room had a slight ammonia smell. When the nurse brought a new tray she hardly acknowledged the fact that most of the food from the previous night was gone. Before she left the room one of the guards pushed a portable toilet inside the door with the toe of his polished boot.

"I want to see Regenbauer," Ted said from his bed. "Tell him I want to see him. Tell him I—goddammit, don't leave yet!"

The door closed silently and locked.

"Goddammit, what are you waiting for!" Ted screamed. But no one answered and no one came.

It was at night, during his sleep time, that he heard the scream. He first thought it was part of a nightmare, that he dreamed it. He sat up in bed to let the sleep wear off and listened.

Ted went to the window and opened it. Silence. Just the cold and the darkness. He broke off an icicle from one of the bars and stood sucking it and listening, straining to hear the slightest sound, but there was nothing but the rustle of pine trees. He closed the windows and climbed back into bed. Had he imagined it? Was it a woman's scream?

Was it Kate?

Days passed. The routine was the same. One meal, one visit from the mute nurse to change food trays. Ted lost track of time. He slept during the day and stayed awake at night, standing at the window in the cold, listening. He'd convinced himself the scream was real, that it was Kate, that if he stayed awake at night, somehow, he could help her. They didn't want him to hear her scream, he told himself. So, if he stayed awake at night . . .

But he wanted to hear it, that's what tortured him. If he could hear the scream again he could verify it was real, that he wasn't going mad. But he never heard it and that made it worse.

He thought about her every waking minute now. He thought about her in that room, alone. He came awake in the middle of the day, sweating through a nightmare in which she was eating sugar. He imagined her on an operating table, her head shaved, her frightened unseeing eyes trying to understand. He saw her in his mind, strapped to a table, nude, screaming as unseen hands touched her, prodded her—doctors in their white coats taking their turn with her. Regenbauer, laughing, forcing himself into her. Kate's body, slimy with the mess of them. Her legs. Her breasts. Her mouth . . .

Stop iiiiitttt!

But he couldn't stop. He couldn't stop his thoughts, he couldn't hold back the images. There wasn't anything else to do with his time. And Regenbauer knew it.

Something woke him. He opened his eyes and blinked at the wall, then rolled on his back. The nurse was standing in the doorway. Ted sat up, glanced around. It was still daylight. He didn't know the time, but it was sometime after noon, he guessed, which was not the usual time for her visit. She only came at night with a tray of food. But she was standing there now, empty-handed.

"Come with me, please." Her expression didn't crack. She didn't show pleasure or sadness or disapproval or even stupidity in that face, just indifference. Ted wondered if she weren't one of the doctor's lobotomy successes. But he didn't dwell on it because then he thought of Kate.

Ted jumped up from the bed. "Is it Kate? Is she all right? *Is she!*"

But the nurse only turned and walked between the guards into the corridor. "This way," she said.

Regenbauer was waiting for him in an office and he was wearing his black uniform. There weren't any mirrors in this room. Behind Regenbauer was a large window with a view of a courtyard and, in the distance, the stables.

"Sit down," Regenbauer said, indicating a chair in front of his desk. He was smoking a cigarette and leaning back in the swivel chair.

"Where's Kate?" Ted demanded.

"I don't like looking up at anyone," Regenbauer said. "Sit down."

Ted sat down. "Where's Kate?"

"Still here."

"Where, goddamn you! I want to see her!"

Regenbauer flicked an ash into a small glass bowl. "You haven't learned much in your stay here, have you?"

"I just—"

"You don't *demand* anything. Not from the staff, not from your nurse, not from your guards . . ." Regenbauer sat forward in his chair, stubbed out the cigarette and looked straight into Ted's eyes. ". . . and most importantly, not from me. Do you understand that?"

Ted nodded.

"I didn't hear."

"Yes," Ted said.

"Yes . . . what?"

Ted glared at the man in the black uniform. "Yes . . . I understand."

"Sir," Regenbauer added. "Yes, I understand, sir."

"Yes, I understand . . . sir."

"Good." Regenbauer pulled a file folder from the top of the desk and opened it. "Now, there are a few things to discuss."

"What about Kate?"

"Later."

"Now."

Regenbauer let out a long indulgent sigh. He glanced at Ted. "She's perfectly safe. You may believe that."

Ted stared at him but said nothing.

"She *hasn't* been harmed."

Ted continued to stare at him. "I heard a scream."

Regenbauer raised an eyebrow. "Did you really?" There was the hint of amusement in his voice. "When was that?"

"Goddammit, I don't care what you do to me! But I won't say another word until I see her!"

Regenbauer closed the folder. He picked up the telephone and spoke briskly into it. When he set the receiver back he looked hard at Ted. "I told you she was safe. But, if you must know for yourself . . ." He shrugged. "She is being brought here now."

Ted straightened in his chair. His palms sweated. He blinked several times to put the room in focus. It was as if he'd just awakened from a bad dream, as if everything would be all right now. He was finally going to see Kate and nothing else mattered. He tried to imagine himself through Regenbauer's eyes: a diry, unshaven prisoner in a grimy inmate's uniform. He'd been locked up for days and hadn't been allowed to shave or bathe or change clothes. The hospital whites they'd given him the night he'd tried to escape were grubby and filthy with the smell of sweat. His hair was a tangled matted mess that hadn't known a comb in weeks and his fingernails were gritty from the iron bars of his window where he'd clung to them as he denied sleep in his nightly vigil to listen for Kate.

But none of it mattered if he could see Kate and know that she was all right. And that was when he realized with savage impact that he could not lie to Regenbauer. Ted would tell him what he wanted to know and tell him gladly—to protect Kate. It was the whole point of his isolation: let Campbell torture

himself with his own ghastly thoughts of what might happen to
her while he sweated away the days on the edge of hysteria in
his little room. Regenbauer hadn't needed to touch her. The
scream, if it were real, had only been the catalyst to electrify
Ted's imagination. Ted suddenly understood Regenbauer's
game with the hopeless clarity of a man whose last psychologi-
cal defense had been ripped from him. Ted *would* talk because
Regenbauer still had a healthy Kate to use against him. Of
course she was safe . . . now . . .

A plump, pig-eyed woman guided Kate into the room and
Ted's heart caught in his throat at the sight of her. She was
dressed in a clean white hospital gown. Her red hair had been
combed and done neatly into a bun. She hadn't any makeup, of
course, and she seemed a bit gaunt and her coloring was pale,
but she hadn't any marks on her that Ted could see.

Ted rushed to her. He took her hand then touched her face.
"Kate! It's Ted. Are you all right? They haven't touched
you—"

At the sound of his voice, she reached for him. "Ted? Is it
really you!" She ran her fingers across his face and touched his
hair and finally wrapped her arms around him. "Ted! God, I
thought they'd—I thought . . ."

"I'm all right. What about you?"

She clung to him, holding Ted tight against her. "I'm fine
. . . really, I'm okay. I was sick for a few days but that was
because I wouldn't eat the puke they served me. But I'm fine. I
don't know what's going on or where I am . . . they wouldn't
tell me anything. They don't even talk to me."

"You are a guest of mine, Katherine," Regenbauer said from
his place behind the desk. He'd lit another cigarette and
glanced at Ted with an expression of arrogant satisfaction.

If there was any doubt in Ted's mind about the power
Regenbauer held over him it was dispelled the moment the SS
major spoke. Kate's reaction was instant terror. She hadn't
known who her captors were, but at the sound of Regenbauer's
voice, Ted saw the frightening dawn of recognition on her
face.

"Johann . . . ?" She said his name in a breathless voice.
Her mouth went slack as she turned her head in his direction.

"Isn't this cozy," Regenbauer said, smiling at Ted, "the
three of us here together."

Ted hadn't anything left to say. Regenbauer was going to win. That was what Regenbauer wanted Ted to understand. The proof of it was here, standing between them, in the way she trembled, in the grip of her hand, in the tears from her green, sightless eyes. Here. Katherine Buchanan, Regenbauer's weapon.

Regenbauer did most of the talking. If they cooperated, he promised he would allow them to see each other. A few days, he said, a week at most of questions and it would be over and they could spend all the time they wanted together, even share a room.

"What happens to us then?" Ted asked. He glanced at Kate. Her hand was on the arm of her chair and Ted reached over and held it.

"Don't be so skeptical," Regenbauer said, "nothing is going to *happen* to you . . . either of you."

"What's going to happen to us, Johann?" Kate said quietly. "You aren't talking to children."

"No, not children," Regenbauer snapped, "spies." He cooled himself with a smile. "Since you are cooperating in exposing a plot against the Reich, we will spare you your lives."

"What does that mean?" Ted said.

"You will both remain here until my investigation is complete," the SS major said. "I will require that Campbell accompany me to Berlin to identify the principal conspirators in a meeting with Standartenfuehrer Heydrich. I doubt there will be a trial, therefore, my need of his testimony will be brief. Then you will be deported, both of you, to the United States."

"And what happens if we don't cooperate?" Kate said.

Regenbauer glanced up from the file he was reading. "Oh, I think you'll cooperate."

Ted tried to read the heading on the file folder that Regenbauer was perusing, but it was too far away to see.

"When you first arrived," Regenbauer said, "you were given a physical by the staff here. Do you recall that, Katherine?" He glanced at Ted. Regenbauer made a habit of looking at him when he was speaking to Kate, Ted noticed. It was as if he thought of Ted as her eyes.

"What about it?" Kate said.

"I have the results of that examination in front of me. You are a wonderfully healthy woman. In spite of your handicap or, perhaps, due to it, your other senses are exceptionally well developed."

Ted moved uneasily in his chair. He didn't like this. Regenbauer was smiling to himself and staring at Ted. He was up to something, Ted didn't know what, but he could feel it coming.

"Very interesting," Regenbauer said as he flipped a page. "They recommend that you not smoke quite so much. And, of course, you've already stopped drinking."

"Hardly by choice." Kate folded her arms in front of her. If her voice were any indication, Ted thought, she wasn't frightened anymore.

"Do you remember where you were ten weeks ago?"

"I don't even know where the hell I am now," Kate snapped, "or even what day it is."

"This is Saturday," Regenbauer replied, "the eighth of February."

"February!" Ted blurted. *"February!* Jesus Christ, how long have we been here!"

Regenbauer ignored the outburst. "This should interest you too, Campbell. Ten weeks ago was approximately the end of November. I assume you and Katherine were together?"

"What if we were? Who cares?"

"Katherine will, I think," Regenbauer said. "Let me tell her why. You may not care what happens to yourself, though it would be a shame to cause injury to such a magnificently healthy woman, but you are not the only person in jeopardy here . . ."

Here it comes, Ted thought. Trot out Nigel Trentlyon and give her a glimpse of what Ted Campbell can be if they put his mind to it.

" . . . There is also the child to consider."

"What?" Ted looked at Kate. Her expression was of dawning awareness and dreadful fear. "What child?"

Regenbauer was watching Kate and he was enjoying it. "I think you will cooperate, yes?"

"What goddamn child!" Ted shouted.

"Yours, I trust," Regenbauer said. "Your woman is pregnant. She is carrying a fetus which is approximately seventy days old. By all signs it's healthy." He nodded at Ted. "Congratulations."

"You bloody—"

Kate caught Ted's arm before he could make a move. He was on his feet and she held him back. "Don't! Ted, don't! They'll only hurt you. It doesn't matter."

"Doesn't matter!"

There were tears in her eyes. "Please, Ted . . . don't let them hurt you. I . . . I already know about the baby. I've known for weeks."

Ted pulled her to him. He closed his eyes and pressed his cheek against her hair. "I'm sorry, Kate . . . Christ, I . . ."

"I wasn't sure at first. But when I missed my . . ." she sighed. "There are unmistakable signs that a woman knows when she's pregnant. I just don't know *they* knew."

"Kate—"

"And don't tell me you're sorry, goddammit! I'm not. It's ours." She pulled back from him and took his hand and stroked it against her face, against the tears. "Promise me you won't do anything. I'd answer his questions anyway . . . whatever he wants to know to keep you safe. We'll tell him and then we'll go home. You can't help the British anymore, you can only hurt us. It doesn't matter . . . I don't care about the bloody war anymore. Just you and the baby . . ."

She tried to smile. Her chin trembled. Ted nodded without a word and kissed her fingers.

"Such a touching scene," Regenbauer said.

Kate turned then, reacting calmly to Regenbauer. "Johann?"

He leaned back in his chair. "Yes?"

She found his voice, looked toward it. She placed her hands over her stomach. "I'm almost sorry this isn't yours. Because if it was I'd know exactly what to do with it." Then she smiled as wide as she could and a tear rolled into the corner of her mouth.

Regenbauer's smile disappeared. He snapped upright in his chair. "Take them out! Get them both out of here!" He slapped the folder shut. "Interrogations begin tomorrow!"

38

HAUSHOFER RUBBED A hole in the frost to see through the station window. Arthur was late and Haushofer was worried. He paced back and forth in the near-deserted train station. Arthur had never been late before. What if he'd been picked up? Haushofer considered leaving, just boarding the next train to the Kurfürstendamm and going home, but he knew he wouldn't do that. He had to wait even if it meant another hour in this godawful cold. The building had no heat and the temperature inside was below freezing. He bent down to see through the window. *Where was that man!*

"Afternoon, Albrecht," said a voice behind him. "Cold bitch of a day, ain't it?"

Haushofer straightened and turned on the heels of his frozen feet.

"I'm late," Arthur Spengler said without apologizing. "Couldn't be helped."

"Did you find them?" Haushofer's face was rosy with the cold.

"No. I gather you didn't either?"

Haushofer shook his head.

"It's been six weeks . . ." Spengler paused to light a cigarette. "He's not hiding, at least not in Germany, yet neither he nor the girl have left the country."

"That we know," Haushofer said. He blew on his hands. "Then . . . ?"

Spengler exhaled. "Then, Regenbauer has them."

The professor closed his eyes. "What do you suggest we do now?" he asked.

"You still want Campbell?"

Haushofer nodded. "If he's alive. If he can still fly a plane." The professor looked closely at the other man. "Hess has already tried once, you know. Last month. He went to Augsberg where he keeps those damned Messerschmitts and flew one of them off into the fog. He only returned because he got lost and had engine trouble. God, what if he'd been killed!"

"Do you think he'll try it again?"

Haushofer shook his head. "No, not on his own. The experience nearly scared him to death. Hess isn't a coward but he's no fool either. He's seen the risk firsthand. He knows the only way he's going to get to Scotland to see the Duke of Hamilton now is for Campbell to fly him there. He's desperate to stop this insane rescheduling of the invasion." The professor looked pleadingly at Spengler. "That's why you must get Campbell! He's all there is left!"

"The only way to find Campbell is to find Regenbauer first."

"Then do it!"

"It's going to cost, Haushofer. You'd better know that."

"Cost?"

"Lives," Spengler explained. "People are going to die if getting Campbell means what I think it does. Regenbauer, wherever he is, isn't going to let anyone just walk up and take Campbell away. Does that bother you?"

"Hess is more important than some soldiers!" Haushofer said.

"Yeah." Spengler nodded. "That's what I thought."

39

From the first question, Ted told the truth. From the first reply, Regengauer didn't believe a word of it.

They were in a room with a tape recording machine and a guard at the door. Ted sat across a table from Regenbauer with the microphone between them. Since the meeting in Regenbauer's office, Ted had been treated differently. He'd been allowed to bathe and shave and they'd given him a fresh set of hospital whites. Regenbauer had even offered him a package of cigarettes.

The first question was the obvious one and Ted was ready —even eager—to get it over with. Regenbauer switched on the machine.

"Who is Pythagoras?"

"Rudolf Hess."

Regenbauer switched off the machine. "We're not playing games now. Just answer the questions."

Ted frowned. "Look, I—"

"I'll tell you when to speak!" Regenbauer snapped. He switched the machine on again.

"Who is the traitor code-named Pythagoras by the British Secret Service?" Regenbauer said.

"I told you . . . Rudolf Hess."

"Hess!"

Ted nodded. "That's right. Deputy Fuehrer Rudol—"

Silence!" Regenbauer slammed the tabletop with his fist. "Have you learned nothing? Did you think I was joking? Do you think I will not do what I say I can? Would you like to see Fräulein Buchanan's head shaved? Shall I let you watch the doctors at work on her?"

"Goddammit, Regenbauer—"

"Who is Pythagoras!"

"Hess!"

Regenbauer slapped Ted with the back of his hand. "You make a fatal mistake if you think—"

"Wait!"

"—I am such a fool—"

"Wait!"

"—as to believe such lunacy!"

They both stopped to catch their breaths.

Ted held up his hand. "Look, if you think I'm going to take a chance on letting your butchers put a finger on Kate, you're fucking crazy! Ask me the questions and I'll give you the answers. I'm not going to lie. *You know* I won't lie! You want to know who Pythagoras is? It's Hess. Rudolf goddamn Walter Richard Hess! I can't help it if he's the fucking deputy fuehrer. You wanted a big catch, well you sonofabitch, you got it!"

Regenbauer shook his head. "Hess," he said to himself. "Impossible."

"It's the truth." Ted sank into his chair. "Believe it, don't believe it, I don't care . . . but it's the truth."

Regenbauer stared at him for some time. He took out his cigarette case and tapped a cigarette against the lid. "You know what will happen if you continue this way?" he said without emotion.

Ted had a sudden vision of Trentlyon in the room behind the two-way mirror. Then the horrible fantasies of what he'd imagined for Kate came flooding back to him. Ted swallowed. He placed his hands on the table to try and calm himself. He was sweating again. He could feel the beads of perspiration on his forehead. He hadn't expected this.

"Look, I . . ." Ted wiped a hand across his face. "I have too much at stake here to lie to you. It's not like I've picked a name out of a hat. I'm telling you the truth. Pythagoras isn't only one man, it is a whole network of agents . . . some in Germany, some in France and Italy and Holland. But they're all in it to funnel information from Berlin to London, to pass information from Pythagoras to Euclid. Pythagoras, the man, is what holds this whole thing together. Without him there wouldn't be any reason for the rest of them. You must see that the man called Pythagoras *must* be important! He is . . . because he's Rudolf Hess!"

Regenbauer nodded. "I see," he said. He puffed on his cigarette and stared somewhere across the room for several moments before he spoke again. "The deputy fuehrer?" He glanced at Ted.

"That's right." There wasn't any reaction from Regenbauer that Ted could see. He just sat there, smoking the cigarette. He has to believe it, Ted thought. He must be convinced because Kate was—

"The Fuehrer's most devoted servant and loyal friend?" Regenbauer asked. "The man at Hitler's side at the Munich *putsch?* The man who suffered with Hitler at Landsberg Prison? The man who helped write *Mein Kampf?* This man is a British spy!"

"Look, let me—"

"I would sooner believe it was Goering or Goebbels!" Regenbauer stood up quickly.

"No, listen—"

"I don't want to hear your lies!" He crushed out his cigarette. "I will make you sorry for this, Campbell . . . and Katherine." He signaled for the guard.

"Wait! No, wait!"

Regenbauer switched the intercom on. "Bring the woman here." Then he spoke to the SS guard and took out his Lüger.

"What are you going to do?" Ted said. He started to rise from his chair but the guard shoved him back. He watched with mounting panic as Regenbauer checked the weapon's magazine then slammed it into the pistol with the butt of his hand. "Good God! *What are you going to do!"*

"I will have the truth."

Regenbauer's menacing stare struck dreadful fright in Ted's brain. *He's going to shoot her!*

"No!" Ted screamed. "Don't hurt her! I'm telling you the truth! Listen to me! It's Hess, goddammit, it's—"

Regenbauer hit him with the Lüger and nearly knocked Ted out of his chair. "Do not speak again without permission!" The SS major's eyes were wild with rage. "Do you hear me! Do not speak or I will put a bullet into her brain! Is that clear?"

Ted's brain reeled from the blow. He held his head where Regenbauer had struck him and felt the sticky gash behind his ear. He looked at the blood on his fingers.

"Is that clear?" Regenbauer shouted again.

Ted grunted acknowledgment and tried to nod. The blow had scrambled his senses momentarily and his eyes watered from the pain, but he understood.

When Kate entered the room she was led by the same matron who had brought her the last time. Her eyes were puffy as if she'd been crying, but otherwise Kate seemed healthy. She didn't appear frightened and Ted wanted to call to her, to reassure her if she needed it, but he didn't dare. He didn't think Regenbauer would really shoot her now, but the man had worked himself into a frenzy and Ted wasn't sure what Regenbauer would do.

"I have a couple of brief questions for you, Katherine," Regenbauer said as the matron guided her to a chair.

Kate turned her head toward his voice. "When do I see Ted again?"

"When I say you can," Regenbauer snapped. "You promised to be cooperative. Just answer my questions."

"All right," she said calmly, "shoot."

Regenbauer glanced grimly at Ted. "First, you know Campbell is part of a British spy operation in Germany?"

She sighed. "Yes, that's why we're here, isn't it?"

"And Campbell told you about it?"

"Yes, yes . . ."

"All the details?"

"Enough, I suppose."

Ted tensed in his chair. Don't try to be cute, he wanted to shout. Just answer the bastard's questions. Regenbauer was slowly pacing in a circle around Kate's chair and he was holding the Lüger loosely, almost carelessly, between his palms, with his little fingers through the trigger guard. Each time he asked a question he would stop and turn toward her with the muzzle of the gun aimed lazily at her head.

"So you know nearly as much about the operation as Campbell, is that true?" Regenbauer was standing driectly in front of her.

Kate shrugged. When she looked up at the sound of his voice she was looking straight at the gun. "I guess so. I only know what Ted told me."

Regenbauer glanced at Ted as if to remind him of his threat. "Who is Pythagoras, Katherine?"

Kate hesitated to moisten her lips and Ted felt the surging of blood pounding at his temples. Tell him! Don't be an idiot! Tell him the truth!

"I . . . don't know," she said. "Ted never told me that."

The gun's report was like an explosion in the small room that echoed in competition with Ted's terrified scream. The blast shocked him straight up in his chair and he hadn't a breath left in his wide-eyed panic when he saw Kate double over in pain with both hands on her ears. Regenbauer had fired the Lüger into the wall, but the muzzle had been less than a handspread from her head.

"Let me ask you again. This will be the last time. Who is Pythagoras?" Regenbauer touched the Lüger to Kate's chin, raising her head. He put the barrel on her throat.

"Tell him!" Ted shouted. He was on his feet, struggling against the guard. "Jesus Christ . . . tell him the truth!"

Kate searched the room for his voice. "Ted? *Ted!*"

Regenbauer swung around to look at Ted. "I warned you, Campbell. I told you what would happen."

"No . . ."

Regenbauer raised the Lüger and aimed it at Kate's head.

"NO! Pleeeease . . . !"

"Don't shoot him!" Kate screamed. She reached for Regenbauer but in the wrong direction. "It's Hess! Rudolf Hess is Pythagoras! Don't kill him!" She was hysterical, crying, screaming, reaching in her darkness . . . "It's Hess . . . Hess . . . *HESS* . . ."

Regenbauer lowered the gun. He was breathing nearly as fast as Ted. "Take her away," he said finally. *"Get her out!"*

"You won't see her again until I have the truth," Regenbauer said after Kate was gone. He's calmed himself, Ted thought. He'd nearly killed Kate and there wasn't any doubt in Ted's mind that he would have if Regenbauer thought it would help. But something held him back. It might have been that Kate believed what she was saying.

"I will get the truth from you one way or another," Regenbauer continued. "You may be sure of that."

"I am telling the truth." Ted hadn't any strength left to press the point. "Ask me anything, if I know it I'll tell you."

"I am only interested in the identity of Pythagoras."

Ted sighed.

"Tomorrow I will speak to the doctors about Katherine," Regenbauer said.

"Doctors!"

"Unless *we* make progress today." Regenbauer found his cigarettes and lit one. "You told her it was Hess—Pythagoras."

"Because it's true."

"You told her to protect the real traitor."

"No."

"I'll give you tonight to think about it. If you persist in this . . ." Regenbauer shrugged. "You will not recognize her when you see her again."

Ted closed his eyes, bowed his head. "What can I say? If I lie to you, if I give you some other name, you'll only find out it's a lie."

"Who is Pythagoras?"

Ted raised his head. "Ask me anything else," he pleaded. "I'll tell you about Euclid. He's running this goddamn thing! James Carstairs. That's Euclid. British Secret Service. He's the one who got me into this. He's the one who planned it all! He set it up—Hess, the Berlin network, bombing London, placing the agents . . ."

Regenbauer frowned. "Bombing London?"

"Yes!"

"You mean Berlin."

"No, I mean London. That was a British operation. They wanted the city bombed to give them a reason to hit Berlin."

"For what purpose?"

"Because Berlin had not been bombed. They knew if it was . . ." Ted took a breath. "They knew Hitler would go into a rage. They figured he would order Goering to obliterate London. It was a strategy to take the pressure off the RAF airfields. A last-ditch effort to stop the invasion."

Regenbauer considered it. "How do *you* know all this?"

"Because I . . ." Ted squeezed his eyes shut. "I was involved in it."

"*You?*" Regenbauer smiled. "How?"

"I flew the plane."

Regenbauer's smile widened. "*You* flew the plane? You were in Berlin, but you flew a British bomber over the capital of Great Britain and bombed it." He shook his head. "Campbell, you are truly amazing. Truly. Bombed London!" The SS major snorted. "When we hang you and your woman remind me to mention this story. Katherine will need a good laugh before her neck snaps."

"You stupid shit." Ted had him. "It wasn't an RAF plane, it was a Luftwaffe bomber. A Heinkel one-eleven. And I wasn't in Berlin, I was in Holland with the Ninth Fliegerdivision, Second Bomber Group!"

"Not possible," Regenbauer said.

"It's possible, all right, because it happened. Check it out. See if Alfred Horn wasn't a pilot on a mission to bomb oil storage tanks at Thameshaven the night of August twenty-fourth. See if he isn't listed missing. He is because *I* was Oberleutnant Horn and *I* bombed London."

"That is idiocy!" Regenbauer said, but he wasn't so sure now. "The bombing of London was an accident. A Luftwaffe pilot off course . . ."

"My ass! The whole thing was a British ploy . . . and it worked. You stupid shit! Even Trentlyon rambled on about it . . . 'Campbell, Campbell, little boy,' remember that? 'Caught in the branches, caught in the trees . . . please don't come out and bomb-bomb me.' I was Horn. *I* was!"

The long ash of Regenbauer's cigarette broke off and tumbled down the spotless black tunic. He was staring at Ted but not really seeing him. His mind was racing over the facts, Ted thought, trying to imagine the logic of such an incredible scheme, searching for soft spots.

"I can prove it, Regenbauer. Right now."

Regenbauer looked at him. He said nothing.

"I saw you," Ted said.

"You couldn't—" But Regenbauer cut himself off.

"Unless I was there?" Ted nodded. "Your plane stopped at Soesterberg airfield, didn't it? You walked out on the grass beside the runway to watch the bombers take off. It was night. You were smoking a cigarette and you'd just come from the operations office and you were watching the bombers. I don't know what you were doing there—but you were there. There's no way I could possibly know that unless *I* was there too. Well, I was. *I was in the goddamn plane you were waving at!*" Ted smiled at last. "You stupid shit."

They beat him then. For three straight days two guards dragged him into a cell on the first floor and beat him with socks filled with sand. Afterwards came the questions. Ted didn't see Regenbauer the entire time. It was as if the SS major didn't want to dirty his hands in the sweaty work.

Then he was left in his room for a few days and when he saw the guards again it was not for another beating. They brought him to the interrogation room where Regenbauer was waiting.

"How did you get to the Soesterberg airfield?" Regenbauer said. His uniform was slightly dusty, as if he'd been for a long car ride.

Ted tried to sit straight, but his ribs and arms were still sore from the beatings and he could only manage to hold himself up by hooking an elbow over the back of the chair. "Where's Kate?" he asked through chapped lips.

"You won't see her again until I'm through with you."

"You haven't . . ." Ted straightened against the pain.

"Not yet. Tell me about Soesterberg."

"The press plane I was on was shot down by an RAF fighter over Holland. I walked and hitched to Eindhoven. From there it was a transport to Soesterberg."

Regenbauer glanced at a sheet of paper. "What were the names of your aircraft gunners?"

Ted looked at him with dawning awareness. "You went to Soesterberg!"

"The names, Campbell."

Ted grunted out a painful breath as he changed position in the chair to see Regenbauer more clearly. He'd been to Soesterberg to check his story, Ted realized. That's where he'd been! Regenbauer's not so sure of himself anymore. If Ted could prove that he'd been on that bomber mission then Regenbauer would have to start believing him. Ted closed his eyes to think back. He was still groggy from the beatings. He remembered the faces now. The nose gunner was the young one. O . . . O something. Olden . . . Orden . . . *Olten!*

"Front gunner was Olten," Ted said. His mouth was dry. "The two in back were, ah . . ."

"You're stalling."

"Christ, let me think! I only knew them for a few hours!" What was Hans' name? Bekker. Bekker and . . . and Rühle!

"Rühle and Bekker!" Ted said excitedly. "The gunners. Olten, Bekker and Rühle."

Regenbauer looked up from the paper. "Baukner," he said calmly. "Baukner, Olten, and Rühle." He folded the paper and slid it in his pocket. "Tomorrow we begin again, the interrogation." He nodded to the guard.

"What about Kate?" Ted asked.

Regenbauer ignored it. "We will not beat you anymore."

Who is Pythagoras?
Rudolf Hess.

The same, every time. Then, gradually, the emphasis of Regenbauer's questions changed. He still wanted to know about Pythagoras, but he wanted to know other things too.

"Who is Spengler?"

"I don't know."

"Who do you think he is?"

"I haven't the slightest idea."

No reproach from Regenbauer. He never displayed his temper again.

"Tell me about Trentlyon."

"I've told you about Trentlyon."

"Tell me again."

Ground that had been covered five and six times before was gone over again. Monotonously.

When did you first meet Trentlyon?
What was his relationship to Carstairs?
Why did they want you?
Who did Carstairs answer to?
What was the nose gunner's name on your plane?
Who is Ultra?

Some interviews lasted only as long as it took Regenbauer to play back a certain portion of a previously taped interview and answer a question about it. Some lasted hours.

"When you proposed this idea about bombing London to Carstairs, Trentlyon was there too, wasn't he?"

"That's right."

"As a matter of fact, every time you saw Carstairs, Trentlyon was also present, yes?"

"Yes."

"Then everything Carstairs knew, that is, everything concerning Pythagoras and MI-6, Trentlyon also knew?"

"You'd have to ask Carstairs that, wouldn't you?"

"But it is reasonable to assume, don't you think?"

"Sure, why not."

Regenbauer had tapes of Trentlyon, too. Miles of tapes, it seemed. And Ted listened to every inch of them.

The secret is the secret . . . must protect Ultra . . . always protect the secret . . .

"What does that mean to you?"

"Same thing it means to you—nothing. You've short-circuited the poor bastard's brain."

"Do you think he's talking about Pythagoras?"

"I don't think *he* knows what he's talking about."

"If Carstairs is Euclid and Hess is Pythagoras, then who is Ultra?"

"I don't know."

"Is he talking about you? Are you Ultra?"

"For the ten-thousandth time, I'm Alfred. I never heard of Ultra."

"Could Spengler be Ultra?"

"I don't know. I never heard of Spengler either."

Ultra is the answer . . . everyone knows . . . no one knows . . .

"Ultra is the answer to what?"

"I don't know! Maybe he's doing a *Times* crossword."

"Who is Pythagoras?"

"Winston bloody Churchill?"

"Good morning, Campbell. I want—are you out of cigarettes?"

"No. I'm going to try to give them up. German cigarettes give me headaches."

"I want to talk about Arthur Spengler today."

"Again? Christ Almighty . . ."

"It would be very clever of the British to lead you to *think* Hess was Pythagoras."

"Clever, all right."

"You agree, then, the possibility exists?"

"Sure. But I wonder who the hell the guy is I've been seeing who calls himself Hess. You don't suppose there's two?"

"Let's say for the moment that I believe you, that Reichs-fuehrer Hess is Pythagoras. When you spoke to him . . . you did speak to him on several occasions, isn't that true?"

"Yes, several."

"But not at the address of Reichdammer Strasse?"

"No. Hess never knew about that."

"When you spoke to him, what did he say? I mean, was he giving you military information?"

"I've told you all this before, Regenbauer. Can't you look it up?"

"Just reply to the question."

"No, he didn't give me any military secrets. Like I said before, Hess didn't want Germany to invade England. He wanted me to act as his intermediary with the Duke of Hamilton. He wanted to arrange negotiations to end the war."

"And Carstairs put a stop to it?"

"He persuaded me that it was useless."

"Useless?"

"Hess didn't speak for Germany, he didn't speak for Hitler."

"So, you didn't speak to Hamilton. You didn't see anyone, except Carstairs, of course."

"So?"

"And Carstairs rehearsed you to lie to the deputy fuehrer, to tell him you *had* met Hamilton and that he put you off."

"He wanted to let Hess down easily, he didn't want Hess to give up. Besides, he left him some hope, if you'll remember. He said they should continue to correspond."

"Carstairs, you mean."

"Yes!"

"I see."

"Campbell, I'm going to put some hypothetical proposals to you this morning and I just want your responses."

"Go ahead."

"Reichsleiter Hess is Pythagoras."

"You don't have to make *that* hypothetical."

"Arthur Spengler is a British agent in Berlin who works for Carstairs but you've never met him."

"I don't know who he is. I've told—"

"A hypothetical case, Campbell."

"Okay-okay. Right, Spengler in Berlin. Fine."

"Trentlyon, because he is Carstairs' deputy, knows many secrets of the British Secret Service, including Pythagoras."

"Yes."

"And something called Ultra."

"Still stuck on that one, aren't you?"

"Suppose Spengler learned that Trentlyon was alive and in German hands. What do you think he'd do?"

"Having never met the fellow I can hardly—"

"He'd try to get him out or kill him, don't you think?"

"I'm sure that's what you'd do."

"Suppose Ultra *is* something bigger than Pythagoras. For the moment, let's just assume that."

"Fine."

"And that it was so important that the English wanted to protect it at all costs."

"I'm getting bored. It's too fantastic."

"Suppose that *you* are the dupe, Campbell. Suppose that this Pythagoras scheme was meant to be a decoy, a trick, a subterfuge to hide the real secret. Suppose you weren't meant to know it. Suppose it was meant for us to think that Deputy Fuehrer Hess was a traitor to protect something else and that you are just an expendable pawn in the trap. Suppose someone —Spengler, I would say—set you up. Pythagoras is real to you because you were an unwitting part of the plan. What would you say to that?"

"I'd call you a stupid shit, but I don't want to get beat up again."

"As I said, it was a hypothetical case. Now, then, about this bombing mission . . ."

And it went on. The questions, the testing, the theories. Regenbauer refused to believe the truth that Ted believed and Ted repeated the same answers to the same questions day after day. Regenbauer had himself a giant-sized problem and that dilemma was Ted's salvation.

Regenbauer wasn't going to kill him whatever he found out. He couldn't harm Ted if he were lying, because Ted was still the only link to the real Pythagoras. And he couldn't afford to hurt Ted if he were telling the truth, because he'd need Ted's cooperation and testimony in proving it. But it was going to take a mountain of evidence to persuade anyone, especially Reinhard Heydrich, that Rudolf Hess was anything but Hitler's

most loyal servant. Ted Campbell alone wasn't enough.
Regenbauer would have to have absolute proof and of that,
Ted knew, there was none. So Ted felt, if not comfortable,
then satisfied. He wasn't going to any meeting in Berlin to tell
his tale to Heydrich. Regenbauer wasn't desperate enough to
resort to that, not with Ted, not yet, not a man who claimed to
have stolen a Luftwaffe plane, flown to England and bombed
London at the request of the British Secret Service. Even
Heydrich wouldn't believe that. And as long as Ted was safe,
so was Kate. Ted thought he knew now something of how
Regenbauer's mind worked. The SS major wasn't going to
harm her because she was the only means Regenbauer had to
keep Ted in line. Besides, it was the only thing Ted could
allow himself to think.

That night Ted was awakened by an explosion that collapsed
his bed. Another blast knocked out the lights. He scrambled to
a corner of the room as the concussion of two more eruptions
shattered his window. He heard the rumble of airplane engines
overhead as another detonation in the courtyard cracked and
broke loose chunks of the ceiling.

Bombers. Ted crouched in the corner with his arms over his
head against the rain of plaster from the ceiling. *British*
bombers. There wasn't any mistaking the sound of Rolls
Royce Merlin engines. An enormous explosion rocked his
room. The wall behind him shuddered. An iron bar from the
window dislodged and clanged heavily to the floor. The RAF
was bombing the castle!

There wasn't time to wonder why they'd come. The place
was a madhouse. He could hear people screaming down
below, then, machine guns. The bombing stopped. Suddenly
Ted realized that this was his chance to get out. Broken glass
and plaster crunched under his slippers as he groped in the
darkness for the iron bar. He sliced his fingers on shards of
glass, frantically searching for it in the debris. It was here. It
had to be here, goddammit, he'd heard it hit the floor.

The bar was longer than he'd expected. And heavy. One end
of it was still attached to a clump of cement. But it didn't
matter. He attacked the door of his cell with all his strength.
He concentrated on the latch, smashing the heavy cement-
crusted end against it until it broke. He ignored the wild
shooting outside. As long as they weren't shooting at him he
didn't care. He wiped sweat off his palms onto his pants and

kept swinging the bar. Each impact seemed to jolt his shoulder out of its socket, but he forgot the pain and kept swinging. Bit by bit the door splintered where the latch had been. He hit it again and again and again . . .

The solid door finally yielded to the savage beating. It cracked against its hinges and collapsed sideways into the hall. Ted's arms ached but he couldn't rest. He half-stumbled down the corridor to the upstairs landing. He carried the bar in both hands. He'd need a weapon. There were fires everywhere. The castle was a shambles. Walls had been caved in by exploding bombs and in the flickering light he saw figures darting frantically out of burning rooms. Where was Regenbauer? That was his first thought, then—where was Kate?

He ran down the stairs. He ran along the route he'd walked a thousand times already, to the interrogation room. He burst into the room to find it burning and empty. The two-way glass windows were all broken and the cells behind them empty.

"You! How did you get here?"

Ted turned. An SS guard was standing at the door. It was one of Ted's escorts, one that had beat him.

"Get back to—"

Ted swung the bar. His rage and frustration finally caught up with him and he struck back the only way he knew how. The guard raised the hand that held the Lüger to deflect the blow but the iron bar crushed through it and connected solidly against his head. His body dropped exactly where it'd stood. Ted grabbed the dead German's Lüger. Whatever happened now, Ted wasn't going to submit to the bastards. He ran down the hall, yelling for Kate. He kicked in doors to burning rooms, but he didn't find anyone. The shooting was inside the castle now. He heard voices screaming orders, but he couldn't understand who they were shooting at. The echoing bursts of machine gun fire were very near. He kept looking for Kate. She was here, in one of these rooms. He fought the smoke like he'd fought it before when he pulled her out of another burning building. His eyes watered with the acrid sting of smoke. He'd find her, he told himself. He'd find Kate if he had to take this place apart stone by goddamn stone.

But he didn't find Kate. He found Trentlyon.

The cell was littered with debris. The outside wall had collapsed and Ted could see the treeline of the forest less than forty yards away. Trentlyon was sitting on his bunk holding a blanket to his chest. His forehead was bleeding. Ted rushed to him. "Trentlyon . . . Nigel, it's Campbell!"

Trentlyon's expression became quizzically amused. "Boom-boom." He looked at Ted in the flickering light with eyes that were unafraid because they had removed fear from him. He pointed to the hole in the wall. "Boom-boom!"

"Christ . . ."

Ted jerked him to his feet. He pointed at the line of trees. "You have to go, Nigel . . . you have to get out!"

Trentlyon smiled and saliva slipped out of the corner of his mouth. He held out his hand. "Please?"

Somewhere nearby a man's scream died in the clatter of machine gun fire. Ted heard running feet in the corridor. He shoved Trentlyon down on the bed. "Stay!" Then he flattened himself against the wall. He held the Lüger trained on the door. If they rushed him, at least he'd get the first one. When he heard the angry, cursing voice in the corridor, Ted suddenly realized that it wasn't Regenbauer or the Gestapo or any SS guard. The voice was yelling in English.

"Campbell . . . Campbell . . . !"

The snout of a gun poked through the doorway.

"Campbell . . .?"

Ted licked his lips. He aimed the Lüger at the weapon. "Who's that?"

The man burst into the room. For an instant they were standing face to face, both with their guns trained on each other. Ted's mouth dropped open. "Moser!"

Moser pushed Ted's Lüger aside. He scanned the room quickly, saw the breached wall. "You gotta get out of here."

"Wha—"

"Move, Campbell! There's an SS detachment less than five miles from here . . . I don't want to wait for them!" He pushed Ted toward the hole.

"Kate's here," Ted protested. "I've got to find her."

"Forget it."

"No! I—"

"She isn't here."

Ted froze. They've killed her, Ted thought. Regenbauer's killed her! The bastard's—

"I don't know *where* she is," Moser said quickly. "They moved most of the medical staff out of here three weeks ago and she went with them."

"Three weeks!"

"You're the only one left here. It's Regenbauer's private hideaway. And before you ask, Regenbauer isn't here either. He leaves this place on Sundays. That's why we set up this coordinated attack tonight. Three Wellingtons bombed it and me and my people cleaned it out because there's only a skeleton guard on duty. Now, I'd love to stay here and chat, Campbell, *but there isn't fucking time!* Let's go!"

Ted stumbled across the rubble to the hole then stopped. "We have to get Trentlyon."

"What!"

"Trentlyon," Ted said. He pointed at the lump on the bed.

Moser grabbed his arm. "Trentlyon's dead. They killed him in Holland six months ago."

"That's him, I tell you!"

Moser cursed him. He went back to the bed and ripped the blanket off the man shaking beneath it. "This isn't—" Then he looked again, squinting in the dim light. "Oh, Jesus God!" He looked quickly at Ted. "What have they done to him!"

Ted didn't have time to respond. He heard trucks.

"They're here!" Moser shouted. He pointed at the treeline. "Get out!"

"But—"

He grabbed Ted by the collar and pushed him through the broken wall. *"Get out!* Go to the trees! *Go!"*

Ted lost one of his slippers in the snow. He ran past a crater, stumbled and skidded to his knees and looked back. Moser was standing in the snow outside the wall. Trentlyon was still on the bed, holding the blanket to him like a child, babbling to himself. Ted heard Moser's steady voice across the cold.

"Nigel, it's Arthur . . . I'm sorry, Nigel. Goddammit . . . I'm sorry."

Ted reached out suddenly, flinging snow in the abrupt movement, as if to stop it when Moser raised the machine gun.

"NOOO . . . !"

The impact of the slugs lifted Trentlyon off the bed and smashed him into the wall. For an instant he hung there, his back against the stones, one leg dangling in midair. Then he fell. The blanket slipped out of his hands and he cartwheeled off the bunk.

Ted dropped his outstretched hands.

Moser ran to him. The SS soldiers were in the castle.

"C'mon!"

Ted stared back.

"He was already dead!" Moser cried. He nodded angrily at the castle. "Do you want to die too!"

"Arthur . . ." Ted said in disbelief. "You're . . . *You're* Spengler!"

Moser jerked him to his feet. "Yes, I'm bloody Spengler . . . we're in trouble. Regenbauer knows everything. We have to get Hess out. *Now* will you move!"

They ran through the trees, Spengler leading because he knew the way. They ran through the powdery snow, over hard frozen meadows, south then east, across a road and past a farmhouse, toward the river Danube. There wasn't anything to do but run now and Ted knew why.

It was a secret in a secret all along, just like Trentlyon said. Only Ted hadn't believed it because he didn't know. But Regenbauer had figured it out. Bit by bit, day by day, with Ted's help, he'd figured it out. The Pythagoras network *was* a ploy to protect something even bigger.

Ted ran without thinking of the cold or the near-frozen state of his bare feet. All those questions about Carstairs and code machines. Questions about Ultra and British subterfuge. Questions he had no answer for.

Suppose you are the dupe, Campbell. Suppose this scheme was meant to be a decoy to hide the real secret. Suppose you weren't meant to know.

If it were true—God, if it were true . . . ! It meant that they were all expendable. All of them . . . Spengler, Haushofer, the agents in Paris and Rome and Lisbon . . . But not Hess and not Ted.

We have to get Hess out.

It was beginning to make sense now. They had to get Hess out because the network was blown. Save Hess. Save Campbell. There was only one reason Ted could be of any use to them now. They wanted him to fly Hess to safety! No wonder he wasn't given a place in the network! A for Alfred. The special code name for a special mission. He was never supposed to be part of the network because . . . because they were going to expose it anyway! Trade the network for Hess and save the bigger secret from detection!

Ted ran mechanically. His legs were numb. He just followed Spengler. It was all a waste of time. Regenbauer knew the

whole dirty scheme. He knew even more than Spengler or
Haushofer. And now Ted knew. Ultra was the secret. Whatever it was it was more important than a hundred lives.
Regenbauer had used Ted to figure it out. Ted ran without
thinking once he realized what that meant. The SS major had
won. It meant he had Hess and he had Ted, despite what
Spengler might think. But it meant more than that. Kate wasn't
safe and she never had been.

40

REGENBAUER SNUBBED OUT his cigarette in the ashtray brimming with dead butts. He uncrossed his legs impatiently and glanced at the Obergruppenfuehrer's private secretary, a lean and officious SS-Haupsturmfuehrer, in whose office Regenbauer had been waiting most of the morning.

"I am sorry, Major," the effeminate fool said in a tone that told Regenbauer he wasn't the least bit regretful, "but Obergruppenfuehrer Heydrich will be with you shortly, I'm sure."

"It is urgent that I see him immediately!" Regenbauer touched the large leather case on his lap. "A matter of utmost security—"

"The moment Obersturmbannfuehrer Eichmann leaves I will remind the Obergruppenfuehrer that you are here. If you'll just be patient, Major . . ."

"Who's Eichmann?"

The secretary sighed. "Reich Central Office of Jewish Emigration."

"Emigration!" Regenbauer's eyes widened. "I've been waiting here all this time while—" He rose suddenly to his feet.

"Major?"

Regenbauer went directly to the door.

"Major! You cannot—"

But Regenbauer hesitated only an instant, then he turned the latch and entered Heydrich's office.

Heydrich was bent over a map table, a young SS lieutenant colonel standing beside him pointing out something on a large chart.

"My general, I must see you at once!" Regenbauer said. He'd taken two or three steps into the office when the harried little secretary rushed in behind him.

"Obergruppenfuehrer!" The captain's short dash had left him out of breath. "He . . . this major burst in without permission! I . . . I told him—"

"Good morning, Major Regenbauer," Heydrich said without warmth. He straightened up from the table. "I assume you have a good reason for this interruption?"

"I do, sir. Gravely important."

"It cannot wait a few—"

"It requires your immediate attention," Regenbauer cut in.

Heydrich turned to the lieutenant colonel. "We'll continue this later."

When they were alone, Heydrich sat at his desk. "Do not *ever* do that again," he said. "Do not ever come into my office unannounced. And do not tell me what requires my immediate attention."

"I'm sorry, Obergruppenfuehrer."

"I have given you a great deal of freedom, and a great amount of power, but do not take the notion that your authority extends to me."

"Yes, sir."

Heydrich leaned back in his chair. "Now . . ." He pressed his fingertips together, touched them to his chin and stared at Regenbauer. "What is this grave news you have?"

Regenbauer explained it all. He began with Trentlyon and the agent called Copernicus and the Englishman Carstairs who ran the Pythagoras network and called himself Euclid. He explained about Campbell and Haushofer and the British spy named Spengler. He told Heydrich about Ultra and Hess and the escape of Campbell. He reviewed the intelligence he'd gotten from the Pole, Fryc, about the operation to break the Enigma coding machine and he described the fraudulent messages he had sent which were responded to by actions of the British as final proof that the secret German coding machine had been compromised. He said that the Pythagoras operation was nothing more than a ruse to protect Britain's real

secret, which was Ultra—an operation which had successfully
cracked Enigma. He pulled pages and pages of proof from his
leather case: transcripts of interviews with Trentlyon and
Campbell and Fryc and Kepler, diagrams, charts, messages
. . . All of it adding up to the indisputable fact that the
English had engineered a way to read top-secret radio traffic
supposedly coded through Enigma.

When he was finished, Regenbauer sat back in his chair
exhausted, dizzy with anticipation. He'd broken a conspiracy
that, if it hadn't been discovered, might very easily have cost
Germany the war. And Regenbauer had done it alone. There
would be no one else to share in the triumph. He stared at
Heydrich, his mouth hinting a smile.

"I think you have been working much too hard, Sturmbannfuehrer," Heydrich said. He rubbed his temples with his long
slender fingers. "I think you should take some time off."

"I will, my general, as soon—"

"You should visit Paris."

"I've seen Paris," Regenbauer said quickly. "I—"

Heydrich cut him off with a harsh stare. "Then rest somewhere else," he said impatiently. "You're tired. You're a
dedicated officer, but you work too hard. I want you to be
rested for the work I have planned for you. I expect to be
appointed deputy Reichsprotektor of Bohemia and Moravia
soon. Lina and I have already taken a villa at Panenske-
Breschen, near Prague. I am very concerned about the Czech
underground there. The Fuehrer is unhappy with von Neurath's
handling of the situation. When I go there I will need a good
intelligence officer to help me wipe out the resistance. I think
you are a likely choice. Naturally, it would mean a promotion."

Regenbauer stared blankly at the Reich security chief. What
was he talking about—Czechs! Regenbauer squinted. He'd just
explained in detail how the British had broken their unbreakable coding machine; how Deputy Fuehrer Hess was a pawn
for the British Secret Service. He had the proof. And Campbell's rescue was the final evidence. Hess must be arrested
immediately! Regenbauer had sweated blood for this moment.
He'd accomplished what no other man in Germany could have
done. And Heydrich sits back in his chair and speaks of
vacations! Regenbauer stared at his superior as if seeing him

for the first time. What kind of fool was he working for! What was Heydrich thinking? *Why wasn't he listening!*

"Sir, I think the immediate question of this British plot should take precedence over—"

"We've discussed this once before," Heydrich said testily.

"About Enigma, yes, but—"

"The Enigma machine has not been compromised," Heydrich said flatly. "It has not been because it cannot be broken. And as for this incredible tale about Hess . . ."

"Tale!" Regenbauer's eyes flashed with sudden rage. "My general, I promise you—"

"Your orders were to look into the possibility that a military conspiracy existed against the Reich, not to implicate the deputy fuehrer as a spy!" Heydrich interlaced his fingers to control his temper. "Rudolf Hess is *not* an agent for the British, Sturmbannfuehrer. You may take *my* word for that."

Regenbauer glanced up from his briefcase. He crumpled a quire of typescript in his hand. He couldn't believe what he was hearing. "Please . . . if you will let me show you . . ."

"It's obvious what they're doing," Heydrich said. "You're too involved to see it. They can't break our codes so they've devised this plan to have us think they have." He wasn't looking at Regenbauer anymore. He was staring at some spot on the ceiling. "Don't you see? If the British can trick us into believing they've learned the secret of our Enigma machine then we would be forced to try some other system."

"No, sir!" Regenbauer tried to overcome the dryness in his mouth. "That's not it! The proof is here . . ." He dug through the briefcase.

The Obergruppenfuehrer sat up angrily in his chair. "The proof is this!" he said. "If MI-6 had broken our top-secret codes—" his cold blue eyes darkened "—where is the *real* evidence of it? If British intelligence is reading our secrets, why do Rommel and his Afrika Korps, outnumbered by the English, push them across the desert and isolate the harbor at Tobruk? Why didn't the English General Wavell's army win at El Agheila or Mersa Brega or Benghazi? Why does the Luftwaffe continue to bomb Allied ships that dare enter the Mediterranean? Why do German armies outflank the British in a move through the Pindus Mountains and compel them to retreat in Greece? In short, why is Germany winning the war!"

Regenbauer put the pages of his report back into the leather case. He didn't look at Heydrich. He said nothing.

"You have wasted enough time on this obsession of yours," Heydrich said after a moment. "Forget it. I want you to take some time off. I want you to rest—here in Berlin, Paris, Rome, take a woman if you like, travel, do something, but *forget this!*"

Regenbauer smapped the briefcase shut. He stood up. "Yes, my general."

"The British are fools to think we would believe such nonsense," the security chief said at the door.

"They are not the only fools, I think."

Heydrich patted his shoulder. "You mustn't judge yourself harshly, Major. We all make mistakes from time to time."

Outside, Regenbauer cupped his hands against the chilly breeze to light a cigarette. He hadn't calmed himself until he'd exhaled the smoke from his lungs into a swirl of wind. *He* wasn't the fool, he told himself. And he didn't make mistakes. Reich security was run by a well-born moron. Heydrich was like all the rest of them . . . highbrow fools. Why hadn't he seen that before? Well, it didn't matter, Regenbauer thought. He didn't need them.

Regenbauer walked down the steps of the Gestapo headquarters building. He didn't need them. He could finish this himself. He flicked his cigarette away. Let Heydrich worry about the Czechs in Prague. There was only one way to prove himself now. Get Campbell.

41 _____

THEY'D BEEN IN hiding for three days. The first night Spengler had found them a shelter in a barn. They'd caught a ride on a vegetable truck to Günzburg where Spengler put Ted up in a second-floor room above a tavern.

Spengler had been quiet and moody after Ted had explained everything he knew or suspected about the trick Carstairs had played on them. He told Spengler about Ultra, at least, his theory that it was some super secret of British intelligence. He didn't know if Spengler believed any of it. Spengler had to leave to contact Haushofer and Ted demanded that they find Kate.

Spengler was gone nearly two days. When he returned he looked as if he hadn't slept the entire time.

"First, you're going to tell me Kate's all right," Ted said after Spengler found a chair. "You're going to tell me where she is and that we're going to see her—that I'm going to see her. Then we'll talk about the next thing."

Spengler wiped his hand across his mouth. "It isn't that simple."

"Where is she!"

"When the medical staff left Grafeneck . . . she went with them." Spengler avoided Ted's eyes. "They went to a camp on the Amper River, north of Munich. They set up shop there to do medical experiments for the Luftwaffe . . . high altitude tests on prisoners—"

"Where!"

Spengler looked at him. "Dachau."

"Da—" Ted's mouth froze forming the word.

"I'm sorry, Campbell."

"The concentration camp!"

"If there was anything we could do . . ."

"We have to get her out," Ted said finally. "We have to get her out!"

"Campbell . . ."

"I can't leave her there! She's pregnant . . . she's . . . she's blind and pregnant! How long can she last in a place like that? Christ, Spengler, do something! You have the contacts! You and Haushofer. Get her out of there!"

"Nobody gets out of those camps. They have her as a communist organizer, that's only one step above Jew." Spengler shook his head. "At least she's only a political prisoner. They're experimenting on the criminal prisoners and the insane."

"You have to do something," Ted said. "Kate's an American citizen. She's—"

"It can't be done, Campbell. If we pressed it they might try her as a spy. A Russian spy or an English spy . . . At least she's alive. Regenbauer didn't kill her."

"You're such a goddamn whiz at getting people out of places! You and your fucking network! Figure something . . . just get Kate out!"

"There isn't a network anymore," Spengler replied. "That's what I've been doing since I left here. They're all gone."

"Regenbauer!"

Spengler shrugged. "I don't know. It may have been Carstairs. I've been checking out that story you gave me. I thought you were nuts, but now . . ." He ran his fingers through his hair. "Now it makes sense. All the operatives are missing. I've tried contacting four of them, but they're just gone. Regenbauer may have gotten to them, but I don't think so. What's crazy is they left all kinds of incriminating evidence about Pythagoras, the network, I mean, not Hess. Still, it wouldn't take anyone with a lot of smarts to figure it out. Regenbauer could do it . . ."

"Regenbauer already knows it. He knows Hess is Pythagoras."

Spengler shook his head. "He couldn't. It's been five days. If Regenbauer knew, Hess would already be jailed. He isn't, though. He's in Munich."

"Waiting for me, right?" Ted glared at Spengler. "I've had a lot of time to think about things these last couple of days. It kept coming back to me—why am I so important? The network's blown, I can't be of any use to you or Haushofer, I can't go anywhere because Regenbauer would slit my throat. So I keep wondering. The only thing I *can* do is fly airplanes."

Spengler looked away from him.

"You want to fly him out," Ted said. "That was my part in this all along, wasn't it? I've been on standby all this time just so I'd be available to get Hess out of Germany if things turned sour. You bastards! Blew up in your face, didn't it?"

"No. You can still get Hess out."

"Sure I can. Look, you idiot, Regenbauer knows! You seem to forget that. I'm not going anywhere near Hess because that's where Regenbauer will be waiting. He *knows* Hess is Pythagoras. Breaking me out of the castle should have proved that to him. If Regenbauer has it figured then the Gestapo knows it too. I don't know what Hess is doing in Munich but he's living on borrowed time."

"Regenbauer's already been to see Heydrich in Berlin," Spengler said.

"There, you see . . . ?"

"But Heydrich didn't believe it." Spengler tried a smile. "Regenbauer got turned down cold."

"What!"

"If Heydrich believed Regenbauer's story then Hess would have been standing in front of Georing and Hitler inside an hour. But it didn't happen. The only German who thinks Hess is a traitor is Regenbauer . . . and nobody believes him."

Ted didn't respond. He stared at Spengler.

"It'll still work. We can get Hess out."

Ted frowned. "Why? If nobody suspects him, he doesn't *have* to go anywhere."

"Campbell, he *wants* to go. But you won't be taking him to Switzerland. That's not the idea."

"What *is?*"

"Hess doesn't know the real reason for all of this. He thinks he's in correspondence with the Duke of Hamilton. He's not a spy, for Chrissakes. He wants Germany and England to be allies against the Soviets. That's all he's ever wanted. He's convinced that he can negotiate a peace with England if he can just see the king."

"Where the hell do you want me to fly—" Then Ted stopped. He gaped at Spengler.

"Right," Spengler said. "Scotland. Dungavel House. Right on the duke's front door. You're the only man who can do it. You're the only man who could fly across Germany, across the North Sea, across the coast of Scotland in the middle of a war and find the damned place at night. You know the route, the country, the towns . . . Hell, you proved you could do it when you hit London."

"Scotland!"

"It'll work. It's the only way. Hess's already tried to go it alone, but he had to come back because of weather. He won't wait later than Saturday. The invasion's set for sometime after the middle of the month. Goering's learned from his mistake last summer. They're not going to repeat it. Hess figures the only way he can stop it is this last-ditch effort for peace and he's willing to risk the consequences. The point is, with Hess in British hands, Hitler's going to think twice about an all-out surprise attack. He'll expect Hess went insane and told them all his plans."

"You're forgetting about Regenbauer. Regenbauer knows the truth."

"I'll take care of Regenbauer."

Ted shook his head. "You're nuts. You and Haushofer . . . and Hess too."

"It's the only way left. All that's left of Carstairs' network is me. And I can't protect you anymore. This is the only way you're going to get out of this country alive." Spengler let out a long breath. "There's one other thing. If what you say about this Ultra is true . . . I mean, if . . . if the Pythagoras run really was just a smokescreen to keep the Germans from the truth, then Hess *has* to go. It makes the point of it work. Heydrich and Goering and Goebbels . . . they'll believe Hess was the leak if he flies off to England. That's what the network was set up for in the first place."

Ted made a face. "Good Christ, you're a company man right to the bitter end, aren't you!"

Spengler waved him off. "What I mean was this. When you get to Scotland—"

"—If."

"When you get there, you'll have to make it seem like Hess made the flight . . . well, alone. You're to go to Edinburgh. Carstairs will be waiting."

"What!"

"You can't be seen anywhere near Hess. You mustn't be picked up. That would ruin it. If they find out here that you flew Hess the whole thing would be pointless . . . that is as far as protecting Ultra. They already know you're involved and—"

"Just where am I supposed to have disappeared to!"

"Dead," Spengler said. "A charred body will be found in your villa after I burn it down."

"Bur—you should be on radio, Spengler! You and Edgar Bergen and Charlie McCarthy. Burn down the villa? Who were you going to use for the body? Any volunteers come to—"

"I was thinking about Regenbauer," Spengler said quietly. "You're both about the same size."

"For a man with few options you sure have some king-sized plans."

"I'll take care of myself. What do you say?"

"I think I'm holding the trump ace, that's what I think." Ted stood up, tested his sore toes on the hardwood floor. "First, you can't pull this off without me, right?"

Spengler exhaled.

Ted nodded. "Right. Second, Hess is the third most powerful Nazi in Germany. Right?"

"What are you getting at?"

"A deal. A trade, if you want to call it that." Ted's voice was calm. "I get Hess out of Germany, you get Kate out of Germany."

"I can't do that! I've already told you nobody can get her out of Dachau!"

"Hess can," Ted said. "If Hess can do anything, he can have a blind woman released from a concentration camp. If the deputy fuehrer of the Third bloody Reich can't do that, then the hell with him!"

"Dachau is run by the SS! Hess isn't even *in* the SS!"

"I didn't say I thought it was going to be easy. Just do it. When I know Kate is out of this country . . . *then* you've got yourself a pilot." Ted raised his eyebrows. "That's the deal. Take it or leave it."

"Today's Tuesday, for Chrissake!" Spengler snapped. "There's only four days until Saturday!"

Ted gave him a hard look. "Then you'd better hurry."

The telephone started ringing as soon as Lowell Grayson came into the office.

"United Press, Grayson." He held the phone in the crook of his neck as he hung his coat on the back of a chair.

"Just answer yes or no. Do you know who this is?"

Lowell whirled back to his desk at the sound of Ted's voice. "Wha—"

"Just yes or no."

"Yes! Where are—"

"Shut up. Do you have a pencil?"

"Yeah."

"Write this down, just the answer. And don't take all day."

"Go ahead."

"Who won the 1936 Academy Award for actor?"

"What!"

"Just write the answer. Last name only."

"Okay."

"Who won the 1934 Rose Bowl?"

"I hope this means somehing."

"Just write."

"Okay."

"What is the very middle of an American football game called?"

"Middle?"

"Yes, goddammit! You know what it is."

"Yeah, but . . ."

"Now, do you have the answers written down in front of you?"

"Sure."

"Look at them."

Grayson looked.

MUNI. COLUMBIA. HALFTIME.

"Now what?"

"Throw out everything in the second two words except the first letter of each and make it all into one word. Do it."

MUNI. C. H.

"Okay."

"It spells a place I want you to go. The main train station at noon tomorrow. It's important, Grayson. I wouldn't call if it wasn't."

"Does any of this have to do with a missing redhead?"

"Everything."

"I'll be there," Grayson said.

"Gluecks speaking."

"Gruppenfuehrer Gluecks, good morning. This is Karl Pintsch, the Reichsleiter's adjutant. I am calling from Munich."

"Ah, Herr Pintsch, how is the deputy fuehrer today?"

"Fine, my general, a slight cold, but fine. Spring is soon coming, yes?"

"And not soon enough, I can tell you. I will be happy when the rain is gone. What can I do for you, Herr Pintsch?"

"It is Emmy Goering's birthday in two weeks, Gruppenfuehrer, and the Reichsmarschal has decided to surprise his lovely wife with a party in Berlin. You know how much the Reichsmarschal enjoys parties and, well, he mentioned the idea to Deputy Fuehrer Hess, who appointed me to oversee the details."

"It is not all tedious work you do, eh, Pintsch?" chuckled the SS general.

"As you might expect, my general, Reichsmarschal Goering wishes this to be a grand affair, but also secret. He would have my head if word of it ever reached Frau Goering and spoiled the surprise."

"My lips are sealed. This then is an invitation, Pintsch?"

"Oh, yes, of course, but there is also another matter and I bring it up with trepidation. When I learned of it and informed the Reichsleiter, he instructed me to see to it immediately. Perhaps it is a mistake, one hears such rumors of nonsense these days, but I must investigate it nonetheless."

"And what is that?"

"Well, you know that the Reichsmarschal has his favorites . . . how should I put this delicately? He is fond of witty companions, especially beautiful women. I do not mean to put too fine a point to it, but there are certain charming ladies he likes to see at these occasions."

"Yes, I understand. But how is that a problem?"

"Well . . . have you ever met Fräulein Katherine Buchanan? An American broadcaster? A lovely, beautiful woman, I can assure you. One of the Reichsmarschal's favorites."

"Buchanan? No, I don't recall the name. I do not go to many parites lately. There is some problem?"

"As Reich inspector of concentration camps, my general, you can put this rumor straight. To be blunt, Reichsleiter Hess has just learned that Fräulein Buchanan is at this moment a political prisoner at the Dachau internment camp! At least, that is what we have heard. Herr Hess instructed me to go directly to Reichsfuehrer Himmler, but I thought perhaps it would be more discreet to contact you, Gruppenfuehrer. If it is a rumor, as I am sure it is, then all is well and I apologize for troubling you. However, if by some catastrophic error the rumor proves to be true . . . well, I thought it best for all involved not to bother Himmler. You know the Reichsfuehrer's temper and—"

"Yes-yes, Pintsch," the voice at the other end said quickly, "you did the right thing to call me directly. Buchanan, you say? Dachau?"

"I can only suspect that it is a silly rumor, Gruppenfuehrer. She is an American, after all. Why would she be at Dachau, I ask myself?"

"I will look into it immediately, Pintsch."

"You will call me, then? The Reichsmarschal has also expressed an interest."

"The Reichsmarschal!" There was a short pause. "I will see to it now, this moment."

"Thank you, Gruppenfuehrer. Heil Hitler."

Kate's eyes fluttered open and she stirred in the bed. As she came slowly out of the groggy sleep she sensed something different—the bed was different, her head was on a pillow, she felt sheets; it smelled different, more antiseptic. She couldn't hear the other inmates. Thy'd moved her again! Where had they moved her to now?

"Kinderfrau? Kinderfrau? . . ."

"The nurse is just down the hall," a voice out of the darkness said. "Shall I get her?"

It came from the right and she turned toward it. Familiar voice . . .

"Who's that!"

"I'm surprised, Kate, old girl. Don't you even recognize an

old drinking buddy?" She felt pressure on the side of the bed near her hand.

"Lowell?"

He touched her hand. "I'm fresh out of ham, but they tell me the chow here isn't bad."

"Lowell!" She grabbed his hand with both of hers. "Oh, God, Lowell! But . . . what? . . . how did you get? . . . where am I? This isn't *that* place . . . ?"

"No, Kate; you're in Munich. Eichendorff Hospital. I've been here since last night."

"Last night?"

"They'd given you something to sleep." He squeezed her hand. "You're a hell of a sound sleeper. So how are you feeling? Hungry?"

"I guess so. But . . . but how did you know? How did you know I was here?"

"Well, actually, Ted called me."

Kate's eyes widened. "Ted!"

"Yes. It's a little complicated and I'll explain it to you in detail, but the important thing is you have to leave Germany. Campbell was very firm about that. He—"

"You've talked to him! Is he all right?"

"He's fine. Worried about you, naturally. You and, ah—" he cleared his throat "—whoever that is in there." Grayson patted the mound of her belly. "Putting the cart about six lengths ahead of the horse, aren't we?"

"I want to know about Ted. Where is he? Why isn't he here?"

"Look, old girl, my part in all this is very small. I didn't actually see Ted, but the man I talked to explained it very carefully. I felt like Robert Donat—hoping the cops didn't find—"

"What do you mean, your part?"

"A bit of intrigue is good for the soul," Grayson said. "You see, I'm booked on a flight Saturday for Bern. Me and a colleague of the female gender. I won't mention any names, but—"

"Wait a damned minute! That isn't supposed to be me, I hope."

"Did I say that?"

"Don't try to be cute. I told Ted I wasn't leaving without him."

"Oh, he's leaving too. Just taking a different route."

"Where is he?"

"I don't know. Really, I don't. I just know that he got you out of that place and that he's seeing that you're escorted out of the country. Someone is still looking for him."

Kate pushed herself up. "Oh, God! It's Regenbauer, isn't it? Ted's hiding . . . but how did he get out of the castle?"

"I don't know anything about castles. I only know what I'm supposed to do."

"But . . . Regenbauer!"

"Just lie back down there. Just rest. You have some traveling ahead of you. Let me call the nurse and we'll get you something to eat. That's it. Everything's going to be fine."

Campbell was clever, but not very clever, Regenbauer mused. He was leaning against the door of the two-year-old Mercedes he'd commandeered from the local Gestapo. Campbell had a lot to learn about codes. Whom did he think he was fooling? Everyone in Germany knew who Paul Muni was. The rest of it was no more complicated than a schoolboy's note. Regenbauer had heard the recording of Grayson's tapped phone call and it didn't take five minutes to understand what Campbell was telling the wire service editor, or where to go.

Johann Regenbauer *knew* Theodore Campbell. He knew his strengths, but more important, he knew his weaknesses. You don't spend four months with a man and not learn something. Campbell would try to get out of Germany; he was on the run now, desperate. He would try to escape because he knew, just as Regenbauer knew, that he was the only man alive in Germany who could corroborate the truth about Ultra. Regenbauer didn't know where Campbell was, but for the moment he didn't need to know. Campbell's weakness was the woman. He would not leave Germany without her or at least without knowing she was safely away. Regenbauer didn't know how he'd gotten her out of Dachau. That *was* clever, however it was accomplished, even well done, but it wasn't enough.

Campbell's plan was pathetically transparent. The newsman Grayson had reserved two tickets on a Munich flight to Switzerland. Fly Katherine to safety, that was the idea. Unfortunately for them, it wasn't going to work. Regenbauer would arrest Katherine and the newsman at the airport. Then he would have Campbell because he'd give himself up to protect her. Regenbauer would have Campbell and he would have Ultra and he would win.

Grayson came out of the hospital. He hailed a taxi. Regenbauer climbed into the Mercedes and followed him, coaxing the supercharged machine through Munich traffic. It was only important to watch Grayson now. Regenbauer had taken the precaution of having a team of Gestapo agents watching Hess's house, just in case Campbell showed up. He knew Campbell wasn't stupid enough to go there, but it didn't hurt to be careful. Besides, Campbell would expect that. He knew Regenbauer would be watching and waiting. The SS major smiled to himself. Why should he disappoint the man.

42

On Saturday, it rained.

Ted had been in Augsberg since Wednesday night, staying in a boardinghouse near the airport. During the day he studied the plan with Spengler, looking for loopholes. There were none. Regenbauer was out there somewhere; Ted sensed his presence. He'd leave with Hess the moment he knew Kate was safely on her way. If there was a weak link, it was Grayson; Ted didn't like depending on anyone else, Kate was *his* responsibility, but he didn't have any choice. It was Spengler's idea, but Ted approved it. Now it had to work because they were committed to it. And Grayson could pull it off, Ted told himself. He could pull it off . . . he *could* pull it off . . .

At night Ted studied the ME-110. It was a plane he'd seen but had never flown. He could fly it all right, but even though Hess had seen to it that the Messerschmitt, and its twin backup, had been fitted with auxiliary wing tanks, fuel would still be a critical problem. The flight to Scotland was almost nine hundred miles; with the added tanks the Messerschmitt's range was extended to a maximum of one thousand. A one-hundred-mile fuel reserve for that distance was taking a hell of a chance. Almost anything could eat it up—bad weather, poor visibility, a hundred things could go wrong.

Hess had gotten him a map of forbidden air zones and Ted plotted a course, zigzagging across Germany, then straight for a point in the Farne Islands off the coast of Scotland and on into the uplands to Lanarkshire. For three nights he moved in a world of gas ratios to piston performance, detachable petrol pods, radio bearings, calculated and recalculated. He really would rather not run out of gas over the North Sea.

That was why his heart sank into his stomach when he got up before dawn to see raindrops on the window. He wanted clouds; cloud cover would help to hide him, but he didn't want rain. The denser the air, the harder the engines worked.

By mid-morning, the rain stopped.

At noon he tried to sleep, couldn't, got up and drew a diagram of the Messerschmitt instrument panel from memory on the back of a map of Germany—anything to take his mind off worrying about what everyone else was supposed to be doing in the next few hours. Grayson would pick up Kate at the hospital at four. They'd go to Grayson's hotel and meet Spengler and go over the final details. Hess would leave his house at five. He and Pintsch would take a leisurely drive around the city, then get on the autobahn and head for Augsburg. Five thirty Ted would walk to the airport. Sunset was at six ten. At six thirty Grayson would put them in a cab to the Munich airport. God, Grayson had to make it work! They left for Bern at seven. Once they were on the plane they were safe. *They just had to get on the fucking plane!*

At quarter past four, Ted wanted to call Grayson's hotel room so badly he nearly sweated blood. He just wanted to hear Kate's voice, to know she was okay, to tell her he loved her.

He was out of cigarettes by five. He was pacing now, alone. There was nothing left to do but wait. Just pace and look at his watch, glare at the second hand and will it to move faster. The plan was set in motion now. There was no turning back for Kate. Hess was in his car somewhere.

Five oh five.

Ted went to the window to check the sky; cloudy, patchy overcast, but no heavy stuff, no rain clouds. It'd be dark in another hour or so. *No, don't look at your watch!*

When the telephone rang, Ted nearly stopped breathing. No one was supposed to call him here. That wasn't part of the plan. Something was wrong! As Ted scrambled to the receiver all he could think of was Kate. Something's happened. Something's happened!

"Hello!"

"Herr Campbell, this is Pintsch. We're at the Reichsleiter's hangar. Can you come now?"

"What's the matter?"

"Herr Hess was a little nervous. He decided to come out earlier. He wanted to look over the plane one more time, carefully."

"That's all?"

"He is a little nervous, Herr Campbell. He's never been a passenger in a Messerschmitt. You will come now, please?"

"I'm on my way."

"What time is it now?" Kate asked. She was sitting in a chair near a lamp by the window. The flower-print dress Grayson had bought her didn't fit well; it was tight in the bust and across her stomach.

"Another hour yet," Spengler said from across the room.

"Everything's fine, Kate," Grayson added.

Kate nodded. "Can I have a cigarette?"

"Sure." Grayson's chair squeaked as he got up. She heard him rip open a new pack of cigarettes, heard the scrape of the lighter. "Here."

She reached for it, found his hand. "I'd normally give you hell for treating me like an invalid, but . . ." She took the cigarette and inhaled. ". . . but right now I don't think I could light a cigarette even if I could see it."

"You're doing fine. It won't be much longer."

"I hope not." She pulled the raincoat from the arm of her chair into her lap. "This hood, you're . . . you're sure my face was covered when we left the hospital."

"Stop worrying, Miss Buchanan," Spengler said. "It's fine. Besides, it'll be dark at the airport."

"Very dark?"

"Dark enough," Grayson said. "Hell, if I'm not worried, why should you be?"

Kate didn't answer. She took another drag on the cigarette, then turned slightly to face the other corner of the room. "Are you nervous at all? You haven't said anything for hours." She couldn't tell if the lamp was obstructing her face, but she wanted to let the other person see her; that was the trouble with being blind. You didn't know if you were looking at a wall or a flowerpot.

"I'm okay," a voice said quietly. "I'm not nervous if you're not."

43

THE MESSERSCHMITT WAS parked on the concrete apron just outside a row of hangars. The setting sun silhouetted the sleek lines of the twin-tailed aircraft and refracted light gleamed in the canopy windows with an eerie brilliance. Across the deserted runway the line of administration buildings ran together in the shadows. Ted walked to the plane and inspected the aluminum auxiliary tank on the starboard wing. It looked pitifully small.

"Herr Campbell."

Ted turned back toward the hangar; Pintsch hurried around the tailfin then ducked under the wing.

"I have your flight suit and equipment ready in the pilots' changing room," Pintsch said. "Everything else is in order."

"Where's Hess?"

"Waiting to speak with you. He's anxious to leave." Pintsch gave a little shrug. "The Reichsleiter is a little nervous . . ."

"We're all a little nervous." Ted ran his hand along the engine manifold. "The plane's been checked and preflighted? Engines started?"

"This afternoon."

"Gassed up?"

"This afternoon."

Ted nodded. "I'll do a check of my own; crank her up, listen to her run." He glanced at the clouds that were drifting in from the northeast. "Ought to be a good night for flying. It'll start cooling off fast now. After dark we'll top off the tanks. I want to have every ounce of fuel on board I can get." Ted looked at Hess's adjutant. "When I've heard from Munich that Grayson's flight is gone, then *we'll* go. We can be on our way in ten minutes."

"I hope there is no trouble," Pintsch said. He wrung his hands. "I hope it works."

"It has to work." Ted glanced nervously across the airfield. "I wish I knew where Regenbauer was . . . exactly where he is right now. If this little trick doesn't work and he gets his hands on Kate . . ." He tried to block the possibility out of his mind.

"The deputy fuehrer's residence has been under surveillance by the Gestapo for the past four days," Pintsch offered.

"Regenbauer's hoping I'll show up. Too bad, isn't it?" Ted smiled, but his heart wasn't in it. "You're sure that they didn't follow you here?"

"Quite sure. It would take an order from Himmler himself to permit the Gestapo to follow Reichsleiter Hess like a common suspect. Anyway, the Security Police know that he comes to Augsburg regularly. It is not unusual."

"Good." Ted glanced at the hangar. The large door was partially open and in the shadows he caught a glimpse of the rounded nose of Hess's standby aircraft. "What about the backup?"

Pintsch frowned. "What about it?"

"If there's anything about this one I don't like, is it ready to fly?"

"There is nothing wrong with this machine," Pintsch said quickly. "You may rest assured. I have seen to it that great care was taken by the maintenance department that one of the aircraft be readied . . . at the expense of the other, if necessary. I saw no reason to have the other plane prepared as well."

Ted sighed. "Let's hope it's enough." He looked at his watch. "I'm going to change and run the check on the 'Schmitt. I'll take fifteen-twenty minutes at the most. Then I'm going to sit by the phone. It's a call I don't want to miss."

"Nor do I," Pintsch replied dryly.

It had been dark only a few minutes when Grayson stepped out of the front door of his hotel. Regenbauer recognized him immediately, waited until Grayson flagged a taxi before he started the Mercedes. The newspaperman was not very clever, either. He held the cab door open, then walked briskly back to the hotel entrance and took Katherine by the elbow and helped her to the cab. She was wearing the same raincoat with a hood to hide her face as she had worn from the hospital. It was a brave attempt, Regenbauer thought, but even with help Katherine couldn't pretend to see where she was going. If anything, she seemed a little drunk.

The taxi pulled away from the curb. Regenbauer slid the Mercedes sports tourer into gear and followed it at about five car lengths. It was obvious that the airport was their destination. The fish was swimming into the net.

"We *will* make peace with England," Hess was saying from his chair in the pilots' lounge. The deputy fuehrer's new leather flight suit was open at the chest, revealing the tunic of a Luftwaffe Oberleutnant. He had been talking almost nonstop since Ted had returned from the final tests of the Messerschmitt. He had psyched himself into a near-fanatic state and translated his nervousness into a recitation of his dream for Germany and a reaffirmation of his devotion to his Fuehrer. He was speaking to himself, Ted realized. And this was the man, Ted thought, who was flying to Scotland, who was going to knock on Hamilton's door at Dungavel House in the middle of Lanarkshire and ask to see the king.

Ted checked his watch. He should be hearing soon; Kate should be on her way. Ted tuned Hess totally out of his consciousness. He could only wait now; wait and pray. He took off tonight with the man who might save England from devastation. It all depended on one phone call. If Kate was caught, she was as good as dead. So was Ted. So was Hess. Hess was the price they'd pay for Kate—Carstairs, British Secret Service, military intelligence, Ultra . . . They'd pay bloody dearly.

They sat in a corner of the airport terminal away from the other passengers. Regenbauer waited outside, smoking a cigarette and occasionally glancing inside. They were huddled together like a pair of sheepherders trying to keep warm over a fire, Regenbauer thought, amusing himself. Katherine was trembling like a leaf. She kept her head bowed with that ridiculous hood shading her face, but she was so frightened that her shoulders shook and strands of her red hair fell into view.

Regenbauer decided to let them board. Katherine would stop trembling when she was on the plane—she would think she was safe. Regenbauer would let them start the engines and fill the plane with passengers and just before they closed the door —that was when he would take them.

He wished Campbell were here. There was probably someone here at the terminal who was going to call Campbell the moment the plane left. Someone to tell Campbell that his pregnant whore was on her way to Switzerland. Regenbauer glanced through the window at the other faces. Well, whoever it was, it would be a message Campbell wouldn't expect.

The passengers were called to board. Grayson and Katherine were the fifth and sixth to walk toward the plane. Regenbauer wondered what she was thinking now. A gust of wind caught her hood and she grabbed for it and nearly fell down. The poor blind bitch. Even Grayson was apparently flustered; he was trying so hard to guide her to the stairs that his hat flew away; he watched it roll into the darkness beyond the tail of the plane.

Katherine negotiated the stairs well enough, Regenbauer thought, and he nearly laughed out loud when she stumbled at the door. Such a long walk for her; maybe she'll remember the way when she returns.

The engines of the Junker snorted; the first propeller turned. Regenbauer had already flashed his SD identity card at the gateman and had four rifle-toting security guards following him across the pavement toward the plane. The passenger manifest listed them as news correspondents: GRAYSON, L., UP, and STEVENSON, ALICE, CHICAGO TRIB. Regenbauer smiled to himself. He made a mental note to find out where she had forged a passport.

Regenbauer had to wait a few moments for the door to open, but he didn't mind. Every second longer was another moment of terror for Katherine.

He drew his Lüger when he was inside the plane.

"Everyone quiet! I am making an arrest in the name of the Reich Security Service!"

Regenbauer moved down the aisle slowly, shining his flashlight in the startled and frightened faces. He saw Grayson; he was sitting in the very back of the plane, his arms protectively around the woman in the raincoat. She was sobbing quietly into his shoulder, her red hair a mass of tangles across her face.

"Up!" Regenbauer pointed the light in Grayson's eyes.

"Look here, you can't—"

"UP!"

Grayson stood up and Regenbauer pushed him into the aisle, then he pointed the light at the woman in the green flower-print dress whose hands covered her tear-streaked face.

There was something about the way she moved. Regenbauer hesitated. He shone his light in her face and she sobbed and turned away. *She turned away from the light!* Katherine was blind! How many times had he seen her stare unflinchingly under the bright lights of the interrogation room? Regenbauer's eyes opened wide. He reached for the hood and ripped it off her head.

"Please don't hurt me," she cried. "Please . . . *please!*"

Regenbauer's astonished expression froze on his face. His mouth was open. He shone his light at her and she covered her eyes. He flashed his glance at Grayson then back at her. He couldn't believe what he was seeing.

It wasn't Kate.

44

THE PHONE RANG.

"Hello—Lowell . . ."

"It worked!" Grayson was breathing heavily, panting. "Regenbauer was waiting for us. He came on the plane . . . must have been following me the whole time, just like you said . . ."

"What about Kate?"

"He went crazy! The sonofabitch went crazy! Hit me with his gun, the bastard. Alice was scared out of her mind from the moment we left the hotel . . ."

"What about Kate!"

"She and Spengler should be halfway to Friedrichshafen by now."

Ted closed his eyes. With Regenbauer following Grayson and the other girl to the airport, Spengler could get Kate to the cottage by the lake. Ted's boat was there; the boat he'd bought when he was recuperating from the broken leg. Even Spengler didn't have to be much of a sailor to get across the lake. It was only eight miles across Lake Constance—to Switzerland.

"Thanks Lowell," Ted said. "I owe you."

"You're not out of the woods yet."

"But you said Kate—"

"I'm not talking about Kate. I told you, Regenbauer went crazy. He left here screaming like a maniac . . . something

382

about you and Hess and, well, I didn't get much of it. He hopped in a car and roared out of here."

Ted glanced at Pintsch, who was drumming his fingers nervously on the arm of his chair. Hess had gone to the bathroom.

"Regenbauer's lost," Ted said into the receiver. "He doesn't know where to look—"

"Will you listen a minute! Look, I don't know where you are. I mean, you didn't tell me and I didn't ask. But if you're anywhere near a place called Augsburg then I suggest you move your ass!" Grayson paused long enough to take a deep gulp of air. "That's what he kept screaming, he kept yelling—"

"Augsburg!" Ted shot to his feet.

"—something about you and Malta or Multra or—"

"How long ago did he leave!" Ted's voice rose. Pintsch looked up sharply; a frown of anxiety creased the space between his eyes.

"I didn't know. . . ." Grayson's voice came back excitedly. "Christ, you *are* at Augsburg! Get out of there, Ted! For Chrissake, get out of Augsburg! I got to a phone as soon as I could, but with all this commotion . . . they delayed the plane. Everyone got off. I couldn't get to a phone—I mean, people are calling—I had to stand in line—"

"How long!"

"Ten—twelve . . . fifteen minutes at the most. I couldn't—"

"It's only thirty miles from there!" Ted's mind was racing. It wasn't over yet. Regenbauer knew Hess came to Augsburg, he knew about the airport, he knew Hess came here to fly occasionally. It wouldn't take him long to figure why he was here now.

"Ted—"

"I'm leaving," Ted said. "Goodbye, Lowell. Thanks."

"Good lu—" Grayson's words were cut off as Ted slammed down the receiver; he whirled to Pintsch, who was standing now, the frown changed to an expression of utter dread.

"Regenbauer? *He* is com—"

"We aren't gonna be here," Ted snapped. He ripped the telephone cord out of the wall. "Get Hess."

The Mercedes coupé shot past a truck on the four-lane autobahn. Regenbauer's knuckles were pale where his hands clutched the steering wheel. He leaned forward toward the windshield like a tightly coiled wire straining for release, his mind gripped in frenzied rage.

Campbell had tricked him! Katherine wasn't on the plane. She had never been meant to be on the plane. She was somewhere else—escaping. Campbell had set him up with the telephone call to Grayson, Regenbauer realized. Campbell knew Grayson's phone was tapped. The code he'd used was *supposed* to be simple. Campbell had planned this. He'd planned the telephone call. He'd anticipated Regenbauer's move. He'd planned the switch. Regenbauer gripped the steering wheel tighter. The switch had been made at the hotel. Kate was gone. Wherever she was, he'd never find her now, Regenbauer was sure of that. Katherine was out of his grasp. But Ted wasn't.

Regenbauer whipped the Mercedes past another car. He knew where Campbell was and what he was doing. A frantic call at the airport had confirmed his guess. Hess had left his house. He'd gone to Augsburg. And he wasn't going to any rally, he was meeting Campbell to fly him out of the country! It made sense now. Campbell wouldn't leave until he knew Katherine was safe. That's why he had to trick Regenbauer into following a red herring. But he'd been *too* cautious, Campbell had. He should have left when he had the chance.

Regenbauer snatched a glance at his watch. He could still stop him. Campbell must have known Regenbauer couldn't call the police or Gestapo to stop them. No one had the authority to demand that Hess not fly, much less to arrest him as a spy. No one else knew that Hess *was* a spy! No one else knew that Hess wasn't just going for a ride in his special Messerschmitt. No one except Regenbauer. He was the only man who could stop them now.

A signpost flashed by. Seven kilometers to the Augsburg turnoff. Regenbauer pressed tha accelerator to the floor. The speedometer needle touched 180 kilometers an hour and the Mercedes almost flew.

The Messerschmitt's engines were roaring. Ted had raced frantically through the final checklist and taxied the aircraft to the runway, where it sat gulping fuel at a gallon a minute. He was ready to go, the plane was ready, but where was Hess? Ted searched the darkness between the runway and the hangar.

Pintsch had told him to get the plane ready, that they'd meet him at the runway with the gear. Ted boosted himself from the pilot seat to the edge of the canopy track, squinting at the night. They had to leave now! Regenbauer was coming! They had to leave *now*!

Then he saw the dark figures struggling with the flight gear at the ditch that separated the runway and the apron taxiway. Hess was limping.

"C'mon!" Ted yelled, but his voice was lost in the roar of engines. He set the brake, cursing. He climbed down to the wing and jumped to the runway.

"We've got to get this plane off the ground now!" Ted grabbed the briefcase Hess was carrying. "What's this?"

"My papers. Letters, notes . . ."

"Christ, it must weigh thirty pounds! This isn't a goddamn airline! Our weight is critical, we can—" Ted frowned as Hess grimaced and supported himself against Pintsch. "What's the matter?"

"The Reichsleiter twisted his ankle," Pintsch yelled.

"Christ!"

"I'm all right!" Hess nodded anxiously at the plane. "Just help me up."

Ted climbed onto the wing step-up and pushed open the Perspex canopy over the rear seat. He pulled Hess's briefcase and the two parachutes onto the wing then extended a hand down for Hess. Then he saw the headlights. They were a mile away, blinking past trees like two cat's-eyes. It was a car, and it was moving like a hurricane, hurtling through the dark on the dirt road that led to the airfield.

"Regenbauer!" Ted yelled. Hess tried to look over his shoulder but Ted pushed him roughly into the backward-facing gunner's compartment and the deputy fuehrer dropped into the seat hard with his parachute in his lap. Hess yelled something that was swallowed in the noise of the engines as Ted closed the canopy.

Pintsch was yelling now, but Ted ignored him. He had to get moving! Regenbauer was here! Ted scraped his shin scrambling into the cockpit. He slammed the pilot's canopy shut with one hand and released the parking brake with the other. The Messerschmitt began to move. Ted jammed the throttle forward and took one last look at the headlights. He could make out the car now; a Mercedes coupé. It was nearly to the hangar.

God, how fast was the sonofabitch driving! Ted jerked his glance back to the instrument panel. The plane was rolling. He pointed the nose down the middle of the runway and switched on the landing lights. Regenbauer would see him now, Ted thought. He'd see the plane now if he hadn't seen it before, but that was too bad. Ted had to have lights to take off. He had to see the runway. Hess was yelling behind him. He was banging on the canopy window and shouting frantically in German.

"Look here! Look here!"

But Ted didn't have to look. Regenbauer sped past the hangar; the Mercedes swerved around Hess's private car, skidding sideways on the pavement until the rear tires found traction. The car raced across the taxi apron toward the runway.

Then it became instantly clear what Regenbauer was doing. Regenbauer was going to stop him the only way he had left. He'd taken an angle on the runway, estimating the speed of the aircraft and the velocity of the car, and aimed at the point in the dark where those two lines intersected. He was going to ram the plane!

Ted had the throttles up full. He should have blown the plugs, he told himself. Both engine cowlings flashed intermittently as the suddenly goosed engines strained to burn fuel after idling so long. The Messerschmitt gained speed, its nose in the center of the runway. Ted didn't have to turn to see the car. He could see it from the corner of his eye. Fly! He held the throttle against the stop. Fly, goddammit!

The ground speed indicator passed ninety miles an hour. Ted felt the fuselage trying to align itself in a level attitude for flight. The tail wheel began to bounce. Ted blinked sweat from his eyes. The plane should be up now! The Mercedes was so close he could see Regenbauer behind the wheel. The car was gaining! The goddamn car was moving faster than the plane! What kind of fucking car—

Then Ted saw the ditch. It was there the whole time, running parallel to the runway, separating it and the apron, but Ted hadn't remembered it was there. Until now. He saw it about the same time the front gears lifted off the pavement, just an instant before Regenbauer's car hit the plane.

The Mercedes left the concrete pavement of the apron at 110 miles an hour. It traveled across the eight-foot ditch and struck the edge of the runway with such force that both front wheel

suspension systems sheared off on impact. The tires exploded.
The car bounced off the pavement in a grinding shower of
sparks. It was airborne for a distance of more than twenty
yards before it slammed back to earth and spun into the soft,
wet ground on the other side of the runway. Both doors swung
open and broke off at the intial impact, and Regenbauer clung
desperately to the wheel to keep from being thrown out of the
car. He heard the cartilage snap at the bridge of his nose when
his face smashed into the steering wheel.

Ted was luckier. Regenbauer had judged the angle correctly,
and Ted felt the jolt as the Mercedes' top colided against the
right landing gear strut when the car passed under the plane.
He nearly lost control then; the left wing dipped dangerously
close to the ground. But the Messerschmitt righted itself and
Ted's last glimpse of Regenbauer as the plane straightened out
was of a dazed figure falling on his knees.

But it wasn't the only thing Ted glimpsed for the last time.
The reason the Messerschmitt had labored so long to get into
the air was because something was on the wing, creating extra
drag and weight, until the collision knocked it away. Ted's
parachute. He saw it flipping end over end until it disappeared
in the darkness. And with the parachute went Hess's briefcase.
In his panic at seeing Regenbauer, Ted had left them on the
wing. Now they were gone.

"My papers! My letters . . . !" Hess's voice was hoarse
from yelling. "Campbell, what have you done?"

That's what he was screaming about!

"Campbell—"

"Shut up!" Ted wiped his sleeve across his face. "It's gone!
Just shut up about it! At least you're still alive."

Getting off the ground had cost them dearly and it wasn't
because they'd lost some papers. Ted had just found what that
cost was. Regenbauer *had* damaged the plane. The right
landing gear light did not go out when Ted pressed the GEAR
RETRACT button. It meant that the Mercedes had bent the strut.
It meant that a landing gear was just sticking out down there,
creating drag. It meant he'd be using more fuel. Ted settled
back in the seat. He glanced over the instrument panel. He
hadn't beaten Regenbauer yet. He had slightly less than five
hours to figure a way to get this plane to Scotland before it ran
out of gas, and do it without killing himself in a suicide

landing in a crippled aircraft and without a parachute. That's all.

Regenbauer had staggered out of the wrecked car and collapsed to his hands and knees on the soggy ground. What had he hit? He'd seen something dark just before the car reached the runway, but he was going too fast to make out anything more than a dark blur. He shook his head. He was sure the car had hit some part of the plane; he'd heard the bang, felt it, but the plane didn't crash. Campbell was gone and so was Hess.

He stood up unsteadily. He touched his face and felt the bloody gash across his nose. At least he was alive. Then he heard a car engine and he looked back down the runway at the light from the hangar. Hess's car. He watched as it roared off toward the dirt road that led from the airfield. Pintsch! Of course, Hess's adjutant! Pintsch knew what had happened here. And Regenbauer could make Pintsch talk.

He started across the runway. He had to get to a phone. Arrest Pintsch, that was the first thing. Pintsch would corroborate that Hess was a spy. Heydrich would have to believe him now. If he could prove that Hess was in the Messerschmitt with Campbell, that Hess was trying to escape from Germany, then there was still time to stop them. Alert the Luftwaffe, Regenbauer told himself, shoot them down. He could still stop—

Regenbauer nearly tripped over the parachute. It was lying in the middle of the dark runway. Then he saw the briefcase on its side a few yards away. It had burst and papers were dancing in the breeze around it. The initials on the broken clasp identified it as Hess's. *The Reichsleiter's briefcase*! Regenbauer leafed madly through the papers. Here was the proof! He found astronomical charts, letters to the Duke of Hamilton and King George, outlines for negotiations, a memorandum of peace between Germany and England . . . Regenbauer felt suddenly dizzy. His mouth went dry. Hess *was* in league with the British! If he'd ever had a lingering doubt, now it was gone. This was the positive proof. In Hess's own handwriting! Why hadn't he believed Campbell!

Regenbauer stuffed the papers back into the briefcase. One of them was a flying map. Campbell's flight plan. It detailed the exact route he would take. And he was going to Scotland!

Regenbauer ran all the way to the hangar. He had to call someone. He had to stop Campbell. In the pilots' lounge he found the telephone that had been ripped away from its cord. Frantically, he searched the halls and changing room for another phone, then scrambled down a corridor to the door leading to the hangar. Campbell had disabled every telephone in the building, but he hadn't disabled everything.

Hess's backup Messerschmitt was parked in the hangar. It had Hess's special markings and was fitted with extra fuel tanks, exactly the same as the plane that had just left. It didn't take Regenbauer a moment to decide his next move. He threw the briefcase and map into the cockpit and kicked away the tire chocks. Calling anybody now, even if he had a phone, didn't guarantee anything, Regenbauer realized. He hadn't the authority to order the Luftwaffe to shoot down a plane. Certainly not one of their own. There was only him.

Regenbauer started the engines. He'd stop Campbell himself! He knew the route Campbell was taking and he could make up time by not skirting forbidden air zones as Campbell had intended. He taxied the plane to the fuel pump. He'd end Campbell's game and stop Hess . . . permanently. He'd kill them both in the air.

45

TED DIDN'T RELAX until he reached the Wadden Zee. Below were the middle West Frisian Islands through scattered clouds. Ahead was the level, slightly curved horizon of the North Sea. He was more than halfway home now; in moments Holland would be behind him. Flying across Germany hadn't presented any of the problems he'd imagined. There had been a lot of radio traffic and it appeared that London was in for another pounding, but he didn't see any bomber formations. He was alone in the night sky with just five hundred miles of sea to cross.

Mentally, he'd solved the problem of the dangling gear. It was bent, which meant it wasn't in a locked position, and the strain it was under now in the slipstream wasn't making it any stronger. If he kept the left gear up, chances were he'd survive a belly landing. The crippled gear should snap as the plane touched down. It was a risk, of course, but the odds favored him . . . if he had enough fuel.

"Are we over the sea?"

Ted had almost forgotten about Hess. He banked the plane. "Take a look. We're on course and on schedule." Actually, Ted thought, the Messerschmitt was running better than he had any right to expect, considering what it'd been through.

"You should not have spoken to me that way," Ted's passenger said over the engine noise. "You should not have."

Ted sighed but said nothing.

"My papers, they are all lost."

"Don't worry about it."

There was silence from the darkness of the rear compartment for a moment then: "You don't understand."

"Regenbauer would have killed us both if I'd waited," Ted
said. "One of us, anyway. You're alive, just be thankful for
that."

"But my papers!" There was fear in Hess's voice. "My
charts . . . the letters! I have urgent things to discuss with the
king. I should have my notes! But now I have nothing. Not
even an identity card in case I am stopped before I reach the
Duke of Hamilton's residence."

He's getting nervous again, Ted thought. He's anticipating
what kind of welcome he'll receive and he's worried. Ted
reached down and pulled his wallet out. He switched on the
map light and ripped open the wallet's leather binding. "Here,
take this." He handed the card back over his head.

"What is it?"

"Just in case we don't go down where I want, use it for your
identification. There isn't a picture so it should satisfy anyone
that you're a Luftwaffe pilot until you can see Hamilton."

"Where did you get it?"

"We all have our secrets," Ted said with a smile. "When we
get down, I'm going to disappear. I'm not taking any chances
of being shot as a spy, anyway. I speak English and I can fade
into the night. So, if anyone asks, you flew this rig to Scotland
all by yourself. Okay?"

The deputy fuehrer didn't reply.

"Hess?"

"Yes, I understand," said the voice from the dark. "Thank
you."

Ted shrugged. "Sure."

"I can't read it in this light," Hess said. "What's the name?"

"Horn," Ted replied. "Oberleutnant Alfred Horn."

Regenbauer had passed the point of no return more than an
hour ago. He hadn't enough fuel left to get back to Germany,
but he didn't care. Getting Campbell was all that mattered.
He'd taken longer than he expected to fuel the plane; and he
had discovered that the plane was not equipped with any
armaments. Finding two magazines for the nose-mounted

machine guns had taken precious minutes—time he now regretted losing. He hadn't caught Campbell in Germany. But he would catch him now, over the ocean.

Regenbauer switched on a light to check the map coordinates again. Campbell was out here somewhere. He had to be close. Farne Island wasn't far away. He had to find Campbell before—

Then he saw it. He'd switched off the light and squeezed his eyes shut to reaccustom his eyes to the dark and he opened them and glanced up at the sky above him. An ME-110 flew at about fourteen thousand feet, skirting a cloud bank. There wasn't any mistaking that silhouette. It was a Messerschmitt, no question. And it was Campbell's! The right landing gear hung at an awkward, clumsy angle, like the leg of a clubfooted duck. He *had* hit the plane with the car! Regenbauer wet his lips. Now he had him.

Regenbauer pulled the stick back and Hess's backup Messerschmitt cut through the night air in a steep inclination toward its sister craft. Regenbauer touched the trigger button lightly. He stared through the target view window, waiting for the other plane to come into sight.

It took Ted only a moment to realize why the clear night sky was suddenly cluttered with fireworks—a stream of Roman candles poured past his starboard wing from below. Only they weren't Roman candles. They were tracer bullets. His reaction was immediate and instinctive. He jammed hard left rudder and slammed the fighter's control column forward. The Messerschmitt heeled over on its back and dove for the sea.

"Campbell—"

"Hold on!"

He wasn't surprised that he'd been attacked, Ted knew sooner or later he'd run into the RAF. He was surprised that he'd run into a patrol this far out; he was still twenty minutes from the coast. Still, he was flying a Messerschmitt 110. He could outrun any Spitfire or Hurricane in England.

He dove a thousand feet, leveled and craned his neck to search the sky above him for his pursuer.

"Do you see him!" Ted shouted.

"Are we hit?"

"No, I don't think—" Then Ted saw the outline of the other

aircraft. It was angling down for another pass. "Christ, there he is! Grab something, Hess!"

Ted began a slow turn to the right—right rudder, right stick —and throttled back. He wanted to give his pursuer a target to concentrate on and allow him to begin his own turn to intercept. Throttling back caused the engines to pop and flash. Ted wanted to be sure it could be seen that he was making a right turn. He paused for the other pilot to begin his turn. *Now*, he told himself.

He switched off his navigation lights, kicked hard left rudder, pulled back on the control stick and rammed the throttle forward.

The Messerschmitt's left wing dropped as if it had been yanked from the ground. The plane rolled and fell on its back in a breath-stopping power dive at maximum speed. Ted was slung into his seat by the positive G-force, but he forced his eyes to focus on the altimeter. At five hundred feet he rolled out. Ted turned back quickly to see the sky behind him. The idea was to fake the turn, then snap-roll in the opposite direction. The other pilot would go for the fake and because Ted'd switched off all his running lights the Messerschmitt would simply disappear from his pursuer's target window. It was a good idea, only it didn't work.

He didn't have to see the other plane to know it was behind him. Tracers were all over the sky. He felt slugs rip through the starboard wing. He put the plane through every acrobatic maneuver he could think of in a desperate attempt to shake the other fighter—he climbed, he rolled, he dove, he looped—but nothing worked. Ted *knew* the Messerschmitt was faster than any RAF plane built. It was faster than anything the British had in the air, even with the drag from his crippled gear. So why couldn't he shake him!

"Campbell! Two o'clock . . . more fighters!"

Ted snapped up in his seat to see over the canopy track. They were there all right. A pair of Hurricanes at two thousand feet, silhouetted against a low-drifting cloud. Christ, was the whole RAF waiting for him!

"Campbell! My God, you must *do something*!"

But there was only one thing left to do.

Ted wiped the perspiration from his hands on his trousers and gripped the control column. He looked out the canopy.

The Hurricanes were coming to meet him. "All right, Hess, hold on to your socks."

"What are . . ."

"I'm attacking."

"Wha—*we're not armed*!"

Ted turned the nose of the Messerschmitt into the Hurricanes. They were below him and he had to dive to meet them.

"Campbell, don't be a fool! Please . . . !"

But Ted ignored Hess. He concentrated on the two Hurricanes. They were flying nearly wingtip to wingtip. If he had any chance at all now it was to dive straight at them and pray they had good reflexes. He was being pursued from both sides. If he couldn't shake them, maybe he could scare them to death.

"You're going to kill us all!"

He almost did. The Hurricane pilots almost didn't react in time. Ted held the stick with both hands. At the last second the two RAF fighters frantically banked away from each other and the Messerschmitt shot through the gap. Ted saw the Hurricanes flash past him. He was so close to them he could have read the planes' identifying numbers if he'd had the time. He held the Messerschmitt in its dive and only pulled it up when he was nearly on the water. He was so low that whitecaps blurred together beneath him. He could lean out and spit at a wave. Then he saw Holy Island straight ahead and he gave the plane all the throttle she would take and aimed straight for it.

Ted was doing 270 kilometers an hour when he crossed the coastline into Scotland. His fuel was desperately low. All that damned rolling and diving had eaten up his reserve. But he hugged the ground as close as he dared. His only hope was that by racing along at this insane altitude, hedgehopping over the dark countryside without lights, narrowly skimming trees and rooftops, he'd lose the RAF fighters. Down here at treetop level his speed was cut in half. But the Hurricanes, if they were still back there, had the same problems. He only hoped that his margin of superior speed was not offset by the drag of the dangling gear. There was also the drag created by his two auxiliary fuel tanks under the wings. The fuel in them was gone now—what little fuel he had left was in the Messerschmitt's main tank. He thought about jettisoning the auxiliary tanks, then decided against it. At this altitude it was too dangerous. The air was too heavy. He wasn't sure how the plane would handle if it was suddenly five hundred pounds

lighter. Get rid of them later, Ted told himself. When he was
safe.

Regenbauer had switched off his lights, wingtip and cockpit,
the moment he saw Ted begin to feint with a right turn. He had
anticipated the dive; it was a familiar fighter pilot's maneuver
and he wasn't fooled by it. He'd followed Campbell's plane
right down to the sea, firing the nose machine guns every foot
of the way. He'd only loaded two of the four nose guns with
one magazine each because that was all the time he'd had.
Now he'd used them up; the magazines were empty.

Campbell was a smart pilot, Regenbauer had to give him
that. This last maneuver, getting down almost to the ground,
had frightened off the British fighters. Anyway, their angle of
pursuit had been too severe to intercept and they had overshot
the correct line of attack. Even if they had recovered in time it
would have been impossible for them to find Campbell because
Campbell had no running lights and they were too far away to
see the faint flashes from the Messerschmitt's exhaust flame
damper.

But Regenbauer was not too far away to see it. He was right
behind Campbell, guiding on the flashes from his engine. They
were two dark blurs in the night, flying in tandem, one behind
the other, climbing up mountain slopes, sliding down the other
side, only meters from the ground. Regenbauer followed
Campbell like a shadow. When Campbell turned east, Regenbauer turned; when he drew down to follow a railway,
Regenbauer was there too, behind him, thirty yards off his tail,
unseen. Regenbauer knew fuel consumption was becoming
critical, and he had jettisoned his auxiliary wing tanks over the
sea. Because of the broken wheel, every mile they flew meant
Campbell was using more fuel than Regenbauer was. Unless
Campbell set down soon, he was going to run out of gas. But
Regenbauer wasn't going to let him land. Maybe he couldn't
shoot him down, but he could keep Campbell from landing.
Regenbauer had him now. Campbell couldn't land and he
couldn't bail out. All he could do was die.

Ted tapped the fuel gauge with his finger. They weren't
going to make it. There wasn't enough fuel to reach Dungavel
House; it was another ten minutes away and they'd be lucky to

get five minutes of flying time out of this aircraft. He'd throttled back to spare some gas, but it just wasn't enough.

"Hess?" Ted leaned around the seat.

"Yes?"

"We aren't going to make Dungavel. I can get within a few miles, but that's all." He waited for a response. The engines were already beginning to cough. "Hess?"

"Yes, I understand," The Reichsleiter's voice came back finally. He sounded physically drained. His voice was almost inaudible against the engines. It was as though fear had been shocked out of him and been replaced by quiet hopelessness. "Are we going to crash?"

"Crash!" Ted exploded then. He wasn't going to die! Nobody was going to die! "I didn't come all this way to get us killed in a goddamn crackup!"

"But—"

"I'm going to belly this aircraft into a plowed field! You understand? You're not going to die . . . and neither am I."

"I'm ready."

Ted took a deep breath, switched on the landing lights. "Okay. You'd better hold on, brace yourself against the bulkhead." He leaned up to see over the instrument panel. He'd gained altitude to about four hundred feet a while ago, now it was time to bring her down. The landing lights wouldn't be much use until he was lower, but at least he'd see small obstacles like—

"Campbell, watch out—!"

Hess saw the other plane first because he was facing backwards, toward the tail, but Ted didn't need to see it, he felt it, a terrific jolt that shuddered the whole cockpit.

"Jesus Christ—"

"A plane, Campbell!" Hess yelled. "A plane is directly behind you! He's ramming his wing into the stabilizer!"

Ted felt another jolt and the Messerschmitt nearly slipped away from him.

"He's backing off! He is—my God! Campbell, it's a Messerschmitt! A German Messerschmitt!"

Ted's stomach flopped. He was bouncing in his seat, trying to hold the aircraft level, and he realized Hess wasn't crazy. Ted was on the verge of panic because he suddenly knew who the other pilot was. It *wasn't* a Hurricane or a Spitfire that had been dogging him all this time. No wonder he couldn't shake it! The cold sweat returned and he felt the numbing aches in his limbs. It was Regenbauer trying to knock him out of the sky! And he was flying the only other Messerschmitt in the world that had the range and the fuel capacity to fly this far—the backup plane. Regenbauer had followed him all the way from Germany and now he was going to keep his promise.

I'll kill you before I'll allow you to make me a fool.

"A Messerschmitt!" Hess was still yelling incredulously. "Who—"

"It's Regenbauer," Ted shouted. "The fucking bastard . . ." He didn't wait for the SS major to make another move. He glanced in the mirror to see that the sister aircraft was far enough behind to climb without colliding, then throttled forward, pulling the stick back.

"What are you doing?"

"I can't land with him back there!" Ted watched the altimeter climb through a thousand feet . . . twelve hundred . . . "Put on your parachute."

"What?"

"Goddammit, just do what I say! Put on your parachute!" The altimeter crawled to fifteen hundred feet. He hadn't come this far to have some lunatic knock him out of the air. Ted glanced in the mirror again. Regenbauer had fallen behind, just enough to keep a safe distance. He was letting Ted have all the climbing room he wanted, and Ted knew why. The sonofabitch wasn't going to let him land but he didn't mind if Ted ran out of gas. The higher he was the further he fell—the ME-110 had all the gliding characteristics of a stick of wood. And because Regenbauer was letting him climb, he must have known Ted didn't have a chute.

"I have it on!" Hess yelled above the straining engines.

The needle was at twenty-two hundred feet on the altimeter and it stuck there. The fuel gauge was bumping empty.

"Pull the canopy!" Ted began easing the plane level. He didn't know where he was precisely, somewhere west of Dungavel, but it didn't matter where he was. "Release the latches and let it blow off!"

"I can't climb over—"

Whatever the deputy fuehrer's last words were, they were lost in the blast of wind as the gunner's canopy blew away in the turbulence of the slipstream. The Messerschmitt was level, flying west, Regenbauer about fifty yards behind him and slightly above and beginning to close the gap. He's not sure what I'm doing, Ted thought. Good. He pulled the throttles back and rolled the plane half over just as Regenbauer hit his landing lights. For an instant Ted couldn't see anything except the powerful beams of Regenbauer's lights. But he saw Hess fall out of the plane. It was all he needed to see.

Ted had done his job; he'd done what he'd promised to do, what he was meant to do. Rudolf Hess was in Scotland.

He rolled the Messerschmitt right side up, still caught in Regenbauer's landing lights, and thrust the throttles forward, pushing the nose toward the ground. He had one chance of staying alive—outrun Regenbauer and ditch the plane in a field. It wasn't a very good chance, but without a parachute, in an aircraft flying on fumes, he didn't have another option.

He put the plane in the steepest dive it could handle, searching frantically for a place to slide it into the ground. There wasn't any place. It was nearly all meadowland, but it was *rolling* meadowland which would, at this speed, tear the plane apart.

He searched for a lake. Christ, there were small lakes all over this country. Lakes and ponds everywhere. So where were they now!

When he spotted the lake it was perhaps two miles away. It wasn't a large lake, but it didn't have to be. Ted glanced at the mirror. Now, if he could just get to it. Regenbauer was closing. His Messerschmitt wasn't forty or fifty yards behind like it was a second ago; he was much closer, twenty, twenty-five yards now. He was gaining and in a few seconds he'd be on him.

How could he be gaining? Ted's eyes raced over the instrument panel. What was he doing wrong? They were flying exactly the same planes, but Regenbauer's aircraft was catching him. Regenbauer was crazy! He was going to kill them both. He was going to win the only way he could now—jam that Messerschmitt straight up Ted's ass. And there wasn't anything Ted could do about it. Ted was going to die. He was going to be rammed by a madman and die in the twisted wreckage. The stark realization of it frightened him. He hoped it would be over quickly. For an instant, he thought of Kate.

Then he saw it. He glanced at his mirror, waiting for Regenbauer's death blow. He could make out part of the SS major's plane in the vibrating reflection. The starboard wing.

There wasn't any auxiliary fuel tank on it.

Christ! The extra tank pods! Ted hadn't jettisoned his. No wonder Regenbauer was catching him. Regenbauer was flying faster because he'd dumped the empty fuel tanks; he wasn't slowed by the added weight and drag.

Ted reached for the pod release handle. His fingers closed over the red-taped lever. Then he realized it wouldn't do him any good just to increase his speed. A desperate last burst of acceleration would only suck the remaining fuel and delay the inevitable by a few seconds. Regenbauer meant to kill him, even if it meant dying himself. If Ted by some miracle could survive a crash landing, he knew Regenbauer would still come after him. The crazy bastard would plow into him on the ground!

It wasn't going to happen that way! Ted hunched forward in his seat. He wasn't going to let the sonofabitch win. He had one chance in ten thousand of staying alive.

Ted jerked the control column back. He throttled up. Both engines choked on the last ounce of fuel, but the plane responded to his final command. The Messerschmitt's nose came up. The maneuver was like trying to brake a runaway train. It wouldn't change anything except for an almost negligible deceleration. But it flattened the Messerschmitt's dive inclination, and that was all Ted wanted.

Only an excellent pilot could have reacted quickly enough to avoid shooting beneath Ted's plane. It was an old fighter's trick to change positions with a pursuing aircraft that was bearing down from behind. But Regenbauer was too experienced a pilot to have fallen for such an obvious ploy. He'd demonstrated that over the sea and by following on Ted's suicidal dive through the Hurricanes. Regenbauer had anticipated nearly every move Ted had made to this point. It's what Ted had counted on: Regenbauer was too smart to be deceived by simple tricks. All Ted had accomplished was to put Regenbauer slightly out of position. His Messerschmitt, instead of being directly behind Ted's, was now behind and slightly below. Exactly where Ted wanted him.

Now Ted grasped the auxiliary tank release lever. The lake was coming up fast. Moonlight shimmered across its surface. Ted could see treetops flashing past nearly abreast of his wings. It's now or never, he thought. Whatever happened now . . . happened. He wasn't flying the plane anymore anyway.

It was just in the air, propelled by sheer inertia. Ted sucked in his breath and jerked the lever.

The Messerschmitt bounced with gentle buoyancy at the release. The right tank dropped away first. It was a miracle that it could miss a plane as near as Regenbauer's, but it sailed end over end past the wing into the darkness. The left tank didn't miss. It tumbled away just as the other tank had, but a split second later. It was in a half turn, its tip pointed at the ground, when the propeller of Regenbauer's left engine ran into it.

The explosion lit up the night. Ted was watching his mirror and the flash blinded him. He felt the blast in his seat as his plane shuddered in the brief concussion. He hadn't expected an explosion. All he wanted was to disable Regenbauer's aircraft, to keep him off his back . . . kill him if possible. The explosion was a surprise until he realized that both tank pods might as well have been bombs. They were empty of fuel but the fumes trapped inside made them deadly missiles. Ted saw Regenbauer's plane cartwheel into the ground and explode. He glanced up in time to see the lake smack him in the face.

The Messerschmitt hit the water at almost a hundred miles an hour. The tailwheel ripped away the moment it touched the water and the main fuselage belly-flopped into the lake, tearing off the crippled gear. The plane bounced twice. The propeller blades peeled back over the engine cowling from the initial impact and the aircraft came to a sudden, skidding halt, its engines hissing and sizzling and its nose bobbing like a buoy in the murky, churned water. Ted's first reaction was amazement; first, that he was alive and, second, that nothing was broken. Then he was galvanzied to action at the sound of water pouring into the open canopy hatch behind him as the plane began to sink.

He released the pilot's canopy hatch and took a last gulp of air before water rushed over his head. He *felt* the plane sinking. He opened his eyes to see if the hatch was gone, but there was nothing to see. It had been a dark night, but this was blackness without depth—cold, wet and absolutely impenetrable. He bounced against the webbing of the seat harness when the plane bumped its nose against the bottom and settled in. The pilot's canopy, Ted realized, unlike the gunner's canopy, which was on a slide, was hinged at the top behind the pilot's seat. If it settled back down and closed over the cockpit, he'd be trapped inside.

He scrambled to get out of the cockpit. His fingers slipped on the harness buckle; he couldn't get it loose. Christ, how many times had he reached down and unsnapped a harness buckle! He was *not* going to drown, he told himself. He had not flown across a continent and outmaneuvered the best SS pilot in Germany to come to Scotland to drown in a goddamn lake!

The buckle came free. Ted wriggled out of the harness. His lungs were ready to burst, but he kicked up, arms and hands extended, out of the cockpit. He broke the surface of the water gasping. His chest was on fire. Then, shedding his shoes and leather flight jacket, he fought not to swallow the oily water while he oriented himself. Regenbauer's plane, what was left of it, was burning back to the east in the middle of a field. He trod water until he had his breath back. Then he swam toward the wreckage, one laborious stroke after another until he reached the shore. He dragged himself out of the cold water and collapsed beside a log, his pulse pounding in his head. He still had to find Regenbauer. If he was dead he was dead. But if he wasn't, if he'd somehow survived the crash, Ted had to find him. He had to finish it.

Ted climbed to his feet. The field was covered with bits and pieces of metal; an engine or part of a wing was burning about twenty yards from the point of impact. He found the broken rudder section of the tail. When he found the fuselage he was amazed that so much of it was intact. By the looks of it the plane had come apart in the air, with the body of the fuselage crashing nearly right side up. He staggered to the cockpit. All the canopy windows had been shattered and he couldn't tell if the pilot's hatch had been blown off. If it had then Regenbauer had survived; it meant that he was around here some-where. . .

Regenbauer was still sitting in the pilot seat. His head hung to one side and his eyes were open. A line of blood extended from his ear down over the black uniform collar. The crash must have broken every bone in his body, Ted thought. He slumped against the fuselage and stared at Regenbauer's body. His seat harness was still strapped tightly across his chest. Regenbauer hadn't worn a parachute either.

Then Ted heard voices. He crouched beside the plane. He saw figures across the field. Whoever they were—farmers, the police, the Home Guard—he couldn't leave Regenbauer to be

found in the plane. Hess's story was that he'd flown to
Scotland alone. If Hess was going to have any credibility at all
then Ted had to get rid of Regenbauer's body. As far as anyone
was ever going to know, Hess had made this trip on a mission
of peace. It's what Hess himself believed. Even if it was the
hopeless act of a desperate man, Ted thought, he was going to
let the deputy fuehrer have his moment. It was Hess who got
Kate out of Dachau.

Ted pulled the limp body out of the plane. There was
something else in the cockpit—Hess's briefcase. He took that
too.

He dragged Regenbauer fifty yards before he stopped to rest.
There were more voices now. He saw more figures in the dying
flames of the burning engines, but they were running toward
the wreckage. No one was headed for the lake. It took an hour
to get the SS major's body to the edge of the water. He stripped
off Regenbauer's uniform and stuffed it in the briefcase then
filled the case with mud from the lakeshore and threw it as far
as he could into the lake.

He'd done all he could do; the secret that had cost so many
lives was safe again, and Hess had been delivered to Scotland.
It was over now. Ted got up from his knees. He was exhausted
and wet and dirty. He looked at Regenbauer's body. Someone
will find him and, eventually, bury him, Ted thought. The
conquering SS officer would finally make his mark on Great
Britain—as an unnamed casualty in a Scottish churchyard.

He left Regenbauer's body at the edge of the lake, on its
face in the mud. He walked south until he found a road and
followed it without wondering where it led. He was exhausted
and cold, his clothes were still wet, but he plodded numbly on,
guiding himself on the rutted shoulder of the road, thinking no
further ahead than the next step in the chilly darkness. And the
next and the next . . .

He didn't know how long he'd been walking or where the
light had come from, but the voice brought him out of his
stupor.

"You there! Hey, now, you . . . where are you going?"

Ted turned around, stumbling in a rut, and was blinded by
the headlamps of a car. He held his hand up against the glare.

"You just stand still now," the voice said. It was a woman's
voice, he realized after a moment, and its owner spoke with a

gruffness that masked a deeper emotion he suspected was fear. "Keep your hands up now. I have a gun here . . ."

He tried to see past the headlights but they were too bright and he wondered why they weren't shielded.

"What are you doing out here?" the voice called from behind the glare. "Who are you?"

"Crash . . ." Ted said, trying to make sense. His voice trembled from the cold and he felt himself shiver. "I . . . had a wreck . . . don't know where . . ." He tried to get the sentences straight in his mind, but all that came out was babble. He suddenly had the vision of being shot as a downed German pilot on a deserted road by a frightened Scottish farmgirl, all because he couldn't speak coherent English. "Please . . . don't shoot . . ." Then he added, as if it made a difference, "I'm American . . ."

"A Yank, is it? All right, then, this way. C'mon now. Let's have a look."

He walked to the car, hands raised.

"Hands on the bonnet. That's it. Nothing cute now. I have a gun."

He could see the figure of her standing behind the open driver's door. She wasn't any farmgirl; she was past sixty at least, and she wore a man's cap with tufts of gray hair sticking out from under. "Please . . . don't shoot. I'm not—"

"You ain't no German, I can see that. What're you doing out here? Don't you mind the curfew?"

He touched his head to the warmth of the radiator, his knees bent to the support of the bumper. "I . . ." But he couldn't manage an explanation. The cold and exhaustion had seeped into him and cut off his brain from his tongue.

She came around the door and Ted saw her gun—a wrench the size of a hammer. "A sight, you are. Scared me rightly, walking beside the road like that. Lordy my, what's this?—" she touched his shirt. "Wringing wet, you are, and cold as thunder. Ran off the bridge at Glen Morrow, right? Not the first one, either. Damn lamp shields. The wonder is you didn't drown too. C'mon, then. Up you go. Hold tight. That's it. Mind your head."

She guided him to the passenger door and helped him inside. It was an old Beardmore touring car with a canvas top and a broken running board and she found a blanket in the rear seat and draped it around him.

"Been a right rowdy night, this one," she said as she climbed behind the ancient steering wheel. "People's out with hayforks and clubs toward Lanark, I hear . . . roaming in the dark, looking for more Germans, if there be any. You're the lucky one, you are, that I found you."

He pulled the blanket tight around him. His teeth chattered but he overcame the cold to ask a question. "More Germans?"

She nodded without taking her eyes off the road. "Plowman up to Eaglesham Moor—" the car shuddered as she shifted gears "—claims he caught himself a pilot. Just drifted down like snow. Hurt his ankle too, they say."

"A German pilot?"

"It's what they say, if you can believe a Scot. Not that I don't, mind. From Gloucester, I am, married a Scot, died at Verdun, bless him. There was a man could spin a tale, I can tell you. A thorough gentleman, the German, I mean, from what I hear. Asked to see his right honorable self, Lord Hamilton. Not that I believe it myself. Never know what a Scot'll tell you."

Hess made it, Ted thought. At least he was alive. He hadn't been shot or stuck like a pig by some angry farmhand. Whatever happened to Hess now, he was on his own. Ted lay his head back on the seat. God, he was tired. It was a hundred years ago that he'd left Augsburg. Two hundred. He wondered briefly what Carstairs was doing, but he didn't really care. Someone was going to be a hero for all of this, probably, and it might as well be Carstairs. It might even be Hess if he ever got to Hamiliton. But it wasn't going to be Ted Campbell. There wasn't going to be anyone pinning a medal on his chest or hailing him as an intrepid war hero. Not now or ever, he promised himself. Not after Anne. Not after London. Not after Trentlyon.

Ted closed his eyes and huddled in the corner against the door. He pushed everything out of his mind and thought of Kate. She and Spengler were in Switzerland somewhere, possibly even in Zurich. In a few days, according to Spengler's timetable, she'd be in Plymouth, after a boat ride from San Sebastian. A few more days, that's all it would be. It kept him warm against the chill in his clothes, the thought of her.

"Lochmaben," the old woman said, startling Ted's eyes open. "That's where I'm going, Yank. Abington's the next town. I can put you off there, if you like. I expect you'll want to be calling somebody, let them know you're not drowned."

Ted stared at the lights on the road ahead. Who did he want to call? *You're to go to Edinburgh. Carstairs will be waiting.* Carstairs.

"Yank?"

"Abington will be fine," Ted said. "How far to Edinburgh?"

She scratched below her hat. "Well, now, couldn't say for sure. It's a long walk, I can tell you, Yank."

He tucked the corners of the blanket under his arms and allowed himself a tiny smile. "Good," he said with a shiver from beneath the blanket. "I wasn't going there, anyway."

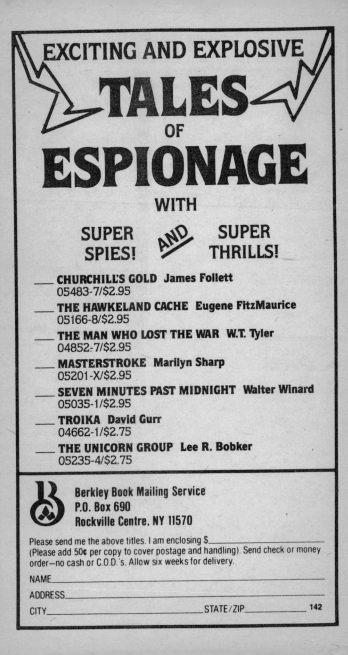